Panic Snap

Also by Laura Reese

Topping from Below

Panic Snap

LAURA REESE

ST. MARTIN'S GRIFFIN

NEW YORK

www.stmartins.com

Library of Congress Cataloging-in-Publication Data

Reese, Laura.
    Panic snap / Laura Reese.
        p. cm.
   ISBN 0-312-24229-8 (hc)
   ISBN 0-312-27275-8 (pbk)
   1. Amnesia—Patients—Fiction. 2. Identity
(Psychology)—Fiction. 3. Women—
Crimes against—Fiction. I. Title.
PS3568.E4314 P36 2000
813'.54—dc21   99-056344
                                        CIP

First St. Martin's Griffin Edition: February 2001

10 9 8 7 6 5 4 3 2 1

In memory of my mother and father

Acknowledgments

My heartfelt appreciation to two very special people: my agent, Barbara Lowenstein, for making the deals, and my editor, Charles Spicer, for nurturing me along. This book is theirs, as much as it's mine.

I would also like to thank the following people for tirelessly answering my many questions: the winemakers, vineyard workers, and cellar rats—too numerous to mention individually—in various Napa Valley wineries; the professors in the University of California at Davis Department of Viticulture and Enology; Jeff Brinkman, winemaker at R. H. Phillips Winery; Lee Philipson, deputy district attorney in Napa County; Mary Reese, Janet Bailey, and Kim Scott, for their singular fields of expertise; and Barb Miller, who read the manuscript in its various forms. And, of course, I'm always grateful for the continuing support of my friends, and of my siblings, Howard, Ben, Mary, and Janet.

The art of our necessity is strange,
That can make vile things precious.
—William Shakespeare,
King Lear

What we call the beginning is often the end
And to make an end is to make a beginning.
The end is where we start from.
—T. S. Eliot,
from *Four Quartets*
Little Gidding

Before
the
Verdict

I must not think about the verdict. I must NOT. But, of course, I do. I can think of nothing else. I keep looking at the clock, watching the time, wondering when the jury will reach a decision. I can see it there, up high, through that narrow slit of a window, plain as day. It's the old-fashioned kind, with a round face and big black numerals and a constantly moving red second hand, ticking off the time. No digital numbers flashing, not on this one. I look again. The red second hand continues its sweep, steady, unrelenting: five hours so far and still no verdict.

Limping from my injuries, I pace back and forth, slowly, from the gray west wall to the locked door and then back again, a short distance, a few steps. The first hour or two wasn't so bad, not really. My lawyers came, gave me a few encouraging words, sat with me for a while. I could tell, despite their words, they had doubts about the outcome, but their presence reassured me. Now, alone, I pace and watch the clock, each hour more difficult than the one before. What do other people think about, I wonder, while they're waiting? What? Mostly, I'm just scared, and I think about that. When I was first arrested, my lawyers assured me the case would be dismissed, it wouldn't even go to trial. They were wrong. My fate, my life, will be decided by a jury of twelve, but what I've learned, over the years, is that justice doesn't always prevail.

I place my forehead against the wall, just to feel the coolness on my skin, the temperature stone cold and soothing, bringing slight relief to this face newly marred. I'm on the second floor of the courthouse building, a guard outside my door. It's a cell, really, but they call it the waiting room, a kind of holding tank for the soon-to-be-judged. Innocent, I go free; guilty, I stay.

Two guards—I haven't seen them before—walk quickly past my locked door. They glance inside the window as they pass, wanting to catch a glimpse of me, curious to see the woman whose crime made headline news. A sharp tension cuts the air, something almost palpable, as prickly as stinging thorns. The guards wait, as do I, for the verdict. Everyone wants it over with.

Placing both hands on the wall, I feel the cool texture of concrete against bare skin. My fingernails, once long and manicured, painted in reds and pinks, are gone now, chewed to the nubs. Earlier, for lunch, I ate an apple, the only food I could manage to eat. A trickle of juice, very sweet, dribbled down my chin. I didn't wipe it off. Instead, I leaned back against the cell wall, closed my eyes, savored that apple as if it was the first I'd ever tasted. I thought about a happier time, the time I realized I was in love, really in love. We took an afternoon off from the winery and went hiking in the mountains, the air fresh and smelling of rich humus and tree bark. He said I had such a carefree manner, my step blithe and springy, like a young girl on a clandestine adventure, that anyone, just by observation, could tell I thought nothing bad would happen that day. *Carefree, blithe, and springy*—not words usually applied to me. My hair was blond and clipped short, a style worn by tomboys or gamines, and that morning I wore scuffed tennis shoes and faded blue jeans and a black T-shirt that said, in cotton-candy–pink lettering, "Sweet . . . but not innocent." I looked like a teenager from the back, he told me, my body slight, my arms slimly muscled, but as soon as I turned around, anyone could see I was a woman, late twenties, maybe early thirties, hard to tell with a face like mine, he said, smooth, no lines, an unusual face, slightly odd, difficult to describe—and here he stroked my cheek, then added—but with a waifish expression, sweet, innocent, vulnerable too, in those pale blue eyes, inspiring protection, wanted or not. His words took me by surprise. Where others, and I, saw a peculiar coldness in my face, he discovered something else.

That apple made me cry.

I sit down. The trial and stay in jail have taken their toll: dark crescents beneath my eyes, from lack of sleep, give me a haunted look, and a heavy air of defeat seems weighted on my shoulders. My hair, grown a few inches, hangs straight and limp. The judge, from the very beginning, denied me bail, and even though Napa County is on a fast-track court system, I've been in custody for almost three months now. If the verdict comes back guilty, I'll be in prison for years. I'll be an old woman by the time I'm released. I may never get out.

As I think about this, my heart races, pounds. "It's okay, it's okay," I mumble to myself, quietly, over and over. "It's okay." I knead my hands, balled up tight in fists, the knuckles white, into the sides of my thighs. Imprisonment, for years and years. It's almost too big to think about, too incomprehensible. This shouldn't be happening to me, not on top of everything else. The world will go on, the seasons will change, the sun will rise on a new day. All without me. No sunshine in a prison cell. I close my eyes, try to squeeze back the tears. My fists dig into my legs. Right now, right this moment, I want to believe in God. Save me, God, I pray. Save me from this. But all I get is a sinking feeling that hollows out my chest. Maybe this is what I deserve. I rock slowly on the edge of the chair. Through the narrow window, I see the clock high up on the wall, another hour gone by. I want to scream. I want to cry.

Instead, I get up and begin pacing again, drag myself slowly from one end of the room to the other. I try to divert myself, try to think of other things. I used to wear beautiful clothes, dresses, skirts, tailored suits, classy slacks, skimpy sundresses, lots of clothes in different colors, a rainbow of hues. Now I always wear blue; blue chambray work shirt, faded blue pants—standard jail issue. I've come to hate the color blue. Slowly, I walk back and forth, to the door, to the wall, back to the door again, my shoes beating out a soundless march, my legs and back aching with each painful movement. "It's okay," I say again, even though I don't believe it.

When I think back, I wonder what I could have done to prevent all of this from happening. Almost a year ago, I met the McGuane family. Seven months later, I was in jail. But it began even before that, with a lifelong search I was powerless to stop. At one time, I would have given anything for my questions to be answered, for my search to be successful. There was no price too high. The reality, however, is the forfeiture of my freedom.

Peering out the window, I see guards down the hall, then I check the clock once more. My hands feel cold, my mouth dry. A few minutes ago, I was sweating; now my palms are clammy. This, I recognize as fear. I swallow, but I have no saliva. This, also, is fear. The time is close, a verdict will come soon. The jury will decide if I am guilty. Suddenly, my skin begins to itch, a frantic call to life, as if all the nerve endings are screaming to be felt. In my ears, the blood pounds, hammers out my panic in a throbbing pulse. "It's okay," I whisper, "it's okay," repeating the words that have become my mantra, my prayer of reassurance, two small words of denial to get me through the day—but it isn't okay. Nothing is okay. I don't want to spend the rest of my life in prison. I was foolish to believe no price was too high. I say it once more, "It's okay," then place my forehead against the gray wall, again feel the cool concrete on bare skin, and wish for a mother, for the warmth of a mother's love, unconditional and always protective. Where is my mother?

I try to think of other things.

A newspaper reporter dubbed me Madame de Sade. And the tabloids, reveling in that sobriquet, pushed it even further—they had me bartering in souls, scourging human flesh, participating in pagan orgies, both bloody and sexual. They turned me into a monster because monsters are easy prey. The truth is much simpler. I came to Napa Valley, to the McGuanes' home, for answers. They didn't know who I was—who I *really* was—and perhaps the truth is never that simple, but no one was supposed to get hurt, least of all me. Two people changed all that. One tried to be my savior, the other my destroyer. I did not foresee who would bring me down. I did not see it coming. I thought I was smarter, wiser, more cunning than the other. I was wrong.

———

I look at the clock one more time. Still, there is no verdict. And there is no one with me while I wait, no family, no friends. I sit on a chair and close my eyes. I remember the opening line of a Dickens story I'd read in college: "Whether I shall turn out to be the hero of my own life, or whether that station will be held by anybody else, these pages must show." For me, there are no pages, no story for others to see. People will remember what is printed in the newspapers. I will remember what I can. Only one thing is for certain: I am no hero.

Panic Snap

CHAPTER ONE

My life began when I was seventeen. Before that, I have no memories. Although borne of a mother, I am lost to her now, and the person I think of as my sole begetter is the farmworker who found me one early morning, unconscious, on County Road 104, south of Davis, in an empty, dew-covered field, my body, like a newborn's, blood-covered and naked. I was airlifted to the UCD Medical Center in Sacramento, where I remained in a coma for nearly two weeks. When I finally opened my eyes, I remembered nothing, not the field, not even my name. The people I'd known, the places I'd been, and the things I'd done, were all gone, vanished, as if they'd taken a vacation without inviting me along. What I had left were vague but certain understandings of the way life worked: although I didn't know why, I knew people ate eggs for breakfast and sandwiches for lunch; I knew, without confirmation, that I could type a letter and drive a car and set a table with all the utensils in their proper order; I also knew, just as surely, that I couldn't speak a foreign language and that if I sat in front of a piano, I couldn't play. Abilities stayed with me; people, places, and events disappeared. For weeks, I'd look around the hospital room, the walls creamy white and blank, a pale pink vase on the table next to the bed, and attempt to picture my life as it was—with a mother, a father, brothers and sisters perhaps, a house with a wide front porch, and a yard edged with yellow roses— but then I'd realize, with a start, that the images came from a magazine left on the bedside table, or from a television program I'd seen the day before, and that my real memories were as white and blank as the hospital walls.

The police attempted, unsuccessfully, to track down the person or persons who left me for dead. They conducted a national fingerprint search, tried to locate my parents, my identity, but no one came forth to claim me—no family, no friends, no one at all. It was as if I'd been dumped from a spaceship, as if I'd come from another planet. I had no past, no history whatsoever. That was fifteen years ago.

I took the name Carly Tyler: Carly from a nurse at the hospital, Tyler from the author of a book I'd read during my recovery, *Morgan's Passing*, about a man who was having identity problems of his own. The name seemed to fit, even if it really wasn't mine.

When I was twenty—more or less; my age had never been precisely determined—when I was twenty, except for a few minor touch-up surgeries, the doctors were finally finished with me. All in all, I couldn't complain about the results. I had no permanent physical injuries, and no one could tell that my face had once been broken in so many different places. For a long time, I walked with a limp, but even that disappeared. A few scars, faint white trails, the stubborn signs of prior damage, still streak across my body in unsuspecting places, the inside of my right thigh, along a rib, beneath my left breast, all of them concrete reminders of what my brain chooses to ignore, the lingering signposts of an earlier time, scar-tissued semaphores leading the way to an, as yet, unknown past. The scars really aren't bad now, barely noticeable unless someone looks very closely, and if that happens, I pass them off as the results of minor childhood accidents: a fall from a tree house, I lie, a tumble off my skates. Except for my memories, I'm intact.

The doctors, successful at patching up my body, couldn't fix my mind. They insisted I continue seeing them—I was a prime case study—but I soon tired of their talk, all their jargon about functional retrograde amnesia, post-traumatic confusional conditions, organic memory defects, dissociative fugue states, psychogenic and hysterical amnesia. They weren't helping me recover my past, and by the time I turned twenty, I was ready for a future, for a life that went beyond hospitals and doctors and tests, for a life that went beyond the newspapers' periodic stories of me, "The Mystery Girl Without a Past." I went to college, I worked, I traveled from city to city, eventually becoming the head chef for a trendy restaurant in Sacramento; and for my friends, I made up memories to fill the void. No one knew I had been the Mystery Girl.

But if I kept my past from others, it was never far from me. What happened that day fifteen years before? And why had no one missed me? Every day, for fifteen years, I asked those questions, never receiving any answers. I moved from one city to another, constantly searching. The doctors had said my actions and behavior might be influenced by the things I'd forgotten, so I always questioned the choices and decisions I had made, scrutinizing them, looking for unconscious motives that steered me toward a particular direction. Why had I majored in English at college and then drifted, without a clear plan, without any prior knowledge, into the restaurant business? Did my parents own a restaurant? Had I, in high school, worked part-time as a waitress? Why did I insist on remaining in northern California? And what about my inexplicable aversions? For no apparent reason, I felt uneasy walking on brick floors and climbing spiral staircases; I always found an excuse not to date large men; I panicked in dark, closed-in spaces. For fifteen years, I kept searching for answers, trying to find connections in everything I did. If I was drawn to a particular place, I would scour the streets for long-forgotten landmarks. If someone looked vaguely familiar, I would quiz him until I was certain we had never met. All to no avail. Not once had I felt the certitude of recognition.

Until last year.

I'm sitting in a diner, but I ignore all the people and noise around me. I sip the last of my coffee, lukewarm and bitter at the bottom of the cup, then reach for my magazine, *Wine Spectator*, lying on the counter in front of me. The magazine is almost a year old and well worn from my constant perusal, the pages ruffled and puckering along the edges, a brownish coffee spill staining the right-hand corner. It doesn't matter. I have five other copies at home, packed away, covered with plastic and in perfect condition. I turn to page ninety-two and gaze, once more, at the picture of a tall, blond-haired man standing in a vineyard, the yellow leaves on the grapevines far behind him like flecks of gold in the midafternoon autumn sun. He's an impressive man, sturdy looking and heavy boned and tanned, his hair as golden as the leaves on the vines. And there's another picture of him in the winery, taken twenty years earlier, his body much leaner, his face not as lined. His name is James McGuane. The article, about his family's small winery in Napa Valley, says he is forty-three. When I was left for dead, fifteen years before, he was only twenty-eight.

I stare at his photograph, mesmerized by his face. There's an air of privileged composure about him, as if he's sure of his place in the world and the world belongs to him. His eyes, squinting slightly in the sun, look faintly amused. The name of the winery is Byblos. A year ago, flipping casually through the magazine, I saw the name and suddenly froze, unable to turn the page. My hand began to tremble as I stared at the word: *Byblos*. I knew that name. It was connected to my past, but in what way I had no idea. When the farmworker had discovered me that early morning so long ago, he told the police I rallied for a few brief moments, slowly opened my eyelids, stared vacantly, then moaned and uttered the single word "bib" before losing consciousness once again. When the police questioned me later, telling me what I'd said, I could think of no significance attached to the word. It meant nothing to me, a child's bib, a lobster bib, a protective cloth, that was all. Now I'm certain I was struggling to say Byblos, a futile attempt to identify the person who had beaten me. Bib, byb—they are pronounced the same. But, even more important, when I first saw the magazine article about Byblos, I *felt* an intense connection. I'd read the article, then read it again and again. No images came to my mind, no memories of the past, just the surety that Byblos, in some way, was connected to me.

And the man—somehow, I'd known the man. I would look at his picture and a feeling of confused familiarity would wash over me, like a hazy dream I couldn't put in perspective, slipping away as soon as I opened my eyes. I'd known James McGuane at one time. I was sure of it a year ago; I'm sure of it now. This man is a link to my past, to the first seventeen years of my life. He could be a friend, or a relative even—or he could be the person who left me for dead. For nearly a year, I stared at his picture, too paralyzed to take any action at all. I debated going to the police, but I realized the folly of that—if they couldn't find the person who'd harmed me fifteen years ago, what chances would they have of doing so now? I still have no memories, no proof, nothing substantial to tell the police. If James McGuane was once a friend of mine, I have nothing to fear. If he was the man who beat me and left me for dead . . . well, I will have to discover that for myself.

I close the magazine, set it aside. The diner is crowded, the room noisy with a steady ruckus of clacking dishes and a crying baby and the pitched rumble of voices competing to be heard. I'm thirty-two years old, and I live in Napa Valley now. I gave notice to my employer in Sacramento and moved here a month ago. This morning, I begin a new job.

I will be the chef for the McGuane family.

The job will allow me the proximity I need. I may not find my answers right away, and I realize I must be cautious, but today marks the beginning of the end of my search.

I swivel on the stool, lean my elbows on the counter behind me, and take in the diner with a sweeping glance—the family of five clambering into the only empty booth; the manager, round and pudgy, with soft white skin, standing at the cash register, taking a customer's money; the wide fuchsia and mauve stripes decorating the walls, making the diner look like a pastel-colored candy shop.

Self-consciously, I reach up with one hand and run my fingers through my hair. It's pale blond, the color of very cold butter. Last week, I cut it—daringly short, above my ears, from a picture I'd liked in a fashion magazine—and I'm still not used to the bare feeling on the back of my neck. I've always kept my hair long, an ersatz security blanket I suppose, to hide as much of my face as possible.

I cross my legs; my skirt, a light floral print, slides up a few inches. Several men are watching me, obliquely, but I don't care. I know men find me attractive, yet I'm not sure why. I'm not beautiful; however, I do have the kind of face—because of my surgeries—that people don't forget: enticing, yet cruel, is how one person once put it. My face, subtly off-kilter, a little asymmetrical, brings up subliminal feelings in others—they sense something is not quite right, but they can't put their finger on it. They take a second look. Some say that my lips, although full and sensual, seem to curl, ever so slightly, in an arrogant sneer. And most people read something aloof and reserved in my high cheekbones and strong chin and clear, almost colorless, skin. A woman, unaware of my surgeries, once told me I looked as cool as stainless steel. I think she meant it as a compliment.

Checking my watch for the time, I turn around. I leave three dollars on the counter, pick up my magazine, and leave. Outside, sunlight glints off the cars in the parking lot, off the chrome and side-view mirrors and windshields in gleaming slants. The sky is a bright, endless dome of blue, with a late-morning white sun shining down and a gentle breeze stirring the air. Small flowers, yellow and white and pale pink, bloom on the side of the road, and a bird trills in a eucalyptus tree. Spring is here, a feeling of renewal and bright possibilities in the air. Finally, I shall know who I am. Walking across the asphalt, I dig in my purse for sunglasses and put them on.

I get in my car—a white convertible—turn off the main road, then head north on the Silverado Trail. All around me, vineyards dominate the green hillsides; they seem to creep across the land, taking over the flat valley floor and crawling up and over the sides of gently rolling hills, straight rows of vines forming quiltlike patterns as far as I can see. But the vines, unlike the grassy hills and early-blooming flowers, are still dormant, the vine canes knotty and gnarled and bare, spread out laterally from tall wooden posts, like men nailed to crosses. Between the rows, yellow mustard plants—growing wild, rioting, shooting up—seem to almost smother the vines. I wonder, not for the first time, if I am doing the right thing. My preoccupation for the truth, for knowledge of my past, is obsessive, blocking out everything else, taking over my life as effectively as the yellow mustard running riot over the vines. But my obsession for the past is not solely for me—it is not, even, primarily for me. It is for the seventeen-year-old girl who lay dying in an empty field south of Davis on County Road 104. While I emerged from the coma, she did not. She is completely gone, a human cipher, a nonentity, not even a remote memory. Nothing of her remains.

Physically, I bear no resemblance to the girl in the field. I've grown two inches since then, and my body has subtly changed with the passage of fifteen years. The doctors warned me that if I regained my memory, I wouldn't recognize myself in the face they gave me, and even my voice has changed. It's pleasant sounding, with a breathless, almost sexy quality to it—but it isn't mine. The surgeon gave it to me, repairing minor throat damage. Nothing belongs to me. The seventeen-year-old was erased, and I appeared. I want her back. I must know who I am and who tried to kill me and why. I need these answers, at any cost.

I push up my sunglasses on the bridge of my nose. I drive with the car top down, the wind blowing on my face, one wrist crooked over the steering wheel. Gazing across the land, I see vineyards everywhere I look, acres and acres of them. And set in the middle of the fields are the wineries, each of them distinct, some as grand as French chateaux, others as cold and gray and formidable as crenelated castles of the Middle Ages, others yet like modern museums and Victorian homes, and some even resembling old American barns, wooden and rustic, all of them isolated, set apart by acres of vines. Some men, field hands I suppose they're called, are working in the distance, not paying attention to the few cars driving up the winery lanes—people coming to visit for a midweek winetasting—and a lone tractor moves slowly on a dirt road, rumbling by, kicking up clouds of dust. The warm wind blows around me, and I feel my vulnerability in the breeze on the back of my newly shorn neck: bare and exposed. I am taking a chance by coming here, I know that. Pushing down on the accelerator, I use the speed to clear my mind, the trees rushing by in a greenish blur.

At Winding Way Canyon Road, I turn right. The land, emerald green from earlier spring rain, seems to undulate: lazy low hills, rolling knolls, waving grasses. Lush and fertile, it looks like a storybook land—if only I believed in fairy tales. Up ahead, on the side of the road, I see a pair of stone pillars, the entrance to Byblos Winery, and continue on my way. A knot of anxiety forms in my stomach as I drive between the pillars. I've been here several times—when Mrs. McGuane interviewed me for the job, as a visitor to the tasting room—and on each occasion I got a similar feeling of apprehension.

A narrow lane, lined with olive trees, leads me to the winery, a huge stone building, ancient, the gray walls almost hidden by crawling ivy and patches of yellow lichen. It is not familiar to me, nothing here is. I'd thought, when I first came to Byblos, that something recognizable might jump out at me, that I would exclaim, "Yes! I've been here! I've seen the lichen-covered walls of the winery before!"

But that hasn't happened. If this place is in my mind, it is hidden from me still, unavailable. I drive farther, about a quarter mile down the winding road. The McGuane property is situated in a small bowl-shaped valley, with vineyards matting the land. The brown vines, old and arthritic looking, stretch out on the trellises like corpse arms. Finally, the lane opens up to a circular driveway in front of the family home, a large, two-story country estate, European, I think, with elaborate dark brickwork and arched windows with paned glass. A shiny black car with gold trim, one of those large 4x4 sport-utility vehicles, is parked in front of the house.

I pull into the circular driveway, stop several car lengths behind the black vehicle, a Jeep Grand Cherokee, the logo says, and turn off the engine. Something sweet scents the air, wisteria perhaps, although I'm not sure. My knowledge of plants is limited. I stay in the car, push the sleeves of my sweater up to my elbows, gazing at the house through my sunglasses. It's surrounded by tall trees, one of which, with its long outstretched branches, reaches up and curls over the house like a leafy, protective umbrella, or perhaps a green burial shroud—I can't decide which. The house is impressive, old-country charm on a grand scale, and it has a solid feel to it, a look of permanence, as if it's part of the land, taking root. This feeling of permanence is completely foreign to me. For most of my life, I was transient, always on the move, always searching, with the bitter knowledge that I could pack up and leave with nothing, with no one, to tie me down.

Taking off my sunglasses, I look around. Although the house is beautiful, and the morning lovely—warm air, birds chirping, wildflowers just beginning to bloom, an azure sky—a distinct feeling of uneasiness overcomes me. There is a strange heaviness to the air, and it feels ominous, as if it's a warning. Involuntarily, I shudder. Goose bumps, although I'm not cold, raise the fine blond hair on my arms. Frowning, I push down the sleeves of my sweater. It is too late for second thoughts now.

I shake off the mood and get out of the car. My job here—cooking lunch and dinner for the McGuanes and their guests—should be relatively easy, certainly easier than cooking in a restaurant. Mrs. McGuane's husband died several years ago, and her adult children, James and his twin sister, Gina, run the winery. I haven't met either of them yet, but know that both live on the estate, Gina in the guest cottage behind the main home, and her brother in another house down the lane. I lean back against my white convertible, looking around. It's taken me fifteen years to get here.

I think I should go inside, but I stall for a few minutes more, knowing that once I cross their threshold, there will be no turning back. I gaze at the house, elegant in an old-fashioned way. The front entry, high and arched, is enclosed in brick, and tall, narrow windows flank both sides of the wooden double door.

Suddenly, the door swings open, startling me, and then I see him, the man in the *Wine Spectator* magazine: James McGuane. He's glancing at a sheet

of paper in his hand, closing the wooden door behind him, preoccupied, and he doesn't see me standing by my car. A wave of panic rushes over me, and
I feel, momentarily, unable to move. Irrationally,
even though it's been fifteen years, even though my
surgeries have given me a face so different from the
one I would naturally have, I think he will recognize
me. And if he'd tried to kill me before, why wouldn't
he do it again? He is a man with much to lose—his
winery, his reputation, his liberty—if he discovers
who I am. Then logic takes over and I push down
my fear. There is no way he can recognize me. I do
not have the face of a seventeen-year-old girl. I do
not have the face with which I was born. I am no
one to him.

Taking a step forward, looking up, he sees me
standing by the car. He hesitates for a moment, then
says, "Hi," smiling uncertainly. He walks toward me.

CHAPTER TWO

He seems almost larger than life. Involuntarily, as if his mere presence is crowding me, I take one step back, intimidated. He's a big man, six-foot-four at least, who looks as though he's used to having his way. His clothes, a long-sleeved pearl-white shirt and black trousers, appear tailored, fitting him perfectly, yet still he gives the impression of bursting out of them, his body substantial and muscular and not easily contained, the physique of a husky body-guard a few years beyond his prime. He takes a last brief glance at the sheet of paper in his hand, then slips it in his back pocket.

"I'm Carly Tyler," I say, "the new—"

"The new cook," he interrupts, smiling, finishing my sentence. As he's introducing himself, I can tell he is giving me a quick once-over, sizing me up, glancing briefly at my flowered skirt and pale pink cashmere sweater, then pausing at my face, find-ing—as do most people—something inscrutable there, something not quite right. And, as do most people, he quickly masks his curiosity so as not to offend. He holds out his hand, big and beefy, like a bear's paw, to shake mine. When I touch his skin, I experience something I hadn't anticipated: excitement, a precarious thrill. It's visceral, something in my gut, and I like the way it feels—very similar, I imagine, to a hunter encountering his prey. I lower my head, not meeting his gaze, afraid I might give myself away. His hand is immense next to mine, and I expect his grasp to be firm, but it's gentle, restrained, as if he's afraid he might crush the bones in my hand. I've known other large men who are like this, wary of their own strength, careful to hold back. But if James is so inclined, he'd have no trouble causing me bodily harm. Perhaps he already has.

"Welcome to Byblos," he says, releasing his grip. His voice is friendly, mildly solicitous, the employer greeting the new employee. He takes a quick glance at his watch. "My mother says you come highly recommended."

Nervously, I smile a little, then shrug. I look for a sign of recognition in his eyes, but there is none. Momentarily, I feel a pang of disappointment. Although I knew it unlikely, possibly even absurd, I was still hoping for a joyous reunion, the long-lost girlfriend finally returns. That was my fantasy—that my prior relationship with James had been good rather than bad, and that, despite a fifteen-year separation and a noticeably altered appearance, he would find in my face, through the sheer power of love, a trace of the person I'd once been. Perhaps, fifteen years ago, on a solitary afternoon walk, I'd been abducted. Perhaps, relentlessly, over the years, James had searched for me. Perhaps. But not likely. Deep down, instinctively, or maybe it's not instinct but rather the struggling attempt of memories trying to surface, deep down I know my connection to him is fraught with malintent, with danger and pain. For us, there will be no happy reunion.

He says something about business in town, and that his mother is waiting for me inside the house, then he turns and heads for his car. He has a John Wayne walk—a sort of slow-rolling stride, self-assured, solid, as if he owns the land he treads upon, which, in this case, he does. Even though I know I'll see him soon, I feel panicked by his hasty departure, as if he's slipping away. After so many years without any clues to my identity, I'm reluctant to let him leave so quickly.

"Wait!" I call out, then realize, too late, that my voice is filled with a desperate urgency. I cringe, admonishing myself to be more careful. I can't afford to make any mistakes.

He turns around and looks at me, quizzical, his head tilted just a notch as if to say, "What?"

A bird trills, then, in a flash of color, it flits to another tree on the far edge of the driveway. I hadn't noticed before, but a large dog, a brown German shepherd, is lying under the tree, his head resting on his front paws, his tail thumping the ground as he watches us. James waits.

"If you have a few minutes," I finally say, and I spread my arms wide, palms up, gesturing around me, "I haven't seen the property yet."

He hesitates a second, looking at me calmly, without emotion. I hear him jangling his keys in his front pants pocket, then he pulls them out, coming to a decision. "Sure," he says, opening the car door. "Get in. I'll give you a quick tour."

He follows the gravel driveway behind the house. I can see, beyond the colorful gardens and a stretch of lawn leading up to his sister's guest cottage, the low, green hills in the distance, vine covered and tree topped. Far away, a large bird—is it a vulture?—circles lazily in the air, its wings spread wide. Leisurely, James drives across the land, pointing out the different vineyards, telling me which grape varietals—zinfandel, cabernet sauvignon, merlot, a little malbec—are planted on which field. Some of the vines are thick and ropy and rough looking, others slender with brittlelike branches, all of them without vegetation. Bright-yellow mustard plants, masses of them, shoot up from the ground, pullulating, making the vines appear even more barren.

He turns now, driving west, pointing out the narrow, curving lane leading up to his house. When I hear him say this—"my house"—I feel a nervous, excited flutter in my chest. I can't see his home from the car, it's hidden behind a small hill, but I realize there's a good chance I may have been inside it. If I was seventeen when I knew James, underage, and he was twenty-eight, he probably kept me hidden from his family—but he may have taken me to his home.

Obliquely, I watch him as he drives. I know, in some misguided way, I am attracted to him—I felt it the moment he shook my hand. I want to reach out and touch him, but of course I don't. What would my psychiatrists and doctors say now?—I find the man who may be responsible for my attack, and instead of revulsion, I feel a seductive pull, a pull as enticing as a warm fire on a rainy day: I want to get close. But I haven't lost sight of who he is and the danger he presents. A warm fire may feel good, but the flames can scorch my skin. I move closer to the door.

Surreptitiously, I take another look. His hair is thick and straight and sun-drenched, golden from many hours outdoors, and although he's a good-looking man, he's more rugged than refined, the kind of man most women want to have around if there's any sign of trouble. He exudes strength. Or perhaps it's power. Once again, I feel overwhelmed. He seems to demand a lot of space, his presence flowing beyond the boundaries of mere flesh. I wonder, when the time comes—and I'm sure it will—if I will be a match for him.

He parks in front of the winery, a massive building of cut stone, mouse gray in color and covered with creeping ivy and lichen, built before the turn of the century, he says, and then he walks me through the building, stopping occasionally to chat with the various workers. In brightly lit rooms with white walls, he points out double rows of cylindrical fermentation tanks, a gleaming filtration system, huge stainless-steel racking tanks with exterior cooling jackets, a glass-enclosed mechanized bottling line. A maze of glass tubing snakes along the walls, for transporting the wine from one location to another. A man, in knee-high black rubber boots, is hosing down the concrete floor. He turns off the water and nods to us as we pass. Then James leads me inside a dank, cool room, the lighting very low, and I see rows upon rows of oak barrels, lying sideways, aging the wine, James says, on the lees. A woody, yeasty smell permeates the air.

We walk outside, blinking in the sudden change of bright light, and I see, next to the building, on a large concrete pad, another slew of winemaking equipment—gigantic V-shaped troughs, hoppers, huge stainless-steel oblong machinery, hoses, and more vats and tanks. I'm sure there's an order here, but it just seems like a jumble of oversized equipment to me. James takes me over to the concrete pad, begins to explain the functions of the large machinery.

"What happened here?" I ask. I'm standing next to the piece of equipment he called the winepress—

a huge cylindrical tank, lying horizontally, secured by a metal frame. A section of the frame is mangled, twisted.

"An accident," he says. "Someone turned on the electrical power not realizing the back door of the press was open. You can't see it from here, but the door is solid steel. When the press rotated, the door took out the dump chute and part of this steel beam. Fortunately, no one was near the door when it happened. A welder is coming out later today to start the repair work."

We both turn as we see a white truck, with dried mud spattered on the sides and on the hood, pull up. A dark-haired woman, very tall and slender, gets out and walks toward us. James introduces me to his sister, Gina, his twin, although, except for the height and eye color, they look nothing alike. He's big boned and brawny, with a rawness to him that's hard to define. She, on the other hand, is striking, dazzling I think, in a sort of flinty, hard-edged way. She has long black hair, thick and wavy, and light green eyes the color of ripened limes. With the way she's dressed, she looks like an urban cowgirl—tight jeans, a red-and-black checkered shirt, the sleeves rolled up to her elbows, pointy-toed leather cowboy boots.

She shakes my hand, a brief, perfunctory gesture, gives me a short smile, then, preoccupied, she turns to James and begins talking about a problem in the winery, ignoring me. Black curls droop over one of her eyes; she tosses her head to get the hair off her face. I run my fingers through my own short-cropped hair. Before I'd cut it, it was nearly as long as Gina's. I continue to watch her, fascinated. Her eyelashes are long and dark, and she has a no-nonsense face, angular and very direct, tanned from the sun. Proprietorially, she puts her hand on her brother's arm and turns slightly away from me.

I lift a hand to shade my eyes from the sun. Next to James and Gina, I feel small and insignificant, dwarfish, stunted in growth. I have to look up at them. They continue talking. James, putting his hand on Gina's shoulder, bends slightly so their heads are closer together, and I get the feeling of a conspiracy, although I can hear they're only talking about a defective pump. A few moments later, they laugh at something, still touching one another, then Gina, rushing into another subject, calls her brother Jimmy. It slides off her tongue easily, affectionately, a name left over from childhood days. This world of effortless familiarity, this world of sibling ease, eludes me. If I have brothers or sisters, they are buried in my past.

Gina gives me a sidelong glance, turns away, then glances once again. I have learned, over the years, not to flinch or bow my head in embarrassment when this happens. I know my face compels others to look, but what I see in Gina's expression is more than mere curiosity. With a start, I wonder if she guesses who I am.

CHAPTER THREE

"I know it's here somewhere," Mrs. McGuane mumbles, peering inside a cabinet. She's nearly seventy, with snowy white hair she doesn't bother to dye.

I smile to myself. I'm used to her frequent interruptions while I'm in the kitchen. In fact, I rather enjoy them. Since I've been here, she's the only family member who genuinely seems to like me. Gina is friendly but reserved, James standoffish. Neither of them goes out of their way to welcome me in their home, and, other than seeing them at meals, we have little contact. At first I was worried that Gina, somehow, had figured out who I was, but I don't think she has. She would not be so calm if that was the case. Besides, if James is the one who left me for dead, it's unlikely he would tell his sister.

I begin sifting flour over a sheet of waxed paper. For dessert this evening, I'm making an almond cake, served with sliced strawberries and fresh mascarpone, a soft Italian cream cheese, which I'll flavor with orange brandy. Mrs. McGuane opens another cabinet door, shuts it, goes on to the next. She's looking for a special serving platter she wants to use tonight.

"Did you check the china cabinet?" I ask.

"Yes, yes," she says, distracted, her forehead scrunched together in puzzlement. She pokes around in the cupboard. "That's the first place I looked."

She's wearing a peach-colored dress with crisply ironed pleats, and as she wanders around the kitchen, it makes a soft rustling sound, like leaves in the wind. She's slightly round in the middle, with barely a waist, and she's very tall, almost as tall as Gina. This is a family of giants. I've never minded being short, but when I'm around the three of them together, I feel unnaturally small.

She walks over to the pantry, goes inside. Even though the kitchen is large and efficient, there's a comfortable feel to it, the room light and airy with paned windows and natural pine cabinetry and cream-colored walls. Three ovens, a professional range covered with a vent hood, and cabinets with pale countertops line one wall. A huge butcher-block island centers the room, above which, suspended from a brass rack, dangles an assortment of mixing bowls, colanders, pots and pans, and various cooking utensils.

When she comes out of the pantry, she looks around, a bewildered expression on her face. Then, quite abruptly, she smiles, remembering. "That James!" she says.

I stop sifting the flour when I hear his name.

"He borrowed it several days ago, and I'll just bet he never returned it."

It's a warm day, and I'm wearing an ecru backless sundress, the hem barely to my knees. A few scars are visible, but only to an observant eye—most would not notice the fine, threadlike lines. I saw James earlier today, and although I know other men would like the way I look—bare arms and legs, sandals, little makeup, lots of skin—he seemed indifferent. He's away on business today, and won't be back until late this evening.

She sighs. "I suppose I can make do with another platter—but that one would've been perfect."

I dump more flour in the sifter. I've been here almost three weeks now, and I still have no clues to my identity. I know I must be patient, build up the McGuanes' trust in me, but I'm anxious for answers. "After I put the cake in the oven," I say, keeping my voice casual, "I can go down to his house and look for it."

"Oh," Mrs. McGuane says, pausing, giving this some thought. Her eyebrows, faint wisps of white, knit together. "I suppose it wouldn't hurt." Then she politely adds, "But I don't want to put you out."

I shrug, as if I have little interest in the matter. "I don't mind," I say. "I'll be through here in a few minutes."

"Well . . . I have so much to do this afternoon. It would be a big help." She touches her temple with her middle finger, rubs it gently, thinking. Her hands, ivory as oyster crackers, are delicate with old blue veins.

"No problem," I say.

Several hoop-backed bar stools line the butcher-block counter, and she sits on one, absently watching me mix the ingredients for the cake, almond paste, butter, sugar, eggs, lemon zest, and a little Grand Marnier. Her forehead slowly creases into a frown, and I assume she's thinking about her plans for this evening. She's having a small dinner party tonight, for a few people in the wine business. James won't be back from San Francisco in time for dinner, but Gina will be here to help entertain.

I think about James's house, hurrying with the cake. I say, "You're lucky to have James and Gina to run the winery. They seem so devoted to Byblos."

She looks up, her face questioning. Her white hair looks soft and fluffy, like a ball of cotton, and her eyes are clear, the skin around them set with a delicate maze of etched wrinkles that seem to splinter and spread out like finely crackled porcelain. Even though I've been here only a few weeks, I'm fond of her already.

"Were they always like that?" I ask. "Interested in the winery?"

Her eyes sparkle with a sudden animation, elfish. She laughs, a soft, pleasant sound. "Oh my, no," she says. "James was an artist, a painter, and he was quite wild, always getting in trouble of one sort or another—just kid stuff, nothing serious, but nevertheless he caused his father and me a great deal of aggravation. We didn't think he'd ever turn around. And Gina, well, she wasn't wild like James, but she had no interest in the winery at all. She wanted to be a biologist, was even set to marry one of her professors. She was working on her doctorate when, out of the blue, she changed her mind—about both the professor and her degree—and decided to learn the family business instead."

"That worked out nicely," I say.

"Yes. Of course, both children grew up here, so they were always exposed to the winery, and they helped out on weekends and summer vacations, but neither of them really had a passion for winemaking. James came home after college—"

"Where did he go?" I ask, interrupting.

"The university over in Davis," she says. "Both James and Gina went there."

As did I, I think.

"Anyway," Mrs. McGuane is saying, "James came home after college—his father insisted on it, he was grooming him to take over the business—but he was young and restless, more interested in women than wine. It seemed James was too irresponsible to run Byblos and Gina too indifferent, and then, almost overnight, both children were entrenched in the business, as if it was their true calling. They both love the winery now, as much as their father did."

"It seems unusual," I say, "that they would both come around at the same time."

"Twins," Mrs. McGuane says, shrugging, as if that word is explanation enough.

"How old were they?"

"When they made the winery their career?" she asks. She gets up and stretches, then waves her hand dismissively. "I don't know," she says. "In their late twenties? Maybe. It was a long time ago."

I can tell her mind is on something else, the dinnerware for this evening perhaps, but the significance of her disclosure does not pass me by. Both James and Gina made dramatic life changes, right about the time I was left for dead. I pour the cake batter into a springform pan, then put it in the oven and set the timer.

"I'll get the spare key to James's house," Mrs. McGuane says, and she leaves the room.

I drive down the lane, passing rows of grapevines. Off to the right, I see the vineyard manager, a burly man with skin as brown and tough as leather, in the middle of a field, inspecting the vines. He lifts his hand to wave as I drive by. Two weeks ago, the vineyard workers disked the fields so the mustard wouldn't compete with the budding vines, and, with most of the yellow-flowering plants plowed under, the fields have a more manicured look now. I gaze at the ring of keys I'd tossed on the passenger seat. I'll have only forty-five minutes before the cake comes out of the oven. Forty-five minutes to search James's house.

On the road leading up to his home, I turn left, then curve around the small oak-covered hillock. Farther ahead, I see another field of vines. In the few weeks I've been in Napa, the vineyards throughout the valley have changed. First, the buds started to swell, then the new growth, delicate and fuzzy, burst forth. Now, although the vines are still gnarly and dead looking, new leaves, young and tender and very green, sprout from the tops of the branches in small clusters, the leaves reaching upward toward the sun. From a distance, the vineyards look like tufted brown bedspreads with straight rows of neat green stitching. With no direct ties to the land, I've never really noticed the change of the seasons before, not really. There's the shedding of winter coats, of course, and the donning of shorter-sleeved shirts as the days warm and lengthen, but, mostly, that is the extent of my seasonal awareness—a gradual shift of weather that signifies a change of wardrobe.

But at Byblos, and all across the Napa and Sonoma valleys, I notice people waking up to spring in a different way. For them, it's the beginning of the growing season, a time of new beginnings, new growth, feverish activity in the fields: disking, pruning, vine training, irrigating, tractors rumbling down the rows, spraying out a fine cloud of mildew-preventing sulfur. There's a sense of expectancy in the air, as fresh as the new green grass growing tall on the hills, as sweet-smelling as the colorful wildflowers coming into bloom. It's the time of renewal and rebirth, a very sexual time, new buds swelling and bursting and sprouting tender leaves, and it makes me think of fresh starts and my own new beginning. I feel as if, like the vines, I am coming out of a long hibernation, a fifteen-year period of dormancy from which it is time, finally, to emerge.

I pull up in front of James's house, which seems fairly secluded, tucked away in the hillock, not visible from the main road bisecting the McGuane property. The house is a tall structure of irregularly cut reddish-brown stones, cemented together with mortar. The building predates the winery, Mrs. McGuane told me, and was built by a farmer out of native tufa rock, compressed ash, from the nearby Glass Mountain quarry. Originally, it was a barn, but when James decided to move out of the main house, he took the old abandoned building and converted it into a home.

I try the front door, high and arched and wooden, slipping in the key and turning the knob. For a moment, I hesitate, feeling anxious at what I might find, then push open the heavy door. I stand in the doorframe and look around, unwilling, just yet, to step inside. The original structure seems intact, barnlike, with wide-open spaces and a high-vaulted ceiling, and the second story is really a mezzanine, a partial story, enclosed by a wooden balustrade, at the same level where the hayloft must have once been. I notice, uneasily—did my aversion to brick floors begin here?—that dark bricks pave the room, laid out in a herringbone pattern, and more bricks frame the arched windows. The room is very Gothic looking, sparse, the rafters exposed; and with no dividing walls, each living area flows smoothly into another. The entire place has a solid, masculine feel to it, stark and cool but elegantly, medievally, dramatic. I take in the stone hearth fireplace, the long wooden table, the dark paintings on the walls.

And then I see it: the black spiral staircase of wrought iron leading up to the second level. Without warning, my breath catches. Despite the open room, a wave of claustrophobia chokes me as I realize, unquestionably, that I've been here before. I can't say that I remember the house or the furniture, but, in some odd way, it's all very familiar, and it makes my skin prickle with fear. Disjointed visions, specks of incoherent memories, fragment the air around me. I try to concentrate on the images, but they slip out of my mind, like evasive dreams forgotten in the light of day. I stare at the wrought-iron staircase, mesmerized.

In the distance, a car horn blasts, no doubt from one of the tasting-room visitors, bringing me back with a startled shudder. Still, something nags at me, in the far reaches of my mind, but I can't bring it into focus. My doctors tried, many years ago, to retrieve my memories. They used amobarbital and thiopental, barbiturate medications, and hypnosis. Nothing was successful. Whatever happened here, in this house, it's something I don't want to remember.

I step inside, then shut the door behind me. As I turn, I notice the large painting on the wall, and take in the details that I'd missed earlier. Black and shades of gray predominate, overwhelm, with a slash of blood-red paint standing out, and then the picture comes into focus and I see, in the murky shadows, a woman down, blood pouring from a wound, a look of surprise on her dark face. I move on, walking slowly around the room, taking a closer look at the other paintings, feeling slightly dazed at what I see. They are all dark, gruesome works, mutilated bodies, faces tormented with some unseen horror, scenes of violence and decay, brutal pictures that rivet me, that challenge the viewer not to turn away, haunting in their sheer savagery. I look closer. The paintings are signed "J.McG." It seems James and I share a common link—we both are fascinated by the morbid, by the macabre. But whereas he, apparently, embraces it, I dread it.

Or do I? His paintings should offend me, but they don't. I feel I understand them, intuitively, and I wish I didn't. A year ago, even a month ago, I would've turned away in disgust. Now the darkness of them beckons, and this frightens me.

I look at my watch. I'm wasting precious time. I decide to start upstairs—I assume the bedroom is there—but then change my mind and cross over to the far right-hand corner, where James has set up a work area with an antique desk, a long walnut credenza, a three-drawer filing cabinet, and several glass-fronted bookcases. There's a back door near the credenza, and a brick-framed arched window that gives a view of the area behind his house. I glance out the window, see a concrete patio, some wrought-iron furniture, and, farther down, a very small building that appears to be some kind of tool or storage shed. It's made with the same reddish-brown tufa rock as his home, and there's a gigantic padlock on the door.

I turn back to James's work area. The desktop is crowded but orderly—stacks of paper in neat piles, and a computer, the screen blank. I sit down and go through his papers: a few unpaid bills, notices of upcoming events, business cards of associates, a letter from a friend in Colorado, inviting him to visit.

I put down the letter, then pull open the top drawer—pens, a ruler, notepads, stamps, tape, address labels. The next drawer is stuffed with files. I rifle through them quickly, just winery business. The bottom drawer is filled with more personal papers, receipts, check stubs, bank statements. Nothing of any use to me. I lean back in the chair. Two framed photos sit on his desk. One is of his mother and father, taken when they were younger, maybe ten or fifteen years ago. His father was big and burly, like James. The other photo is of James and Gina, also when they were younger, early twenties perhaps, their arms around each other, both smiling at the camera, looking as if nothing could harm them. Again, I see their easy familiarity with each other.

Picking up the photo, I gaze at James. His smile is faint, and he seems distracted, or maybe bored. The picture fails to capture his essence, the restrained intensity of his presence. Why, I wonder, am I attracted to him? Sure, he's good-looking, but I sense it's more than that. I scrutinize the photo, as if it could provide the answer. What is it, James, that makes me want you?

I hear the crunch of car tires on dirt and gravel. Startled, I jump up, dropping the picture frame on the floor. Crossing the room quickly, I peer out the arched window, then grimace at what I see. The black Cherokee is there, parked under the shade of a tree. James opens his car door and gets out. He glances at my white convertible, frowning a little, then starts for the house.

I dash back to the desk, check to make sure all the drawers are closed, then straighten up the piles of paper. I pick up the letter I'd read, from his friend in Colorado, trying to remember where James had laid it. I place it next to the business cards. No, it wasn't there. I move it to the other side of the desk. Regretfully, I look at the filing cabinet, which I didn't have time to search.

The doorknob turns, just a small scraping noise

that seems to reverberate in the large room. I bend
down to pick up the photo I'd dropped. With a sinking feeling, I notice a long, slender crack in the glass,
running lengthwise down the frame. Hearing the
door swing open, I hurriedly set the photo on the
desk where I'd found it, tilt it slightly so the crack
isn't as noticeable.

"What are you doing here?" James says.

Spinning around, I bang my hand against the side
of the desk, spilling some of his papers on the floor.
James is standing at the open door, in the doorframe, filling it. He's wearing a dark-colored suit, the
jacket of which is slung over his shoulder, hooked
by his thumb. Backlit from the outside light, his face
is in shadow, unreadable.

"You startled me," I finally say. "I thought you
were gone for the day."

He closes the door, lays his jacket over the back
of a chair, then walks over to me. Instinctively, as
he gets closer, I draw back against the desk. He looks
at me, at the way I shrank back, taking it in without
saying anything, then bends down and picks up the
papers I'd dropped on the floor. For such a large
man, he moves easily, with a confident grace. His
neck is thick, his shoulders broad. He's a man of substance, with a solid, meaty look about him. He tosses
the papers on the desk.

"I finished early," he says. "For once, the meeting
didn't drag on." He has a low, soft-burred voice,
soothingly lush, sensuous, as if all the vowels were
wrapped in velvet. I don't ask to which meeting he
is referring. "And you?" he says. He stares at me,
waiting for an explanation.

"Your mother gave me the key," I say. "You borrowed a serving platter she wants to use this evening." I look at him evenly, forcing my voice to
remain calm. "I was just looking for it."

He gazes down at the desk, not saying anything, although I can see he is wondering why I would search for a serving platter in his work area. His glance flicks over the computer, the stacks of paper, the open letter. I force myself not to look at the cracked picture frame. He puts his hands on the back of the desk chair and slowly pushes it in.

"It's by the front door," he says, then crosses the room. I follow him.

He says, "I put it here so I'd remember to bring it back."

Next to the door, the platter sits on a low wooden table. The ring of spare keys is on the other end of the table where, apparently, I'd placed them. I feel myself blushing, feel the heat rise to my cheeks. He watches me, notices my embarrassment, but doesn't comment. I should've seen the platter—and would have, if I'd truly been looking for it—the second I walked through his door.

He picks up the platter and hands it to me.

"Thanks," I say. "I guess I didn't see it." He doesn't believe me, I can tell. Mumbling that I have a cake in the oven, I turn around to leave. As soon as I step outside, I let out a long sigh of relief, glad that I'm out of there. Then, suddenly feeling his hand on my shoulder, I tense up.

"You're forgetting these," he says as I turn around. His arm outstretched, he holds out the ring of keys to me. The gesture almost seems a challenge, as if he is daring me to take the keys, as if he has nothing to lose by me having access to his privacy. There must be twenty-five or thirty keys on the metal ring, spares for every lock on the estate, kept at the main house for emergencies.

I hesitate, feeling awkward.

He says, "My mother shouldn't have asked you to go inside my house when she knew I wasn't home." He shrugs casually, then adds, "But that's not your problem. I'll speak with her."

Again, he holds out the keys to me. When I still hesitate, he says, "Here," and places them in my palm.

I turn around and leave. As I'm driving away, I see him standing in the doorframe, watching me, a questioning look on his face. He's wondering what I was really doing in his house, why he found me looking around his desk. He thinks I'm harmless, I'm sure. An advantage to being a woman small in stature is that people often confer an innocence that isn't always there, as if a diminutive size somehow precludes guile. He shouldn't have trusted me with his house key, though. I intend to make a copy for myself.

CHAPTER FOUR

I sit in the glider on my front porch, the swing seat moving slowly back and forth as I watch the setting sun, the western sky a ruby blush the color of a young red wine. It's been two weeks since I retrieved the serving platter from James's house. If he's discovered the cracked picture frame, he's said nothing to me. And although I haven't used it yet, I keep the copy I made of his house key on my own key chain, with me always, waiting for another opportunity to search his home. Tonight I will have that chance.

The floorboards creak beneath the weight of the glider. As the sky darkens, the nearby trees and shrubs lose their color, becoming formless and shadowy. I rented a small, furnished house in the city of Napa, from a professor on sabbatical in Europe. It's set far back from the sidewalk, a quaint bungalow-style home built in the 1920s, with stucco walls, dark shutters, and a clay-tiled roof. It's a modest structure with nothing special about the house except the abundant vegetation that engulfs it, swallowing it. A dense wall of tall oleanders surrounds the property like a fence, making the house and driveway invisible from the street; bougainvillea drip down the low, wooden railing enclosing the porch; ivy climbs up the walls, twists around the corners, scales the chimney. An old weeping willow arches close by, its drooping branches rustling against the stucco. The house seems draped in greenery, heavily laden, overtaken by climbing woody vines, creepers, and grass that has been allowed to grow exceedingly high, each blade waving in the nighttime breeze—a house in camouflage, concealed, just as I.

In the dark, I drink coffee, waiting for the hours to pass. A seven-pound hand weight—a remnant from my years in physical therapy—is next to the glider, and occasionally I'll pick it up and do biceps curls to strengthen my arms. Street noises—a car door slamming, a whining ambulance siren, kids shouting—become less frequent. The sounds are muffled and flat, as if the dense foliage of my yard is filtering out the sharp edges and clear tones, slowing down the sound waves so nothing distinct passes through. This entire place has a solemnness to it, hushed, like a morgue. Faintly, in the distance, I hear the deep hooting call of an owl. As time passes, the night grows cooler, and I hug my arms to my chest. I think of James, of what I will find in his house tonight. I think of him.

When it is very late, I change into dark jeans and a black sweater, then drive out to Byblos. Mrs. McGuane goes to bed early, and Gina, most likely, at this late hour, will also be asleep; James said he was staying in San Francisco for the night. I park far away from his house, down by the winery, then get out of the car and start walking, keeping in the shadows of the olive trees that line the main road. Even if someone should see me, it wouldn't raise any concern. The McGuanes, by now, are used to my irreg-

n his hand, he wields a whip; it's long and
with several thongs of leather dangling from
ndle. A woman, naked except for very high
is bound to the spiral staircase, her hands high
her head, lashed to the wrought iron, her feet
on the floor, ankles tied to the bottom of the
se. The black iron railing presses into her
She has long curly reddish hair, and bright red
‹, long legs and a narrow waist, and I can see
hat she is not in need of help. When I first
l, just a brief glance actually, before I backed
surprise, I thought James was hurting her,
g her the way he may have once beat me. But
can tell that is not the case. There is no blood,
maged flesh, no broken bones. Her face is not
l by his fury, and she does not cower in fear.
d, she leans against the staircase railing, re-
not fighting against her restraints. Her eyes
osed, and when James strikes with the whip, I
e one who flinches, not her. She merely parts
ps, as if to let escape a soft sigh. She is no one
gnize. He strikes her again, and once more I
. I don't like pain, observing it or receiving it.
lready had too much.

puts his hand on her back now, gently, and
down to whisper something in her ear. His
caresses her back, slides down her reddened
‹k, then down farther onto her thigh. He's
ng black slacks and a belt, but his feet are bare.
‹oman tries to lean into him, tries to rub her
against his, but he quickly draws back and
; out. She cringes this time, not expecting the
lets out a small gasp, and he strikes again and
his shoulders rolling, his muscles tensing as
aws back and then releases.

rce myself to watch. He wipes the sweat from
ow with the back of his arm, then strikes her

ular hours. Although breakfast is not my responsibility, they find me in the kitchen early in the morning, and sometimes late at night, and even on my
days off. I set my own hours, coming and going as
I please. They don't complain—and why should
they? Never have any of their previous cooks put in
so many hours, served them so well. I putter around
the kitchen, work outside in the fruit and vegetable
gardens, provide them meals and snacks for which
I'm not responsible. Mrs. McGuane—Charlotte, she
asked me to call her—will take a midmorning coffee
break with me, and sometimes we'll go to the market together. Even James and Gina seem to accept
my constant presence. They are used to me being
around, in the house, in the gardens, at the winery,
always somewhere on the property, visible yet unobtrusive, like a piece of furniture.

The narrow lane leading up to James's home is
straight ahead, a meager divide in the vineyards
faintly illuminated by the light of the moon. The
night is dark, with a chill in the air, and pinpoints
of starlight dot the clear, black sky. I cross the road,
then head up to his house. I'm used to walking. I've
been walking for years now, miles every day, another part of my physical therapy that has become
a daily habit.

The road is unevenly paved, and curves around
several small hillocks covered with large hulking
boulders and several ancient oak trees, the foliage
mushrooming at the top. The surrounding fields,
planted with grapevines, fade quickly into a blackness that seems never ending, and it all looks unearthly this time of night, dark and deserted, each
madrone tree on the edge of the road a threatening
moon shadow, like a man in black, stalking.

I stop abruptly. I hear a noise coming from the
vineyard on the right, some kind of movement. I

peer into the blackness, wary, then I relax when I see two dogs, both of them black-coated hounds with drooping ears. The McGuanes have several dogs besides the German shepherd I'd seen here on my first visit. They're handy in the vineyards, James had explained, keeping the rabbits and deer from eating new leaves. Both dogs pad up to me, tails wagging. They know who I am and do not bark. I kneel down and pat one of them on the head, rub him behind the ears.

"It's just me, Blue," I whisper. The other hound nuzzles my leg, sniffs at my pants and then my shoes. "Hiya, Chica," I say, petting her, scratching her chest. I get up.

"Go away now," I whisper, but they ignore me. The dogs circle my legs, wagging their tails, rub up against me as if they want to play, then, apparently, both hear a noise because they freeze, their heads cocked. They run off down the vineyard, out of sight. I hear nothing. They are after a rodent, I think, some kind of nocturnal animal.

I continue up the road, listening for any strange noises. As soon as I turn the last bend, I see James's house and stop. My disappointment presses down on me: his Cherokee, a boxy shadow of black, is parked in front. He isn't supposed to be here tonight. Crouching down by the side of the road, I watch the dark house, feeling frustrated. No outside lights are on, but I see a faint glow, almost imperceptible, coming from behind the closed curtains on the lower level. It's so faint, so indistinct, that I think he must use a dimmer switch, turning the lights low while he sleeps. There's no possibility of searching his house now. Another night, James, I say to myself, another night.

Getting up to leave, I notice that the light is dimmer still, then, a second later, it grows stronger. It's

wavering, oscillating behind the cur
candlelight. Curious, I walk closer to
ping carefully so I won't make any no
the trees, hide behind his car, then cr
area as quickly as I can. I reach the firs
the drapes are tightly drawn, no
through. The second and third windo
impenetrable, but the drapes on th
slightly parted, just a sliver in the mid
fabric edges don't touch, enough to see
barely. I step closer, put my eye to the w
the center of the room, candles bu
wooden table and from the fireplace
from several spots on the floor. A
warms the room, soft and diffuse, and
ally fades as it reaches for the corners
fuzzy and increasingly dark where the
doesn't extend. I put my hands on the l
window, feel the hard stone, then shift an
face closer to the glass, trying to see mo
over to the right. An elaborate brass ca
six-branched, sits on the floor, all tapers
flames shimmer, casting elongated flutt
ows across the brick floor and up the w
in the drapes cuts off my peripheral visi
wearing blinders, and so I see the room
section by section. I shift my angle on
through the window, then take in a sha
what I see.

I draw back quickly, stunned. I don't
to do. A shaky uneasiness creeps over
run away, but I feel rooted to the spot.

I look again, my pulse quickening. Ja
his shirt off, his back golden from the
glistening with sweat. He has a threa
ence, his body large and strong like
powerfully built, knots of muscle visib

again. Still, she does not call out, does not fight against the restraints. I can see she is trying to take the pain he gives her. Her body, tawny by candle-light, seems to yield under his blows. I no longer have to force myself to watch. I am mesmerized by the woman, by her control, by her acceptance of the pain. I cannot help but stare. She looks exquisite.

James, however, wears quite another expression, his face dark, flushed, consumed with a violent pas-sion. He seems oblivious to everything around him, a massive bulk of a man, almost menacing in the way he looms, scowling, his concentration fixed on the woman, on what he's doing to her, lashing out against her bare skin, laying down the red marks of his passion. His movements are precise and delib-erate, giving the impression that he is in command of the situation, but his face looks otherwise, as if it wouldn't take much for him to lose all control.

I pull away from the window, disturbed by what I see. I've gone through too many surgeries, was in too much pain, to ever forget how vulnerable hu-man flesh is. Violence is not a vague concept to me; I know very well what it can do. And yet . . .

I walk away, not worrying they might hear me. They're too engrossed to notice anything outside their personal sphere. I go back down the road, turn the first bend leading away from his house, think-ing. I'm not sure what to make of the scene I just saw. I should have been repulsed, but I wasn't. I am frightened by James, to be sure, frightened of his intensity, frightened that my involvement with him must continue. But while part of me—perhaps most of me—feels only dread at what I saw, another part is fascinated. Watching the woman, and her will-ingness to comply, so obvious, intrigued me. More than that, it aroused me. I do not pretend to under-stand why.

I hear a twig crack. I stand still, instantly alert, feeling my muscles tighten. Turning around, I expect to see James, but no one is there. I take in the shadowy madrones and the vineyards extending into blackness and the length of road visible in the dark night, my nerves on edge. Still, I see nothing. I continue walking, slowly, although my impulse is to flee. Nervously, I glance over my shoulder. I still don't see anyone but get a strong feeling I'm being watched, observed. My tennis shoes break the silence with soft, muffled footsteps. Then I hear footsteps that don't belong to me.

Quickly, I turn around. My heart pounds with a sudden release of adrenaline. On the hillock, walking out of the shadow of an old oak tree, I see someone. I peer into the night, trying to make out who it is. My pulse races. In the blackness all I see is a dark shadow, tall, formidable, coming down the hill. I want to call out, but I don't. He takes another step, closer still, then I see who it is: Gina.

"What are you doing here?" she asks. Her hair is pulled back, and her denim jacket, not buttoned, hangs loose. She has a small notebook in her hand, which she shoves in her pocket.

My heart still pounds, although I'm glad it's Gina who found me and not James. "Why did you hide like that?" I say, more sharply than I intended. "You scared me."

She walks toward me, silent. I realize now my predicament, so I give her a story about my car stalling by the winery and the walk to James's house for help. She watches me as I speak, her face impassive. She hooks her thumbs into her belt loops, shifts her weight onto her other foot, her hip jutting out.

"And did you get it?" she asks finally.

I look at her, not understanding.

"Help," she says.

I scratch the back of my neck. "No," I say. "I didn't knock. It looked as if he had company."

She starts walking down the road, back toward my car. I fall in step beside her, walking fast to keep up. "I couldn't sleep, either," she says, her tone matter-of-fact. "I was working at the winery, in the office. I heard a car pull up, and when I went outside to investigate, I saw you on foot, crossing the road toward James's house."

I don't comment on this. I wait for her to continue, but she doesn't. She won't tell me how much she knows. If she followed me all the way, then she must've seen me staring in his window. On the other hand, she may have stopped at the hillock and waited for me there. We walk down the curving road, both of us silent. The night air is cool, invigorating. We pass around another bend in the road. Gina slows down, then stops. She turns to me.

"I see the way you look at my brother," she says. "You stare at him when you think no one's watching." She delivers this in an accusing voice, as if I had committed a crime. I start to protest, but she dismisses my denial with a brusque wave of her hand.

"Let me give you some advice," she says: "Stay away from him."

The bluntness of the warning startles me. "Why?" I ask.

She stares at me, her hand planted on her hip. Then she sighs and looks off into the distance. "He's hard on women," she finally says, softly, almost a whisper. She turns and walks off down the road, disappearing around a bend.

I follow, not knowing what to make of her cryptic response. When I reach the main road, I head down to the winery.

Gina stands in front of my convertible, leaning

against the hood. When I walk up, she says, "Get in and see if it starts."

The engine, of course, turns over on my first attempt.

She leans down, rests her hands on the door. She says, "I didn't mean to sound abrupt back there."

I shrug. "That's okay," I say, and I turn on the headlights. She doesn't move back, still leans against my car.

"He was married once," she says quietly. "Did my mother tell you that?"

"No," I reply, genuinely surprised. No one mentioned a wife.

"It was a long time ago. James loved her very much. He's never been involved, seriously, with a woman since—he's had a lot of girlfriends, but they've meant nothing to him. James never got over his wife."

I nod, now understanding Gina's previous warning. "How long since they divorced?" I ask.

"They weren't," she replies. "His wife died shortly after they were married."

My car, suddenly, seems too small. "How did she die?" I ask, my voice barely louder than a whisper.

Gina's lips form a hard, straight line. She says, "We don't talk about that." She straightens up, then adds, "Ever," and walks away.

ular hours. Although breakfast is not my responsibility, they find me in the kitchen early in the morning, and sometimes late at night, and even on my days off. I set my own hours, coming and going as I please. They don't complain—and why should they? Never have any of their previous cooks put in so many hours, served them so well. I putter around the kitchen, work outside in the fruit and vegetable gardens, provide them meals and snacks for which I'm not responsible. Mrs. McGuane—Charlotte, she asked me to call her—will take a midmorning coffee break with me, and sometimes we'll go to the market together. Even James and Gina seem to accept my constant presence. They are used to me being around, in the house, in the gardens, at the winery, always somewhere on the property, visible yet unobtrusive, like a piece of furniture.

The narrow lane leading up to James's home is straight ahead, a meager divide in the vineyards faintly illuminated by the light of the moon. The night is dark, with a chill in the air, and pinpoints of starlight dot the clear, black sky. I cross the road, then head up to his house. I'm used to walking. I've been walking for years now, miles every day, another part of my physical therapy that has become a daily habit.

The road is unevenly paved, and curves around several small hillocks covered with large hulking boulders and several ancient oak trees, the foliage mushrooming at the top. The surrounding fields, planted with grapevines, fade quickly into a blackness that seems never ending, and it all looks unearthly this time of night, dark and deserted, each madrone tree on the edge of the road a threatening moon shadow, like a man in black, stalking.

I stop abruptly. I hear a noise coming from the vineyard on the right, some kind of movement. I peer into the blackness, wary, then I relax when I see two dogs, both of them black-coated hounds with drooping ears. The McGuanes have several dogs besides the German shepherd I'd seen here on my first visit. They're handy in the vineyards, James had explained, keeping the rabbits and deer from eating new leaves. Both dogs pad up to me, tails wagging. They know who I am and do not bark. I kneel down and pat one of them on the head, rub him behind the ears.

"It's just me, Blue," I whisper. The other hound nuzzles my leg, sniffs at my pants and then my shoes. "Hiya, Chica," I say, petting her, scratching her chest. I get up.

"Go away now," I whisper, but they ignore me. The dogs circle my legs, wagging their tails, rub up against me as if they want to play, then, apparently, both hear a noise because they freeze, their heads cocked. They run off down the vineyard, out of sight. I hear nothing. They are after a rodent, I think, some kind of nocturnal animal.

I continue up the road, listening for any strange noises. As soon as I turn the last bend, I see James's house and stop. My disappointment presses down on me: his Cherokee, a boxy shadow of black, is parked in front. He isn't supposed to be here tonight. Crouching down by the side of the road, I watch the dark house, feeling frustrated. No outside lights are on, but I see a faint glow, almost imperceptible, coming from behind the closed curtains on the lower level. It's so faint, so indistinct, that I think he must use a dimmer switch, turning the lights low while he sleeps. There's no possibility of searching his house now. Another night, James, I say to myself, another night.

Getting up to leave, I notice that the light is dimmer still, then, a second later, it grows stronger. It's wavering, oscillating behind the curtains, as if it is candlelight. Curious, I walk closer to his house, stepping carefully so I won't make any noise. I stay near the trees, hide behind his car, then cross the exposed area as quickly as I can. I reach the first window, but the drapes are tightly drawn, no cracks to see through. The second and third windows are equally impenetrable, but the drapes on the fourth are slightly parted, just a sliver in the middle where the fabric edges don't touch, enough to see through, just barely. I step closer, put my eye to the window. Near the center of the room, candles burn from the wooden table and from the fireplace mantel and from several spots on the floor. A muted glow warms the room, soft and diffuse, and then gradually fades as it reaches for the corners, becoming fuzzy and increasingly dark where the candlelight doesn't extend. I put my hands on the ledge of the window, feel the hard stone, then shift and press my face closer to the glass, trying to see more, looking over to the right. An elaborate brass candelabrum, six-branched, sits on the floor, all tapers ablaze. The flames shimmer, casting elongated fluttering shadows across the brick floor and up the wall. The slit in the drapes cuts off my peripheral vision, as if I'm wearing blinders, and so I see the room piecemeal, section by section. I shift my angle once more, spy through the window, then take in a sharp breath at what I see.

I draw back quickly, stunned. I don't know what to do. A shaky uneasiness creeps over me. I want to run away, but I feel rooted to the spot.

I look again, my pulse quickening. James is there, his shirt off, his back golden from the candlelight, glistening with sweat. He has a threatening presence, his body large and strong like a tree trunk, powerfully built, knots of muscle visible under the skin. In his hand, he wields a whip; it's long and black, with several thongs of leather dangling from the handle. A woman, naked except for very high heels, is bound to the spiral staircase, her hands high above her head, lashed to the wrought iron, her feet spread on the floor, ankles tied to the bottom of the staircase. The black iron railing presses into her belly. She has long curly reddish hair, and bright red lipstick, long legs and a narrow waist, and I can see now that she is not in need of help. When I first looked, just a brief glance actually, before I backed off in surprise, I thought James was hurting her, beating her the way he may have once beat me. But now I can tell that is not the case. There is no blood, no damaged flesh, no broken bones. Her face is not ruined by his fury, and she does not cower in fear. Instead, she leans against the staircase railing, relaxed, not fighting against her restraints. Her eyes are closed, and when James strikes with the whip, I am the one who flinches, not her. She merely parts her lips, as if to let escape a soft sigh. She is no one I recognize. He strikes her again, and once more I wince. I don't like pain, observing it or receiving it. I've already had too much.

He puts his hand on her back now, gently, and leans down to whisper something in her ear. His hand caresses her back, slides down her reddened buttock, then down farther onto her thigh. He's wearing black slacks and a belt, but his feet are bare. The woman tries to lean into him, tries to rub her body against his, but he quickly draws back and lashes out. She cringes this time, not expecting the whip, lets out a small gasp, and he strikes again and again, his shoulders rolling, his muscles tensing as he draws back and then releases.

I force myself to watch. He wipes the sweat from his brow with the back of his arm, then strikes her again. Still, she does not call out, does not fight against the restraints. I can see she is trying to take the pain he gives her. Her body, tawny by candlelight, seems to yield under his blows. I no longer have to force myself to watch. I am mesmerized by the woman, by her control, by her acceptance of the pain. I cannot help but stare. She looks exquisite.

James, however, wears quite another expression, his face dark, flushed, consumed with a violent passion. He seems oblivious to everything around him, a massive bulk of a man, almost menacing in the way he looms, scowling, his concentration fixed on the woman, on what he's doing to her, lashing out against her bare skin, laying down the red marks of his passion. His movements are precise and deliberate, giving the impression that he is in command of the situation, but his face looks otherwise, as if it wouldn't take much for him to lose all control.

I pull away from the window, disturbed by what I see. I've gone through too many surgeries, was in too much pain, to ever forget how vulnerable human flesh is. Violence is not a vague concept to me; I know very well what it can do. And yet . . .

I walk away, not worrying they might hear me. They're too engrossed to notice anything outside their personal sphere. I go back down the road, turn the first bend leading away from his house, thinking. I'm not sure what to make of the scene I just saw. I should have been repulsed, but I wasn't. I am frightened by James, to be sure, frightened of his intensity, frightened that my involvement with him must continue. But while part of me—perhaps most of me—feels only dread at what I saw, another part is fascinated. Watching the woman, and her willingness to comply, so obvious, intrigued me. More than that, it aroused me. I do not pretend to understand why.

I hear a twig crack. I stand still, instantly alert, feeling my muscles tighten. Turning around, I expect to see James, but no one is there. I take in the shadowy madrones and the vineyards extending into blackness and the length of road visible in the dark night, my nerves on edge. Still, I see nothing. I continue walking, slowly, although my impulse is to flee. Nervously, I glance over my shoulder. I still don't see anyone but get a strong feeling I'm being watched, observed. My tennis shoes break the silence with soft, muffled footsteps. Then I hear footsteps that don't belong to me.

Quickly, I turn around. My heart pounds with a sudden release of adrenaline. On the hillock, walking out of the shadow of an old oak tree, I see someone. I peer into the night, trying to make out who it is. My pulse races. In the blackness all I see is a dark shadow, tall, formidable, coming down the hill. I want to call out, but I don't. He takes another step, closer still, then I see who it is: Gina.

"What are you doing here?" she asks. Her hair is pulled back, and her denim jacket, not buttoned, hangs loose. She has a small notebook in her hand, which she shoves in her pocket.

My heart still pounds, although I'm glad it's Gina who found me and not James. "Why did you hide like that?" I say, more sharply than I intended. "You scared me."

She walks toward me, silent. I realize now my predicament, so I give her a story about my car stalling by the winery and the walk to James's house for help. She watches me as I speak, her face impassive. She hooks her thumbs into her belt loops, shifts her weight onto her other foot, her hip jutting out.

"And did you get it?" she asks finally.

I look at her, not understanding.

"Help," she says.

I scratch the back of my neck. "No," I say. "I didn't knock. It looked as if he had company."

She starts walking down the road, back toward my car. I fall in step beside her, walking fast to keep up. "I couldn't sleep, either," she says, her tone matter-of-fact. "I was working at the winery, in the office. I heard a car pull up, and when I went outside to investigate, I saw you on foot, crossing the road toward James's house."

I don't comment on this. I wait for her to continue, but she doesn't. She won't tell me how much she knows. If she followed me all the way, then she must've seen me staring in his window. On the other hand, she may have stopped at the hillock and waited for me there. We walk down the curving road, both of us silent. The night air is cool, invigorating. We pass around another bend in the road. Gina slows down, then stops. She turns to me.

"I see the way you look at my brother," she says. "You stare at him when you think no one's watching." She delivers this in an accusing voice, as if I had committed a crime. I start to protest, but she dismisses my denial with a brusque wave of her hand.

"Let me give you some advice," she says: "Stay away from him."

The bluntness of the warning startles me. "Why?" I ask.

She stares at me, her hand planted on her hip. Then she sighs and looks off into the distance. "He's hard on women," she finally says, softly, almost a whisper. She turns and walks off down the road, disappearing around a bend.

I follow, not knowing what to make of her cryptic response. When I reach the main road, I head down to the winery.

Gina stands in front of my convertible, leaning

against the hood. When I walk up, she says, "Get in and see if it starts."

The engine, of course, turns over on my first attempt.

She leans down, rests her hands on the door. She says, "I didn't mean to sound abrupt back there."

I shrug. "That's okay," I say, and I turn on the headlights. She doesn't move back, still leans against my car.

"He was married once," she says quietly. "Did my mother tell you that?"

"No," I reply, genuinely surprised. No one mentioned a wife.

"It was a long time ago. James loved her very much. He's never been involved, seriously, with a woman since—he's had a lot of girlfriends, but they've meant nothing to him. James never got over his wife."

I nod, now understanding Gina's previous warning. "How long since they divorced?" I ask.

"They weren't," she replies. "His wife died shortly after they were married."

My car, suddenly, seems too small. "How did she die?" I ask, my voice barely louder than a whisper.

Gina's lips form a hard, straight line. She says, "We don't talk about that." She straightens up, then adds, "Ever," and walks away.

CHAPTER FIVE

I wake up early in the morning, my heart beating fast, so fast I can hear the blood pounding in my ears, and my chest aching from not enough air, as if I'd been running and running and running all night long. Sitting up in bed, I suck in the air, breathing rapidly through my open mouth, trying to catch my breath. I had another one of my dreams, another one of my nightmares. I'm prone to nighttime awakenings, to sudden starts from dreams gone bad, but for the last several years, I'd been sleeping undisturbed. The bad dreams had disappeared, disappeared for so long I thought I was through with them, like an old dress I'd finally outgrown. But they are back, the dreams, ever since I first saw James's picture in the *Wine Spectator*.

Or maybe they never left. Maybe they were sneaking around in my head all the time, just waiting for a chance to catch me off guard, waiting for me to think, I'm done with this, No more nightmares, and then—*Bam!*—hit me with a bad one just as I'm thinking everything is going to be okay.

Feeling calmer now, I look around the room, rubbing my eyes. The glowing red numbers on my clock say 4:11. The night is still black, a couple hours remaining till morning. Sometime during the night, I kicked the blankets off my bed, and the sheet is twisted up on the side. I'm wearing an oversized, baggy T-shirt, the bottom of it almost to my knees. I put my hand under the shirt, feel my skin. It's damp, slightly slick with sweat.

I get up and walk through the dark house, my bare feet padding on the carpet down the hall. Murky shadows fill the corners of the room, but I don't need to turn on a light. I'm accustomed to midnight navigating, and the dark shadows don't scare me—all my nightmares are locked in my mind, the kind I can't see. In the kitchen, the linoleum is cool beneath my feet. I lean against the refrigerator door, a cold metallic panel, and let it cool my skin. Closing my eyes, I rest my forehead on the door. I'm so tired.

A few minutes later, I hear a muffled creak and jerk up my head, startled. I peer straight ahead, in the darkness of the kitchen, trying to discover the source of the noise. I listen. Silence. For moments I stand there, not moving. Still, no noise, no more muffled creaks. It was nothing, I finally decide, relaxing, just the house with all its moans and groans, the walls and pipes settling into place like the many creaky bones of an old animal shifting about, making itself comfortable.

I go back to bed, wondering if sleep will come, worrying about another nightmare. I never remember them. As soon as I wake, the dreams vanish, leaving me exhausted, frightened, but never knowing why. The doctors told me my failure to remember them, like my enduring amnesia, is a defensive measure: I bar them from consciousness to avoid anxiety I cannot—or choose not to—endure. I don't know if this is true. But I do know my nightmare tonight was triggered by the thought of James's dead wife.

I watch a hawk glide effortlessly, a dark movement against the clear blue sky, then land in a vineyard far away. Grapes are not the only plants harvested at Byblos. Mrs. McGuane, leaving most of the vineyard and winery management to her children, prefers to work out here, in her vegetable and fruit gardens behind the main house. Narrow paths run through the gardens, dividing them into sections, and, depending on the time of year, they are planted with beds of lettuce, sweet corn, carrots, onions, tomatoes, cabbages, peppers, zucchini, and potatoes, supplying fresh vegetables most of the year. She has a full-time gardener to help her, and between the two of them I'm learning a little about gardening myself. I plan meals with the gardens in mind, using fresh produce as much as possible.

Bending over, I pull a few weeds growing among the vegetables. I should be cutting off more of the artichoke heads—the plants border the gardens—but I can't stop thinking about James's wife. Did she die the same way I was supposed to have died? A vague sense of foreboding begins to weigh heavily on me. I feel I am getting in too deep. What match am I against James? And how does Gina figure in this, if at all?

I look over at Mrs. McGuane, who is kneeling by the asparagus bed, the spears, straight and thick, shooting out from the ground like a bed of nails. She cuts the stalks several inches beneath the soil surface, inserting a long serrated kitchen knife into the ground. I'll serve the asparagus tonight with dinner, steamed, a little melted butter drizzled on top. She lays the spears in her basket. A big floppy straw hat is perched on her head, to protect herself from the sun, and errant wisps of white hair curl down her neck. Her stomach, a slight bulge, pouches out from under her belted blue dress in a very comforting way. This is how Betty Crocker would look, I think: motherly, soft all over. I wonder about my own mother, but realize she probably wasn't like Mrs. McGuane at all. My mother didn't search for me when I was missing, or if she did, she didn't look very hard.

"Mrs. McGuane," I say, calling over to her, then I correct myself. "Charlotte," I try again, the word feeling uncomfortable on my tongue. "Has James ever been married?"

She doesn't answer me right away. She puts the knife in her basket, rearranges the asparagus. Finally, she looks over at me and says, "Yes, but it was a long time ago."

"What was her name?"

Mrs. McGuane gets up, then walks over to the bed of leeks. The green leaves are tall and spiky, and the white stems protrude from the ground. "Her name was Anna," she says. "Anna Maria Monicelli. She and James were married for only a short time." She doesn't say anything else. A few minutes pass. She lifts the leeks out of the ground, gently, with a fork, and places them in her basket.

"She died?" I prompt her.

Slowly, Mrs. McGuane rises. She comes over to me and places her hand on my arm. "Dear," she says, "please don't mention this to James. It happened such a long time ago, but it's still very painful for him. He doesn't like to talk about it, and he doesn't like anyone else talking about it, either." She looks over my shoulder.

"Here he comes now," she says, and I turn to see

him walking across the patio. Quietly, she adds, "No more talk of Anna," and she walks off toward him, swinging her basket, her blue dress swishing at the hem. He lifts his hand to me in recognition, not quite a wave.

I watch them. They go over to the far end of the patio, where it's covered with a shady arbor, the lattice roof dripping with pale violet wisteria. Stones, irregularly cut, pave the patio, and large terra-cotta pots are set randomly, planted with trees—lemon, bay, pomegranate, and a ballerina apple. The picnic furniture is shaded under the arbor, with a pitcher of iced tea sitting on the table. Mrs. McGuane pours her son a glass. James, working in the winery with Gina today, transferring some of last year's harvest of white wine from oak barrels into stainless-steel tanks, is dressed in jeans and a light-brown T-shirt, with splotches of perspiration dampening the front. He has the shoulders of a bulldog, square and solid, and his T-shirt stretches tightly across his chest. He stands by the table and drinks the tea in a few gulps. He and his mother talk for a few minutes, then she leaves, going inside the house. He pours himself another glass of iced tea and sits down. This one he drinks slowly, gazing in my direction while I pull weeds.

I go over and sit at the table. James gives me a curious glance—I'm not sure what it means—then he leans back in the chair. We sit in silence, both taking in the view. The yard is a profusion of flowers and color, most everything in full bloom—orange poppies and blue lupine, tall bearded irises, velvety pansies, yellow and red roses, purple bougainvillea. There are no blocking fences dividing the property, so the view from behind the main house extends to the southern edges of the McGuanes' small valley, from the fruit and vegetable gardens to the lawn leading up to Gina's cottage to the stretch of vineyards nestling against the distant rolling hills.

Abruptly, James turns to me and says, "You were at my house last night." He watches me, waiting for a response. "Gina told me."

I feel my heart beat faster, my pulse racing.

"Why were you there?"

I hesitate, wondering how much Gina told him. "My car stalled at the winery," I finally say. "I walked to your house, to get help."

He cocks his head a little, listening. He fills up the chair, his legs spread, both palms resting on his thighs. When I don't continue, he prompts me, saying, "And then?"

I stall, feeling I'm on dangerous ground. Did Gina watch me at his house or not? I reach for the pitcher of iced tea, pour myself a glass. I take a drink, then decide not to risk a lie. "I started to knock but . . ."

He waits for me to continue. When I don't, he says, insistent, "And?"

"I saw you." I pause, then add, "And the woman."

He doesn't respond, and in the silence I hear a buzzing insect, the far-off drone of machinery, birds chirping in the trees. The noises seem loud, determined, as if they're filling in the tense silence.

But James doesn't appear uncomfortable at all. He pours himself another glass of iced tea. He takes a sip, watching me over the rim of his glass, a look of detached amusement on his face. Despite his T-shirt, I see him as he was last night—skin bare, golden in the flickering candlelight, muscles tense and hard as he wielded the black leather whip, striking a woman who seemed to welcome the pain. Unbidden, a rush of excitement goes through me.

He starts to get up.

"I want you to do that to me," I say suddenly,

surprising myself. I start to back off, to tell him I didn't mean it, but then I stop. I *did* mean it. This will get me what I want. My heart races at the mere thought of the pain—I know I won't endure it well, not like the woman last night.

"I want you to hurt me," I say, then feel my face go warm, blushing from the words. "The way you hurt her."

He looks at me, not blinking. His eyes are a yellowish green, like Gina's, the color of ripened limes. Slowly, he walks around the table. He puts his hand on my shoulder. "You don't know what you're asking for," he says softly. "You have no idea." He removes his hand.

"Forget about it," he says, and he walks away.

But I don't forget about it. All day—while James is at the winery, transferring wine from oak barrels into stainless-steel tanks, while Gina is in the vineyard, supervising the leaf thinning—all day I think of little else, and while I make dinner, I formulate a plan.

A gush of warm air washes over my face as I open the oven door. Using a towel, I remove a rhubarb pie—the fruit fresh from the garden—and set it on the counter to cool.

I go into the bathroom and splash cold water on my face. I dry myself with a towel, avoiding the mirror. I have a problem with mirrors. I know my facial scars are more imagined than real, but when I look in a mirror I see myself the way I looked fifteen years ago. Cross-stitching sutures, like miniature train tracks, covered my face, painful whenever I moved, and my jaw, broken in six places, was wired shut. The doctors, without a photograph to show them what I looked like, worked forever on the remains of my face—my eye sockets, my nose, my chin and jaw and forehead, the shape of my mouth—patching, sewing, removing crushed bones, adding fillers, sculpting it into what I have now. Only a few facial scars remain, almost invisible, near the hairline, under the chin, close to my ear, but I still see hideous scars crisscrossed on my face, Frankenstein scars. I suppose I'm like those newly slender people, forever imagining themselves fat.

Wary, I gaze into the mirror. I'm tired of seeing myself this way, without my own face, without an identity. James has never looked into a mirror without recognizing the face staring back. He says I don't know what I'm asking for, but he doesn't know what he can give: my identity. Later tonight I will begin the process of claiming back what is rightfully mine.

CHAPTER SIX

I knock on James's door. His windows are covered, but they glow faintly from the inside light, the steady glow of electricity. No candles tonight. Although it was only yesterday I spied through his windows, it seems a long time ago. This time I didn't sneak up to his house, and I didn't wait until after midnight. I drove, parked my car next to his, and it's barely nine o'clock.

When he opens the door, my resolve falters for just a second. In his presence, I get a clear sense of my own inadequacy. I push the feeling all the way down, then say, "I don't want to forget about it."

He looks at me, one hand on the door, his blond hair slightly damp. Although I left the main house soon after he did, he still, apparently, had time to shower and change. He looks as if he's going out for the evening—gray dress slacks, long-sleeved maroon shirt, a faint trace of cologne, something musky. He doesn't seem surprised to see me. He opens the door farther. "I've been expecting you," he says.

Although he doesn't invite me in, I squeeze past him, stepping into his house. Automatically, I lay my car keys on the table by the door, as if I'd done it many times before. The lights are dim, the paintings on the walls too dark to see clearly. Upstairs, in the loft, a brighter light illuminates what I assume is his bedroom. "What made you think I'd come?" I ask.

"Just a hunch," he says, and he shuts the heavy door. It closes with an ancient sound, a hollow thud, like the sealing of a tomb. "This afternoon, on the patio, you looked as if you were unwilling to let it go. I didn't expect you so soon, however, not tonight."

I walk over to the stone hearth fireplace. A long black leather couch and three large chairs are arranged in front of it, in a U shape, with an Oriental carpet in the center. Taken by itself, his furniture appears hugely out of proportion, oversized, yet in this room, which seems as large as a medieval hall, it fits right in.

"Sit down," he says, switching on a light.

I choose one of the chairs. He sits opposite me, on the leather couch, and he runs his fingers through his damp hair, gazing at me directly, openly. His jaw, square, solid looking, is like a chunk of granite. There's a power to his presence, and he seems as he always does—sure of himself, a man who doesn't hesitate if action is required. I'm still wearing the clothes I've had on all day—paisley walking shorts, a long vest, a white knit top—and compared to him, in his tailored slacks and elegant shirt, I feel dressed down, wilted. Patiently, he waits for me to begin.

"What I saw last night," I say. "I liked it. I'm not sure why . . . but I did." I know I sound unsure of myself, my sentences chopped, my voice tentative. I say, "I really liked it."

James leans forward, places his elbows on his knees, then rests his chin on his interlocked fingers, looking me over. I feel awkward in his silence, as if I'd said something wrong.

"You don't know me." He says this quietly, but it sounds like a warning. "Not at all."

I shrug, as if I'm unconcerned.

He gazes at me for a minute. Finally, he says, "I don't get involved with inexperienced women. Things can get . . . out of hand. Do you understand what I'm saying?"

I can tell he doesn't expect an answer. He leans back, drapes his arm along the back of the couch.

I get up and sit next to him. Having never played the seductress before, I'm unsure what to do next. Tentatively, I place my hand on his chest, feel the smooth fabric of his shirt, feel the heat of his body coming through.

He slowly smiles. He says, "Gina warned me about you."

"What did she say?"

"That you'd be trouble."

I slide my hand over the contours of his chest, the planes of muscle firm against my palm. He allows me this touch but doesn't utter a word. I say, "It sounds to me like she's jealous."

"Maybe you're right," he says, smiling a little. "Maybe you're right." He adds, "Still, she made a point—you're not the type of woman I get involved with."

I say, "This is something I want." I hesitate, searching for the words to convince him, then add, "Something I need."

He watches me, thinking. Finally, he shakes his head, a small movement. He says, "You don't know what you're saying."

"Maybe not. But I want to learn."

I can tell, by the way he's looking at me, as if he's reassessing me, assigning a new value to my worth, that he will not refuse me now. Embarrassed, I gaze off to the side.

He puts his hand under my chin, forces me to look straight in his eyes. "Are you sure you want to do this?" he asks. "Because once we get started, I may not let you back out."

My breathing becomes shallow, anxious. "I won't back out," I tell him.

He nods, his hand still under my chin. "All right," he says suddenly, making up his mind. "I have to make a call," and he walks over to the desk, picks up the phone. After he punches in a number, I hear him talking to someone, saying he can't make it this evening. As soon as he says this, I feel a sudden twinge of panic. I didn't think we'd actually do anything tonight, especially when I saw he was dressed to go out. I assumed we would begin another day.

He hangs up the phone. "Come here," he says, walking over to the wrought-iron staircase.

Slowly, I rise. I say, "I told my neighbor I was going to be here tonight, with you."

He chuckles, a low amused laugh. "There's a term for that," he says. "It's called a silent alarm—you tell friends where you'll be and that you'll check in at a certain time; if you don't, they notify the police." He unbuttons the cuffs on his maroon shirt, then rolls up his sleeves, taking his time, first one, then the other.

"Except I don't believe you," he adds. "I don't think you told anyone at all." He rests his hand on the black railing of the staircase. "Now come over here."

When I reach the staircase, he points for me to go up. As soon as I start to climb the stairs, he wraps his hand around my arm, making me stop. I feel the strength of him, of his fingers pressing into my flesh.

"Do you really think anyone can help you now?" he asks.

Feeling uneasy, I walk up the stairs. The upper level, like the lower, is open, without dividing walls, the only partition a high brick barrier screening off the bathroom. A wooden balustrade runs along the length of the loft, and the floor, also, is planked with wood. As with the main level, my first impression is one of medieval elegance—exposed rafters, lots of space, a brooding darkness even though a light shines in the far corner. On the left, I see his sleeping area, an extra-large bed, dark wooden furniture, a long trunk on the floor; on the right, the brick-enclosed bathroom; and in the center, a spacious painter's studio, an easel pushed off to the side, a table cluttered with brushes in glass jars and squished tubes of paint, a stone hearth fireplace, similar to the one downstairs, a couch and two chairs, and an enormous arched window, framed in brick, where the loft door must have once been. Stacks of canvases lean against the balustrade and the brick barrier.

I go over to the studio. In the middle, near the large window, a hoist-and-pulley device is suspended from the rafter in the ceiling. And from the hoist hangs a contraption of chains and clips and metal bars and black leather straps. It seemed part of the studio at first, but now I see that it isn't. With my eyes, I follow the hoist line, see that the rope is tied off on a metal cleat that is bolted to the wall.

James comes over and stands behind me. Faintly, I smell the muskiness of his cologne. He doesn't touch me, but I feel his body close to mine, almost brushing against my clothes. "That's a harness," he explains. "For suspension bondage. I don't usually keep it out, but I used it last night. After I whipped her."

I reach out and touch it, the smooth leather, the chain slightly cool. I finger one of the clips.

"That's called a panic snap," he says. "It's a quick-release device, in case something goes wrong." He reaches over my shoulder to show me how it works. With one hand, he slides up part of the clip. Instantly, the hook drops open and, with a thud, the leather harness falls to the floor. "A panic snap can get you out of a dangerous situation," he says.

A panic snap. My amnesia is like that, allowing me to escape a dangerous situation. It's my own quick-release device, so I don't have to face the truth. But the past is still there, and something did go wrong. A panic snap didn't save me from that.

Reaching up, I touch the clip again. The hook, empty of the harness, dangles open. The contraption, the hoist and chains and metal bars, frightens me. "Maybe we could save this for another time," I say.

He closes the drapes on the loft window, then walks over to the trunk and sits down. The trunk looks antique—dark wood, intricate hand carving on the panels—and it's very large and sturdy, with metal rings secured on the bottom. He says, "Lesson one, Carly: You don't make the rules, I do."

I don't say anything.

"Do you understand?" he asks. There's a slight edge to his voice, a tightness.

I nod.

"Good," he says. "Now take off your clothes."

I hesitate for a minute.

The corner of his mouth lifts in a wry smile. "You look as if you're being forced to swallow bitter medicine," he says, folding his arms across his chest. "Don't tell me you're not enjoying this—isn't this what you wanted?"

I don't reply. I kick off my sandals. I take off my vest, then the walking shorts. I start to fold them so they won't wrinkle, but change my mind and let them fall to the floor. I pull the knit top over my head.

"The rest," he orders when I hesitate.

Reaching around my back, I unhook my bra, slip it off, then slide down my panties. I step out of them, drop them on the pile of clothes. Anxious, I wait for what comes next. I want to cross my arms, but I don't. I just stand there, feeling ill at ease.

He stares at me, taking his time. I shift to my other foot. He looks at my arms. I'm strong for my size, my biceps toned and fairly well defined from my habit of lifting weights. He motions for me to come near. I walk forward.

"Closer," he says. When I get to him, he reaches over to a chest of drawers and turns on another lamp. He continues looking at me closely, inspecting my body as if it were a blueprint to be carefully studied. He doesn't touch me, not once. With each passing minute, my discomfort increases. I feel my scars expanding, snaking across my body, as purple as varicose veins. I realize this is all in my mind. Most of my scars have disappeared, and even the remaining few, from the deeper, more serious wounds, are faint after fifteen years of healing, just thin white lines, delicate, like fine thread.

He tells me to turn around, looks at me from behind, then, when he's finished, has me turn back again. Still, he keeps his hands off me.

He looks at my face next. It's unnerving to have someone stare for so long, taking in every detail, every defect. The doctors took special care with my face, using extra-small stitches and frequent dressings so the scarring would be minimal. The few facial scars that do remain are hidden—buried in the hairline, behind my ear, under the chin. Even after all these years, I embarrass under scrutiny.

Finally, softly, he says, "There's a vulnerability about you—around the eyes."

I think, Of course I look vulnerable—you fractured my eye sockets in several different places.

He examines the rest of my face. I stare off to the side, barely able to endure this. Other than my doctors, no one has looked at me this closely, nor for this length of time.

When he's finished, he leans back slightly. Only now do I look at him. "You have a few scars," he says.

Immediately, I tense, fearing, although I know it's unlikely, that he's guessed who I am. My heart pounds. "I was a tomboy growing up," I say, making my voice sound natural.

He puts his finger on my skin, and I jump, startled by his touch. He traces the scar on my hip.

"Not many men notice them," I say, talking out of nervousness. This is true. I like to keep the lights off while I'm making love. If men notice, they see them the next morning—but even that is rare. Men, I've found, aren't as perceptive on the morning after.

"I noticed," he says. He traces another scar, the one near my waist, his finger moving slowly, lightly, like the gentle brush of a feather. I hold my breath.

He looks up at me and says, "Are you nervous?"

I nod.

"Good," he says. "You should be." He places both hands on my waist, holding me firmly. He bends his head and—surprisingly—licks the scar, his tongue a wet glide, a sliding glissando of moist flesh over flesh, the gesture so sensuous it almost makes me relax, almost makes me give in to the gentle movement of his tongue. And then he bites me.

I suck in my breath, a short gasp, feeling the sudden sharp sting of pain. He holds me securely, his hands spanning my waist so I can't move away, watches me as I look down and see the impress of his teeth marks on my pale skin. His bite didn't draw blood, but it wasn't gentle either. It hurt.

He holds me tighter and starts the process again, licking and biting. He goes from one scar to the next, and then the next. I clamp down on my lip so I won't call out, but after a few minutes, I start to cry, silently, angrily, just a few tears, a quiet protest against his biting teeth. I don't cry for the pain—he isn't biting me that hard—but for the gross unfairness of the act, the infliction of fresh wounds directly over the old. I hide my scars, he magnifies them. It doesn't seem fair. He sees my tears, but he doesn't stop. He turns me around and continues, his hands grasped firmly around my waist.

When he's finished, he lifts me onto his lap. He looks at the teeth marks on my body, so much more pronounced than the scars. Tomorrow I'll have many bruises. He puts his hand on my face, feels the wetness of my tears. He's so much larger than I, that I feel like a child sitting on his lap.

"Is this what you wanted? What you *needed?*" he asks, pointing to the teeth marks on my inner thigh, his voice mocking.

I knock his hand away.

"I guess not," he says, and he quickly puts his arm under my legs and carries me to the bed, tosses me down. He goes over to a chest of drawers, opens one, pulls out something. I lie still where he threw me, watching him, the immensity of him, then feel a sudden burst of panic, wanting to be anywhere but here. Unable to stop myself, in a gut reaction to fear, I scramble to the edge of the bed and start to get up. But he's beside me, circling my waist with his arm. He turns me over and shoves me down roughly, my face smashed in the bed covers, then puts something around my wrist—a leather cuff, I see, with a rope attached—then ties it off to the headboard.

"I warned you I wouldn't let you back out," he says, pinning me down.

Physically, I know I'm no match for him. He holds me easily. I struggle not to fight against him, not to show my fear.

"Why don't you—" I begin, but quickly, without warning, he slaps a gag on my mouth. Automatically, I reach up with my free hand. He grabs it, attaches a cuff, ties it off on the other side of the headboard so I'm face down, my arms spread. This happens so fast, it shocks me. He goes to the foot of the bed, grabs my legs, and pulls, sliding me down until the ropes on my wrists stretch taut. I try to speak, but my words, under the gag, come out muffled, unheard. He cuffs and ropes my ankles, tying them off to something beneath the bed, my legs spread wide. I'm too scared to feel the embarrassment of this position.

He returns to the head of the bed and looks down at me. His shirt is disheveled, untucked in the front, and a tuft of blond hair falls in his eyes. I'm breathing heavily, the gag tight on my mouth.

"Calm down," he says, brushing back his hair. He watches me for a minute, staring at my face. He reaches for the pillows—there are four of them—and tosses them to the foot of the bed. He turns, crosses the room, walks behind the brick partition closing off the bathroom.

I pull against the restraints, but the ropes, secured tightly, don't budge. I hear the toilet flush, then the sound of water running while he washes his hands. When he comes out, his shirt is straightened and tucked inside his pants. He turns off the light above the studio, then comes over to me. He removes the gag. I force myself to remain silent.

"That's better," he says. He lays the gag on the oak chest, then pulls a whip out of the drawer. It's the same one he used last night—a short handle to grip, many black leather straps, each about two feet long.

"This is called a flogger," he says, then he leans over and puts the handle next to my lips. "Kiss it."

The handle is wooden, shiny with varnish, rounded, and with a knob at the end. Reluctantly, I lean my head forward, brush my lips against the wood.

"Now lick it," he says.

I look up at him.

"Go on," he says. "Lick it. You're going to be great friends with this whip."

I stick out my tongue, barely touch the wood. He watches, runs his hand along my outstretched arm, then he picks up the whip. He walks behind me. My muscles tense, getting ready to feel the sting of the whip, but it doesn't come. I twist my head around. He bends over and takes the cuff off my left ankle, then he takes the one off my right. I pull my legs together, still looking back at him.

"If you kick," he says, "I'll put them back on. Do you understand?"

I nod.

He gets three pillows from the floor. "Roll up," he says, tapping me on the side. When I don't move, he says it again, "Roll up," putting a stern edge on his voice.

I lift up, and he pushes the pillows under my hip, then reaches around and pulls them through from the other side, until they're squarely beneath me, raising my buttocks in the air. I clench my jaw with indignation, humiliated to have my ass pushed up like this, elevated, on display, as if I were offering him a morsel, a tidbit, on a serving platter.

I look back at him. He has the whip by the handle, his wrist turned over, dangling the straps, shaking them loose, it seems, and then he steps back with his right foot, draws back his arm like a baseball pitcher getting ready to throw. I squeeze shut my eyes, feel all my muscles clench, then gasp as the straps hit my flesh, my arms pulling against the ropes, a burning pain slashing down my right buttock. Before I have time to recover, he strikes me again, the left buttock this time, and I gasp once more, feeling the pain. He strikes me over and over, rapidly, each blow a racking jolt of pain that stabs at my flesh, almost unbearable, and then the pain of my surgeries comes flashing through my mind, and then, abruptly, the memory of the greater pain, lying still, almost dead, but feeling the broken bones and cut flesh and damaged skin, blood all around, sticky warm blood, blood in my mouth, darkness all around, and I'm waiting to die, wanting to die, but I didn't, and I am here, and now I am sobbing, begging him to stop, crying out his name.

He sits on the edge of the bed, places his hand on my back. "Breathe deeply," he says, but I am still sobbing. He leans closer. "Breathe," he whispers, drawing out the word, and he rubs my back slowly, his palm warm on my flesh, a gentle move I don't expect from him.

"Breathe with me," he says, his voice a soft whisper. And I begin to hear the rhythm of his breath, slow and deep, the exhale a long, leisurely release of air, a gentle sea breeze, a warm soughing of wind, and I close my eyes and breathe with him, his face close to mine, sharing the air. We breathe together, minutes go by, maybe more, his palm laying down lazy circles on my back.

When he straightens up, he reaches for the whip.

"No!" I say.

"Yes," he replies. "There is more."

"James, please—"

"Shhh," he says, placing his fingers over my mouth. When he sees I won't say anything more, he sets down the whip and reaches over and takes off the right wrist cuff, then the left.

I think he's changed his mind, there won't be any more, but then he moves me down to the very edge of the bed, has me get up on all fours.

"If you fight me," he warns, "I'll put the cuffs back on."

He moves my knees apart, then tells me to go down on my elbows. Once again, my ass is in the air. I turn my head, see him pick up the whip. My body tenses.

He puts his hand on me, on my hip, my buttock, my thigh. "Relax," he orders, "breathe."

I think of the whip. I think of the pain.

"Breathe," he says again, his hand still on my haunch, and this time I close my eyes and try to relax. Several minutes go by before the touch of his hand leaves me. Again I feel the sting of his whip, the slashing pain on my ass. I clench my hands into fists, drawing them close to my body. He leans over and pulls out my arms, pries open my fists.

"I don't want to see you tightening your muscles," he says, "or tensing your body." He pauses, then adds, "Settle in, Carly, because I'm just beginning."

I close my eyes again, waiting for the whip. When it comes, I jerk, feeling the pain, but this time I concentrate on my breathing and I relax before the next blow arrives. He strikes me again, on the top of my back, and I shudder, wanting this to be over, but he whips me again and again, on my ass, my back, my thighs, and I wait for the memory of that earlier long-forgotten pain to return, the darkness and blood and the feeling of death in every broken bone, but it doesn't come. It is gone, faded away. The pain I feel now is of a different kind, sharp and burning, the pain of the here-and-now, and as I concentrate on my breath, my gasps begin to come out as low groans, and I keep my fingers unfurled, telling my-self the pain will lessen the more I relax.

But it doesn't. I feel each strike painfully, and sometimes I forget to breathe, and James leans over and reminds me, then he hits me again, and again, and again. I don't know how long this continues, I've lost all sense of time, and it takes me a minute to realize when the blows have stopped. I wait, ex-pecting more, but nothing comes. My buttocks feel warm and prickly, tender. I wait longer, then finally allow myself hope that he is through.

When I open my eyes, I see him walking toward me from the bathroom, his shirt unbuttoned, a glass of water in his hand. I dare not move. As he gets closer, I see he is flushed, and beads of sweat linger on his chest and face.

He gulps the water, watching me, sets the glass on the armoire, then takes off his shirt. His chest is broad, muscled, lightly tanned, with not much hair. I want to ask him if I can move, but I'm afraid to speak, afraid to disturb the silence. He slips off his shoes and socks, then picks up the whip. I close my eyes, waiting, knowing more is still to come. He's not finished with me yet.

He begins again, and the pain starts all over. There is a rhythm to the way he whips, although he breaks it up, surprising me with three rapid strikes within a sequence of slow hits. The pain mounts, a crescendo of blows, while he moves from side to side, slowly, striking me from here, lashing out from there, placing each stroke deliberately, like an artist covering his canvas, and then, despite the pain, or maybe even because of it, I notice something strange within myself, acceptance, perhaps, or something more urgent than that, some kind of temptation or hunger that comes from deep inside, a feeling too disturbing to acknowledge. I concentrate on my breath.

Then I feel his hand move between my legs, insinuating, and I open my eyes and forget to breathe. His fingertips brush against the lips of my vagina. I hold my breath, waiting, tense. Not once this evening has he touched me in a sexual manner.

"Spread your knees more," he says, pushing them apart farther with his other hand. He lays his palm on my buttock, and I feel the heat of my own flesh, the hotness left behind from the scourge of the whip. With his other hand, he slides the tips of his fingers along the opening of my vagina, barely making contact, a brushstroke touch. I remain motionless, apprehensive, waiting, but he neither penetrates nor causes me pain. The muscles in my back and shoulders, down my legs and in my calves, are tight, taut, and I feel the bare touch of him, teasing it seems, or torturing, and then I remember his appeal, forgotten in the pain, but it's coming back to me now, and I realize—or maybe I knew it all along—that I want him to fuck me.

As if he could read my mind, he pushes a finger inside me, twists it around. He puts in two fingers, and I relax, accepting him.

"You're dripping," he says. He removes his fingers, and, leaning forward, with one knee on the bed, he shoves them in my mouth. I suck his fingers to the knuckles, tasting myself, smelling myself.

"Don't move," he says, taking his fingers out of my mouth, then he gets up, standing behind me. I hear him unbuckling his belt, the rustle of a sliding zipper, his pants falling to the floor, then more movement as he steps out of his underwear. I try to turn around, to look at him, lift up on one elbow, but he puts his hand on my back and shoves me down.

"There's nothing here you need to see," he says, and his fingers are inside me again, palpating. I hear him go down on his knees, and I think he is going to fuck me now, but instead he slaps my ass sharply with the palm of his hand. I tighten up, let out a sudden cry, surprised by the unexpected pain. He keeps his fingers inside me, moving them around.

"This feels better, doesn't it?" he asks.

I nod, not sure if he is referring to the pain or the pleasure, too afraid to ask. He slides out his fingers and goes to my clitoris, rubbing gently. He hears me sigh, a soft moan.

"You like this?" he asks, and I nod again, closing my eyes. He continues rubbing, then uses his other hand on me as well, his fingers hard and cool and pushing against me, determined, trying to wedge inside my vagina but not succeeding, and I feel myself growing wetter, wanting more, impatient, so I press back against him, then abruptly realize it is not his finger pushing against me, but something else, something hard and round: the wooden handle of the whip.

"James?" I ask, uncertain, a slight protest.

"Quiet," he commands as he continues to work it inside me, twisting it in bit by bit, nudging, prying me open with the whip that had caused me so much pain, and then, unexpectedly, I feel myself getting even wetter, yielding to the thought of this violation, wanting it, wanting more, and all of a sudden the handle slips in easily, slick with my own juice, and then he fucks me with it, his other hand still on my clitoris, rubbing, until he makes me come.

When he removes the handle, he puts the rounded knob up to my lips. I know what he wants, but I don't comply. I've had enough of the whip for one evening.

"Suck on it," he orders, and he shoves it in my mouth, holds it there, makes me gag. He pushes his penis inside me and fucks me roughly, his hands on my back and head, holding me down, getting what he wants, watching me suck the wooden handle of his black leather whip.

When he is through, he leans down and kisses the back of my shoulder—the only kiss he has given me tonight—and then whispers in my ear. "You don't understand anything yet," he says, "but before I'm finished with you, you will." He kisses my shoulder again, then adds, "And you'll give me what I want."

I don't ask him what that is.

CHAPTER SEVEN

Instantly, when I wake, I sense something is wrong.

Then I remember last night, and I remember where I am. Although I'm not facing him, I know he's beside me, still sleeping. He makes no noise, but I feel the closeness of him, the rolling dip in the mattress, the warmth of his nearby body; even the odor of the air is different, weighted, a masculine smell.

Carefully, I roll over. James is sprawled on the bed, lying on his stomach, one arm under his head, the other, palm up, by his side. Although the bed is king-sized and extra-long, it barely seems large enough for him. A white sheet, tangled at his waist, covers his lower body. Rising to my elbow, I watch him sleep, inspect him the way he inspected me last night. His back is tanned and lightly freckled, and his flesh seems packed on, in solid slabs, the muscles firm even while he's asleep. I look closer and see he has his own set of scars: a jagged one on the back of his left shoulder, and another on his upper arm, both out of view when he's shirted. The scar on his temple I've seen before, this one round, a small indent the size of a quarter. His doctor wasn't nearly as good as mine—but then I suppose men tolerate scars better than women. I can't imagine James being bothered by his at all.

He moves, shifts his body to the right, and I hold my breath, hoping he won't wake. His forehead creases into a slight frown, then he turns onto his side, dragging the sheet with him, eyes still closed, still asleep, and he settles again, with a sigh. Smiling a little, I look down at him, at his face, placid and unaffected while he sleeps, almost childlike, vulnerable. Then I think of last night, how he fucked me. There was nothing childlike about that. I reach over and touch him lightly, place my fingertips on his shoulder, feel the warmth of his skin. I want him again. Through his sleep, he must feel my touch because he moves slightly, brings his arm up to his chest, pulling the sheet from my body. With a start, I see the ugly bruises where he'd bitten me last night. They cover my torso in dark, angry splotches, some of them with a bluish tinge. I almost start to cry out, but then I see the leather whip lying on the floor, the long black thongs in a tangled heap, the knobbed end of the handle shiny and smooth. I need to get out of here.

Quietly, slowly, I get out of bed. Just as I start to cross the room, James makes a noise, a soft moan. I freeze, holding my breath, waiting, but he doesn't stir. The whip, a tangible reminder of last night, taunts me. Just to make sure I haven't roused him, I wait a few more seconds, anxious, then cautiously walk over to the middle of the loft and pick up my clothes, still crumpled in a heap from the night before. I take a quick glance back at him. He's still sleeping.

Carrying my clothes and shoes, I tiptoe down the spiral staircase. In the morning air, his house appears cool and precise, grayish, almost stark. From each of the arched windows, outside light seeps through the curtains, shines across the room in long tubular columns, from which dust motes, like sprinklings of fine powder, float lazily in the air. I get dressed in a hurry, then grab my car keys from the entrance table and open the front door. A shaft of bright light streams into the room. Looking back, I hesitate, suddenly remembering the cracked picture frame. I go over to the other side of the room. His desk looks the same as the last time I saw it: computer with a blank screen, stacks of paper in neat piles, a ceramic dish filled with paper clips and rubber bands, pens and pencils in an upright plastic container, and the two framed photos pushed toward the back, out of the way. The photo of James and Gina is still on the desk the way I'd left it, tilted slightly toward the right so the crack in the glass isn't as noticeable. I pick it up. Chances are, James never even noticed I'd broken the glass.

Abruptly, I look up. I hear him rustling around upstairs, in bed. I place the picture frame back on the desk where it belongs, angle it to the right, then cross the room quickly. I can't face him this morning.

"Carly?" I hear him mumble, his voice thick with sleep.

I rush out the door, slamming it shut behind me.

After I go home and change clothes—long white pants to cover the bite bruises on my thighs—I return to Byblos and go out to the garden. Artichokes are coming up all over. We have a superabundance of them. Every day, for the last two weeks, I've been serving them—cold with mayonnaise, warm with hollandaise sauce, marinated and tossed in a salad, chopped up in frittatas and crab crêpes, baked with Monterey Jack cheese and green chilies and garlic;

I've tried them in soups and appetizers, served them chilled, steamed, curried, sautéed, and boiled; made a dilled artichoke and bay shrimp purée, baked the hearts in a casserole with mushrooms and Swiss cheese and white wine, stuffed them into sweet green peppers with feta and onions and orzo—but I barely make a dent in the crop. I freeze the hearts and the edible pulp from the leaves to use in future months. We give away artichokes by the bagfuls, to visitors, to guests, to anyone at all. Still, we have more.

A cool, refreshing morning breeze passes over me while I work, and the sky is a powdery blue. I cut choke after choke, assiduously. The plants are ferny-looking and tall—nearly as tall as I—with arching silvery-green leaves, the artichoke buds fat and swollen and the scales tightly closed. As soon as the scales open, the artichoke turns into a giant purple thistlehead—a stunning display of color, but not good for eating. I cut the stalks two inches below the buds, then drop them in a large wicker basket, slow but steady work. The gardener would've cut them this afternoon, but I wanted to be alone, out of the house. I'm still confused about last night and don't want to run into James just yet. If he and I had sex before, when I was younger, I don't remember it, not at all. And I feel I should have—that kind of sex one doesn't forget: a little rough, a little scary, and supremely pleasurable just because it was rough and scary. My response alarmed me. My passion came unexpected, unbeckoned, a passion that caught me off guard in its sheer intensity. And of course I noticed the absence of a kiss, the utter lack of romance. He kissed the back of my shoulder, lightly, but not once did his lips touch mine. Somehow, I feel cheated.

I cut another artichoke head, trying not to think

about what came before the sex, but still it goes through my mind. It wasn't pleasant at first—I certainly hadn't enjoyed it as had the red-haired woman bound to his staircase, giving in, willingly, to his touch with the whip—but toward the end I felt myself accepting the pain and humiliation, and I felt a stirring deep inside, something alien, that I couldn't, or wouldn't, identify, a feeling, as I think back on it, that even now makes me blush. The sensation was disturbingly erotic.

And the experience last night gave me something else: my first memory. When I cried last night, it wasn't from the sting of his whip, but for the pain of my earlier beating. It came back to me in a flash—lying still, almost dead, yet feeling my broken bones and cut flesh and warm blood, hurting so badly I wanted to die, with nothing but blackness surrounding me. When the farmworker found me in the empty field, I was lying in a newly dug hole, half-buried, as if the person who put me there was interrupted before he could finish the job. Perhaps the blackness came from there, from lying in the hole. Neither it nor the field are in my memory; the police informed me how I was found after I woke from the coma.

Cutting another artichoke bud, I think about the hole, my intended grave. I shudder. On Monday, I say to myself, I'll go to the county recorder's office. I'll find Anna Maria Monicelli's death certificate. Anna Maria McGuane, I correct myself. Only two days until Monday. Two days until I discover how James's wife died, and whether her injuries were similar to mine. Even now, foolishly, I am hoping for a happy ending. I want James to be innocent of all crimes, of his wife's death and his attempt against me. But I fear he will not be.

I gaze at the long row of artichokes bordering the

garden. There are more of them down by James's house, a few on the east side of Gina's cottage, and others close to the winery. They are spectacular; live sculptures in green. Mrs. McGuane told me she planted so many just because she loves to look at them, and she laughs at my urgent, futile attempt to cut every artichoke bud before it can flower. Dried, the thistle makes a wonderful flower arrangement, she said, but still, irrationally, I rush to cut all I can, rush against nature, against time, as if time, *my time*, was running out.

Artichokes, of course, for dinner—a quiche with Swiss Gruyère cheese, onions, artichoke hearts, and chives. I set the table, only the three of them tonight, and put out a salad and bottle of champagne, a sparkling wine from Schramsberg, a neighboring winery in Napa Valley. Mrs. McGuane loves champagne— she doesn't believe in reserving it for special occasions—and will drink it with almost anything. Back in the kitchen, from the bay window, I see Gina leave the guest cottage and then walk determinedly across the lawn toward the house, her long black hair blowing in the wind.

I return to the dining room, bringing the warm dish of quiche. Mrs. McGuane, arranging a vase of fresh flowers, smiles as I come in. "That looks delicious," she says.

Blossoms in yellow, pink, and blue brighten the room and give off a delicate, fresh spring scent. I hear the kitchen door slam.

A few moments later, Gina enters. She nods to me, a brief gesture, and her lips turn up slightly, not quite a smile, then she crosses the room and kisses her mother on the cheek.

"Sorry I'm late," she says. "I had to finish up some

things at the winery." She looks as if she'd dressed hurriedly: no makeup, still wearing jeans and cowboy boots but with a satiny rose-colored blouse instead of the usual T-shirt, her hair tangled from the wind. She glances at the table. "There're only the two of us tonight," she says to me.

"Oh," I say, trying not to sound disappointed that James won't be here. I cannot deny the desire I felt last night, nor the confusion. I move the vase of flowers slightly to the left. Looking up, I see Gina staring at me, a suspicious expression on her face.

"James went to Sacramento on business," she says, watching me closely. Then adds, "He won't return until the middle of next week."

I shrug.

"I'm sorry, dear," Mrs. McGuane says to me. "I completely forgot to mention it."

Sitting down next to her mother, Gina says, "Since you've already set the table for three, why don't you join us this evening?"

"Yes, of course," Mrs. McGuane adds. She pats the table with her hand. "Sit," she says.

Mrs. McGuane and I have shared meals before, but this is the first time with Gina present. I feel a bit awkward, intruding on a family dinner, but Gina looks up and gives me a warm smile.

"Please join us," she says again. "If you don't, Mother will harangue me the entire meal about the Jeffersons' boy."

"The Jeffersons' *boy*," Mrs. McGuane says, "is nearly forty—a suitable age for you."

Gina gives me a look, rolls her eyes.

Her mother raises a hand in capitulation. "All right," she says. "I won't say another word." She shakes her head.

"Keeping notes about the winery?" I ask Gina, nodding to the pad of paper she has in her breast pocket. Gina, I've noticed, is never without pencil and paper.

Before she can answer, her mother smiles and says, "Gina keeps a notebook with her in case inspiration strikes. She's a poet—although she refuses to let anyone read her poetry."

Gina, not commenting, frowns at her mother, crinkling up her nose.

I reach for the bottle of champagne that I have chilling in a silver bucket and open it. The cork comes out with a pressurized pop, and I pour each of us a glass. The champagne smells wonderfully yeasty, like freshly baked bread, and tiny bubbles stream up to the top of the flute-shaped glasses.

"Very nice," Mrs. McGuane announces after she tastes it. She looks up at me, and I can tell another lecture is forthcoming. "In Europe," she says, "only bottle-fermented sparkling wines made in the Champagne district of France can call themselves Champagne. Sparkling wines in Italy are called *spumanti*, in Spain *cava*, and in Germany *Sekt*. California winemakers, even though we have no labeling restrictions on the term *champagne*, almost always use the term *sparkling wine* or Napa Valley Champagne." She takes another sip. "In conversation, of course, everyone uses the terms interchangeably."

Recently, Mrs. McGuane has begun educating me on some of the simpler aspects of wine, acting as my teacher, as if I was going to remain at Byblos for a long time. While she elaborates, I take a sip. The texture is smooth and creamy on my tongue, and it has a fruity, citrus flavor. Normally, I enjoy the tidbits of wine information that Mrs. McGuane dispenses, but, with Gina here, I find it difficult to concentrate. I sit down. I cut and serve the quiche, wondering if Gina knows I had sex with her twin. Then it crosses my mind that, perhaps, he's told her.

Abruptly, knife in hand, I look up, sniff the air. Something is wrong. Then the smoke alarm goes off, a loud squealing sound coming from the kitchen. Gina is the first to react. She kicks back her chair and crosses the room, running. I follow, close behind. When she opens the kitchen door, I see yellow flames shooting up from the stove and running along the countertop. Trails of smoke curl up toward the ceiling.

Quickly, Gina grabs the fire extinguisher from the cabinet, pulls the ring pin, aims the nozzle at the largest flame. White powder bursts out, dousing the fire. She squeezes the trigger again and again, blasting the flames along the countertop, not stopping until the fire is gone. When she's finished, a layer of white powder covers the range and counter. We stand there, not speaking.

"How . . ." Mrs. McGuane falters, not finishing her sentence. She's standing at the doorway, one hand clutching at her blouse, her face ashen. "How . . ." she begins again, her voice barely audible, and again she doesn't finish. She just shakes her head, slowly, still in shock, not believing what she sees.

Gina points to a pile of black cinders on the stove. "A dish towel must've caught fire," she says. "Or maybe a pot holder. Then the flames jumped to the counter." She steps forward, turns off the front burner on the stove. They both look at me.

"I'm so sorry," I say. "I—"

But Mrs. McGuane, recovered from her initial shock, interrupts. "We've never had a fire here!" she snaps. Her face is red now, furious. "Never! How could you be so careless? Give me one reason why I shouldn't dismiss you immediately," she demands, but then she stomps out of the room before I can reply.

Gina eyes me evenly. She says, "My mother is deathly afraid of fires. When she was a young child, she barely escaped from a burning house."

I go over to the stove, inspect the damage. The countertop will need to be replaced, also the bottom wall of a charred cabinet. The fire looked worse than it actually was, though, most of the flames fueled by a long row of cookbooks I kept along the countertop.

"I don't know how this could happen," I say, upset. "I would never leave a towel on the stove top. And I would never forget to turn off a burner. Never." I look over at Gina. "You were the last one in the kitchen," I say.

She shrugs. "I didn't see anything."

"You came inside the house through the kitchen door."

"Yes," she says, "but I was late for dinner. I didn't look around. I didn't notice anything. I went straight to the dining room."

She comes over to me, puts her arm around my shoulder. "Nobody got hurt," she says. "It could've been worse." We gaze at the blackened counter.

She says, "You seem pretty shaken yourself. Why don't you go home? When my mother calms down, I'll talk to her."

CHAPTER EIGHT

In the county recorder's office, I wait, impatient, at the front desk while the woman makes me a copy of Anna McGuane's death certificate. The woman gives off an air of confusion: her hair a gray chaos of short, crimped curls; her dress a wrinkled green material with wide, flaring gores, one side of the collar skewed. She looks at the newly extruded copy from the machine, then shakes her head.

"We've been having problems with the copier," she tells me. The gold chain attached to her glasses dangles in two big, glittery loops beneath her ears.

"It doesn't have to be perfect," I say. All I need is to see how James's wife died, and it seems as if it's taking forever. First, I had to wait while the woman helped an elderly man with his business, then, when it was finally my turn, she had trouble locating Anna's death certificate, and now that she's found it, the copy machine isn't working properly. "As long as I can read it," I say, "it'll be okay."

Reluctantly, the woman comes over with the copy. I've already filled out a form and signed it, so now she takes my money, counts it slowly. Finally, she offers me the copy.

"Thanks," I say, grabbing it from her. I head toward the door, skimming the certificate. Accidental death. Head trauma from a twenty-foot fall. A bunch of medical and forensic terms I'm not familiar with. Date of death.

Blinking, I check the date again, feeling my heart pound. I stare at the document, at the date of death. My palms feel clammy, my mouth dry. The vein at my temple throbs out an abnormal pulse, rapid with panic or fear or maybe both: Anna, James's wife, died one week before I was beaten and left for dead.

I go outside and sit on the steps in front of the building, try to calm down, watch a few cars slowly passing by, a woman pushing a stroller down the sidewalk. It's quiet out here this morning, peaceful, the building cool under the shade of tall trees. Two birds, in pleasant, fluttering warbles, begin singing each other a song, each, it seems, trying to outdo the other. I look at the death certificate, the paper trembling slightly in my hand. It doesn't tell me as much as I'd like. I still need more.

Suddenly, I get an idea. I call out to the woman pushing the baby stroller. She turns her head, looks around to see who's calling her, then settles her gaze on me.

"Do you know where the library is?" I ask.

The woman, wearing a formless, baggy dress, is young and pale. She has limp blond hair, which she now hooks behind her ear. She nods eagerly, tells me the library is nearby, and points up the street while she gives me directions, moving the stroller back and forth with her other hand. The woman wants to chat, even offers to show me the way, but I thank her quickly, tell her I can find it, and head up the street.

Inside the library, I go through the *Napa Valley Register*, the main local newspaper for this area.

Anna died more than fifteen years ago, and the library keeps the newspapers from that period on microfilm. Each reel is for one month. I run the appropriate reel through the machine, going quickly until I reach the day she died. I have a computer at home, and by comparison the microfilm machine is slow and awkward, a bulky piece of low-tech equipment. I move the reel forward, to the next day, and there, on the front page, is the story of her death. I read the article: "Anna Maria McGuane, 25, daughter-in-law of prominent Napa Valley vintner James McGuane, Sr., died yesterday in an accidental fall from a catwalk inside the Byblos Winery. Apparently, she slipped on the platform, then slid beneath the guardrail. She died instantly, hitting her head on the concrete floor. . . . Witnessing the accident, and also present on the catwalk, was her husband, James McGuane, Jr. . . ."

I skim the article. Anna, it says, was also from a prominent Napa Valley family that grew and sold wine grapes to local wineries. There's a picture of the winery, one of the catwalk as it looked back then. I print out a copy of the article, then return the microfilm and leave.

As I'm driving back to Byblos, I wonder if I knew Anna. I also wonder if she was pushed from the catwalk rather than fell. It would be easy to do. The catwalk was high and narrow, with a thin guardrail that didn't offer much protection. A large man such as James would have no trouble shoving her under the guardrail.

I drive north on the Silverado Trail, barely taking in the view, thinking. Fifteen years ago, I, also, suffered a head wound. The doctors and the police, working together, speculated how I may have been injured. There were bruises all over my body, as if I'd been badly beaten, and the side of my head had been hit—hard—with a blunt instrument. But the other wounds, they said, the broken bones, the shards of embedded glass, were consistent with a long fall—as if I'd been shoved through a high window.

Or from a catwalk, I think now. And the shards of glass could've been from wine bottles on the winery floor. Perhaps I was meant to die in the same manner as Anna.

I pass through the double stone pillars of the Byblos entrance, absently wave to a few people working in the vineyards as I drive by, then turn on the winding road leading up to James's house. The top of my convertible is down, and the wind whips through my short hair. Looking around at the vineyards, I note the changes. The vines, although still neat and orderly, are in a state of rapid growth, the leaves a vibrant, refulgent green, young and tender. The rows are like processions of restrained schoolchildren, tramping in obedient files up and over the hills yet just waiting to be released, waiting for the time they can let go and finally run amok. They are like me, waiting for the order to disintegrate.

When I reach James's house, I stop. I didn't expect to find his black Cherokee here, and it's not. He's still in Sacramento. The small pane of glass which I'd bought earlier is sitting on the seat, next to the copies of the death certificate and newspaper accounting of Anna's so-called accident. I pick it up and go inside his house, knocking first before I use my pilfered key. I stand inside the doorway, call out his name just in case, but no one is here. Quickly, I replace the glass in the picture frame, then glance over at the three-door filing cabinet. This would be an ideal time to go through his files and search his home again, but I'm expected back at the main house.

Reluctantly, I lock the door. As I'm walking back to my convertible, I hear another car coming up the road. I stop, listening. Yes, it's definitely coming up this road. I run back to my car. Frantically, I search in the glove compartment—toss aside a few maps, some white napkins scrunched up in the corner, a tire-pressure gauge, a pair of small binoculars. Under all this mess, I find a pocket knife. I grab it, then rush over to the artichoke patch beside James's house. I cut one of the heads just as a car turns the corner. It's Gina, in her white, mud-splattered truck. She pulls up to my convertible, watches me from there.

"Hi!" I call out brightly. I hold up the artichoke head I'd just sawed off the stalk with my not-so-sharp pocket knife. "I thought I'd cut some of these since James is gone."

Smiling at me, she brushes back her hair, then looks down at my car, at the front seat. She holds her gaze there, frowns just a little.

With alarm, I remember the death certificate on the front seat. "Gina!" I call out, walking toward her.

She looks up.

"I could use some help," I say, waving my knife toward the patch of tall artichoke plants. "Do you have a few spare minutes?"

She shakes her head. "No, I just came by to see if everything is okay between you and my mother. I saw you drive up here a few minutes ago."

Nodding, I put my hand on her truck door, lean against it. "Thanks for talking to her," I say. "I thought she'd fire me. She had every reason to—I still can't understand how it happened."

"It was just an accident."

I gaze at Gina, her light green eyes, wondering. She was the last person in the kitchen. "I guess so,"

I say. "I told her I'd pay for the damages, but she refused."

Gina pats my arm, then shifts the truck into reverse. "Don't worry about it," she says. "Mother was talking about getting new cabinets anyway." She backs up and drives away.

I look at the front passenger seat of my car. The maps and crumpled white napkins and pair of binoculars partially cover the death certificate and newspaper article. The words **Certificate of Death** are visible in large bold letters, but the rest of the paper is covered. Gina didn't see much, if anything at all, but I realize I was lucky. I can't afford to be so careless—not with James, nor with Gina.

CHAPTER NINE

I don't go to the winery at all this week. After learning how Anna died, I'm not ready to see the catwalk again, not just yet. I stay in the McGuanes' home, hiding out. Every day I like the house more and more. Mrs. McGuane—I still have a hard time calling her Charlotte—did the decorating herself, and although most of the furnishings are expensive and chosen with careful deliberation, the house has a warm, comfortable feel to it, homey with potted green plants and colorful wall prints and vases of fresh-cut flowers from her garden. James still hasn't returned from Sacramento.

I walk through the wide hallway and down the two steps into the living room. It's a collection of soft colors—off-white plush sofa with pastel pillows, a light pearl-gray carpet, dusty-blue stuffed armchairs. Sunlight, from the back ceiling-to-floor window, floods the room. I come in here frequently. It isn't the décor that pulls me in, but the portrait on the wall.

I cross the room, look once more at the painting. It's a family portrait of the McGuanes. Mother, father, the two kids, all of them looking much younger. When I asked her, Mrs. McGuane said it was painted sixteen years ago—only one year before I was attacked. Lightly, I run my finger over James's face. This is how he would've looked when I knew him, younger, fewer lines on his face, an open expression not yet jaded by time or experience, his hair even blonder than it is now. It's a nice portrait, but every time I see the picture, a shudder comes over me, a feeling that the air is growing thick, making it difficult for me to breath. Vague, amorphous images—fluid, without definite form—try to take shape in my mind, but they are out of reach, and then, like delicate wafts of smoke, they just drift away. The harder I concentrate, the more elusive the images become. The doctors told me my memories might return in snatches, a bit vague, perhaps not in sequence, just precious bits of recall sneaking out from under the barricade of amnesia. Or they could come out in a rush. In truth, the doctors were uncertain how, or if, my memories would return. Despite its popularity in both film and fiction, my type of amnesia is extremely rare, with no definitive process of recovery. The memories may never come back.

"Are you alone?" I hear Gina say.

Startled, I turn around. I hadn't heard her walk in the room. She's been at the winery again, wearing her uniform of tight blue jeans, boots, and a T-shirt, this one brand-new, with the Byblos logo printed on the front. Her hair is swept up in a bushy ponytail, with loose coils of black tendrils plastered against her sweaty neck. Most every time I see her, visible signs of her labor are present—dirt from the vineyards smudged on her cheek, dusty or muddy shoes, dark splotches of wine staining her shirts. She practically lives at the winery.

"You're alone?" she asks again, coming toward me.

Although it's not as deep, she has the same voice as James, soft-burred and lush, each vowel wrapped in velvet. I nod, hoping she didn't see me touch the portrait, tracing my finger over her brother's face.

"Dinner will be ready soon," I say, and, nervously, I rattle off what I'm serving—grilled lamb topped with a wine sauce of cabernet sauvignon, black currants, and fresh basil. For dessert, I thought I'd try a zabaglione poured over marinated peaches and pears.

Gina listens, a slight smile at one corner of her mouth, her arms folded casually across her chest. Her skin is lightly tanned, her eyebrows dark and dramatic. In the portrait, she has a very playful quality in her expression, a carefree look in the light-green sparkle of her eyes. None of that remains. She's a beautiful woman, but there's nothing carefree or playful about her.

"You're too good for us," she says.

I tilt my head, curious.

Her smile widens now, and she reaches for her back pocket. "Here," she says, and she shoves out her arm.

Looking down, I see a sheet of folded paper in her hand. I take the paper and open it. The name and phone number of a prominent San Francisco restaurant are scrawled across the top. A man's name is written below.

"He's the owner," she says. "A friend of mine. You can start there next week—at triple the salary you're getting here. It'll be a good career move for you."

I finger the paper. Of course I recognize the name of the restaurant, one of the finest in the country. I've dreamed of working in such a place; every chef has. I give the paper back to her. "I'm not looking for a job," I say. "I have one."

Her smile disappears. She hesitates for a moment,

then says, "I've seen your résumé, Carly. You don't belong here."

When I don't reply, she shakes her head a little, confused. "Well . . . so much for surprises," she says, shrugging. "I thought I was doing you a favor." She starts to leave.

"Gina," I say.

She turns back to me.

"Thanks for recommending me to your friend. I appreciate it. I'm just not looking for another job right now. I like it here."

She comes back to me, puts the paper in the left breast pocket of my blouse. "Think about it," she says, her voice soft, almost sisterly. "It's in your best interests."

She walks off. I hear the front door open and close. Alone now, I feel a faint pang in my heart, a yearning, a need to have someone—a sister maybe—who truly does care about my best interests.

Again, I look at the McGuane portrait, their smiling faces, and I wonder if, somewhere, in someone's house, packed away in an attic trunk perhaps, if I'm included in a family portrait. Was my picture taken long ago? Did I, at one time, understand the interaction between parent and child? Between brother and sister?

No, I don't think I did. How could I? Family relationships seem foreign to me now, so odd, so far beyond my grasp.

I cross to the other side of the room, to another picture. Family portraits may confuse me, but this picture I understand—and it also draws me in. It's a reproduction of a Picasso, a very sensual, erotic painting, a nude woman, voluptuous and curvy, sitting in a dark chair. The first time I saw it, I assumed there was a man in the print, hovering behind the chair, staring down, but then I realized the woman was alone. She has two heads, one dark, the other light, and skewed breasts and a black painted slash for genitals. Sometimes I feel like that myself: disjointed, out of whack, with dark and light sides of my own, not necessarily balanced. This picture I can understand.

CHAPTER TEN

"Where do you store the old records?" I ask Patsy Wilson. She's the office manager at Byblos, a woman in her fifties, and she's wearing a blue-checked blouse that stretches tightly across her chest, the buttonholes straining. Plump and curvaceous, she always gives the impression, like an aging stripper, that she's about ready to pop out of her clothes.

She's by herself today, and she breezes around the room, from the computer to the fax machine to the file cabinet in the corner. I'd just dropped off a plate of date-nut bars, and she picks up another one before returning to her desk. Occasionally, I'll bring snacks for the people in the winery—cinnamon brunch rolls, spiced madeleines, poppy-seed butter cake, a fresh pear kuchen. I enjoy surprising them with food, but mainly it's an excuse for me to wander around.

"Records?" Patsy repeats, looking up from the computer. Powdered sugar, from the date bars, dusts her upper lip. She hits a button on the computer, and the printer next to it begins churning out a document. "What kinds of records?"

"Employee applications, that kind of stuff. Where do you keep the records of all the people who worked here, say, fifteen or twenty years ago?"

She grins. Red lipstick smudges one of her front teeth. "Honey," she says, "those were thrown out years ago."

I shrug, trying not to show my disappointment.

"Are you sure?" I ask her.

Patsy, reading one of the pages coming out of the printer, nods. "We keep them for seven years, but after that they all get tossed." She glances over at me. "Why the sudden interest?"

"No interest," I say, shrugging again. "I just wondered where you kept everything. It looks pretty crowded in here."

"You're right about that," she says. She turns back to the page she was reading.

I'm about to ask her another question, but the phone rings. She looks up and says, "If you want to know more about employee records, ask Gina or James. They could tell you," and then she reaches for the phone.

"Ask me what?" I hear James say, and I turn around to see him standing at the door, leaning his shoulder against the doorframe. With the noise of the printer and the phone ringing, neither Patsy nor I heard him come in. He's dressed in charcoal slacks and a sport coat, with a dark-blue button-down shirt open at the collar, but what I'm really seeing is the image of him as he fucked me from behind, remembering how much I liked it, and, watching him now, I feel that heavy desire come over me again when what I really want is to appear as cool and detached as he. Behind me, I hear Patsy talking on the phone, answering questions, ignoring both of us.

"Ask me what?" he says again. There is no change

in his voice, no knowing glance to indicate what occurred last week.

Flustered, I say, "Nothing. It isn't important."

He gazes at me evenly, without emotion, then steps aside and holds the door open. "I'll walk you back to your car," he says.

His Cherokee is parked next to my convertible. At the far end of the building, two men, wearing jeans and knee-high black rubber boots, are hosing down some stainless-steel equipment.

"Are you having second thoughts?" I ask him.

"Second thoughts?" he repeats, giving me a sidelong glance, not understanding.

"It's been a week since . . ." I hesitate, not sure what to call our sex. "I thought maybe you'd reconsidered Gina's warning—that I'm a woman who'd cause trouble."

We stop in front of my white convertible. He looks down at me, his head cocked to the side. "No," he says finally. "I haven't changed my mind."

I nod. I should've known he's a man of no regrets, no second thoughts, the kind of man who, once he makes a decision, always stands by it.

"Have you?" he asks, but the question is rhetorical. He knows what my answer will be. I see the faint smile lift his lips, see the amusement in the sparkle of his eyes. "Well?" he asks.

I shake my head. At the end of the building, the two men finish cleaning the equipment. One of them turns off the faucet. He says something in Spanish to the other man, then they walk around the corner, disappearing. James and I are alone now.

He opens my car door but wraps his hand around my wrist before I can get in. His touch, just his fingers pressing gently against my wrist, makes me tingle with desire. Disturbingly, my attraction for him grows. As if he can guess what I'm thinking, what I'm wanting, he leans down and, unexpectedly, kisses me on the lips—a real kiss.

He whispers in my ear, "You didn't work here fifteen years ago."

I pull back, bang into the car door.

"Don't bother searching for your employment records," he continues, "because there are none."

As I hear this, a chill goes through me. He releases my arm but doesn't move. His sheer presence pins me against the car.

"Did you actually think I'd never figure it out?" he says.

I cannot speak. I feel the metal of the car against my back, against my legs.

"As soon as I fucked you, I guessed who you were. Your appearance may be different, but your responses aren't."

He reaches out. I shrink back, try to ease away, but his body blocks my path. When I look up at him, he puts his hand on the side of my face, then lets it slide down to my neck. His touch immobilizes me, makes my body go rigid.

"I feel your pulse racing," he says, stepping closer, bending down his head so it's near mine. His hand circles my throat, a firm pressure. "I feel your fear," he whispers.

Still, I'm unable to reply. My pulse pounds in my ears.

He searches my face, his eyes penetrating. "There is no resemblance," he says, more to himself than to me. He turns my face, scrutinizes it, then releases it. He says, "If I hadn't fucked you, I never would've known."

Finally, I'm able to speak. "People are nearby," I say, choking out the words. "If I scream, they'll hear."

He looks down at me, smiles a little. He says, "You don't know anything, do you? You have no idea what happened fifteen years ago." He shakes his head. "It's not what you think. Not at all."

"Tell me what happened," I say.

He lifts his hand again, lightly brushes his finger across my lips, as if he can't believe the change in my appearance. "You were so naive," he says, staring at my mouth, "but also incredible. You'd do whatever I asked of you."

"And then you tried to kill me."

He watches me, continues to study my face for prior recognition. "No," he says.

I move to the right, try to get away from him. Lightly, he places his hand on my shoulder, a restraining move even though he uses no force. He doesn't have to. The threat of him is enough.

"What happened to me?" I ask.

He looks over my head, gazes across the field of grapevines. "I'll tell you," he says, "but you'll have to do something for me." He still stares across the field, a faraway expression on his face.

"What?" I ask, apprehensive.

He looks down at me. "Finish what we started," he says. "I was your mentor then. I taught you things no one else could. But we were interrupted. Something happened before I could finish. I want to take you the rest of the way."

I shake my head.

"You have no choice," he says. "Why did you risk returning to Byblos?" Not waiting for my reply, he answers his own question. "To find out what happened—and I'm the only one who can tell you."

He hesitates, then says, "You won't regret it, not in the end. And you'll get all the answers you need."

"I could tell your mother," I say.

He laughs, a short derisive sound. "Tell her what?

That something happened to you fifteen years ago and I'm responsible? That won't get you what you want. She didn't know you then, neither did Gina. I'm the only one who can fill in your past. Besides, I doubt my mother would believe you. Your credibility with her is lacking at the moment. I hear you almost burned down her kitchen."

"I didn't—"

He stops me from talking, puts his fingers on my lips. "Telling her won't do you any good, and neither will going to the police. There's nothing here to connect you to me. No one would believe you. But I can help you. I know the truth. Give me what I want, and I'll give you all the answers."

An icy sensation, a cool recognition of foreboding, goes through me as I listen to him speak. I tell myself to leave now, to reject his challenge, but I stand rooted to the spot. I am foolish to even consider his proposal, this I know, and my consent would imply I have nothing more to lose. The truth, however, is that there's always more to be lost. There is no absolute depth, no final end, to pain or misery or suffering. More can always follow. I know this—and still I do not turn away. My desire for knowledge is greater than my fear.

"What's my name?" I ask him. "My real name."

He traces my jawline with his finger, searching, it seems, for vestigial evidence of the young girl who used to be me. "You've been Carly for fifteen years," he finally replies. "For now, let's keep it that way."

He steps back, begins walking toward his car. "Come to my place tonight," he says over his shoulder. He's not asking, but telling me. He adds, "Come early."

CHAPTER ELEVEN

At the top of the spiral staircase, I hesitate. I'm wearing a short jade dress, a simple design with narrow shoulder straps and sparkling sequins, and darker-than-usual makeup: lipstick the color of plums, slightly smudged black eyeliner. When I arrived, I found a note taped to his front door, telling me he'd be back in a few minutes and to make myself at home. With that kind of an invitation, I went straight inside, planning to search his house once more. I don't trust him to tell me the truth about my past. I debated if I should go through the filing cabinet, but decided against it—too risky if he came home soon—so I went upstairs.

The loft is as I remembered it—brick-enclosed bathroom on the right, sleeping quarters on the left, a messy painter's studio and a stone hearth fireplace in the middle. Drapes cover the large loft window, so I walk over to the armoire and turn on a lamp. As before, the studio is the only area of his house in disarray. Stacks of canvases are everywhere—leaning against the table, crammed into the narrow walkway to the bathroom entrance, shoved up against the brick wall, lining the balustrade.

Splotches of paint splatter the easel, which is empty now, and the table is still cluttered with squished tubes of paint, a few scattered drawings in pencil, an array of paintbrushes in different sizes, some of them soaking in liquid-filled glasses. Something seems to be missing, and then I remember the black leather harness. The hoist is still in place, near the arched window, but suspended from it now is a benign-looking hanging chair made of dark rattan and plush burgundy cushions, an innocuous piece of furniture that could be placed in anyone's home.

I begin flipping through the canvases stacked up against the brick barrier to the bathroom. All of them are similar in theme to the ones hanging on the walls downstairs—dark and brooding, disturbing images of violence, each signed with his initials, J.McG. Moving on, I quickly go through the stacks leaning against the wooden balustrade, then the ones by the table. I'm about to leave the paintings and check his dresser drawers, when, stuffed behind an armoire, I find more canvases. I drag them out, skim through them rapidly. More of the same dark images. But then, near the end of the pile, a painting catches my eye. It's different from the others, the only one of a young girl.

Excited, I pull it out of the stack, take a closer look. The girl is small, as I am, and has long black hair, the same color as my hair when I woke from the coma, a cheap dye job. She's sitting outside at a wooden table, a picnic table, it looks like, with a stretch of grapevines in the background. Her skin is pale, and there's something vulnerable about her posture, slouched a little, as if she's overwhelmed. But her face . . . her face startles. It's grotesque, her features contorted, unrecognizable, her mouth red and twisted into an angry moue, her eyes narrow slits of rage.

For accuracy, the painting is useless to me. No one could form a realistic picture of the girl based on this. It's much too deformed, too abstract. Still, my discovery excites me. This girl must be me.

Hearing the door open, I shove the paintings back behind the armoire, then walk over to the balustrade. I look down and see James just outside the door, bending over, brushing dirt off the cuff of a pant leg. A gust of cool air blows through his hair, flattening it on one side of his head. Behind him, I can see that the sky, which had been a lovely blue and nearly cloudless when I arrived, is turning dark, very gray and hazy. He's dressed as he was earlier in the day, charcoal slacks and a sport coat, a dark-blue shirt open at the collar.

"I'm up here," I call to him.

He raises his head, glances in my direction. A fleeting look of annoyance flickers across his face, then disappears. He closes the door.

I add, "You said to make myself at home."

He crosses the room, bounds up the spiral staircase two steps at a time, combing his fingers through his hair, straightening it out. When he reaches the top, he pauses for just a brief second, glances around the loft, then comes over to me.

"I was looking at your paintings," I say. "I hope you don't mind."

He stands close to me, and I'm made to realize again, acutely, how much larger he is than I. He towers over me, his body like a shield, blocking out the lamplight, and, involuntarily, I take a step back, feel the balustrade behind me. I look over the railing—a very long fall, like the one the doctors said I once took.

When he puts his hand on my arm, I jerk a little, startled, and clutch the railing. He gives me an odd, questioning look but doesn't say anything. He leans down and brushes his lips, lightly, against my bare shoulder.

"Yes, I do mind," he says. "I didn't give you permission to look at my paintings," and he lets his hand trail down my arm, then he crosses the room, takes off his jacket, and lays it on the antique trunk.

"Sorry," I say. "I didn't think you'd mind." I hesitate, then add, "But since I've already looked, may I ask you a question?"

"Go ahead."

I want to ask about the young girl, but don't dare to. He'd hidden that painting from me. Instead, I say, "They're all so very dark, so bleak, that . . ." I don't finish with my question. I'm not sure how to phrase it.

James walks over to the table. Slowly, he goes through the stack of paintings leaning against it, a slight frown creasing his forehead.

I say, "They're so . . . disturbing."

"Yes." He nods, absently, turning to another canvas.

"It's almost as if you're obsessed with . . ." I pause. "With the macabre," I say, then add, "with violence."

"Precisely," he says, still going through the paintings.

I wait for him to elaborate, but he doesn't. I say, "Is that why you like the . . ." I falter. It seems I'm having trouble putting together sentences this evening. "Why you like the whipping?" I ask.

He laughs softly, leans the stack up against the table, then looks at me. "That's a complicated question," he says.

I wait for more of a response, but again he doesn't elaborate.

"I guess I don't understand," I say.

"I know." He comes over to me. He says, "But

someday you will." He takes my hand and leads me to the other side of the loft. He pushes aside his jacket and sits on the antique trunk, then pulls me down to sit on his knee. I don't like this position, again on his lap, as though I'm a small child. "Someday soon," he adds.

I hear a threat in his words—whether it's intentional, I'm not sure. I look at him, at his steady green eyes, no uncertainty in them, then at the texture of his skin, slightly grainy up so close, a stubble of beard showing. I am intensely conscious of his rugged appeal, of his hand at my waist.

"I don't like people snooping in my house," he says.

"I wasn't—"

He puts his fingers up to my mouth, silencing me. "Did I tell you you could look at my paintings?" he asks.

"No. But—"

Again, he interrupts. Changing the subject, he says, "Tell me about the photo on my desk, the one of Gina and me."

I give him a confused look, as if I don't understand, but my heart is beating so fast I can hear it pounding in my chest.

"Don't lie," he warns me.

I'm not sure what to say.

He puts his hand on my leg, on my thigh. The bite bruises from last week have healed; I fear now he is about to give me more.

"The day you were here searching for my mother's serving platter," he says, "I noticed that the glass covering the photograph was cracked. Then, miraculously, a few weeks later, the crack disappeared."

Still, I say nothing. My heart beats wildly.

"Well?" he asks, waiting.

"I don't know anything about it," I finally say. I shrug. "You have a cleaning lady, don't you? Maybe she broke it accidentally and was afraid to tell you. Maybe she fixed it without saying anything."

James shakes his head. He indicates for me to get off his lap, then he stands up. "I'm going to take a shower," he says. "I won't be long."

I nod, relieved he's dropped the subject of the broken glass. I watch as he unbuttons his shirt and tosses it on the bed, then removes his shoes and socks.

He turns to me, and I smile, but his face is stern and he says, "I told you not to lie to me. It would've been easier for you if you'd told the truth. Now I'll have to punish you."

I start to protest, but he says, "Wait for me," and he goes into the bathroom. I hear the shower running, sounds of him taking off his belt and slacks, then stepping under the water. I sit on the bed, listening, wondering, worrying what my punishment will be. I could leave—and I do consider it—but instead I sit on the bed and wait.

He's naked when he comes out, carrying his slacks and belt in one hand, a towel in the other, reaching up to dry his hair. He walks toward me, drops his clothes on the bed, continues to towel his hair. Still sitting on the bed, I reach out, touch the skin on his thigh. It's warm from the water. He has no modesty, no scars he cares to hide. He looms over me, a bulk of masculine flesh, powerful. I place my other hand on him also, one on each thigh, the muscles hard, like plates of iron under the skin, but what I'm really noticing is his penis, semierect, and wondering how we will fuck tonight. I feel my desire for him, and wish it wasn't so strong. I lean forward, place my face against his flesh, smell the sweet, clean fragrance of mild soap. His pubic hair is soft against my skin. His penis, built like the rest of him, thick and meaty, grows harder, rubs along my cheek. I turn my face, place my mouth at the juncture of penis and groin, suck the flesh. I feel his hand on my head, and I know he's watching me, looking down. I slide my mouth lower, along the shaft of his penis, silky smooth and fresh smelling, then put my tongue on the tip of him, caress it with my lips. He pulls back, restrains me with his hand.

"You want to suck my cock?" he says, but it's more of a statement than a question. His throaty voice, guttural with desire, makes me want him more.

"Yes," I say, and I start to pull him closer, my hands around his thighs, but suddenly he turns me over on the bed and plants his hand on my back so I can't move.

"Stay like this," he orders.

I'm bent over the edge, my legs dangling, my face pushed into the bedspread. He yanks up my dress to my waist, then pulls down my panties. I feel them around my ankles, hanging loose.

"We have some unfinished business," he says. He reaches for his belt, doubles it over. "You lied to me," he says, and he brings the belt down across my buttocks, striking me hard.

I scream, shocked by the pain, much worse than the week before. "No," I say, shaking my head, "I didn't lie—"

But he hits me again, and once more the pain evokes a scream. He leans down, puts his face next to mine.

"You'd be wise not to say a word," he tells me. "We both know you lied, and your denials only anger me more."

The look in his eyes—determined, heartless—frightens me. I remember how he appeared the night I spied on him with the red-haired woman, as if it wouldn't take much for him to lose all control. I keep my mouth shut.

He pulls back, and seconds later I feel the pain of his belt once more, searing. I try not to scream, but still it comes out. Tears water my eyes. I don't know why the belt hurts me so much more than his whip—the construction, perhaps, or increased force—but it does. Soon I am sobbing, tears streaming down my face, each blow feeling as if it's cutting deep into my flesh.

He leans down again, puts his hand on my face, wipes away my tears. I look at him through sodden eyelashes. He caresses my cheek.

Softly, he says, "Tell me you want more."

A sob chokes out of me. "I can't," I say. "I can't take any more."

He continues to stroke my cheek, his touch gentle. "Tell me to hit you again," he says, insistent.

I shake my head, my eyes watering.

"Say it," he says. "Ask me to hit you."

His touch is gentle on my cheek, but I know he won't relent. Worse, I fear what will happen if I don't say the words he wants to hear. Tears roll down my face.

"Hit me again," I whisper, the words barely coming out.

He gazes at me, his touch soft but his eyes still cold. "Would you like me to hit you harder this time?"

My body quivers against the bed. He is a blur now, my vision marred by silent tears. I know what I have to say, but I can't take any more pain.

"Say it," he orders when I don't reply.

"Yes," I say, the sound a choked sob. "I want you to hit me harder."

And I wait for the pain to come, but instead he turns me over, climbs on top of me, straddles my face. His penis juts out, fully erect, turgid with passion derived from pain, my pain, and he shoves it between my lips. He fucks my mouth deeply, one hand behind my neck to keep my head plastered to his groin, making me choke as he thrusts fast and hard, his penis all the way inside, making my eyes water again, until he finally comes, spurting down my throat.

Later, I roll over and look at the angry welts running across my buttocks. They are red and ugly, and they still burn. "You hurt me," I say.

James slides down lower on the bed. He kisses my ass, runs his tongue along the length of a welt. "Yes," he says. "And I'll hurt you even more."

CHAPTER TWELVE

I've lost my battle with the artichokes. Purple thistles, glorious in their triumph, bloom all over the
garden. I walk between the plants, appreciating
their beauty yet feeling somewhat defeated. My disappointment, I know, is not caused solely by the
blooming thistles. I thought I would be further along
by now. I thought, by immersing myself in once-
familiar surroundings, my memory would come
flooding back. And I thought, most definitely, that
being with James, having sex with him, would jog
old feelings, shoot me back to an earlier time. But
that hasn't happened. I am still very much in the
present, involved with a man who exclusively holds
the key to my past.

Hearing a motor, I turn and see Gina coming up
the gravel driveway behind the house. When she
spots me by the artichokes, she applies her brakes.
Bits of gravel, like spittle, spew out from under the
tires of the white truck. She waves a tanned arm at
me.

I walk over, place my hands on the door, and look
at her through the open passenger window. Once
again, she's wearing blue jeans and a T-shirt, a small

notebook and pencil in the front pocket. Her black hair, falling down to the middle of her back, is secured with a barrette, and a red baseball cap shades her eyes from the sun.

"You've failed," she says.

"What?"

She points a finger toward the purple-thistled garden. "The artichokes," she says, laughing a little at my confusion. "I could've told you we'd never eat them all, but you seemed so determined to use every last one of them."

"Oh," I say. "Well, yes. I suppose I was." I shrug.

She laughs again, a friendly sound. "Artichoke casseroles, frittatas, crêpes . . . in soups, salads, appetizers . . . baked, sautéed, steamed—I think I can speak for the rest of the family when I say we'd be happy to forgo artichokes for the rest of the year."

I smile, a sheepish grin, I know. "I guess I got carried away," I say, looking over at her. There's an easy manner about her, one hand draped casually over the steering wheel, a warmth in her eyes I hadn't really noticed before.

"Get in," she says. "I'll take you for a ride."

Seeing the front seat, I hesitate.

With a sweep of her arm, she clears the mound of trash—the dog-eared magazines and empty Styrofoam coffee cups and scraps of paper—off the front seat. Everything falls onto the floor. Reaching over, she turns the handle and opens the car door. "Get in," she says again.

I slide inside, barely have the door closed before Gina starts off down the lane. She goes around the house, then down the main road to one of the vineyards. Making a sharp right, she swerves between a row of grapevines. She drives fast, the vines flashing by in a greenish blur. At the end of the row, she turns onto a deeply rutted dirt road that winds up to the top of a hill. She slows down here, but still I hold on to the door and the front dash, wishing I'd fastened my seat belt, feeling every bounce and bump as the truck jerks along, dust swirling in a brown cloud behind us.

At the top of the hill, she maneuvers the vehicle so it rests under the shade of an ancient oak tree overlooking the McGuane property. She turns off the engine. The dust settles, and in the still air I can hear the soft humming of insects. Long, lacy threads, hanging like Spanish moss, drip from the oak—although I've learned from the gardener it's not really Spanish moss at all, but lichen. Gina, her hand again draped casually over the steering wheel, looks out at the small valley, a rolling patchwork quilt of vineyards. I wait for her to speak, but she doesn't.

I settle in. James and I haven't told anyone of our involvement. We didn't discuss this, we didn't agree to keep our union a secret, it just came about. We don't hold hands in public, we don't kiss, we don't act as if anything has changed. It seemed better this way, since what we have is neither a romance nor an affair—and what we have cannot be shared with other people.

I look over at Gina, who's staring out the front windshield. I don't think he's even told her, but I'm not certain of that. Sometimes I'll see her glancing from him to me, as if she suspects a change has taken place, but she's said nothing. She keeps her suspicions to herself. A black bird, large and glossy, lets out a raucous call.

Finally, still gazing out the window, Gina says, "My family has owned this property for more than half a century. I grew up here, helped my father expand the operation, increase production. Because of our location, we're in a unique position in Napa

Valley. We have several different microclimates on our property."

She looks over at me, sees my blank expression, then patiently explains. "Different grape varieties grow better in some areas than in others. Here, at Byblos, we have six different soil types, and we even have different climate conditions on the different vineyards. All of this—the soil, the slope of the hill, drainage, sunlight, rain, temperature, wind, and a thousand other factors—all of this influences the grapes. The French call it *terroir*, the natural conditions of a certain place that give the grape its distinctive flavor. Because of our varying microclimates, a cabernet we plant on a south slope will taste differently from one planted on the flat land next to it."

I listen to her, surprised at this little discourse.

"We've worked hard over the years," she continues, "trying to distinguish our wines from the ones produced at other wineries, always maximizing quality over quantity. We make great wines here, but it's not easy work. Like all forms of agriculture, we're dependent on the weather. If we get frost in the spring, new buds can die. If we get an early rain before harvest, the grapes may not have a chance to ripen fully, or they may become waterlogged, which will dilute the flavor."

She looks out across the vineyards, across the small bowl–shaped valley that comprises the McGuane property. Quietly, she says, "Growing grapes . . . it involves more than just implementing the latest viticultural and winemaking technology. Winegrowers are like parents, always worrying, nurturing, wanting the best. It's truly a labor of love."

Although Gina speaks with little emotion, I hear the pride in her voice, sense her passion for Byblos.

I've never lived anywhere long enough to feel impassioned about it. I've never had the chance. Under the shade of the oak, the air is cool, pleasant. I say, "Why did you bring me up here?"

She turns and faces me. The baseball cap casts a shadow over her eyes. "To show you what I love," she says quietly. "Loving something—caring about something—it grounds you, gives you a sense of purpose."

Embarrassed, knowing I may well destroy her home, I look away.

She starts the engine and heads back down the hill. The ride is rough, the truck bouncing up and down, and Gina has to swerve abruptly to avoid the many deep ruts in the road. She seems perfectly at ease behind the wheel, even though I feel I'm being knocked around in a carnival ride. She downshifts, and the engine groans into a lower gear.

"Can you take it a little slower?" I say, shouting over the noise of the truck.

She just smiles, her eyes watching the road. The front right wheel dips into a rut, tilting the truck, then it bounces back up. She turns off the rutted road and speeds down another dirt pathway, this one flat and adjacent to a field of vines.

Finally, she slows down, looking closely at the vines as we pass. I'm amazed at their growth since I've come to Byblos. When I arrived here, the vines were grayish brown and knotted and bare; now they're covered with leafy vegetation, shining greenish gold in the sun. She stops the truck, reaches over the seat, and pulls a handheld magnifying glass out of the glove compartment. Without saying anything, she gets out of the truck and goes over to the grapevines, looks at the leaves through the magnifying glass.

"What are you doing?" I ask from the truck.

She doesn't hear me. Out of nowhere, it seems, the two black-coated hounds appear.

"Hey, Blue," Gina says, petting one, then the other. "Hey, Chica. You chase any rabbits today?"

Across the road, I can see the vineyard manager. And farther down, off to the right, are the ivy-covered stone walls of the winery. Three cars are parked in front, and another one, a blue BMW, drives slowly up the lane—visitors to the tasting room. I get out of the truck and follow Gina, who's striding down the row in her black leather boots, periodically stopping to check the leaves. I'm wearing a flowered sundress and sandals, not practical clothing for a vineyard walk. The dogs meander down the row of vines, sniffing the ground. I watch Gina, her expression intent as she peers through the glass lens, her nose and forehead wrinkling in concentration. She goes on to another vine.

I follow, watching her silently. Her father named this place after one of the ancient nature goddesses, the Lady of Byblos. He thought a tribute to goddess worship, with its emphasis on fertility and reproduction, was appropriate for a winery. The Lady of Byblos was a triple goddess. She created, preserved, and destroyed. How far would Gina go, I'm wondering now, to save the winery?

She walks back toward me, inspecting everything carefully as she comes, the vines with their bright green leaves, the drip irrigation system, the trellis wires, the soil. She pulls a tool out of her back pocket and adjusts one of the wires, securing it against a wooden post. Her arms, lean and slimly muscled, flex as she works.

When she finishes, she comes back to me, smiles, starts to say something, but doesn't. Instead, she gazes out across the vineyard, over the rows of leafy vines. A smudge of dirt streaks her left cheek. She puts one hand in her front jeans pocket, looking flustered, slightly embarrassed. Her skin is tight and tawny, the color of a young deer. She touches the bill of her cap, pulling it lower over her eyes.

"This is my dream," she says finally. "Byblos," and she nods toward the rows of vines.

She turns back to me. "You have a dream, too, Carly. I know you do. I can help."

She has no idea what my dream is—retribution. Absently, I pick a leaf off the vine and play with it between my fingers. I don't know what to say. I start to ramble, to tell her that my dreams are simple, that I like Byblos and her mother, and that I enjoy cooking for her family.

But she isn't really listening. She's crouched on the ground now, on her knees, and is fiddling with the irrigation system, the black plastic tubing stretched from stake to stake.

When I'm finished rambling, she says, "Let me help you," in a way that dismisses everything I've just said. She continues with the irrigation system. Her T-shirt strains across her shoulders and back as she works, revealing the faint outline of a thin bra strap. Her hands, blunt, lightly scarred, toughened by the sun, pull deftly on the black tubing. When she gets up, she wipes her hands on the back of her jeans.

"Why do you want to help me?" I ask her.

"I like you. Besides, you'd be a good investment." She moves down the field away from me. She calls out, "Check the truck, under my seat."

I watch her leave. Although friendly to me, she's an enigma, as mysterious now as when I first met her. Something I've noticed about Gina: she has no friends. No boyfriends. No close girlfriends. When she's not at the winery or working in the vineyards, she's at home, in her cottage, alone, writing her poems, Mrs. McGuane told me.

I return to the truck. The ground is dry and dusty, with prickly weeds shooting up. Dirt covers my sandaled feet, and a stray pebble has worked itself between my toes. When I reach her truck, I open the door and shove my hand under the seat. I find a zippered blue bank bag. A note is taped to the front: *You should be working for yourself.* I open the bag. It contains money, a lot of money. Hundred-dollar bills, secured in packets wrapped with a label that says "$10,000" on it. There are five packets. Fifty thousand dollars. I've never seen this much money. It's not a fortune, but enough to make a down payment on my own restaurant. Enough money to work for myself rather than someone else, every chef's dream. I'll never get another opportunity like this again.

When I look up, I see that Gina is far down the row of vines. I gaze in the direction of the McGuanes' home, hidden by the curves in the road and the roller-coaster land, the hills studded with dark-green clusters of live oaks. The sky, bright blue and cloudless, glistens with a wet, shiny look, as if it's glazed. Down the road, a field was recently plowed, and the warm air takes on the loamy smell of freshly upturned soil. It's quiet, the silence broken only by an occasional singing bird and buzzing insect, and the air remains windless, very calm. But I sense this surface serenity at Byblos will never last: someday, perhaps soon, something bad will happen here. Why else would Gina hand over fifty thousand dollars?

I look again at the money. A wistful longing that I cannot suppress comes over me. I want the money. Regretfully, I zip up the bag and leave it on the seat.

I turn and walk out of the vineyard. I know it would be prudent for me to take the money, to leave Napa Valley now, but I can't. I must know everything about the young girl left half-buried in an empty field. For everyone else, she's dead. For everyone else, she's forgotten. I'm the only one who cares. That young girl no longer exists, but still she exerts a hold on me that pulls, that keeps me at the McGuanes' as if her grasp extends from the grave. I can't leave, not just yet. We have business together, she and I: wounds to heal, scores to settle. *That* is my dream.

CHAPTER THIRTEEN

"Did you tell Gina about us?" I ask. I walk over to
the black leather couch, sit down.

"No," he says, shaking his head. He's working at
home this afternoon, entering information on his
computer. "But then words aren't always necessary
between Gina and me."

He makes a final entry, glances once more at the
computer screen, then comes over and sits next to
me. The cushions sink under his weight. He puts his
hand on my leg.

"She offered me fifty thousand dollars," I say.

He lifts one eyebrow, makes no comment.

"So I could open my own restaurant," I add.
"What do you think it was—a gift or a bribe?"

His hand strokes my leg. "Gina's intentions have
always been sincere," he says. "Did you take the
money?"

"No."

He nods, apparently not surprised.

I say, "Don't you think it's odd that Gina never
dates?"

"We're very close," he says, as if that is explanation enough, and he leans over to kiss me, but I'm not through with Gina yet.

Breaking away from him, I say, "Perhaps her intentions aren't all that sincere. Maybe she wants to get me away from you."

He drapes his arm across the back of the couch. "It may appear she's overly possessive when it comes to me," he says, "but it's only because she's afraid."

"Afraid of what?"

But James only shakes his head, smiles cryptically. "It's no concern of yours," he says.

By his closed-off expression, I know he won't say anything further. Gina may be possessive, but since I've been here, I've noticed that he, also, is protective of her. It's subtle, but, unobserved, I've glimpsed James treating his sister with great care, solicitous of her needs, even comforting her at times, as if Gina— strong, unbreakable Gina—were as fragile as a paper doll. Perhaps this is some kind of twin bonding; perhaps it is something more.

Reaching up, I lightly trace the scar on his left temple. "How did you get this?" I ask.

He raises his hand, puts his finger on the scar, shrugs. "I got it a long time ago," he says, standing. He takes my hand and pulls me up, drawing me near. "Let's go upstairs," he says. "I have a surprise for you."

I stall. I'm not sure if I'm ready for another surprise. "Wait," I say, and he looks down at me, head tilted, wondering why I hesitate. I don't know what to say, so I say nothing at all. My palm goes to his chest. He's wearing a light-colored shirt, linen I think, a tint of blue, the fabric smooth and almost cool to the touch. A flush of warmth rises to my face. I want him, and it embarrasses me that I am so transparent. His nearness challenges me.

He watches, says nothing as I undo the buttons and pull the shirttails out from his slacks. I push his shirt open, gaze at him, then place my hands again on his chest, move them slowly, feel the skin, mostly smooth, beneath my fingers, the broad expanse of his shoulders, the gentle rise of the pectorals, the light whorl of hair surrounding the firm jut of his nipples. I've never been so physically aware of a man before. He's not the best-looking, nor the fittest, man I've been with, but his appeal—rugged, rawly masculine—goes down deep. I feel crushed by him, overwhelmed, although his hands are by his sides, not even touching me. A picture of him with other women flashes through my mind, followed by an unfamiliar ache in my chest, which I recognize as jealousy. He sees other women besides me, and, until this moment, I haven't really cared. Now the idea of him touching another woman, fucking her instead of me, agitates my mind.

I push the thought away, concentrate on him. Under my palms, I feel the heat of his body. His skin holds a valence: I need to touch it. I need to touch him. I look into his face, his pale green eyes, the color of jade, and think that I am a fool. My desire for him mars my judgment.

"Tell me what you want," he says. His voice is flat, controlled, and I find this maddening, yet I know he wants me. I can sense it under my fingertips, in the tight restraint of his body.

"You," I whisper. "I want you to fuck me." And I hear the sound of my own voice, softly burred, the words steeped in desire. My feeling for him is elemental, basic. I just want him to fuck me.

"Now?" he asks. "Here?"

But his questions aren't really questions at all. He knows the answers, he just wants me to say it again. He wants me to beg. "Yes," I say.

Abruptly, he grabs both my wrists, holds them tightly, removes them from his chest. "I think what you really want," he says, "is to distract me." Provoked, he snaps out his words at me. "You want me to fuck you so I'll forget about the surprise upstairs."

I shake my head, but he's half right. I could live without the surprise, but I most definitely want him to fuck me.

He loosens my hands. "Go upstairs," he says.

I walk up, slowly, a bit apprehensive. Immediately, as soon as I reach the top, I see the portrait of the angry young girl, the portrait I'd discovered hidden behind the armoire. It's propped in his easel, in the center of the room.

"Strictly speaking," he says, "I suppose this isn't a surprise. You've seen it before."

I don't even consider lying, not after what happened the last time. I nod. I walk over to the painting, stare at it. "Is this me?" I ask.

He comes over.

Putting his hand on my face, he traces my lips with his index finger. Even after all these weeks, I still cringe, inwardly, when he pays too much attention to my face. My scars haunt me, but he seems only intrigued, trying to make out, in this new physician-made visage, a hint of the young girl I once was. He runs his finger along my jawline, his hand large and iron-grip strong, a prodigious weapon. I try not to think of the damage it can do— possibly has already done—to my face. I think instead of the slow progress I am making. In the last two months, even though I'm far from the truth, I've gotten closer to my past than I've ever been before.

"You still don't know what I want from you," he says. "You have no idea."

"Why don't you just tell me?" I've asked him this before, but he's refused to say.

He takes his hand off my face, looks at the girl in the painting.

"She wasn't as slow a learner as you," he says. "In fact, she understood, almost from the beginning, exactly what I wanted. And she gave it to me."

He crosses the room, shrugging out of his shirt, tossing it on the trunk, then sits on the edge of the bed. He bends over, takes off his shoes and socks. He says, "Shall I tell you a story about her?"

I nod, eager.

He slides back on the bed, resting his back against the headboard. He thinks for a minute, as if he's trying to decide what to tell me, then says, "When I first met her, we were in the middle of a very hot summer." Stretching out his legs, he closes his eyes, remembering. He is silent for so long that I think he's changed his mind about the story, that perhaps he has dozed off, but then, after a minute or two, he opens his eyes and looks around the room.

He says, "I didn't have air-conditioning installed back then, and the loft got especially hot in the summer. She'd been up here many times before, but this was the first time I'd decided to paint her. A nighttime breeze, a very welcome breeze, blew through the open windows, stirring up the warm, heavy air. The electricity went off, a power outage, so I lit an oil lamp. It flickered, and there wasn't really enough light to paint by, but I began sketching her anyway."

"You're talking about me?" I ask, interrupting, but he silences me with an irritated glance.

"I painted her while she was near the fireplace. She was squatting on the floor, her back to me, cleaning up the remains of our food. Her hips were visible under the loose material of her dress, and they swayed slightly from side to side. We'd just eaten up here—ripe tomato slices sprinkled with cinnamon sugar; a few sweet, juicy figs; some yellow gourds seasoned with garlic and butter—and oily scents of grilled garlic lay heavy in the warm air.

"She hummed a melody I'd never heard before, something slow and soft, while she picked at the food remaining on the plates. She was young, very small and slender, but still her ass was a provocative sight, amply fleshed, pear-shaped, a bottom that begged to be touched and squeezed, the soft skin pinched gently—or not so gently—between my fingers. Staring at the spread of her hips, her ass swaying like some animal soon to be mounted, reminded me of how I'd fucked her the previous time, and I felt myself getting hard. I told her to come to me.

"The girl, still on her haunches, turned around, and then she smiled when she saw what I wanted. She rose, sliding her hands down her hips. Outside, I could hear my father's dogs, the gravel-crunching sounds of their steps beneath the open windows. The girl—"

I interrupt again. "What was my name?" I ask, and I picture myself in this room with James, all the windows open, an oil lamp flickering, throwing golden shadows on the walls, making the corners dark and full of mystery.

"The name isn't important," he says, annoyed again at my interruption. "Do you want to hear this or not?"

"Yes," I reply.

He crosses his legs at the ankles, then begins once more. "She came to me, stood before me, her black hair loose, twisting in curls almost to her waist. She had trusting eyes, light blue and innocent, and a face completely without guile. She was naive and unsophisticated, although I'm certain she wouldn't have described herself as such. She knew very little about the world, very little about men; she only thought she did. I'd had her pierced, and a silver nose ring, curling down to her upper lip, hung from her right nostril."

I almost interrupt again, but keep silent. In the hospital, my face was too smashed up to tell if my nose had been pierced.

"She reached up and removed the nose ring," James is saying, "and set it on the low table containing the oil lamp. Smiling, she untied the sash at her waist, then let her clothing, a cream-colored dress, fall off her shoulders and slide down to the floor, where it gathered around her ankles.

" 'How do you want me?' she asked.

"I stared at her in the glow of the lamplight, her pale skin, the seductive droop of her small breasts, her hips and soft flat belly, the fuzzy delta of golden pubic hair."

I breathe sharply when I hear this. Golden pubic hair—blond. Her waist-length hair was dyed black, as was mine. In the hospital, during my recovery, my hair—where the doctors hadn't shaved it—was two-toned, blond near the scalp, black elsewhere, the natural color gradually replacing the dyed. This girl in the portrait is me.

James continues. "She was all gentle curves and flesh, malleable, I knew, under the pressure of my touch. She came closer, her arms hanging languidly at her sides, her shoulders thrust back, displaying herself, proud of her young flesh. A tiny bell was fastened to an anklet adorning her foot—it was like the nose ring, another gift from me—and it tinkled as she approached.

"Again, she asked, 'How do you want me?'

"At the time, I was engaged to another woman, a woman who didn't tantalize me nearly as much, and as I stared at this girl's nakedness, I knew, with her, I could do whatever I pleased. She was mine, totally. I'd ensnared her as surely as if she were an animal caught in a cage—yet she had no idea I'd both baited and set the trap. 'The same as last time,' I told her."

Even though the room is warm, I shiver when I hear his words. James beckons for me. I go to him, sit on the edge of the bed. I think of how I once was, my slight body, the innocent face, a face not yet weathered by troubles or time or the treachery I was soon to see. I imagine myself as I was then, and it's as if I'm seeing a friend I'd presumed long dead, a teenage ghost who used to be me.

"Over there," he says, pointing to the studio, "I had a braided oval rug, and the girl took my hand and pulled me to the floor. She removed my belt. I smelled a flowery perfume in her hair and the scent of dinner on her skin, cinnamon and garlic. I watched her flesh bend and roll as she worked to remove my shirt, then my shoes and socks. Lightly, I put my hand on the dip of her waist, feeling the smooth young skin, her soft, yielding female flesh.

"She reached over and touched the vein at my temple, smoothed my brow. Softly, she said, 'You don't love her. You know that you don't. I'm the one you want.' She stroked my face, then added, 'I'm going to make you forget about her. Tonight you'll have only the pleasure of me. Your mind won't have room for any other woman.' "

James looks at me and says, "Her voice was lulling, coaxing. She knew how to charm, but it wasn't affected. It came from the heart. Pleasing me was her desire. As soon as I told her what I wanted, she would comply—even if she didn't understand why I wanted it."

He reaches over and holds my hand. He says,

"With her fingers, she massaged the crown of my head, gently rubbing my scalp. She brushed the hair away from my eyes, then picked up my hand. 'James,' she whispered, bowing her head to kiss the palm of my hand. 'My Master.' "

When I hear him say this, I shiver again, a slight frisson of fear tinged with something else, something inexplicably sexual. I can't believe I once uttered those words.

" 'Master,' she whispered again, giving me what I wanted. She unzipped my pants, and I raised myself so she could slide them off me. My penis was swollen, hard with desire for this young woman who knew so well how to take care of me."

He gives me a sideways glance, and I understand clearly the implication is that I don't know how to take care of him at all. This is, of course, the point of the story.

He begins again. " 'You need me,' the girl murmured, and she ran her hands along my stomach, down my thighs. I breathed heavily as she touched me, aching to fuck her, yet wanting to prolong it as long as possible. Her hands slowly explored the texture of my skin, roaming over my body as if they were trying to memorize every inch through tactile sensation: my chest, my stomach, the length of my legs."

I think of how I, earlier, downstairs, had done the same, my palms canvassing every nuance of his chest, unconscious gestures mimicking hers, and I feel my face redden with embarrassment. I glance at James, but, continuing with the story, he doesn't notice.

"She settled her hands on my thighs and gazed adoringly at my penis. 'I like this,' she said, almost reverently, grasping it at the base. With her tongue, she moistened the tip of my penis. She looked up at me and said, once again, 'You need me,' and then she leaned forward and took my cock into her mouth.

" 'Yes,' I said, feeling the wetness enclosing me. 'I need you.' I started to shut my eyes, enjoying immensely how this young woman sucked my penis, how it felt as if it was being dipped into a pool of sweet warm honey, but, suddenly, she released me. 'Not yet,' she said. 'You wanted to do it like last time?'

" 'Yes,' I answered, and I raised myself to my hands and knees.

"She got behind me, placed her palms on the insides of my thighs, encouraging me to spread my knees farther, to open my ass to her. I felt her hands, so firm and sure of their movements for one so young, stroke my thighs, rub and caress them, then move up to my buttocks and begin kneading them, almost tenderizing, as if they were slabs of precious meat. Her tongue made a long, slow slide along my right buttock, then she repeated it on the left.

" 'Do you love me?' she asked. Her words circled around my flesh, annoyingly I thought, ferreting out my love like hungry birds searching for seed.

" 'Yes,' I answered, but only because I knew she wanted to hear it. It was part of the snare.

" 'You are my life,' she murmured. 'From the beginning, I knew it. My life belongs to you. *I* belong to you.' She embraced me, wrapped her arms tight around my torso. She whispered into my flesh, 'I am bound to you for all time. I will always be with you.' "

I sit quietly next to James, not understanding how someone, even someone quite young, could've spoken those words. The melodrama of her speech saddens me.

He says, "I sighed when she said this, wishing her words away. I wanted her tongue, not the rest.

" 'James,' she murmured.

" 'That's enough talking,' I said, and I heard the young woman laugh softly.

" 'Ah, my Master,' she said, a tease in her voice now—no reverence this time. 'You're so grumpy when I ignore your cock. You whine like a little boy.' She took my ass flesh between her teeth, biting me gently.

"I started to reproach her, but then felt her tongue once more on my body, sliding over my buttocks. She kissed every space of flesh, made my skin ripple with anticipation, then spread my buttocks and ran her tongue down the crack in the middle, slowly, and, just as slowly, came back up again. I let out my breath, a lust-felt sigh. Once more her tongue made the descent down the divide, as slow as a slimy snail, lingering, lingering, taking her time, until she reached my asshole—Satan's hole, she whimsically called it, the dark, winking eye of evil. This time she didn't pass it over, but lapped at it as if she were an animal, licking it over and over, like a dog tonguing a wound. She caressed my testicles with one hand, the other still spreading my buttocks, then left my balls to reach down and pull on my penis, her tongue still lapping. Her hand slid smoothly on my cock—she must've used spit to moisten it—as she tongued my asshole.

"I murmured my approval, then settled down on my elbows and let her continue. She circled the hole with her tongue, wetting it, massaging it, the most hidden part of my body—'It's the brown pit of everything forbidden,' she once said with a smile—then she pushed her tongue inside as if it were a worm, wiggling its way home.

"I closed my eyes, relishing her tongue inside my bowels. Even on this part of me, the most profane, she showed her obedience—something my fiancée would never do—and I thought, This is how it should be.

"I reached under my legs and felt my testicles. I must've grunted or mumbled a few words because she hesitated for a second, wondering if I wanted something else. 'No,' I said, 'don't stop yet.'

"So she continued, moving her tongue inside and out, steadily, her hand on my penis keeping rhythm with her tongue. I arched my back, lifting my ass more to give her better access. Reaching around with one arm, I clasped the back of her head. 'Go deeper,' I ordered. 'I want your tongue in all the way.'

"She obeyed, kept her head plastered to my ass, her tongue squirming inside me, wiggling around, licking and poking, pushing in and out until I couldn't stand it anymore."

I see it all very clearly, not from memory but from his words—him moaning, a low guttural sound, as she increased the speed of her hand, pumping on his cock, her tongue jammed in his shadow part, the dark cavern of his soul.

James says, "I told her it was time and I grabbed my penis from her, almost ready to come. She removed her tongue from my asshole, quickly rolled over on her back, and slid between my knees. The bell on her anklet tinkled as she moved. I shoved my cock into her mouth, then thrust hard and deep, just in time, as I came into her mouth."

I imagine him on the oval rug, still above her after he ejaculated, leisurely massaging his penis in the depth of her mouth, sighing contentedly now that he was through, before he extracted it.

He says, "I rolled over on my back, stretched out

on the rug, tired. She curled up next to me, draping her arm across my chest and her thigh over my leg. I allowed her this—even though my body was sweat slicked, and her touch, welcomed earlier, now seemed oppressive in the stifling heat of the room. The girl curled closer to me.

" 'I like doing that,' she said, 'putting my tongue there. And I really like it when you come in my mouth.'

"When I didn't say anything, she added, 'When I taste your semen, it's as though you're giving me the core of your being, your very essence. It's a blessing, a treasure, like you're giving me life.' "

Her words, so very misguided, are painful for me to hear. This man didn't give her life, but took it away. How could she—I—not see him for who he was?

James turns to me and says, "Do you think you can do that?"

It's not the tongue-fucking to which he is referring, I realize, but the attitude. Slowly, very slowly, although I should've guessed it weeks before, I begin to understand what he wants from me: my worship. He wants what he received from the young girl, her total—and willing—compliance, her almost godlike devotion.

Again, he asks, "Do you think you can do that?"

Where is the line, I wonder, between wanting to please someone and needing to? Stepping over that boundary, simply the thought of it, I must confess, both titillates and repulses—a response I hadn't anticipated. Will my passion, like the girl's, ease into surrender? "I don't know," I tell him.

He gazes at me, then nods. "We'll see," he says.

He is silent now, still holding my hand, waiting for my reaction. When I don't say anything, he adds, "The girl and I had nothing in common. I was fond of her, but not in love. Her attitude drew me in. By nature, she was compliant. She wanted to please me. I showed her how, then pushed her to please me even more. I was twenty-eight—"

"How old was she?" I blurt out.

He reaches over, touches his fingers to my cheek. "Younger," he says, his voice unnervingly even, restrained. He adds, "And I've already told you twice not to interrupt me."

Although he barely touches me, I feel as if he's slapped my face, the look in his eyes more quelling than any reproach. I won't interrupt him again.

"I was twenty-eight," he continues, "and up till then my relationships with women were . . . more traditional, you might say. With her, I learned, quite accidentally, that they could be different." He pauses, then adds, "Neither of us understood what we were getting into. It was new for both of us. Her instinct was to please, to submit herself to me—only she didn't know to what extent. The longer we were together, the more I required from her. The longer we were together, the more she gave . . . and she gave with pleasure."

When he's through speaking, I say, "What about the painting? I don't look very happy in that. I don't look like I wanted to please you. That picture doesn't tell the story of a woman in love. I was angry, enraged."

A smug look crosses his face, then disappears, a look so brief I wonder if I imagined it. "That came later," he says shortly, "after things had changed."

"What things?" I ask, but James just shakes his head.

"It's not important," he says. "*She's* not important—only the story. You asked me what I wanted. Now you know."

We stare at each other. I don't like what he's asking of me, and he knows it. I am the first to turn away, unable to hold his gaze any longer. I fold my hands in my lap, look at them stupidly. I toy with a fingernail, pick at the edge, nervously chip away the light pink polish. Many years ago, I responded to this man with an almost godlike devotion, and my love for him—if that's what it can be called—led not to salvation or transcendence or to any of the other things that the transforming power of love putatively achieves. It led to ruin. I suppose I can understand how a young girl could fall under the sway of his influence. He's undeniably charismatic—I feel it myself—but there's something monstrous under the veneer.

He stands up, takes off his slacks and underwear, then returns to the bed. He gets up on his hands and knees, and offers me his backside. "Give me what I want," he says, and I know, this time, he is referring to the tongue-fucking.

I look at him, his ass in the air, two mounds of exposed flesh, waiting for me to comply. I know the game he's playing, I understand the challenge. I'll tongue-fuck his asshole, Satan's hole, a name more appropriate than I ever could've realized, but if he thinks I'll sincerely worship him, he's mistaken. I am no longer an impressionable seventeen.

I get behind him and begin, timorous at first, awkward with my own ineptitude. The punctilio of ass-licking is beyond my sexual purview. I think of the young girl, her ardor, the way she sojourned at his asshole, slavishly accommodating his needs. The lupine hunger of her tongue required no encouragement, and now I feel myself grow jealous at her proficiency. In imitation of her, competing with myself, I slide my tongue down the divide of his buttocks. He has a moist, paludal smell, fecund, faintly malodorous, redolent of places forbidden. My hands go to his haunches. Firm muscles under the skin. Hip, buttock, thigh, the flesh untouched by the sun, not like the rest of him. Here, it's lighter. Still massive and solid, though, indestructible. He is colossal, a leviathan before me.

I spread his buttocks. The umber-hued hole beckons. It is puckered with exiguous grooves and ridges, a tight crumple of pursed flesh that he offers as a sanctum, a holy place. I put my tongue on him, tentative at first, a brief swipe, then another. I settle in for the duration. I lap at him as the girl had, lave his asshole with the saliva in my mouth, taste the sweet acridity of him, finally push my tongue inside.

He moans.

I feel the desire in him, the slight tremble of his flesh, and this makes me work harder, sliding my tongue in farther, feeding the grasping, sloe-eyed hole, and it comes to me then, this resonance of something long forgotten: a renascent passion to please. My response is visceral and unbidden, too complicated for words. I lick and suck him, shove my tongue in his bowels, a vortex pulling me in, while my mind spins. I feel transported to someplace dark and crepuscular, to a feral world where ancient passions hold sway. I keep my tongue inside him, moving, tasting, pushing for lower depths. I am an adjunct in this sex, a mere appurtenance to another, and even as I tongue him deeper, willingly now, needing more of him, even as I do this a distant tocsin rumbles in my brain, sounding the perils. I'm on precarious ground here, traversing the slippery scarps of James's scree-ridden soul.

CHAPTER FOURTEEN

All day, I have this nagging feeling that we're being observed, followed. I feel a dark, shadowy presence with us, hovering nearby, but whenever I look around, no one suspicious is there.

"Tell me about Anna," I ask Mrs. McGuane.

She sighs, then sips her wine, not answering. Since I hadn't yet visited any of the local wineries, she insisted we go on a winetasting tour, and now we're taking a break between wineries, eating a late-afternoon lunch on the lawn at Clos Pegase, a winery in the northern edge of Napa Valley. Earlier, we stopped at the Oakville Grocery, a century-old general store that had been converted into a gourmet market and deli, and filled a picnic cooler with lunch supplies—herbed Brie, sliced smoked turkey, olives, San Francisco sourdough baguettes, fresh fruit, and a few chocolate truffles—and at Clos Pegase we purchased a bottle of their reserve chardonnay. The food, spread out on a red-checked ground cloth, is already half-eaten.

"Anna," she says finally, sighing again, shaking her head. Wisps of white hair frame her temples. Her face clouds up, then a look of uneasiness settles in, a tight, pinched look that creases the fine wrinkles around her eyes. She's wearing a navy-colored skirt and a short-sleeved creamy-white knit sweater. Reaching up, she fiddles with the pearl button at the collar. She watches a few cars pull into the parking lot, watches people walk toward the columned entrance of the winery.

Patiently, I wait. I spread Brie on a piece of sourdough I'd torn off from the loaf, then eat it. I lean back on my elbows, my wineglass in one hand, gaze absently at the winery in front of us. It's totally different from Byblos or, for that matter, from any of the other wineries I've seen in Napa Valley. It's like a monumental Greco-Roman temple, but with a very contemporary, twentieth-century look, a fawn and terra-cotta–colored building of precise geometries, sharp angles and flat surfaces and monolithic columns. Adjacent to the building, trellised vines are flush with bright green leaves.

I shake off my earlier apprehension. There is no sinister, lurking presence here, just modern sculptures dotting the winery grounds—startling, looming masses that seem to erupt from the earth itself, springing forth like nature gone mad: a seven-foot, wrinkly bronze thumb; a white marble sculpture of soft curves and surreal, amorphous form; a bountiful cluster of breasts resembling a purple bunch of grapes, ripe and plump.

I take a sip of the chardonnay. It has a smooth, butterlike texture, and a slight touch of vanilla, which, I've learned from Mrs. McGuane, comes from the oakiness of the wooden barrels. Something else she taught me: wine is similar to great music—the more I know about it, the greater my appreciation and enjoyment. A wonderfully aged cabernet is like a Beethoven symphony, classic, resonating, deep, and complex; whereas a pinot noir is more like

Chopin, romantic, sensual, exquisite; and a sauvignon blanc is pure jazz, lively and brazen, full of sass.

Mrs. McGuane turns to me. She says, "You and James are having an affair, aren't you?"

Surprised, I say nothing. I nod.

"I thought so," she says, and she stops fiddling with the pearl button on her sweater. "James hasn't mentioned it, of course, he's always been reticent to discuss his girlfriends with me, but I've noticed a difference in the way he looks at you. It's more personal, more intimate. Gina and I have both noticed the difference."

Reaching over, she gently touches my hand, then holds it in hers. Her hand is much larger than mine—she is much larger than I—and, although she's almost seventy, there's a sturdiness about her that no one would confer upon me. Next to her, I appear fragile, breakable, without substance.

She smiles, her hand still on mine. "I'm very fond of you. You're aware of that, aren't you?"

I nod. She and I have reconciled since the kitchen fire, although, ever vigilant, I've caught her checking the stove burners before she goes to bed.

"I think you would be good for James," she says. "He'd be lucky to have someone like you in his life, but I'm not entirely sure if he'd be good for you." She pauses, not used to this line of conversation, then laughs nervously. The sound sticks in her throat.

"James is a wonderful man," she continues, absently picking at her sweater, not looking at me. "He's honest, straightforward, hardworking. Everyone likes him. I just hope—"

She stops abruptly in midsentence. "Isn't that James?" she asks, uncertain.

I turn quickly. "Where?" I say, not seeing him.

Squinting, Mrs. McGuane peers into the distance.

"I must be mistaken," she says. "James and Gina have business in San Francisco today."

I scan the far edges of the winery. If he was there, spying on us, he's gone now. Turning back, I see a dark blue sedan speed up the road. Suddenly, it swerves over to the curb and stops, the engine still running.

"You were about to tell me something," I say to Mrs. McGuane.

She smiles apologetically. "I suppose I'm interfering when I shouldn't. It's no wonder my son keeps his women friends a secret from me. I just hope . . ." For the second time today, she doesn't finish her thought.

"Hope what?" I ask.

Once more, she reaches over and pats my hand. Her eyebrows, snowy white, furrow into a frown. A look of concern passes over her face. "I just hope he doesn't hurt you, dear."

A sickening feeling settles in the bottom of my stomach. "What do you mean?" I ask.

She looks down at her lap, uncomfortable. She says, "He doesn't seem to stay with any woman for very long. In my day, we would call him a heartbreaker, or a womanizer."

She coughs faintly, squares her shoulders, and her expression turns defiant. "In his defense, however, I don't think he deliberately sets out to hurt anyone. He tells me he just hasn't found the right woman." She shrugs a little, finished with his defense.

"Anyway, you've become very special to me, a friend, and I thought you should know this about James. I would just hate to see you get hurt." She smiles, then adds, "And I'd hate to lose you as our cook as a result of it."

"I like Byblos," I say. "I'm not planning to leave."

Actually, I haven't given much thought as to what will happen when I finally uncover the truth.

I didn't think about his family. Of course, I'll have to leave. Neither Gina nor Mrs. McGuane will want me around when James goes to prison.

I nibble on the last of the smoked turkey. Long, thin wispy clouds, like brushstrokes of white paint, settle in the sky. The summer day has turned slightly cool, and I'm glad I'm wearing long pants and a light pullover sweater.

We are quiet for a while, reclining on the grass, enjoying the last of the chardonnay. I did not expect to find friendship at Byblos. The only woman with whom I've ever felt a closeness is Mrs. McGuane, a woman much older than I, old enough to be my mother. In the hospital, I bitterly resented my mother's absence. As I got older, I accepted the fact that circumstances could've kept my parents away— I catalogued numerous explanations to justify their absence, some of them reasonably logical, others absurdly far-fetched—and I learned to be not so bitter and to grant them a generosity of spirit that I didn't always, sincerely, feel, but it's still difficult for me to accept that not one relative, not a single friend or acquaintance or even a schoolteacher, came forward to claim me, that there was no one who cared. What kind of a person was I who could inspire so much neglect? Was I a monster? Was I so hated that no one bothered to report me missing?

Uneasily, I brush away this thought, think instead of James. He confuses me, frightens me, and, inexplicably, makes me desire him more and more every time we are together. My attraction is irrational, and dangerous, yet I long to touch his skin, feel his body next to mine, his penis inside me, taking possession. As I gaze out at the vineyards, with their bursting early-summer growth, the branches shooting out a yard's length, clusters of tiny green berries, like sweet baby peas, clinging to the vines, as I gaze at them, I find myself thinking of how James sucks me in, making me feel that ancient pull toward sex, making my blood, like the sap in the vines, warm with desire. Lust, that age-old need, betrays me, drives me to crave the one man I should flee.

Shifting on the grass, I lie down on my side, prop my head on my elbow. Lazy-moving clouds blow slowly across the sky. I lift my hand to shade my eyes, then look at Mrs. McGuane and say, "Tell me about Anna."

A light frown creases the papery skin of her forehead. Avoiding my question, she reaches for a chocolate truffle and pops it in her mouth. She chews slowly, deliberately. When she's finally through, she says, "There's not much to say."

Annoyed, I sit up, brushing the bread crumbs off my pant legs. "Why won't James talk about her?" I ask. "Why won't anyone?"

She sighs. She works her jaw. At last, she speaks. "James loved his wife very much. He prefers not to mention Anna, and we accommodate him."

She pauses, then says, "Her death was a tragic accident, and I think he feels he's somehow responsible, although, of course, he wasn't. She simply tripped on the catwalk and fell under the railing. Her head hit the concrete floor, killing her instantly. James couldn't have prevented it, yet he's never gotten over her death, not really."

Mrs. McGuane thinks we are through with Anna, but I still have questions. "What was she like?"

She gives me a patient, patronizing look, and, once again, reaches over to pat my hand, this time dismissively. I see the blue car again, moving forward in a sudden, jerky rush, then turning left into the far end of the winery's parking lot. The car is long and big, an older model, with tinted windows, and it moves lumberingly across the paved lot, weaving just a little, and I hear the sound of music, the low-pitched bass tones, loud but muffled, seeping out from behind the closed windows.

"Dear," she says, sighing, "it was a long time ago. James loved her and planned to spend the rest of his life with her, and then, abruptly, it all changed for him, his entire life changed. If he wants to tell you about Anna, he will. But don't press him. I don't think a person ever, completely, gets over the loss of a spouse." The sad way she says this, gazing off into the distance, a watery look in her eyes, I suspect she's thinking about her husband.

I watch the blue car. Did James really love Anna, as everyone claims, or was he instrumental in her death? As I ponder this, I keep my eyes riveted to the car. It's coming toward this end of the parking lot, going faster now, picking up speed, misjudging the distance of the curb straight ahead. A visitor to the tasting room, I think, with too much to drink. I anticipate the slamming of brakes, the swerving fishtail of the car as it jerks to a stop, but it doesn't come. The car jumps the curb, a loud scraping sound follows, and then careers toward us on the grass. I sit up straighter, tense. I expect the car to change direction— even drunkards could see us sitting in the middle of the lawn—but it doesn't. It barrels forward.

"The car!" I yell, rising to my knees. Mrs. McGuane, still thinking of her husband, turns around, confused. She sees the car, but, stunned, doesn't react. I grab her shoulders, her arms, pull. Suddenly, she's startled into action, helping me. We both tumble over onto the grass. The blue car charges forward, swerving, driving over the red-checked ground cloth. The picnic cooler goes flying, sounds of shattered wineglasses pierce the air, leftover food is smashed under the tires. The driver stops, hesitates just a moment, then makes a hurried, wide arc across the lawn, bumps over the curb, crosses the parking lot, and roars off down the road.

I spend the evening with Mrs. McGuane, who, although not hurt, has several bruises from where I yanked her, and several more from our tumble. Still shaken from this afternoon, we both wanted company. Neither of us noticed the license plate, and the darkened windows concealed the driver. The police, whom we called at the winery, and Mrs. McGuane concluded our mishap was an accident, a drunken driver, but I'm not convinced. Finding my solace in cooking, as usual, I bake two loaves of spiced-pumpkin raisin bread for tomorrow.

By the time I leave Byblos, it's dark outside. I drive across the valley floor, pull into my driveway, and park in front of the secluded bungalow. Both the house and driveway are completely hidden, surrounded by a thick wall of tall oleander bushes. I walk up the flagstone path to the front door, then abruptly halt. Before I left this morning, I'm sure I turned off all the lights in the house. But now one is shining in the living room; I can see it through the curtains.

On guard, I walk up the porch steps, taking each one slowly so I won't make any noise, avoiding the creak on the right side of the third step. The front door is ajar, open just a crack. A burglar has broken into my house, I think, and I need to leave immediately, go over to my neighbor's for help. Irresolute, I stand there, ready to flee, yet telling myself that a burglar wouldn't leave the front door open, wouldn't turn on all the lights to announce his presence. The blue car suddenly comes to mind.

I take one cautious step forward. Holding my breath, a sense of dread tightening in my chest, I peer through the crack in the door.

CHAPTER FIFTEEN

I lean my forehead lightly against the door, still peering inside the house. Gina, with a drink in her hand, is sitting on the couch, an overstuffed almond-colored sofa, very old, with antimacassars on the rolled arms to hide the places where the fabric has worn thin. Gina, in contrast, is stunning, wearing a sleek powder-blue jumpsuit, her hair tumbling down her shoulders in black, silky tangles. I swing the door open and go inside.

"I see you've made yourself at home," I say curtly, setting my things, a stack of mail, two food magazines, my purse, on a table by the door.

She cocks her head, surprised by the tone of my voice. "I'm sorry if I startled you," she says. "The door was open." Her lipstick is a bright candy red, like a maraschino cherry. "Were you expecting someone else?"

"No," I say, shaking my head. Subtly, I gaze around the room, wondering if Gina has searched it, wondering if she went into the bedroom and found anything I've hidden away, the old newspaper articles about my attack and subsequent amnesia, the pictures of me recuperating in the hospital, the extra copies of the *Wine Spectator* that profile Byblos, each wrapped with a protective covering.

"Where was James this afternoon?" I ask.

She ignores my question. "I heard about your near miss," she says. "That's why I came over—to see if you're all right."

"Your mother saw James at Clos Pegase."

She looks at me blandly, then, as she discerns the point of my question, the corners of her mouth tighten slightly. "She was mistaken."

"Right before it happened," I add, "as if he knew it was about to occur, as if he wanted to watch."

Bringing the glass to her lips, she takes a drink. "He was in San Francisco all day, with me. Ask him."

Would Gina lie for James? Yes, I think, she would. Of course, she would. They'd both lie for each other. It crosses my mind that perhaps they're in this together, and what chance do I have against the both of them? I feel rooted to the floor, unable to move forward, unable to back away, my legs heavy, like leaden ingots, weighted down from my own impotence.

"What's going on, Carly?" She leans forward, a look of concern on her face. "Why would you think James had anything to do with the accident this afternoon?"

I sigh, then attempt a smile, shake my head. "I don't," I manage to say. "It just surprised me when your mother saw him there."

Gina shrugs. "Her eyesight isn't very good, not for distances." She changes the subject. She glances around the living room. "Unusual house," she says, waving her glass in the air. "Who are you renting from?"

"A professor," I say. "He's on sabbatical for a year."

Gina crosses one sleek leg over the other, lightly

bounces her foot. She's wearing calf-high blue suede boots. "Apparently," she says, "the professor likes the feel of the outdoors." She looks around once more, swiveling her head. "Very unusual."

I nod. The house is small, all the walls painted in muted greens and browns, and the kitchen and bedroom frescoed with pale leafy ferns, rambling tendrils, mossy boughs. But I wouldn't call the house unusual; I have different words for it. It's dark and shabby, cluttered, with no empty spaces. A two-foot brass horse stands at the side of the brick fireplace; in one corner of the room, a split-leaf philodendron grows unrestrained in a heavy terra-cotta clay pot; bookshelves are jammed together against the walls; and a brown braided rug covers the floor. On the walls, which are painted a forest green, with tacky gold-trim crown molding around the top, hang a huge, straw-weaved fan and four garish African masks. There is no airiness in here, no tasteful décor that defines the McGuanes' family home.

"How did you know I lived here?" I ask.

She takes a sip of her drink. The ice cubes clink against the glass. "Mother mentioned it," she replies.

"And you said I left the front door open? That's odd. I would never leave my door unlocked—just as I would never leave a stove burner on."

Gina shrugs, not really paying attention, staring at the four African masks on the wall. "Uh-huh," she says, looking at the brass horse now. "It was open." She pushes the black curls away from her forehead, turns back to me.

I sit in the armchair across from her. "I didn't see your truck," I say.

"It's parked around the corner."

I lean back in the chair, sink lower in the cushions, feeling uncomfortably small, irritated that all the McGuanes, this family of giants, can shrink me simply by the mere power of their presence. "So what's on your mind?" I ask her.

She doesn't answer right away, gives me an embarrassed smile. She swirls her drink, then looks in the glass. "James seems to attract a lot of women," she says finally. "I suppose they think he'll make a good catch—a wealthy Napa Valley vintner, every girl's dream."

Again, sloppily, she swirls her drink. A few drops of liquid spill onto the collar of her blue jumpsuit. I'm beginning to think she's drunk.

"Fifty thousand dollars is a lot of money for someone like you to turn down. It made me wonder." She pauses for a moment, then continues, her voice gentle. "He'll never marry you, if that's what you want. He'll dump you when he gets bored with you, just as he did with all the others."

My set of hand weights are on the floor, next to her, and she rolls one of them back and forth with the toe of her shoe. "I'm not saying this to be cruel," she adds. "I just thought you should know."

"Thanks for the warning."

She takes a drink, looks me up and down. "He tried to stay away from you when you first came here," she says. "I could tell he wanted you, but even James knew it could get awkward with you working at Byblos. He would've left you alone. You shouldn't have . . . you shouldn't have initiated things with him."

I rub my eyes. It's been a long day and I'm tired. I'm not in the mood for discussing this with Gina, who surely would never understand what's happening between James and me. "I can take care of myself," I say.

"Can you?" she asks quietly. Her face seems to stiffen a little, to take on an uncomfortable, guarded look, and she shifts her gaze away from me. Slowly, she traces her finger around the rim of her glass. She says, "I watched you with him."

"What do you mean?"

"The same way you watched him with that other woman, through the curtains." She adds, "A few nights ago."

A few nights ago. I get a creepy feeling in my stomach, knowing we'd been observed. I remember what happened a few nights ago, and a flush of embarrassment colors my face. We were in the living room, downstairs. I was unclothed, James fully dressed. He likes me that way, vulnerable, exposed. I hate it. Although my scars are imperceptible now, I've lived with them too long to willingly uncover my body for a long duration. He knows the reason for my modesty; he knows that nudity, my nudity, embarrasses me, and he uses it against me. He makes me parade in front of him, showing off my flesh. That night, he gave me a red-ribboned box and said to open it. Inside lay a black, silver-studded dog collar. It was a hideous thing, unwieldy, thick, wide, a big silver buckle, cumbrous in my hand.

"Put it on," he said, standing in front of me.

I hesitated. I knew the significance of this: a symbol of ownership, a symbol of submission. I fingered the black leather, the large silver studs, smooth, cool to the touch, embedded in the surface. Despite my anxiety of where this would lead, a rush of excitement shot through me. I shuddered, terrified of the latent desires, *my* desires, trying to break free. I reached up, fastened the collar around my neck. It felt bulky and crude, hung heavy.

He gazed down at me, his arms folded across his chest, taking in the picture of me, naked, wearing a piece of leather that proclaimed his ownership, my blond hair so short it covered nothing, not even the top edge of the stifling collar. James loomed over me, rocked back on his heels a little, still staring. His clothes, the marble-white tailored shirt to fit his broad shoulders and massive arms, the taupe Dockers, his clothes bulked him up; my nakedness diminished me. I looked off to the side, daunted by his penetrating gaze.

"That looks nice," he said, "but it's not quite right." Reaching over, he tightened the silver buckle until the leather was snug against my skin.

I closed my eyes, a wave of confusion sweeping over me. The raw smell of new leather, the feel of it around my neck, cinched, proprietorial, not unwelcome—it all seemed so natural, me wearing his collar. I bowed my head against his chest, wanting to yield, feeling the erotic pull of my submission, but then, in a panic, I pulled back, afraid to give in, afraid to return to that forbidden place of my past. I stepped back, stared up at him, defiant.

His face hardened. He left me, went over to the kitchen area, came back with a metal dog dish. Inside the dish was leftover take-out Chinese food from our dinner earlier that evening, hoisin-flavored beef. He set the dish on the rug.

"Now get on the floor," he said. He added, "On your hands and knees."

I didn't move. I felt the warmth flood to my cheeks, felt the humiliation of what he asked. He was going to treat me like a dog, make me eat out of the dish like a dog, using my mouth, my teeth, to grab the meat. He thought that would break me, make me bend to his will. Any eroticism I'd felt earlier disappeared. I didn't move.

He began rolling up the sleeves of his shirt, slowly. When he finished, he said, once again, "Get down." His voice was so quiet I could barely hear it, his tone so unmistakably threatening I couldn't miss the intent.

"No," I said. "I won't do it."

I expected him to shove me down, force my face in the dog dish, but he didn't. No, that wouldn't be good enough for him. He wanted me to go to the dish willingly. He crossed his arms, stared at me, waited for me to obey.

Finally, after several minutes, both of us waiting for the other to make a move, he said, "You're not going to do as I asked?"

I shook my head.

"All right," he said, and he took my arm, firmly, and led me over to the kitchen. He cleared the long, tiled counter, then lifted me and set me on it. The tiles were cool against my buttocks and the backs of my legs. He lashed my hands above my head, to a railing behind me, and my feet, spread wide, to the cabinets below. He crossed over to the sink, filled two copper tea kettles, and set them on the stove. He turned on the burners, then came back to me. He put his hand against my cheek, caressed it with care.

"I'm going to punish you severely," he said, his voice not angry but instructional: I had a lesson to learn, a price to pay for my refusal.

He continued, "I'm going to make you cry, but your tears won't convince me to stop. Only one thing will get you down from here, when you ask to eat out of the dish."

I felt a drop of sweat on my forehead. He caressed it away. I thought he'd whip me for my refusal, but he had something else in mind. Apprehensive, I tried to stall for time.

"I have to pee," I said.

He cocked an eyebrow, called my bluff. "Then do it," he said.

I waited for him to remove the ropes, but he didn't. "You have to untie me," I said.

"Pee here . . . on the counter."

I looked down. My legs were spread, lashed to the cabinets below, the pale blue tile of the counter visible in the V of my thighs. "I can't," I said. "Not here."

He slapped me across the face, a sudden sharp sting.

I gasped.

"Pee!" he commanded.

I looked down again, imagined myself urinating on the countertop, a yellow puddle forming between my legs. I couldn't do it. There was something infantile about the act, wetting myself. The humiliation stopped me. "I can't," I said again, my head lowered.

I prepared myself for another slap across the face, but it didn't come. I looked up at him. A disgusted expression covered his face. I'd failed him again.

"You will do as I command," he said, his voice low, a twitch at his temple.

Scared, I didn't say anything. I tried to pee, but couldn't.

He lowered the burners under the tea kettles. Without saying a word, he left the room, went up to the loft, then came back a few minutes later. He was carrying a thin plastic tube, a foot or so long, with a clear bag attached to one end.

"This is called an In-and-Out catheter," he said, standing in front of me. He leaned down, put his hand between my legs, used his fingers to spread my vaginal lips, prodded around.

Although I had little recollection of it, I knew the nurses catheterized me in the hospital. "James—"

"Be quiet," he interrupted.

Quelled by his sharp tone, I shut my mouth. The tube, still in his hand, appeared greasy on the tip, as if he'd applied a lubricant.

"If I choose to control your bladder," he said, peering between my legs, using his fingertip to separate the folds of my skin, holding them apart, "I will. If I choose to control any other bodily function, I'll do that also. And you'll obey."

I felt the tip of the catheter against my skin.

"One way or another," he added, "you will obey."

He inserted the plastic tube inside the small opening of my urethra, slid it inside. Immediately, the clear plastic bag, which he'd set on the blue tile between my thighs, began to fill. I squirmed on the counter, self-conscious. The ropes restrained me. Holding the catheter in place, he watched closely as my urine ran down the tube and into the bag, the bag collecting the yellowish fluid. My face flushed. I was helpless in this gross invasion, the tube sticking out of my body proof of that. I squirmed again. The catheter didn't hurt, but it felt strange inside me, slightly uncomfortable, like an itch I couldn't scratch. The embarrassment, the loss of control, was worse.

When he'd emptied my bladder, he slipped out the catheter tube, set it and the bag aside, on the counter next to me, a reminder.

"You can always disobey," he said, "but it won't do you any good. In the end, I'll get what I want . . . always." He paused for a moment, then said, "Now, for the other matter," and he turned up the burners under the tea kettles.

Momentarily, I'd forgotten about the dog dish. "Let me go," I told him.

"What did you say?" he asked, turning around, a look of scorn on his face. "Are you giving *me* an order?"

"No. It's just . . . I've had enough for tonight."

"I'll decide when you've had enough," he said, and he put his hand on my breast, squeezed it hard until I groaned.

"That hurts," I said.

He didn't reply. He reached across the aisle between the counter and stove, picked up one of the
tea kettles. He tipped it over, dripped a little water
on his palm, then held the spout over me, over my
genitals. I tensed, pulled against the ropes, tried to
close my legs, but I couldn't. Warm water poured
over me. I gasped, shocked at first, afraid it would
burn, but it didn't. He poured more, bathing my vagina with warm water. It dribbled down my thighs,
formed a puddle between my legs that made me
think of my urine. He returned the kettle to the
burner, picked up the other one. Putting his hand
on my clitoris, he stroked me, then used his fingers
to separate my lips, to hold me open. He put the
spout close to my vagina. I didn't breathe. I could
feel the warmth of the kettle, so near it was to my
flesh. He tipped it over, and the water trickled out—I
sucked in my breath as it hit my skin—then it came
faster. It was warmer this time, almost hot. He put
his mouth on me, licked my clitoris, licked the water
off. He switched kettles again.

"This is going to hurt," he said as he tipped it over
me.

I flinched. The hot water brought a strangled
shriek from my mouth. Tears wet my eyes. Again,
he put his hand on me, used his fingers to keep me
open. He dribbled more water over me, over his fingers, and I whimpered, watched my genitals grow
bright pink from the heat. He licked me again, his
tongue cool compared to the water.

"You know where this is going," he said, looking
up. "Are you ready for the dog dish?"

I hesitated. I wanted to give in, I knew it would
be easier on me, but the degradation held me back.

"Are you?" he asked again.

Once more, I hesitated. I looked at the kettle on the stove, steam coming out of the spout. He grabbed it.

"Yes!" I shouted.

"Too late," he said, and he poured the water on me, cruelly. I screamed at the pain, but he didn't stop. My acquiescence wasn't enough for him now. He wanted satisfaction, he wanted retribution—I could see it in his face—and he kept the water on me, a determined look in his eyes, no hesitation as he switched kettles, making me scream with pain and fear, over and over, the water hotter with each application, almost scalding my vagina and the insides of my thighs, until I was crying hysterically, afraid he would go too far, afraid he would let the water boil, scorch my skin, afraid he was out of control. I begged for the dog dish, pleaded for it, blubbered like a baby. I told him I wanted to eat like a dog, told him I really really wanted it—and I did. I would've promised anything for him to stop.

"Did you enjoy watching?" I ask Gina now, sarcastic, embarrassed that she saw me catheterized and punished by her brother, then eating out of the dog dish, embarrassed that she saw me break under her brother's will. And not only that, but she must've seen what happened later, how I, shamelessly, even with the skin between my legs tender and raw and red, even after the degradation—maybe even because of it—how I still wanted him to fuck me, how I begged for that too.

She puts the glass to her lips and empties it, then pulls herself up and crosses the room. She walks with exaggerated carefulness, the way people who are drunk often do. She goes into the kitchen—she's found the professor's liquor cabinet—and returns with a fresh drink in her glass, whiskey maybe, or scotch, the liquid a light bronzed brown.

I slip off my shoes and curl up in the armchair. "James will be angry when I tell him you've been spying," I say. Outside, faintly, I hear an owl, its soft hooting call.

Gina sips on her drink slowly, watching me over the rim of her glass. Finally, she says, "He already knows."

She gives me a sheepish smile, seeing the surprise on my face. "He's a bit of an exhibitionist—and I like to watch." Shrugging, she adds, "We're compatible that way."

I look at her, incredulous, not speaking. I hear the owl again, and the rustle of the willow tree against the side of the house.

"The offer still stands," she says. "The fifty thousand. You should have your own restaurant." She plays with her hair, winding a black curl around her finger.

"I can't leave," I say. "You'll have to share James with me—and I think he's falling in love." I see the flicker of discomfort in her eyes, see her grip the glass tighter. "Your brother is in love with me," I repeat, although I'm not sure this is true.

"You don't belong here," she says quietly. "You shouldn't have come."

I don't reply. I had no choice but to come. My nightmares brought me. For years, after I came out of the coma, I'd wake up in a sweat, night after night, my heart pounding hard, not remembering my dreams yet the panic staying with me, the awful, chest-tightening feeling that was as loud as a scream, telling me I had to set things right. And then, finally, after so many years without clues, I saw James's picture in the magazine, and something clicked, a small, cloudy haze of recognition, and of course I had to come. Byblos is my chance—perhaps my only chance—of putting the nightmares to rest. The clock on the wall chimes.

Gina tries to set her drink on the coffee table, underestimating the distance between glass and table, releasing it too soon. It drops to the surface, making a loud thunk as it hits the wood, the drink sloshing over the sides of the glass. She stands up, walks over to me, and places her hand on my shoulder.

"You won't get James," she says softly, leaning down, her hand gentle on my shoulder. "Reconsider my offer."

CHAPTER SIXTEEN

When I feel a hand on my shoulder, I let out a small, surprised scream, jerk around, see James behind me.

"You're jumpy today," he says. "I didn't mean to scare you." A slow grin spreads across his face. "Your lips are purple," he says.

I wipe my mouth with the back of my hand. I've been outside picking blackberries for the last hour and a half, and it's impossible to pick them without sampling the fruit. My palms are stained a bluish purple, and I imagine my mouth looks the same. I'm wearing cutoffs, a tattered pair of jean shorts suitable for berry picking, and a pink tank top. I wipe my hands on the back of my shorts. "You startled me," I say. "I didn't hear you walk up."

"You look like a little kid," he says, "your face and hands smeared with berry juice, even your tongue is purple. You look like you ate more than you saved." He leans down, kisses me, lets his tongue linger on my lips. "You taste sweet," he says.

Shading my eyes from the sun, I gaze up at him, confused by his show of affection, embarrassed by my own disarray. My skin, too pale, too delicate to ever tan, emits the faint chemical aroma of sunscreen; my knees, from kneeling in the berry patches, are scratched and covered with dirt; my cutoffs, ragged and stained. James, by contrast, is tanned, neat, and smartly dressed, his light-colored shirt clean and crisp, his slacks without smudges of dirt, his expensive leather shoes polished.

"Can I come over tonight?" I ask him. This is the first time I've invited myself to his home. Afraid he'll refuse, I quickly add, "I thought we could have dinner together. Just the two of us. I'll cook. There's a new dessert recipe I want to try."

"Sure," he says. "That sounds nice." He reaches into his pants pocket, pulls out his keys, takes one off the ring. He holds it out for me. "Here's my house key," he says. "I have some business this afternoon. I won't be home until seven-thirty or eight, so let yourself in. I'll be there as soon as I can."

I knew he'd be gone. Mrs. McGuane told me earlier. "Thanks," I say, taking the key.

"Just leave it on the table," he says. "By the front door," and I blush slightly, knowing he doesn't want me to keep the key, knowing I have a stolen copy of it on my own key ring.

As he leaves, I watch him walk away. There's something heroic about his stature; he still seems, to me, larger than life. He crosses the garden, walks toward the main house. I like to see him in motion, the slow roll of his shoulders, the sureness of his step, the thick muscularity in his thighs. He moves like a jungle animal, a powerfully built cat, with confidence, with grace, yet giving the impression he's always on the lookout, ready to pounce. There is no hesitation in his step, no self-doubt to give him a tentative gait. I wonder what it would feel like to possess that kind of self-assurance. Suddenly, I remember something.

"James!" I call out.

He turns around.

"Why did you come out here?" I ask. "Why did you want to see me?" Between us, the sky is blue, expansive, and I feel we are worlds apart.

"I'll see you tonight," he calls back, not answering my question, and he turns to leave, walks through the vegetable garden that is spread out before us like a feast: to the right, a block of sweet corn, growing straight and tall, with trails of summer squash and zucchini in bright golds and greens snaking along the ground; farther on, beets, potatoes, peas, rad-ishes, cucumbers, and carrots; and then there is the lettuce patch, a frilly, bronze-fringed mix of loose-leaves, curly endive, and lobed arugula, several rows of pale green crispheads, a few crimson radicchio, a ruffle of butterheads, and, filling in the interstices, a ferny feathery collection of herbs.

I hear a door slam and turn to see Gina come out of the cottage. Last night, as soon as she left my house, I checked the bedroom closet to see if she'd found my hidden cache. I keep all the information about myself and Byblos securely locked in a suit-case. It appeared untouched, everything in exactly the same order as I'd left it.

She walks across the lawn now, strides past me, nodding her head and smiling wanly instead of say-ing hello. She doesn't look well, her skin dull, her eyes shadowed with dark circles. I imagine she's hungover. Normally, even when she's in dirty jeans and a T-shirt, she still has a dazzling look about her, hard-edged yet elegant, lots of drama in those dark eyebrows and gorgeous green eyes. Today, how-ever, she just looks sick.

She goes over to James, who is waiting for her on the patio. They exchange words, heated it seems, then she shoots a quick glance in my direction. He puts an arm over her shoulder, directs her into the house.

I return to my berry picking. The gardener planted strawberries, blueberries, raspberries, and blackberries, many different varieties of each, and they vary greatly in color, texture, and flavor. My favorite are the blackberries, deliciously warm and smelling like jam in the midafternoon sun, juicy purple nuggets sweeter and more luscious than candy. Of all the berries, blackberries seem to be the most wild, the most untamed, the renegades of the garden, prickly and thorny and spreading uncontrollably. I fill my container but not without a price, my fingers scratched and bleeding.

I carry the grocery bag into James's house, leaving his house key on the entry table. His refrigerator is Spartan, the contents indicative of someone who doesn't spend much time cooking at home; a few condiments, mustard, mayonnaise, catsup, salad dressing, several cans of soda, a quart of milk. His cabinets are equally uninspiring, an opened box of cereal, two jars of pasta sauce, a few spices, a container of coffee. I put the groceries away, then look at my watch. I'll have plenty of time.

In the living area, I stop in front of the couch and fireplace and rust-colored oriental carpet. A shiver goes through me as I remember the sordid details of the last time I was here. I tell myself I complied under duress, but I know there's more to it than that. I shake the thought out of my mind. Better if I don't dwell on it, better if I don't scrutinize my motivations too closely.

I pass on to his work area. The first time I searched it, James interrupted me before I got a chance to look in the filing cabinet. I pull open the first drawer. All of the folders are labeled with clear plastic dividers, the labels indicating a particular business function of the winery. I inspect each folder, carefully, so I won't miss anything, but see nothing of interest to me. I'm not sure what I'm looking for, but I'll recognize it if I see it.

I open the second drawer, find more documents about the winery, business papers, old tax returns. I go through them all, tedious work, examining each paper to see if it will throw any light on my past. When I finish with the last folder, I look at my watch again. This is taking much longer than I anticipated. I slide open the final drawer. Before I begin reading the first folder, I take a cursory glance at all the titles. There, way in the back, I find what I'm looking for: a folder labeled "Anna Maria McGuane."

Excitedly, I pull it out. I settle into James's desk chair, open the folder. He has a copy of the death certificate, her obituary notice, the front-page newspaper article reporting her death. I have my own copies of these, and don't take the time to reread them now. Next, I find copies of her birth certificate, social security number, her high school and college diplomas, her driver's license. In the back of the folder are two bulky manila envelopes. The first contains documents belonging to her parents, whom I see had died in a car accident when she was eight years old, and various other personal papers belonging to Anna. I go through all of them, piece by piece, stitching together her history, creating a picture of her life, a mosaic vita from miscellaneous scraps of paper. She lived with her grandfather after the accident, who, along with his two brothers, owned several large vineyards in both the Napa and Sonoma valleys. Judging from the many snapshots—holding his hand, riding in his tractor, sitting on his lap—she adored him. Each picture shows her smiling, laughing. She was a cute little girl, curly dark hair, brown eyes, and she grew up to be an attractive woman, slender and long-legged, a playful smile, a gracefully curving neck. There is a Girl Scout picture, at a camp-out in the woods; then the prom picture, her hair piled on top of her head, a long satiny gown; a snapshot while she's working in the vineyard, another standing by one of her grandfather's trucks, the gondola filled with recently picked grapes. I read a newspaper article about her grandfather. Although he was one of the largest growers in the area, he didn't make wine himself, but rather sold high-quality grapes to local wineries. Then I see a copy of his will. When he died, Anna, his only grandchild, inherited all his property, all his money.

I open the second manila folder. Inside, I find a copy of Anna's will. I read it carefully, making sure I understand it, then lean back in the chair, thinking. James had a motive, a reason to kill his wife: he was her sole beneficiary.

For dinner, we have grilled sea bass with a lemon caper sauce; a salad of baby greens, freshly cut from the garden; and portobello mushrooms, sautéed in garlic and sherry, on a bed of creamy polenta. The meal, for me, seems oddly uncomfortable, and I have to choke down each awkward bite. I'm not used to a domestic arrangement with James. Our relationship is basic, primal, not intended for small talk at the dinner table. The day-to-day shared ramblings, the routine, the quotidian—they're not within the realm of our experience, and I have trouble sitting here, sharing a meal, pretending that it's a perfectly normal thing to do.

James, however, seems at ease. It appears he doesn't mind the domesticity at all.

Finished with dinner, I lay down my fork. We're sitting at one end of the long wooden dining table, a table that could easily accommodate twelve, a table—with its hard-backed chairs and dark wood and simple, austere style—that reflects the stark, medieval loftiness of the room. I try to concentrate on his words, but I'm still thinking of Anna's will tucked away in the back of his filing cabinet. James made a small fortune when his wife died.

I finger the flimsy strap on my dress. Earlier today, I'd showered and changed into a clingy, peach-colored stretch-lace slipdress. He's talking about the Carneros district in the valley, explaining how it's cooler and much more suitable for growing the pinot noir grape. When there is a lull in the conversation, I say, "Does Gina know who I am?"

He looks at me, raises one eyebrow, then takes a drink of his wine, a creamy, oaked chardonnay I'd chosen for tonight's dinner.

I play with the fork on my plate, push around the polenta I hadn't finished. "Does she?" I ask again.

Holding the wineglass at the base, he slowly moves it in small circles on the table, contemplating me. I wonder what he's thinking, but his eyes, cool, intensely green in this light, offer no clues.

Finally, he says, "No. I didn't tell her."

"I thought you and Gina didn't keep secrets."

He shrugs. "There's no reason to tell her."

I go to the kitchen and get dessert out of the refrigerator, a chocolate-raspberry tart, made with fresh berries, both white and milk chocolate, and a buttery cookielike crust. I serve it with a sweet dessert wine, a late harvest Riesling. When we're almost through eating, I say, "Gina paid me a visit last night."

"Oh?" James says, curious, looking up from his plate.

"Did you know that she watches us?"

He takes another bite, finishes his dessert, then pushes the plate away.

"Through the curtains," I add. "She spies on us through the cracks in the curtains. At night, when it's dark outside."

He gives me a look, but says nothing.

"She tells me you know."

A smile, which I'm unable to read, starts at the corners of his mouth, then goes nowhere. He rises to his feet.

"Don't worry about Gina," he says. He comes around the table, pulls me up, kisses the base of my neck, then tilts my head so I'll look up at him. "Leave her to me," he says.

I say nothing, well aware he still hasn't answered my question. I just nod my head. He lifts me, easy for him, and carries me up the spiral staircase.

Something between us has changed. It began the evening of the dog dish—maybe even earlier—and came full circle tonight. I stand in the bathroom, looking at myself in the mirror, wondering how, and why, this change occurred. James's bathroom is a walk-in looking glass. From the outside, all one sees is a wraparound, serpentine brick wall. Follow the brick, past the balustrade edging the loft, then left down a narrow hallway that goes to the back end of the house, and one finds the entrance at the rear, no door, just an opening in the brick wall. Inside, the curving room is open and completely mirrored, from ceiling to floor, revealing every flaw, every nuance of blemished flesh, not a room for the timid, not a room where modesty can prevail. A huge marble tub, long enough for James, large enough for two, lines one wall; a toilet and double vanity line another; and on the far wall, an open shower, dormitory style, with two gleaming stainless-steel showerheads. Black tile covers the floor, and a drain lies in the middle.

Looking at myself from behind, I see the rosy blush of flesh inflamed, my ass reddened from the repeated slap of James's hand. And there are the other marks, from the whip, long thin imprints scoring my buttocks and thighs, a deeper red, the scarlet trails of my endurance. Tonight, for the first time, I didn't fight the whip. I took what he gave me, and when he asked if he should stop, I hesitated for only a moment, then said no, give me more. And he did. He had me bent across the table in his studio, like a criminal in front of a cop, my legs spread wide, hands folded behind my head. "You want your cunt fucked?" he asked, pushing his fingers inside me roughly, working them around, then shoving a finger in my ass, and I said yes, fuck me, but instead he stepped back and started again with the whip. I gasped each time he struck me, felt tears well up in my eyes, felt my exposure and vulnerability, afraid I was sinking to a depth lower than I could bear, but I never asked him to stop. I accepted it, accepted it all, each humbling lash of the whip, disconcerted I'd asked for more, baffled I was willing to prolong my pain, and yet wanting it still, wanting him, confusing the two, pain and pleasure all mixed up, and when he finally fucked me, it was even better than all the times before.

I look at my marks again, at the rosy-red rouge of my ass, so prominent now, like the swollen red rump of a female chimp in heat, and the sight of it seems sexual, alluring, and then a new feeling comes to me, something strange, something unfamiliar: pride. I could take everything he gave.

I splash cold water on my face, go back out to the loft. James is sitting on the antique trunk, waiting for me, gazing down at the floor, in thought. Even now, naked, relaxed, a slight slump to his shoulders, even now his presence is formidable, intimidating even in his nakedness, and I have to tell myself it's all a facade, that he will bleed like any other man, that he is vulnerable like any other man, and if I was to take a closer look, if I could wipe away the hold he exerts, I would see him as he really is, a man in his forties—flawed, imperfect, lines from too much sun edging his eyes, a few extra pounds, a sag here and there, but I cannot sidestep his hold and the imperfections have no diminishing effect and, still, to me, he appears larger than life.

In one hand, he holds several lengths of rope, with cuffs attached to the ends. When he looks over and sees me watching him, he straightens up and says, "Come here."

I walk over, past the studio and couch and hanging rattan chair, past the stone fireplace, then stop before him. He runs his hand, the one without the ropes, along the length of my thigh.

"Do you trust me?" he asks.

Surprised by this question, I say nothing.

"Do you?" he asks again.

Thoughts leap through my head. Do I trust him? No. How could I? Just because we reached a higher level with the whip, that doesn't mean my opinion of him has changed. He hurt me once, hurt me badly, and he could do it again.

"No," I say, honest, shaking my head slightly, my voice low, quiet. "I don't trust you."

He is pleased, I think, that I told him the truth,

even though I'm sure he would have preferred a much different answer. "We haven't gotten very far, have we?" he says.

I think of my response tonight, how I accepted the whip. "To me," I say, "it seems that we have."

He keeps his hand on my thigh. His touch feels like a statement, possessive, a declaration that my thigh belongs to him. "Tonight," he says, "we'll go even further."

A frisson of fright goes through me, a small tremor, a dread of the unknown. But the other feeling is there also, lurking in the background of my soul: excitement, the expectation of something new. Nevertheless, fear predominates, and I feel myself stiffening, pulling away. His hand is a brace, restraining me.

"Do you trust me?" he asks again.

I wish I could say yes—it's the answer he demands—but I can't. We both know it would be a lie.

"I want you to trust me," he says. "Someday you will."

I doubt if that will happen, but I remain quiet, feeling silence is prudent.

"I have something for you," he says. "But since you don't trust me, I'm going to tie you up first."

I look at the ropes in his hand. He's tied me up many times before. Still, it terrifies me, makes me feel completely out of control, at his mercy. Each time, I try not to show my fear, but he can sense it, he can smell my panic as if it were a perfume. The act itself, the binding, is not violent, nor is it painful like the whip, but the sensation of restraint, of knowing I am truly helpless, unable to defend myself, unable to fight back, that sensation is horrifying. It takes me to the edge, makes life seem, in some bizarre way, more real.

"What are you going to do?" I ask, my voice

barely a whisper. He pulls me closer, between his legs. My palms rest on his thighs. His muscles are like granite, unyielding.

He takes one of the ropes, attaches the cuff around my right wrist. I think about resisting, but know, from prior experience, from the first night we were together, that a fight between us would be useless. A drop of sweat, a drop of fear, rolls down my temple. James sees this.

Quietly, patiently, he says, "Anytime you want out of our"—he pauses for a second; I think he's going to say relationship, but he chooses another word—"arrangement, just say so. You can end it anytime you like."

His offer is an empty gesture. He knows I need him, the answers only he can provide. And the outlawed pleasure, I need that too. He knows I won't call it off.

Timidly, I hold out my other hand. He cuffs it, then reaches down and attaches cuffs to both my ankles. Standing up, he tells me to lie on the trunk. He's never asked this of me before. It's built like a coffin for a very large person, long and fairly wide, sturdy, and when I lie down it feels as if I'm lying on top of a wooden casket, uncomfortably hard. He walks behind me, slides me up so my head is near the top edge. The trunk is longer than I, by several feet. Large metal rings are secured to the bottom edges of the trunk, and I watch James as he loops each rope through the rings, then ties off the rope so I can't move my arms or legs.

He gets a chair from the studio and puts it near my feet. Next, he goes over to the dresser, then comes back with a wooden box in one hand and a long black extension cord in the other. He sits at the chair, by my feet. I watch him, lifting my head, straining to see, dreading what will come next. The box is slightly larger than a cigar box, and he opens it, pulls out a small holder, a metal bracket, and sets it on the trunk. Then he takes out some kind of tool with a short electric cord. He rests it on the metal holder, attaches the extension cord, goes over to the wall, and plugs it in. I watch him, then I look down at the foot of the trunk. The tool looks like a glue gun, with a wire on the tip. It's difficult to see it clearly from my position on the trunk. I feel another drop of sweat slowly slide down my face.

"Don't worry," he says, and he comes over to me, bends down on one knee. He works his thumb on my forehead, gently, in small circles, then leans down and kisses me.

"Don't worry," he says again, but his words provide neither comfort nor reassurance.

I look down at my feet, at the metal holder, and see a thin trail of smoke rising from the wire tip. A surge of panic suddenly goes through me. "What's that?" I ask, breathless, my voice muffled, but I think I know. It's some kind of branding tool. He's going to brand me, brand me like a cow, give me another scar.

"James?" I say, but he puts his fingers to my lips.

"Shhh," he says. "It'll be okay."

"Please don't," I say, begging, and the words come out choked. I feel tears water my eyes. I don't want another scar, I don't want that kind of pain.

He looks down at me, watching, observing, seeing the fear that I know is in my eyes. I am silent, trying not to cry, but my eyes water. His forehead creases just a little, as if he's confused, as if he doesn't understand me. He takes an index finger, runs it lightly under my lower eyelashes, first one eye, then the other. His fingertip is wet with my tears. I see his face soften a little, a gentle look of compassion, and I think perhaps he will change his mind.

But he doesn't. His expression turns to resolve.

"It'll be okay," he says once more, and he gets up, moves a lamp onto the trunk, shines it on my feet. He goes to the bathroom. I hear water running in the sink. I pull on the ropes, but, as I knew they would be, they are tight, firmly attached. When he comes back, he's carrying a small glass of water. He sits in the chair at the foot of the trunk. He gives me a quick glance, combs his fingers through his hair, then pulls the chair closer to the trunk, angles it away from me, leans forward, hunches over my feet. I cannot see what he's doing now. His bare back and shoulders block my view.

"James?" I say.

I feel his hand on my ankle, and, nervously, I jerk my foot, wincing. I try to pull away, but the cuff is secure around my ankle.

"Stop," he says firmly.

I brace myself for the pain. "James?" I say again, a plea for mercy.

He ignores me. I feel him readjust the cuff, move it up my leg, then he attaches something else to my ankle. I breathe heavily, breathe with fear. He fiddles around by my ankle, hunched over, working closely. I can see nothing except his bare back, the jagged scar on his left shoulder. After a few minutes, I feel something else next to my skin, something cool and smooth. He stops, looks back at me.

"Don't move," he says, then he returns to his work. Even though I strain, I still can't see anything. After a minute, he stops. Without turning around, he says, "This is important. No matter what you feel, you mustn't move your foot. Do you understand? You have to hold completely still." His voice is serious, intent.

"Do you understand?" he says again.

I nod, but he doesn't see this.

"If you move," he says, "I'll hurt you."

Squeezing my eyes shut, I wait for the pain to come, trying, desperately, not to move, clenching my teeth so tightly my jaw begins to ache. Whatever he's going to do, I tell myself, it couldn't be any worse than the pain I've already suffered. I feel my chest rise and fall with each struggling breath, feel my heart beating too fast, the sound roaring in my ears, my body slick with the sweat of fear. It seems so warm in here, like an oven, stifling, claustrophobic. I can't breathe, can't get enough air into my lungs.

Suddenly, something warm and wet splashes my left foot. Involuntarily, I jerk, let out a small gasp, then wait for the pain that James said would come if I moved. I wait, and I wait, but he does not reprimand me, and he does not hurt me as he'd promised. I feel it again, warm liquid, a slow dribble, and then I remember the glass of water he brought from the bathroom. I bite my lip, confused, anxious, still waiting. After a few minutes, I feel something else against my ankle, not liquid but warm, very warm, and growing warmer. It doesn't burn me, but I feel the heat, the hotness, against my skin. Then a soft cloth. I look down. James's back and shoulders are still blocking my view. I see his elbow moving, feel the cloth rubbing against my skin, rapidly, back and forth, as if he was polishing silver.

When he finishes, he leans back in the chair, looks over at me. I don't understand what just happened. I lift my head, but the ankle cuff blocks my view. I cannot see what he has done. He removes the cuffs from my legs, then reaches over and removes the ones from my arms. I sit up, see an elegant gold ankle bracelet, the links about a quarter-inch wide, around my ankle. It is not a dainty, slender chain, but something more substantial, something that will resist the wear and tear of time. There is no clasp, no fastener to remove it. I look at the tool in the metal holder. I know what it is now. It's a soldering gun, and he'd soldered the anklet so it wouldn't come off. I think of the girl in James's story, the tinkling bell on her ankle bracelet. My anklet doesn't have a bell, but the implication is quite clear: he is duplicating his actions, doing to me now what he'd done once before. My chest tightens. I know the ending to that story, if not the details.

"You're not to remove this," he says, his hand wrapped around my left ankle. Then he adds, "Ever."

Numbly, feeling my world is spinning out of control, I nod my compliance, and then he leans down and kisses my ankle, the inside of my foot, and I know he's going to fuck me again, and I want him to. He pulls me onto his lap.

"Say you belong to me," he says.

I look at him, puzzled by the request. Without conviction, I say, "I belong to you."

He breathes into my neck. His hand goes down my leg, his fingers pause on the anklet. "Again," he says. "Say it again." His voice is a soft command.

"I belong to you."

Pulling me closer, he slides his penis inside me. "Again," he whispers, urgent now.

"I belong to you."

"Again."

"I belong to you," and this time, as I say it, I know that it is true. For whatever reason, for whatever insanity that holds me here, I belong to him. I'll know the truth, I'll see him punished, but still I belong to him. He has taken possession. The proof lies around my ankle.

CHAPTER SEVENTEEN

For two weeks now, Byblos has been busy bottling last year's chardonnay. Inside the winery, as I get closer to the glass-enclosed bottling room, the noise gets louder, the machine clanging and groaning like some overgrown freaky animal of modern technology that hasn't yet worked out its kinks and peculiarities of iron and tin and stainless steel. Several workers line the machine, helping it out, upending boxes of empty bottles. The bottles crash onto the conveyor belt, then they chug along, rattling and clinking, protesting all the way up the line, submitting to a new assault at each stage, first purified and purged, then filled with wine, corked, capsuled, and slapped with a label, and finally sent back where they came from, inside the box.

I stand outside the glass, off to the side where Gina can't see me. She's by the labeler, checking the bottles to see if the Byblos labels are glued on straight. She's wearing a sleeveless plaid blouse, her arms slender and tanned, the muscles clearly defined. She's a feminized, and much more refined, version of James, both of them strong and willful, she radiating elegance whereas he gives off a whiff of the untamed. Sliding both hands in the pockets of her slacks, she leans forward slightly, examining a label. She's built like a model, tall, very long legs. I glance down at my own legs. I'm wearing a short plum-colored skirt, plenty of skin visible. Calf-high boots judiciously cover the chain around my ankle.

Immediately, from just thinking about the golden anklet, a surge of pleasure rushes through my veins. It is dissolute and abasing, but pleasure nonetheless. The chain is on me always—when I shower or bathe, when I sleep, when I cook or work in the garden, a light pressure against my skin, constant, lingering, from day to day, every day, a sign of possession as indelible as a brand. I can remove it with wire cutters or pliers, but I don't. That would break our bond—something I cannot yet do. So the chain stays, a symbol of my surrender, of my appurtenance, a mark of ownership as surely as a serial number stamped on private property.

I belong to him.

He could've done something much worse that night, something to cause me physical pain. Instead, he left a psychological scar, his signature in the form of gold links, unbroken, letting me know what I will become: chattel. His chattel. I cover it when I leave my house, wear socks or shoes with a high top, long slacks or skirts that nearly reach the floor. No one sees the anklet but James and me.

Watching the bottling machine, I realize I have no life outside of Byblos, outside of James. I go home only to sleep, shower, and change clothes. Byblos is my life. Retribution is my goal. In between, James and I fuck.

Gina still scrutinizes the bottles, nodding her head slightly in satisfaction. Her curly black hair, gathered up in a silky ponytail, bobs as she moves. Then I spot James, crouched down behind the machine, fiddling with something on the side of the conveyor belt. They'll be occupied here for a while, I think. Time enough.

I walk to the other end of the building. Even here, there's a lot of racket from the bottling machine. A couple of winery workers—cellar rats is what they call themselves—quite suddenly appear, walking out from between a row of stainless-steel tanks. I didn't hear their footsteps over all the noise. They give me a friendly nod and a flip of their hand.

Up ahead, disappearing around a corner, I see the man I'm looking for. His name is Ed, the cellar manager, a friendly but shy man who's been with Byblos for years. He's tall and skinny, with rough, wrinkled skin and a gray walruslike mustache that droops. He's always been nice to me, from the beginning, even though we've never had a conversation lasting more than a few minutes. I glance back at the bottling room. James and Gina are still busy.

Going after Ed, I see him just as he's leaving the building, the door closing behind him. I cross the room, step outside, look around. I spot him at the gray circuit-breaker panel, flipping a switch, then he walks over to the large concrete pad of winemaking equipment, the names and functions of which are now becoming familiar to me—the receiving hopper, a huge V-shaped bin where the grapes will be dumped when they're ripe; the stemmer/crusher, which removes stems and gently breaks the skins; and the giant new Diemme press, for extracting juice from the must.

I follow him through the steel maze of equipment, all of it much larger than I, past the empty hopper, past the crusher. He goes over to the winepress, takes a couple steps up the platform. I glance around. We're alone out here. The press looks like a mammoth cylindrical steel drum turned on its side. It's secured by heavy steel beams, and a metal platform goes up several feet so workers can climb inside the gigantic machine when it needs to be cleaned out.

"Can I talk to you, Ed?" I ask, climbing up the few steps, holding on to the railing. He turns around, surprised to see me.

I stand next to him on the platform. "You've been here twenty-two years," I say.

I see a faint smile behind the grizzled mustache. The wrinkles around his eyes deepen. "Twenty-one," he says. "Next month."

"Longer than anyone else," I say.

He nods, gets a wrench out of the toolbox he'd brought up with him. He starts to loosen the nuts on the metal grate in front of the press.

"Then you knew Anna," I say. "James's wife."

He stops, looks over at me. "I knew her," he says. "Knew her granddaddy, too."

"Nobody will say anything about her."

"Not surprising," he says, and he turns back to the metal grate, works another nut.

"Can you tell me about her?" I ask. He doesn't say anything. I lean against the railing, watching him work. His hands are leathery and gnarled, the fingertips stained with grease.

Finally, he says, "She knew grapes, more than most. Picked it all up from her granddaddy." He pauses. I hear birds nearby, chirping, and the distant rumble of a tractor in the fields. Several minutes go by. Ed works on the metal grate.

"I liked her," he says abruptly, breaking the silence. "She was a good girl. She had a good laugh."

He's quiet again.

"Did James love her?" I ask.

"Don't know about those things," he says, curt. "I just work here." He removes a section of the metal grate blocking the press, sets it aside. There's a small oval-shaped door on the back side of the press—everyone calls it the manhole door since this is where workers climb in to clean the machine between runs. The press is rotated now, so the door is near the top. Ed reaches up. The small opening is like a submarine hatch. He cranks it open.

"Were you in the winery when she fell?" I ask.

He jerks around but doesn't answer. He looks beyond me. I turn. James and Gina are there, walking by. She's speaking to him, and she smiles at us as they pass. James watches, his eyes blank, without emotion. He leaves with Gina, not saying anything.

I look at Ed. He's kneeling on the platform now, staring inside the toolbox, intent. "I forgot something," he mumbles after a few moments, rising, and he heads down the stairs.

"Ed?" I say.

He pauses, his hand on the railing. I see his back stiffen. "I wasn't here that day," he says, not turning around. He walks off toward the winery. I have more questions for him. I look at my watch. Mrs. McGuane is having a luncheon this afternoon, and I need to get back to the house fairly soon. I gaze out across the vineyards. The leaves are vibrant green. The vines, full of vigor, festoon the trellis wires like decorative green garlands, winding down the long rows.

After ten minutes, when Ed still hasn't returned, I sit on the platform where he'd been working. I dangle my feet over the side, on the green metal dump chute. If the chute wasn't in the way, I could easily jump to the ground, only a few feet. I look up at the huge machine. When harvest comes, after the grapes are put through the stemmer/crusher, they'll be dropped into this press so the remaining juice can be extracted. I see the hopper down below, beneath the chute. Unexpectedly, I hear the big machine groan, then the cylinder begins to rotate. This isn't supposed to happen. When workers are cleaning or repairing the machine, the press is always turned off and locked down, and then the circuit breaker switched off.

As I scramble to my feet, I feel metal slamming into my back, a sharp pain that takes my breath away, makes me lose my balance. I fall over the edge, into the green chute, and crash against the side of the moving press. Flailing out, I scramble for the top railing, miss it. I hold on to the edges of the chute, the metal digging into my palms. All of a sudden, I think of the opened manhole door. I remember, vividly, the winepress accident James described when he gave me a tour of Byblos on my very first day of the job.

Desperate, I glance around. I see no one. I scream for Ed. There's an emergency shut-off button—like a panic snap, I think, the image racing through my mind—but it's at the front of the machine. I cling to the chute. The press drum rotates. Looking up, I see the manhole door reach the top, then disappear from view. It'll clear the other side, but when it gets near the bottom of the rotation, the door will fall open, and as the press continues to rotate, the heavy steel door will drag along the ground, scraping the concrete, tearing apart and crushing anything in its way, the dump chute, a body . . . my body. Frantically, scrabbling, I try to pull myself up the chute. My boots slip and slide on the metal. I see the door coming toward me, dragging along, the raucous screech of steel against concrete jarring my mind. The noise of the machine is like a death knell, beckoning. I reach up, lunge for the metal grating, grab hold. My arms, from years of lifting weights, are strong, and I manage to lift myself. I crawl onto the platform, my heart beating against my chest. I gasp for air.

Moments later, I hear the press grumble to a stop. Ed bounds up the platform steps. My heart still slams against my chest. I can't speak. I hear him asking me questions, if I'm okay, how did this happen, but I still can't speak. Finally, I sit up, shaking. I see the section of grating he'd removed earlier, lying on the platform. That's what hit me in the back. It fell over when the press started.

"I could've been killed!" I yell at him, angry, still scared, getting my voice back. "I could've been killed!"

He looks stunned. "I didn't turn it on," he says, clearly distressed.

I'm still shaking. I try to think, try to put my mind in order. My heart still beats rapidly, my hands tremble. "It was locked down," I say. "How could the press start if it was locked down?"

Ed looks off to the side, chagrined. He has a stricken look on his face. "I didn't lock it down," he confesses. "I was only going to work on it for a minute."

I stare up at him. He knows better. The lock-down is part of OSHA regulations. He was cutting corners, saving a little time. He looks down at me, his old eyes full of remorse.

"I'll find out who turned on the breaker," he says finally, and he trudges down the platform steps, his shoulders stooped, heavy with guilt.

For the first time, I feel I'm in real danger. I decide it's time for the police.

"Are you all right?" James asks. There's a look of concern—specious, I think—on his face. He's changed clothes for lunch, I notice.

He says, "Ed called a minute ago—he told me what happened." He tries to put his arm around me, but I back off.

"I have to fix lunch," I say, and I walk away, not telling him I'd called the police. I hear voices coming from the living room—Mrs. McGuane's guests.

In the kitchen, I throw together a quick salad of red leaf lettuce, fresh figs, walnuts, and blue cheese. Nervously, I look at the clock. I wonder when the police will arrive. I straighten my skirt. Although covered by my clothes, huge bruises, ugly purple splotches from where I crashed into the winepress, mark my right thigh and shoulder. Maybe it was an accident. Maybe not. I need a safety net, an insurance policy to protect against future harm. James will be less likely to hurt me if he knows the police are watching.

I go into the dining room. Mrs. McGuane is at one end of the long table, James at the other, Gina by his side—their usual arrangement—and the guests in between.

I watch James and Gina, one of them light-haired, the other dark. Still, there's no mistaking the family connection, the firm jaw, the same lime-green eyes, the height, the strength, the aura of power they possess. They are an impressive pair, he in his Italian silk jacquard tie, she in a shimmering dress, form-fitting and tinted the color of cinnamon. She calls him Jimmy—no one else does, not even his mother—and, even now, I feel a twinge of envy at this show of intimacy.

I serve the salads. If James feels awkward around me, in front of other people, he doesn't show it. He seems perfectly at ease, charming, witty, telling a story about his first years in the business, something about leaving the grapes on the vines too long.

He glances at me, and I see an unfamiliar warmth

in his eyes. I see his affection for me. I begin to doubt myself—perhaps the incident earlier was only an accident. As he's speaking with his guests, he gives me a friendly smile, and, discreetly, his gaze follows me around the room. I have trouble reconciling the man in front of me now with the man I'd formed in my mind, the one who tried to kill me many years ago. My perception of him wavers. It's like a modern art trompe l'oeil painting that shifts and changes focus depending on how I look at it—I'm staring at a vase one minute, two men in profile the next. This is my perception of James, wavering, shifting back and forth between the nice guy in front of me now and the killer he could be.

I uncork a bottle of wine. As I pour it, Mrs. McGuane introduces me to her guests. I hear the doorbell ring. A minute later, the housekeeper, a sturdy woman with very dark bushy eyebrows, enters the room, walks over to James, leans down, and quietly whispers in his ear.

He nods, listening, his expression indecipherable to his guests. Gina, however, gives him a curious look. Instinctively, she knows that something is wrong. She knows her twin, his expressions, his moods, all the feelings that are somehow tied into her.

"Excuse me for a moment," he says to the people at the table, sliding back his chair.

I set the bottle of wine on the table. "Is that the police at the door?" I ask him. The room suddenly falls silent. "I called them about the accident," I continue.

"Yes," he says, all warmth gone from his eyes now. "Perhaps we should both speak to them." To the others, he puts on a false smile. He says, "This'll take only a minute," and he walks around the table, comes over to me.

Appearing confused, Gina also rises from her chair, follows us out of the room. We walk down the hallway, pass the living room.

"What accident?" Gina asks her brother, but he doesn't reply. Apparently, he didn't relay Ed's message.

James puts his hand on my elbow, a definite pressure, intimidating. I look up at him. He stares straight ahead, his lips pressed together in a hard line. We go to the front of the house. Two uniformed policemen, one in his thirties, ruddy cheeked and blond, the other older, with gray-streaked hair, are standing in the foyer.

"Thanks for coming," I say. "I'm Carly Tyler, the person who called."

Before I can explain further, Mrs. McGuane enters the foyer, still holding her linen napkin, a concerned expression on her face. "There was an accident today?" she asks James, ignoring the police. "Why wasn't I informed?"

"It wasn't an accident," I say, answering for him. "I think someone's trying to kill me."

Mrs. McGuane frowns, her thin white eyebrows coming together in confusion. "What?" she says. "Kill you? Why on earth would anyone—"

I interrupt. I tell the police of the blue car that nearly ran me down at Clos Pegase, then I tell them about the winepress. I lift my skirt and show them the bruise on my thigh. James watches me, coolly. The policemen listen, but their skepticism is obvious. I'm paranoid, they think, overreacting, blowing this all out of proportion. I wonder if I am. They ask me if I have any reason to believe someone would want me dead, if I have any enemies. I look over at James. He folds his arms, stares at me icily.

"No," I say. "No enemies. But it seems odd—I move to Napa Valley and soon after I arrive, I'm almost killed. Twice. It seems more than a coincidence."

Mrs. McGuane slides over to me, puts her arm around my shoulder. "How frightening for you," she says. "It must have scared you to death when the press started, but of course it was an accident."

"I'm not so sure about that."

The older policeman starts to fill out a report. He asks me more questions, about the blue car, about the winepress. He tries to assuage my fears, but I don't relent.

"I'll pass this information on," he says finally, still writing, "and tomorrow someone will contact you." He scribbles on the report, shifting to his other foot. He says, "I'm sure there's nothing to worry about, but you might feel safer staying with a friend tonight."

Despite his manner, his skepticism is still obvious. It doesn't matter. The safety net, albeit a tenuous one, is in place.

Night covers Byblos like a blanket, warm and comforting. The house is quiet. James and Gina are gone, and Mrs. McGuane fell asleep nearly an hour ago. Although she believes the incident at the winepress was accidental, and the blue car manned by a drunken driver, she insisted I spend the night with her. I admit I find solace in the main house late at night, alone, the lights dim. There's a sense of safety and shelter here, as if I could snuggle down and be protected forever, as if I'm under the aegis of Charlotte McGuane. But I know this is an illusion. She cannot protect me now any more than she could have fifteen years ago.

Earlier this evening, I baked a coffee cake for tomorrow morning. The kitchen, still warm from the oven, smells of apples and cinnamon and freshly baked cake. I'm unable to sleep, so I make a cup of hot herbal tea. I lace it with honey and a squeeze of lemon, and take it out to the back patio, quietly sliding shut the glass door behind me. It's cool and refreshing out here. Although summer days at Byblos are hot, sometimes stifling, the nights can be thirty to forty degrees cooler. Stringy wisps of sea fog, like gossamer, float and dance in the night air. The moon, luminous, golden tinged, casts shadows across the land. I head for the patio table.

Abruptly, I stop. I listen. I thought I was the only one out here, but I hear voices, agitated whispering, coming from around the corner of the house. I walk closer, not making any noise, listening carefully. I recognize the voices now. It's James and Gina, arguing, their whispers heated. I've never heard them angry with each other before. Still, I can't make out their conversation. I move closer.

"No!" I hear Gina say to her brother. "I won't risk Byblos. We could lose it all."

James's reply comes to me muffled, inaudible. He speaks urgently but softly, his voice low. I move closer, then hear the crunch of pebbles beneath my feet. It's a crumbly, gravelly noise, not loud, but, to me, it sounds like crashing boulders.

James and Gina suddenly appear, from around the corner, both of them with startled expressions on their faces. I glance from one to the other. Neither says a word. Gina recovers first, smiles uncertainly.

I start to back away, toward the house. "I thought you'd both gone home," I say. I lift my mug of tea. "I just came out here to enjoy the night air for a minute. I'll leave you two alone."

"No," James says, and I see the abrupt change in his face, his composure regained. He puts his hand on my arm, detains me. "We were finished," he says.

Gina throws me a suspicious glance, wondering, I'm sure, how much I heard, then she and James exchange a long look—the meaning unclear to me.

"Good night, Gina," he says firmly.

She hesitates for a moment, indecisive, glances at me, only a brief glance, but the worry in her eyes is obvious, and then she gives her brother a curt nod and heads back to the cottage. She strides across the lawn, her body, tall and lean, a silhouette in the moonlight.

James walks me over to the picnic table, his hand clasped firmly around my arm. He pulls out a chair, has me sit. He's still wearing the clothes he had on this afternoon, but his silk tie is loose, draped around his neck, and his shirt is unbuttoned at the collar. He pulls up a chair next to me. We are silent. Nervously, I sip my tea. Feathers of fog, magical, almost supernatural, drift eerily in front of us, like numina of the night. The right side of James's face is dark, murky from a moonshadow, making him look sinister.

He says, "You think I tried to kill you fifteen years ago. Why didn't you tell the police that?"

I am quiet for a while. "I don't know," I say, shaking my head. "I guess because I knew they wouldn't believe me."

He grabs my arm, jerks me toward him in a sudden move. His face is inches from mine. "They wouldn't believe you?" he says, repeating my words, his voice a tense whisper. He glares at me, then releases my arm quite suddenly, as if he can't stand the feel of my flesh one second longer, as if *I'd* betrayed *him*. He leans back in the chair.

"You don't know anything," he says. "No one is

trying to kill you. Not Gina, not me." He stares. I glance away.

He grabs my arm again, forces me to look at him. "I'm the only person who can fill in your past," he says, his voice tight. "The only person—and if you pull another stunt like the one this evening, you're out of here. Don't think my mother can stop me from firing you. *I* run Byblos."

He relaxes his grip on me, slides back his chair, stands up. "Let's go," he says, and he pulls me up.

"Your mother wants me to sleep here tonight," I tell him.

He doesn't listen. He holds my hand, pulling me along. My car is parked around the side of the house, his is next to mine. Our footsteps crunch in the gravel driveway.

When we get to the cars, he says, "I'll follow you."

I start to say something, not understanding why he wants to follow me, but before I do he says, "We'll go to your home tonight. I want to see where you live."

The cool night air seems tense, jagged and dangerous. He's never shown any interest in my home before. He opens my car door. I stand there. I don't get inside.

"Your mother says I should stay here," I protest.

He looks down at me, his face half-covered in shadow, his expression unreadable. "Get in," he says, the tone of his voice resolute, unyielding.

I look away. The fog is thicker over the vineyards, kind of spooky the way it presses down, like a lid, as if it's trapping us here. "Some other time," I say. "My house is messy."

He puts his hand firmly on my shoulder, guides me into the car. "Get in," he says.

———

A narrow, brick-lined entryway opens onto the cluttered living room. With a quick, assessing glance, James takes in the two-foot brass horse reclining against the fireplace, the split-leaf philodendron growing wildly in the corner, the antique copper clothes boiler, the books jammed together, the African masks hanging on the walls, the set of weights on the floor.

We go off to the left, through an arched doorway, to the kitchen. The professor's love of nature brings a smirk to James's face. With all the kitchen walls painted to resemble the outdoors, and the ceiling an overcast canopy of gray, it's like stepping into a shady bog, mysterious: a huge marshland tree, frescoed across the south wall, spreads its branches behind the beechwood table; muted watercolors of swaying ferns and tall, swampy grasses smother everything in sight, reaching around the creamy-white kitchen appliances, around the refrigerator, the stove, sink, and cabinets; a painted mud hollow, dark and choking, is visible in the background; and birds, with wings spread, hover on the plaster, caught in midflight.

James sits on one of the beechwood chairs, forces me to my knees. I look up at him, his face brusque, more hard than handsome. Without him saying a word, I know what he wants. I unzip his pants, take out his penis, then hesitate when I feel his hands on my shoulders. I don't move. Slowly, he unbuttons the top of my blouse, just the two top buttons. He tucks my collar inside the blouse, then his fingers go around my neck.

"I used to control your breath," he says. "I'd put my hands around your neck and squeeze. You trusted me with your life."

His fingers press into my neck, threatening. "The first time," he says, "it frightened you. I could see it in your eyes, the panic, the terror when you thought you were going to die. You couldn't breathe. You tried to push me away, your hands clawed at my chest, but I wouldn't let go. I kept squeezing until you passed out."

I don't look at him. I feel his fingers around my throat.

"After the first time," he says, "you became more . . . generous with your neck. You offered it to me whenever I asked, but still, right before you'd pass out, there was always a look of panic in your eyes."

He pauses for a minute, his hands still circling my neck. "I would fuck you," he says, "and choke you at the same time. The first thing you felt from a lack of oxygen was euphoria. It gave you a feeling of bliss, rapture. It gave me power—the power of life and death." Again, he pauses. "Your life. Your death. It was in my hands."

I feel both thumbs on the base of my throat. Closing my eyes, I imagine the two of us together, long ago, and a brief picture of the past emerges, a made-up picture, a vision of him controlling the very air I breathed, of me offering my bare neck as a sacrifice. I picture the necklace of bruises, purple on my pale flesh, tokens of my misguided love. I allowed him to choke me. I wanted his touch. A tremor of fear goes through me. My stomach clenches, knots. He could do it now, he could squeeze, and there would be no way for me to fight back. I am powerless against his strength.

I look up and find him staring at me. The scar at his temple makes him look tough and unyielding, hardbitten by experience. I've asked him several times how he got the scar, but he refuses to talk about it. He says I'll learn in due time.

"You were eavesdropping on Gina and me," he says. His green eyes are cold, expressionless.

I cannot speak. His hands do not tighten, yet they feel like a noose around my neck, choking. I stare at him, frightened of what I know he is capable.

"What did you hear?" he asks, his voice even.

I shake my head. "Nothing," I manage to say, a shaky whisper. "Nothing."

He plays his fingers on my neck, tightening, releasing. I breathe heavily, afraid each breath may be my last. "You purposefully mentioned the police in front of my dinner guests," he says. He leans forward, puts his lips lightly on my forehead, a brief, burning kiss. He says, "Don't ever embarrass me like that again."

I hear the threat in his voice, unmistakable. His penis juts out at me, hard, erect.

"Suck it," he says.

His fingers around my neck are a warning. My heart beats fast with the sense of danger that will come if I don't suck him the way he wants. I put my tongue to his flesh. I take him into my mouth, work on his penis with an urgency galvanized by fear. I think of myself at seventeen, imagine how I sucked on him then. I take him deeper into my mouth, picture the young girl licking his balls and running her tongue along the shaft of his penis, then going lower to his asshole and swirling her tongue there, lapping at it, dipping her tongue inside, and then, quite suddenly, a heady time- and space-displacing sensation overtakes me. I feel a slender connection between my dead past and the living present, one providing life for the other, an umbilical cord pulling them together. I am that young girl, and I feel her need for James even as his hands circle her throat, and I feel his hands on me now, and I know I'm on the edge of something dangerous, the precipice between life and death, his fingers menacing, gently squeezing, and this proximity to danger makes me feel alive, more alive than I've ever felt before, sensations exaggerated, more intense, and I'm super-aware of his penis filling my mouth, every contour of it, the ridge around the top, the needle-eye slit of an opening, the serpentine vein, the silky-smooth texture, and this super-awareness makes me tingle, and then my own fear foolishly metamorphoses into desire, and I need him just as did she. I breathe in his earthy male odor. I suck on him slowly, deeply, wanting all of him in my mouth, all of him in me, despite the danger, despite the risk. I can feel myself sinking lower, pulled down bit by bit, and I can do nothing but go along. I plaster my face to the swale of his loins, his penis deep in my throat. I suck him harder. I suck him fast. I suck on him as if my life depends on it, suck on him until he comes inside me, the taste viscid and salty and sweetly bitter in my mouth, the taste glorious because I am conscious and I am alive, and while I'm swallowing, while his hands still clamp around my neck, holding me to him, I remember what the young girl—what I—had once said: his cum is the taste of life itself.

CHAPTER EIGHTEEN

I ring James's doorbell for the third time. He asked me to drop by this afternoon, but still there is no answer. One of the black hounds comes loping up the road, her tongue drooping. I pat her when she nuzzles my leg.

"Hiya, Chica," I say, scratching her behind the ears. "Where's James?"

But the dog isn't interested. She pads over to the shade of a tree, flops down.

Both James's black Cherokee and Gina's truck are parked in front. I find it odd that neither of them answers the door. I try the doorknob, a cautious twist, just to see if it's locked. It is.

I glance around. It's warm this afternoon, the air hot and heavy. I'm wearing a tank top and shorts, but still I feel the heat. The dog pricks up her ears, lumbers to her feet, goes off down the road in a slug-gish trot. Even Chica feels the heat. She disappears between a row of vines. The vineyards at Byblos are lush and green now, the berries, once only the size of peas, are ripening and swelling with juice and just beginning to change color. This change of color,

James told me, is called veraison. The green berries will turn an almost see-through greenish white for green grapes, and turn into a deep purple for red grapes. Once they've changed color, harvest is only a month and a half away.

Looking at the house, I wonder if James and Gina are inside, and if they are, what they could be doing. The drapes are drawn shut, the arched windows covered. I step closer to one of the windows, careful not to make any noise. I hold my breath, keeping quiet, apprehensive at what I might find.

But I find nothing at all. There is no crack between the curtains, no peephole for me this time. I walk over to the next window. I feel an unwelcome surge of jealously, imagining the two of them together. I step up to the sill. Again, no partition in the curtains. A twig cracks.

Nervously, I glance around, but no one is in sight. I see the winding road, the ancient oaks and the madrones and the olive trees; I see sunflowers nodding their yellow heads; I see the Cherokee, Gina's white truck, my convertible, grapevines in the distance. The air, heavy and still in this heat, seems weighted down. The sun blazes. Everything is quiet. I turn back to the house. I check the other windows, but the drapes cover them completely. Just as I'm deciding to try the back windows, the front door opens. James and Gina step out.

"I knocked," I say. "You didn't answer."

I'm talking to James, but Gina answers. "We didn't hear you," she says. Her hair is carelessly bunched up in a rubber band, with long strands of curly black hair hanging loose on one side, giving her a blowsy, unkempt presence. She plucks at a loose thread on her blouse, then gives me a nervous smile. She adds, "The music was too loud."

I didn't hear any music.

"Gotta go," she says, and quickly gets in her truck and drives off.

"Why did you ask me here?" I say, turning to James.

Instead of a reply, he tosses me his keys.

I give him a quizzical look, not understanding.

"The storage shed," he says. "It's all yours," and he goes back inside the house.

My heart pounds with excitement. I walk around to the back. The shed, like the house, is made from irregularly cut, reddish-brown stones, and the door is always kept locked—with the biggest stainless-steel padlock I've ever seen. I've asked James what he keeps inside, but he always replies with a vague answer, tools, equipment, odds and ends. Yet a normal lock would not suffice for these odds and ends. The storage shed is more secure than his home.

At the shed, I go through James's key ring and pick out the key that looks as if it would belong to a huge padlock. It works. Quickly, I remove the padlock, set it on the ground, then go through his other keys, trying one after another, to find the key that belongs to the lock on the door. After four attempts, I find the correct key. I push the door open. It creaks. The noise seems to reverberate in the hot air. I open the door farther. Peering inside, I see the darkened room, the closed-in space. The sole window is covered, boarded up. A feeling of claustrophobia comes over me. I want to turn around, but I don't. I step inside before I change my mind.

Except for three crates, nothing is in the shed. I try the edge of one of the crates. It's nailed securely. I'd need a crowbar to open it. All of the crates—which are almost as tall as I am, as wide as they're tall, and maybe two feet deep—are tied with rope.

Then, on the last crate, I see a red-painted crowbar. I pick it up.

All at once, a gut-clenching uneasiness comes over me. The shadows seem to press in on me, bringing to the surface my old fear of dark, closed-in spaces. My breathing, labored, comes in fits, panicked spasms. The room is too small, too dark. I have to get out of here. Backing out of the room, I'm near palsied with fear, my movements jerky, stuttering, my pulse thundering in my ears. I push against the door, squeeze through, shut it, then keep my hands on the door, holding it closed, keeping the nightmares at bay. I breathe the warm afternoon air, lots of room out here, I tell myself, lots of space, and I begin to relax now, my breath coming slower. I turn around, lean against the door. The crowbar, still in my hand, gives me an idea.

I go to the side of the shed, to the covered window, and pry off the boards, all of them, then go back inside. Muted sunlight filters through the dusty window. The room is still murky, but not as dark as before. I turn back to the crates—nailed shut and then unnecessarily tied with rope, as if to provide double protection from whatever lurks within.

I choose the crate nearest the window. I untie the rope, let it fall to the floor, then use the crowbar and try to pry the side board loose. It doesn't want to come. I keep working the crowbar, finally feel the nails give a little. I wedge it in, work it some more. I pry until the board, with a deep moaning creak, comes loose. I set the crowbar aside and use my hands to pull off the board completely. I lay the plank on the floor, then turn back to the crate.

Anxious, taking a deep breath, I pull out the packing material, white sheets of cloth, dingy and fusty smelling, and let it all drop to the floor. Inside, I find a stack of paintings. I slide out several. They are of the young girl, similar to the painting I found behind his armoire, the girl who was me. Her hair is long and black, her skin pale, a vulnerable look in her bent posture, but her face is unrecognizable, twisted in rage and fury, distorted beyond human proportions. I pull out the rest. More pictures of me, each of them different in location or position, yet similar in theme, a girl made ugly by anger.

I set aside the paintings, frustrated with the discovery. I was hoping to find something more concrete. I wanted clear evidence of James's guilt, evidence that would hold up in a court of law. The pictures prove nothing.

I open the second crate, find more paintings, pull them out. The girl—they are all of the girl. I look at each one, amazed at James's preoccupation, his obsession with her . . . his obsession with me. I arrange all the paintings around the shed, line them up along the walls. I stare at them, fascinated, a little queasy. When did he paint them—while he and I were lovers? Or after he'd left me for dead?

I pick up the crowbar, pry it under the board on the third, and final, crate, expecting to find more of the same. The nails are rusty and groan as I pull them out. I lay down the crowbar, tug the long piece of board with my hands, yanking it loose. I hear the shed door squeak.

The board still in my hands, I turn around.

James stands there, blocking the doorway, his body, like the stone structure of this shed, solid and unbreachable. He coolly looks over at me, at the opened crates, at the sheets of grimy white packing material, at the paintings scattered around the room.

"Why did you paint so many?" I ask him.

He ignores me, changes the subject. "You

shouldn't have called the police," he says. "It didn't do you any good, did it?"

I don't reply. A detective, following up, came out to see me earlier today, a nice man in his late forties, but said there was nothing, really, he could do. The accidents appeared to be accidents. There was no evidence, no indication at all, that someone was trying to harm me. He gave me his card, said to call if anything else happened.

The plank is heavy in my hands. It's nearly as tall as I, reaching to the top of my nose. I look out over it.

He walks toward me in that slow, sure way he has, each step a statement of his authority, as if nothing in this world could ever quell him. I grip the plank, daunted. He unbuckles his belt. He slides it out from the belt loops, doubles it over in his hand. It's thick and stiff, like a weapon.

"You deserve to be punished," he says. "I'm going to beat you for calling the police."

I watch his hands, can't keep my eyes off the belt. I hold the plank in front of me like a shield.

"Put it down," he says, then he smiles when he sees me hesitate, smiles snidely, as if he'd enjoy a confrontation. "Put it down," he repeats, his voice as unyielding as steel.

A few heartbeats go by. I want to do as he asks—I know it will go easier for me if I do—but my hands won't obey. They are clamped around the plank, my knuckles white. "Are you going to hurt me?" I ask, my pulse racing.

He steps forward, pries the plank out of my hands, lays it on the floor. "Yes," he says.

He drapes the belt around his neck, as if it were a tie. He pulls my tank top over my head, then removes my shorts and sandals and underwear. I stand before him, immobile, my stomach clenching. Placing his hand on the side of my face, he says, "You like to be hurt."

He moves his hand lower, to my breast. He squeezes my nipple, pulls on it. Looking down, he watches me. He's a man marked by the sun, his skin deeply tanned yet his hair lighter now than a month ago, bleached from hours spent outdoors, the pale blond color of flax. He's wearing a short-sleeved shirt. I reach up, put my hand on his arm, feel the muscle of his biceps, the skin warm.

I lean against him, close my eyes. He works my nipple, rubbing it between his fingers, pinching it sharply, pressing down, then tugging at it. He switches to the other nipple.

"Say it," he says. His hand goes down between my legs. He insinuates a finger inside me. I ask for another. Working as one, his fingers feel like a snake, sliding around, twisting, opening me up. I push closer to him. "Say it," he repeats.

I know what he wants to hear. "I like to be hurt," I murmur, and I shudder because I know that it is true. I thought I was through with the pain and violence, through with it fifteen years ago, but apparently I'm not.

"It's in your nature," he says, as if he could read my mind. He takes me over to the window, has me grip the stone sill, spread my legs. He leans down, and I feel his mouth on my ass, the wet slide of tongue and lips, feel his fingers inside me, pushing. I know he'll fuck me, but not now, not just yet. He'll punish me with the belt first. The inevitability of this, knowing there is no escape, makes me feel much calmer. I relax, waiting for it to come. I want it to come.

He says, "Tell me again."

"I like to be hurt," I say.

He leans down and kisses me on the shoulder. "Good girl," he says, as if I were a small child being congratulated for telling the truth, then he straightens up and brings the belt down hard on my ass.

I scream.

He brings it down harder, and I scream again. Soon, he has me crying, the belt hot and cruel on my ass, but I do not resist him. I take what he gives me. I take the pain because I know the fucking, afterward, will be even better. Or perhaps I take the pain for some other reason. Maybe it is in my nature. I don't know. Maybe it is.

He gives me more, more than I think I can stand. My thighs and buttocks feel raw, abused, and my tears flow freely. Once again, he lashes out with the belt. I cringe. I cry. My body is slick with sweat; my fingers, white knuckled, grip the windowsill. Through tear-soaked lashes, I see the pictures of the girl scattered around the shed. We are becoming one, she and I, we are becoming one. The belt cuts across my ass. I let out a strangled, sobbing shriek. The girl watches, approvingly, a witness to my submission, and then James is turning me around, dropping his jeans, and lifting me up. My legs lock around his hips. Without preamble, he fucks me against the shed. He fucks me fast, hard, bores into me like a rutting animal. He makes grunting, peremptory noises, animal noises. I cling to him, take the brutal pounding of his penis. His face—by the sheer intensity of desire—is wildly contorted, and I understand I'm just a receptacle for him at this moment, nothing more than an available cunt, a vessel to receive his cum, but instead of feeling used, this insight excites me, and I become caught up in the ferocity of his fucking, the brutishness of it, his flesh slamming into mine, and I want more, demand more, even while the rational part of my mind, the part concerned with self-preservation, is glancing out the dusty window, wondering if Gina is there, watching.

"I'm going to get something to drink," I say to James. "Do you want anything?"

We'd just taken a shower, and I watch him as he lies on the bed. Timidly, I put my hand on his chest, feel the planes of muscles under the soft skin. His eyes are closed, but I see a faint smile. I move my hand to his leg, to the firmness of his thigh. I like to touch him—more than that, I feel an almost ineffable need to touch him, to feel his flesh.

"No," he murmurs, his eyes still closed. His lashes are long and sensuous, curving upward.

I grab the shirt he'd thrown on the trunk, the one he was wearing earlier, and put it on. It's short-sleeved, with thin maroon stripes, and the tails go down below my knees. The shirt carries his smell.

In the kitchen, I open the refrigerator and look inside. I take out a few oranges, squeeze them, pour the juice into a glass, then walk to the back part of the house. It has a severe, grave feel to it, the lighting dim now, shadows sneaking around the corners, the brick floor cool under my bare feet. I take a drink, look at one of his paintings on the walls. None of them, thankfully, are of me.

I hear James, the muffled sound of his bare footsteps as he crosses the room. He stands behind me, and I can tell that he, also, is gazing at the picture.

"Your paintings," I say, turning to look up at him. "They're so dark. All of them."

He nods slowly. He wears nothing, but his nakedness does not discomfort him as mine does with me. His scars, visible or psychic, need no concealment. He wears his flesh easily, his stance conveying a sense of confidence and unchallenged authority. He is the scion of Byblos.

I gaze at the picture again. Undeniably, it's fascinating, the violence mesmerizing. It draws me in, makes me want to keep staring.

James says, "You were in love with me before."

I glance up at him. I think of the other paintings, the ones of me in the shed, in the crates, the ugliness in my face. "I didn't look like I was in love," I say. "Not at all."

He takes my hand, leads me up the spiral staircase. When we get to the top, he goes over to the antique trunk, opens it, pulls out a length of rope, comes back to me. "Put your hands out," he says, and he begins tying them together in front of me.

"I don't paint pretty pictures," he says, winding the cord around my wrists. "Surface realities don't interest me. I want to know what's underneath, the tension below the calm, the darkness under the light." He knots the rope, pulls it tight. He goes over to the trunk again, begins looking for something inside. He takes out the blankets, the extra pillows, the whips he keeps in there, the lengths of rope.

"Love," he says, still searching in the trunk, "is typically portrayed as this beautiful, soft emotion, as a place where tenderness prevails. But love doesn't always go there, and it doesn't always lead one to an exalted state of bliss."

He looks over at me. "Do you know what I mean?" he says. A nerve at his temple throbs. "You have to dig deeper, go beneath the surface."

Something about the tone of his voice worries me. It's all wrong—distant, unfeeling, a cold finality in it that I haven't heard before. He seems miles away from me, remote. He pulls another blanket out of the trunk.

"What are you doing?" I ask, but he ignores my

question. His lips are pressed together in a tight, severe line. The trunk is empty now, everything piled up beside it, and it comes to me, all of a sudden, that he wasn't looking for anything at all. He was emptying the trunk. I get a panicked feeling when I realize what's coming next. The rope around my wrists chafes. I back away.

"Why did you want me to see all the paintings in the shed?" I ask him.

"Sometimes," he says, and he watches me closely, the way a cat will watch a mouse, just biding its time, "sometimes, love is violent and destructive. Sometimes, it's obsessive." His eyes are ice-cold, too objective, calculating. I try to think, try to stop the panic from creeping up. He stares at me, waiting. The air between us is thick with tension. He says, "And sometimes, it brings death."

I edge for the stairs, start to bolt, manage to get in a couple of feet before I feel his arms around my waist, grabbing me. I try to break free, but, easily, he picks me up. He carries me the few feet to the antique trunk. I struggle, but my hands are tied and he holds me tightly. I scream as loud as I can, hoping someone will hear. He bends over, sets me down, my legs scraping the wooden sides.

"Don't do this," I say. I beg. I plead. I try to get up, but he places his hands on my shoulders and pushes me down. I scream out, kick him with my legs. He fumbles with them, shoves them inside, and slams the lid shut. I hear the lock click.

At first I am silent. It's pure black in here, no light at all seeping through the trunk. The blackness is absolute. I hear my heart beating, a loud thumping sound that registers my fear. I grope in the dark with my legs, feel the smooth sides of the trunk. He's taken everything out. I start to breathe in jerky spasms, gasping for air, feeling my claustrophobia close in on me. With my legs, I kick at the lid. It doesn't budge. I kick again, then begin screaming. I yell, I curse, I pound the trunk but get only a muffled *thud thud thud* and sore feet for all my efforts.

I try to calm down, try to breathe slowly, but I can't. Tears roll down my cheeks. Everything is black, utterly. I feel light-headed and nauseated. The trunk seems to move, whirl around and wobble, get smaller and smaller, but I'm sure it's only the terror taking over my mind. Minutes pass, hours maybe, I can't tell. The blackness obliterates everything, squeezes down on me like a weight, suffocating, and I'm sobbing and banging my head against the wood, and then I feel something pressing against my eyes, and I think of blood, blood in my eyes, blood all around, with every part of my body hurting, hurting so badly it goes beyond the word *pain*, and I can't move or speak, but I feel the bumps, the bumps in the road, each one jarring, and everything is so dark, so black, and I try to move one part of me, my finger, just my finger, to assure myself that I still exist, that I am real, but my finger won't move, and I'm squished in here, all broken bones and sticky blood, wrapped inside something, a carpet, a blanket, I don't know, but confined, with everything closing in on me, in the trunk, not the antique trunk but the trunk of a car—his car?—the blackness overwhelming, the rusty metallic stench of my own blood mixed with the ammonia smell of urine that I also know is mine, confined in an area so tight that my world, even my terror, finally ceases to exist, and all I pray for now is death, the sweet release of death.

"You've come between me and Gina," I hear him say, a faraway sound that brings me back, back to the loft and the antique trunk, away from the disjointed image that invaded my mind. I am in the trunk, locked in the trunk. The blackness expands, goes on forever. He has defeated me, I realize, and I may never get out of here.

"You've upset Gina," he says. "I don't like that."

The sides of the trunk are closing in. I want to know the truth before I die. Guessing, I say, "You took me to an empty field in the trunk of your car." My voice is muffled and weepy, and the words come out with difficulty. I sigh, a choked sound, then say, "You were going to bury me."

James doesn't say anything.

With my legs, I feel the sides of the trunk, the top, the bottom, built like a coffin. The blackness collapses in on itself, stifling me. My flesh itches, itches all over.

The silence is long, intolerable. I roll over on my side, rest my cheek against the wood. I think he will kill me now, finish what he began fifteen years ago, and there is nothing I can do to save myself. I press my body against the side of the trunk, just to feel something solid next to me. It's cool, hard, and brings no comfort. I thought I was so smart, calling the police, but James isn't afraid of them. My body feels leaden, heavy. I don't want to think of what will come next. I open my mouth to speak, but nothing comes out. I try again. "Tell me what happened," I say numbly. "I need to know the truth."

There is a moment of quiet, then, his voice hushed, he says, "Do you remember anything else?"

I shake my head, but of course he doesn't see. "No," I say.

He is silent.

The blackness engulfs me. I'll never see light again. "I need to know what happened," I say.

I wait. He won't deny me this, I know he won't. He can't.

He is quiet. I listen for noises. I know there must

be noises—the house creaking and settling, a groan coming from the pipes—but here, in the trunk, nothing comes to me. The blackness annihilates, wiping out everything.

"Tell me," I say, needing to hear a voice, needing to hear the truth.

Instead, I hear the click of the lock, then the sound of the lid being opened. I blink, blinded by the light in the room. He reaches down, lifts me out of the trunk, carries me over to the bed. He takes the rope off my wrists. Slowly, astonishingly, it sinks in that he isn't going to harm me.

He says, "Do you know why I locked you in the trunk?"

I don't answer.

A faint smile lifts his lips. "Simply because I can," he says. "I'll do whatever I want—and you'll let me. That's the nature of surrender."

I don't say anything. I feel too disoriented to speak, feel I may cry—with relief, with anger—if I open my mouth. We sit. For minutes, we just sit.

"You were going to bury me," I say finally.

He sits next to me on the bed. "I didn't say that. You're only guessing. Eventually, I'll give you the truth, but not yet. You and I still aren't finished. You have a lot more to learn."

I'm still wearing his shirt. It's damp with sweat. He lays his hand on my leg. He says, "I hope I'll never have to choose between you and Gina." He leans closer. I feel his breath on my neck. He whispers, "Because I'll choose her."

Nervously, feeling cowed, I play with my hands in my lap, not looking at him. I start to get up. He pulls me back down. He says, "Gina told me what you said—that I was falling in love with you."

I don't say anything.

"You're right about that," he says softly. He presses his lips to my forehead. He says, "I am in love with you."

The words reverberate in the air, going round and round, like an echo. I don't speak, and in my silence the words remain undiluted. They stay out there, whirling around above me, foreign, unfamiliar. I've never heard those words before. Never. I don't know what to do with them.

CHAPTER NINETEEN

I'm not very helpful today. Feeling rather listless in the warm air, I follow Mrs. McGuane around the garden. She's wearing a wide-brimmed hat to protect herself from the sun, a cartwheel hat, and her dress, a pale yellow, goes down to the middle of her calves. She seems to have enough energy for the both of us. She cuts an eggplant at the stem, its skin dark purple and smooth and so shiny it looks polished. This is the best time of the year for summer vegetables, and we harvest them daily—glossy eggplants, tender summer squash, finger-sized carrots, peppers, potatoes, broccoli, and green beans. We pick everything as it ripens, eating it the same day, giving away what we're unable to consume.

"There was a tangy, ripened one that I particularly enjoyed," she says now, cutting another eggplant, placing it in the basket. We went to a goat-cheese tasting earlier today in Sonoma, and she's talking about the cheeses we tried. She spends a lot of time with me now, even more than before. Since my so-called accidents, she's been protective of me, almost maternal. It's not a feeling I've experienced before.

She meanders to another section of the garden, nattering away about cheeses, the mild fresh ones with a lemony aroma, the aged ones, pungent and nutty. I listen, but really I'm thinking of James, and what he said yesterday: he loves me. And then I think of the opened crates and all the pictures scattered around the shed. I think of his obsession for me.

"Why, Carly!" Mrs. McGuane says, her tone changing. "That's lovely."

I think she's referring to the fennel, the tall, feathery masses of it, and the few ladybugs and lacewings flying about, but then I see she's looking at my feet. The cuff on my left pant leg is turned up on the side, exposing the gold chain. Although she has no idea of its significance, I'm embarrassed she's seen the ankle bracelet. Quickly, I smooth down my pant leg.

"That's charming, dear," she says. "You should wear it with a dress, to show off your ankle. Let me take a closer look."

She bends down, lifts my pant leg. "Exquisite," she says, fingering the chain.

I hold my breath, feeling nervous, hoping she doesn't notice it has no clasp, no way to remove it from my ankle.

"It suits you," she says. She straightens up. "It just occurred to me that you never wear jewelry."

"No," I say. "I guess I don't." When I got out of the hospital, I never wore earrings or necklaces or rings, never wore anything that would cause people to take a second look. Even after my scars healed I couldn't bring myself to wear jewelry, thinking it would only bring scrutiny. I wear a watch, that is all. And now the chain.

"You really should," I hear Gina say, and I turn around, startled, wondering how long she's been standing there. She reaches out, as if she's going to touch my face, but then she pulls back her hand, changing her mind.

"Earrings would look nice on you," she says. "Your hair is so short that . . ." She doesn't finish the thought.

Ever since I turned down her fifty-thousand-dollar offer, and ever since I called the police, there've been subtle changes in her behavior, an edginess, and sudden losses of composure. If James is concerned about the police, he hides it well. Not so with Gina. Her emotions are closer to the surface, more exposed, and now there's a frazzled look about her all the time, her appearance slowly deteriorating by the day. She's wearing faded blue jeans that are scuffed on the knees, and a sleeveless blouse missing a button.

"You look pale," Mrs. McGuane says to her daughter. "Aren't you feeling well?"

Gina gazes at the distant hills, the vineyards backing into them. Absently, she says, "I haven't been sleeping. It's hectic right now, trying to get everything ready for the crush."

By the crush, I know she's referring to the harvest, but Gina isn't worried about that. The harvest is still a long way off. Her loss of sleep has nothing to do with crushing grapes. Mrs. McGuane nods, tells her to take it easy, that nothing is more important than good health, then she wanders off, carrying her basket.

Gina waits until her mother is out of earshot, then says, "I saw her looking at your ankle."

I don't respond.

She kneels on the ground, raises my pant leg. She hesitates just a moment, the cuff in hand, says nothing, then I feel her fingers on my ankle, a gentle touch, sensuous, her skin warm on mine.

"Why don't you want me here?" I ask her.

She doesn't reply. Her finger, between the gold chain and my flesh, moves slowly around my ankle, her touch as light as a feather stroke.

"James made one of these for me," she says finally, her voice so quiet I can barely hear. "I took it off," she adds. "In the end."

"Why?" I ask her.

She smooths down my pant leg, then stands up. "He asks for too much," she says, looking away. "If you stay, you'll find that out." She shifts to her other foot, sighs.

"Are you jealous?" I ask. "Of me?"

When she hears this, she turns to me sharply, frowning. She opens her mouth to say something, then closes it. She works her jaw. Hard lines crease her forehead. Then, in a weary sigh, as if life is too much effort, her face softens. The hardness fades. She reaches out and, in a tender gesture, puts her hand on my cheek. She holds it there a second, then walks away, over to the cottage, one hand shoved in the back pocket of her jeans.

I hear Mrs. McGuane say something. "What?" I ask, turning around. She's kneeling on the ground, over by the block of sweet corn. I walk to her.

"The zucchini," she says, looking up at me. "How many will you need for tonight's dinner?" Dark sunglasses hide her eyes.

I look at the ground beside her, trying to concentrate. Zucchini and pumpkins and variously colored squashes—pale green, bright yellow, fiery orange—trail the ground between the rows of corn, winding through the tall stems. I glance back at the cottage, but Gina is gone.

Leaning down, I inspect the zucchini. "Pick only the tiny ones," I tell Mrs. McGuane, "four or five of them." The smaller ones, I've learned from recent experience, are the most flavorful. I watch as she cuts them from the stem with a sharp blade, but my mind is on Gina and the golden anklet she once wore.

"Why don't you move into the house," Mrs. McGuane says suddenly, glancing up at me.

"What?" I say, confused.

"You're here all the time. There's no need for you to rent a house in town. Not when I have so many empty rooms."

Her unexpected offer stuns me.

When I don't reply, she says, "Well, dear, think about it. You don't have to make up your mind right away."

Move into her home? Why not, I think. I like it here, I like Mrs. McGuane. My gaze goes to the garden. Butterflies drift and swoop through the fragrant lavender and the yellow asters and the grayish-green rosemary that smells like tea. I see a hummingbird, with brilliantly colored wings, dart among the showy fuchsias, dipping its long bill into the bell-shaped flowers. The McGuanes' garden is full of life and energy.

Why not move in, I think again.

And then I remember why not—because one of Mrs. McGuane's children will be going to jail. She won't want me anywhere near her when that happens.

I hear gravel-crunching noises. I look up. The black Cherokee pulls around the driveway, then stops near the patio. James gets out, walks over to us. He's dressed in dark slacks and a tailored salmon-hued shirt, the color setting off his deep tan, and he appears as invincible as always, his stride long and sure, his arms as large as oars. For some reason, I take pride in his stalwartness, and just seeing him makes my gut tingle with anticipation, makes me think of fucking and—despite the risk—of what he'll require next. Who has the greater obsession, I wonder—he or I?

"Gina's not feeling well," Mrs. McGuane tells him. "Touch of the flu, I suspect." She's still kneeling on the ground. She places one hand on her waist, looks up at him. Gloves, made of soft leather, cover her hands. "I'm sure she'll be fine in a couple of days."

James dangles his keys, a worried expression on his face. His twin is not holding up well. He looks beyond the stretch of lawn, over at the cottage.

"She's resting," his mother says. She follows his gaze to the cottage, then turns back to him. A few wisps of white hair have fallen out from under the big hat. "Don't you go over there. I told her to get a few hours' sleep."

James nods. "That should help," he says absently. "She hasn't been sleeping."

But he knows what's really bothering Gina, and it's not the flu, and it's nothing that can be helped by a few hours of sleep. Her sickness comes not from disease, but from me. My presence is like a cancer, eating at her, taking her over, making her ill.

He stuffs his hands into his pants pockets. A lock of blond hair falls over his creased forehead. When he sees his mother watching him, he relaxes his face—a conscious effort—and gives her a smile.

"More zucchini?" he says, scanning the plants at her feet, but I can tell he isn't at all interested in the garden vegetables today. He only pretends to listen as his mother tells him I'm making a ratatouille for dinner.

She gazes at the winding trail of squash. She cuts another zucchini, places it in the basket, then stands up, grunting a little. James reaches forward to give her a hand.

"Stiff bones," she says. She straightens her hat,

pats the skirt of her dress. Her leather gloves make a soft soughing sound against the cottony material. She turns and heads for the onions and green peppers.

I pick up the basket, but neither James nor I follow her. He crosses his arms in front of his chest. He stares down at me.

"Will you be coming for dinner tonight?" his mother calls back over her shoulder.

"No," he says, still looking at me. "I'm busy."

She floats away in her big floppy hat, giving us a wave with the back of her hand, a trilling of gloved fingers in the warm summer air.

James steps closer. "Come over tonight," he says, making it sound like a command. "Right after dinner."

He walks away, not allowing me the chance to refuse. At this point, however, a refusal is beyond me.

CHAPTER TWENTY

I stand at his doorway. James hasn't yet invited me in. I can wait. I'm in no hurry. I have an uneasy feeling about tonight, that he ordered me here for something more than just sex. Outside, it's still light, the sky, in the far horizon, a dusky rosy hue.

He looks down at me, his eyes clear and, in this early-evening illumination, a deep, rich green. He smells lightly of cologne, a spice-and-dried-leaf smell, a faint pleasant odor, not the least bit over-powering, but his presence is—the black shirt and slacks; the rugged hardiness of him, his thick arms and muscled shoulders; and the look on his face, darkly mysterious, intense.

He swings open the door, steps aside for me to enter. I feel as if I'm walking into a trap. He am-bushed me last night—I never saw it coming—im-prisoned in the antique trunk, and he could do it again. A rush of apprehension goes through me, then a corresponding rush of excitement. Life on the edge is more complicated than I'd imagined. I con-sidered not coming tonight, but only briefly, and only halfheartedly. I need this drug he proffers. Even apart from him, I feel his pull. He's like a magnet, attracting. Walking past him, I brush against his arm, feel the soft fabric of his shirt.

He closes the door behind me. It shuts with a hollow slam, sealing me in. The sound makes me feel, once again, that I've entered a trap. I try to shake off the feeling. I'm wearing something sexy, a slinky red dress with spaghetti straps, but I don't think he's noticed. He seems preoccupied, looks at me as if I could be either friend or foe.

I walk into the living area. It's dim, lit only by a soft light from a brass floor lamp in the corner. Upstairs, a light shines in the loft. I go over to the leather couch, then stop when I see the painting leaning against it, the picture that was hidden behind the armoire. That damn portrait again. I cannot take my eyes off her. She dominates the room, takes it over. She's like a vortex, sucking everything in. This was me. The anger, the ugliness, the pain. The picture could've been painted when I woke from the coma, when I saw my scars, and the body and face that seemed so foreign, and the legs that wouldn't work, when I realized my parents would never come. I was full of anger and bitterness, my face distorted beyond recognition. The attack made me wary not only of people but also of life. It put me on autopilot, never really living, never really loving.

James walks up behind me, puts his hand on my shoulder, his fingers touching the base of my throat. "Do you still think I'm the one who tried to kill you?" he asks.

His fingers on my neck feel like a condemnation—and if I answer incorrectly, I will know their censure. I'm not sure how to reply, so I say nothing, nothing at all.

He says, "If I wanted to, I could've killed you last night."

I wait, wondering what will come next. The room

grows dimmer as the outside light darkens. Through an arched window I see the sun sinking below the horizon. The girl stares at me. Her face is distended with rage, yet her vulnerability shows through in the skin so pale, and in her posture, slouched, as if she's overwhelmed by her predicament. The paintings on the walls portray death and destruction but in a generalized way, as if James is making a comment about the nature of man. This painting and the ones in the shed are more specific, more concrete, a comment about one person, a comment about me, my anger, my destruction—portraits by an artist obsessed with one subject alone.

Finally, his voice low, he says, "You'll learn more about her tonight."

He moves his fingers along my throat, a soft caress. He places his other hand on me also, and they form a gentle noose around my neck. I feel stiff and unbending, knowing the strength in his hands, realizing the vulnerability of my position. I also feel the rush, the flirt with danger that makes me come alive.

I reach up, put my hand on his arm but don't try to pull it away. I move closer, feel him against me, feel his shirt against the bare skin of my shoulders.

"I chose you to be my pupil," he says. "We played a game—you worshiped me, I controlled you. It worked out well, we both got what we wanted."

The girl's eyes are red-rimmed and ruined. I look as if I got much more than what I'd bargained for.

He says, "In the end, I could do whatever I wanted. You never protested. I controlled everything about you."

His fingers are a gentle pressure around my neck. I'm wary of what he's leading up to. He wants to control my breath, I think, choke me, put bruises on my neck as he did fifteen years ago. He wants to control the air I breathe. "Why did you choose her?" I ask, stalling.

He doesn't answer immediately. The darkness of the room gathers, creeps up. I feel his breath against my cheek. Finally, he says, "My father kept a journal. He was obsessive about it, not letting a day go by without making an entry. It was as if his life had no validation unless he could put it down on paper. Every evening before bed, every single night of his life, no matter how exhausted he was, he'd sit in his study, recording the day's events. For him, it was a compulsion. He could no more discard his journal than you can ignore your past."

Inclining my head toward the picture, I say, "What does that have to do with you choosing her?"

Shadows darken the corners of the room, making the silence seem profound. "You can't always choose your obsessions," he answers quietly. "Sometimes, they choose you."

He takes my hand and leads me up to the loft. He sits on the bed while I stand in front of him. Except for the blondness of his hair, his presence is dark, foreboding. He removes my clothes, one piece at a time, my shoes first, then my red dress, my panties. I'm not wearing a bra.

He says, "I'm going to humiliate you." He adds, "The way I did fifteen years ago."

My first reaction is relief—there will be no choking tonight—but quickly trepidation takes its place. I know the quelling influence embarrassment can have. Bending forward, I place my hands on his shoulders, lean against him. I feel myself trembling, nervous of what he's planning. "You don't have to do that," I say, and even to me my voice sounds small and scared. I'm speaking in a whisper. "I'll let you do whatever you want."

He reaches down and places his hand around my

ankle. He runs his finger along the gold anklet he'd placed on my foot. "Let me?" he says, and he smiles just a little. "You *belong* to me. I can do whatever I want. I don't need your permission."

He moves his hand up my leg, up my thigh, to my waist, a smooth, gentle movement. The blackness of his shirt sleeve makes my skin appear even more pale than it is.

"You sound just like you did fifteen years ago," he says. "At first, you didn't understand the difference. You thought you were giving me something, letting me do what I wanted. You had to learn you couldn't give me what was already mine. I'll teach you that again. Tonight."

I wait for him to continue. The tingle I feel is fear, but it's also something else: life, a heightened awareness of life.

He unbuttons his shirt cuffs, rolls up the sleeves. He says, "Have you ever seen an enema?"

I stare at him, then shake my head. I know what they are, of course, but I've never actually seen one.

He says, "There're several different kinds. Some are quite simple, a nozzle attachment hooked up to the showerhead, where I control the temperature and flow of water at the faucet. The downside of that setup is that it allows only water enemas. Sometimes, I like to add a little coffee in the water—which I can't do with that setup. Sometimes, I'll add a little wine." He shrugs. "It depends on my mood, on what effect I want the person to experience. Coffee will give you a rush, wine will get you drunk."

He says all of this in a matter-of-fact tone. He is the teacher, I am the pupil. He pulls me closer, brushes his lips across my stomach. The catheter wasn't humiliating enough—now he intends to give me an enema. I don't want to do this. I'd prefer a whipping.

"Then there's the fountain syringe," he continues. "It's similar to a hot water bottle with a long hose. The bag holds two quarts of liquid and is hooked overhead, from the ceiling or from a stand. Insert the nozzle in someone's rectum and gravity takes care of the rest. You can even buy a heavy-duty, gallon-sized bag."

He pauses a moment. His gaze goes to my breasts. I think he will suck them, but he doesn't. "I've experimented with all of them," he says, "but my favorite is the bulb syringe enema. It's very simple, a plastic bulb or bottle on one end, a nozzle on the other. I find it's more personal than the others. There's more contact. I direct the flow of liquid by squeezing the bulb, and it goes in as fast or as slow as I wish it to."

He slides his hands around to my buttocks. He holds me as if I am his possession. *I belong to him.* I've uttered those words. He says, "You've used a turkey baster, haven't you?"

I nod.

"In a pinch, that'll work also. Sometimes, one must improvise."

By his blank expression, I can't tell if he's kidding or not. His hands play with my buttocks, squeezing, releasing. I don't want to do this.

"There's a long history of enemas," he continues. "Ancient Egyptians used them, and enemas were extremely popular in the aristocratic courts of France in the seventeenth and eighteenth centuries. It was part of their daily regimen."

Again, he looks me over as he speaks, my breasts, my naval, the blond pubic hair between my legs. He looks at me as if it were the first time. The words he spoke last night go over and over in my mind: *I love you.*

"Some of the early solutions contained tobacco,"

he says, "which gave the receiver an instant jolt of nicotine. In fact, one of the most popular treatments for reviving women who had fainted was to blow smoke into their bowels with a pipe."

He pauses for a second, his gaze lingering on the scar at my hip, his handiwork from years past, then says, "People have eroticized enemas probably for as long as they've been around. Some enemas can be dangerous, however. Different solutions can irritate the lining of the intestine or, even worse, they can kill."

He tightens his hold on me, looks now into my eyes. He says, "But, with a little research, with a little experimentation, one learns what is safe and what isn't."

He stands up. Wrapping his hand around my arm, he walks me toward the bathroom. He says, "You hated the enemas at first. When I was finished, I made you squat over the drain and evacuate in front of me. You found the utter lack of privacy, the fact that you had no control over your own bowels, degrading. But it humbled you. It made you more submissive, more willing to depend on me since you had no choice. Your humiliation was erotic—not for you, of course, but for me."

He takes me inside the bathroom, flips on the light switch. Instantly, I'm reflected in all the floor-to-ceiling mirrors. My nakedness glares back at me. The brightness of the room makes me squint. James, fully clothed, looms next to me, towering, taking up a lot of space. The black tiles on the floor gleam. On the counter, I see two enemas.

He goes over to the sink and begins washing his hands.

"I don't want to do this," I say. "I can't. It's too . . . demeaning."

He doesn't say anything. He washes his hands.

It's just an enema, I tell myself, but I can't get past the indignity. His strange love mystifies.

He turns off the water, reaches for a blue towel, dries his hands. "Come here," he says.

I stay where I am, shifting from one foot to the other. I don't want to make him angry, but I don't want the enema, either. I don't know what to do.

A heartless smile crosses his face. "You look exquisite," he says coolly. "Naked . . . nervously bobbing from one foot to the other . . . your breasts jiggling slightly . . . a look of sheer panic on your face—you are lovely, but you've waited too long."

He grabs my arm, pulls me over to the counter, shoves me face down. "Your reluctance is tiring," he says. He keeps his hand on my back, pinning me to the counter. "Shall I beat you into submission?"

Bending over, he places his head close to mine. He whispers, "I thoroughly enjoy beating you. You have an ass that practically begs to be slapped: round, plump, heart-shaped, so pale my hand leaves an immediate mark."

I wait for the pain, but instead he caresses my ass. Closing my eyes, I take in the luxury of his touch, wishing he was fucking me. I've already surrendered to him, I know that I have. I'm at his mercy, utterly, a junkie for this drug that only he can give.

"I'm sorry," I say quietly. The counter tile is cool on my cheek. I feel James's lips on my neck, feel the warmth of his breath.

"That's better," he says, and he straightens up, leads me to the center of the room. He places his hand on my back, has me bend over, put my palms on the floor. I see my reflection in the mirrors. It's all too clear. I turn away, stare at the black-tiled floor.

"Spread your legs," he says, and he puts his own leg between my feet, forces me to spread them. "You look quite delightful with your ass up in the air," he says.

He walks away, over to the sink, gets something out of the cabinet, then comes back to me. In the mirror reflection, I see him putting lubricant on his fingers. He lets the tube fall to the floor. He slides his greased fingers, one, two, and then three, inside my ass. He works them, twisting, moving them around.

I push back toward him, wanting more than just his fingers in my ass. He reaches around with his other hand, first slides his fingers over my clitoris, then slips two or maybe three into my vagina, his other fingers still wedged in my ass. I feel so full, stretched out, as if he might tear me apart, but he keeps his thumb on my clitoris, rubbing it the way I like, keeping it up until it makes me moan, makes me forget the discomfort and want even more. Abruptly, before I can come, he removes his fingers, goes back to the sink. I hear the water running, and know he is filling the syringes. This time, I don't protest.

He turns off the faucet. I glance in the mirror. He returns, carrying both enema syringes. I feel the tip of the nozzle entering me. He squeezes the bulb. The water makes a very soft, gurgling noise, and it slushes inside me, warm, pleasant, erotic in a soothing kind of way. This surprises me. I hadn't expected it to be erotic. I don't resist him at all. He squeezes again. The water enters me in a pulsing, sensual flow. He empties the enema, then immediately inserts the second. I watch him from the mirror, standing behind me as if he was a quarterback waiting for the snap of the ball, shoulders squared, bulldog strong, sleeves rolled up, forearms tanned and sinewy, working. I close my eyes, relax. I think of him fucking me. He removes the nozzle.

"I'm not finished with you yet," he says softly, seeing I'm ready to fuck. "I'm just getting started."

He goes back to the sink, refills the syringes, then once again deposits the contents in my ass. He does this several times. I start to fill up, feel waterlogged and uncomfortable. The eroticism of it is gone now. I hear the rustle of a zipper, then his penis is inside my ass, and he's fucking me, but I'm so full I can barely stand it. He ignores my discomfort. He pumps inside me, grasping me by the hips, holding tightly, hammering away, his cock like a giant syringe now. I think he will come inside my ass, but he suddenly pulls out. He goes over to the counter, watches me. I start to straighten up.

"Did I say you can move?" he asks. He leans against the counter, arms folded.

I return my palms to the floor. "I can't hold it in any longer," I say, squirming around. My ass is sore. I feel I'm about to burst. He doesn't care. He seems to enjoy my distress. Seconds, agonizing seconds, go by.

"All right," he finally says. "You can let it out."

I clean myself, feeling humbled as he said I would. When I come out of the bathroom, I see he's hooked up one of his leather harnesses. He's naked now, and he crooks his finger at me. I cross over to him. The contraption is on the end of a heavy-duty bungee cord, dangling from the rafter in the ceiling. He puts me in the harness, on my back like a turtle tipped on its shell, with my legs strapped and spread. I look up at the ceiling, feeling . . . I'm not sure what. Helpless, yes, but also as if I'm on some kind of pornographic carnival ride, just swinging and bouncing along at the end of the bungee cord, naked and available with my thighs held open, watching the room tilt and sway. I'm glad we're in the loft, away from Gina's prying eyes.

James kneels in front of me, steadying the harness with his hands. He kisses my ankle, the gold chain around my leg. It's solely possessive, his kiss, bereft of any sentiment or warm feeling. He pulls me closer to him, his face inches from my crotch. I reach out, touch his cheek—he has the kind of flesh that compels one to touch and explore—then put my finger on his lip, trace it lightly. His mouth is cruel, arrogant, no softness in those lips, no forgiveness. He removes my hand, places it between my legs.

"Play with yourself," he orders. I hesitate for only a moment, then begin. I touch my nipples, gently at first, then squeeze them more firmly, until they are hard. He watches while I masturbate, while I rub my clitoris, while I slide my fingers inside me and pretend it is him.

He gets up and takes my picture. The flash startles me. I didn't realize he had a camera nearby. The photo, a Polaroid, extrudes from its slot. James lets it fall to the floor. He walks around me, watching, the camera still in his hand. He doesn't say anything, and neither do I. I know what he wants. I look at him, at his penis, fully erect, and the sight of it, sticking out, hard and meaty, bouncing a little as he moves, the priapic sight of it gets me wetter.

I close my eyes, reinsert my fingers, feel the wetness. I can hear him moving around me, taking pictures, some close up, others farther away, and I rub myself faster, almost ready to come, when I suddenly feel him beside me, those immense thighs wedged between my legs, then his penis probing, going deeper, and he grabs the harness, using it to bring me closer, slamming his penis inside me, so hard it makes me gasp, and he fucks me fervently,

and as he does, instead of worrying about my predicament, strapped in a contraption from which
only he can set me free, instead of worrying about
the man who might do me harm, all I can think
about is him, wanting more of him.

Afterward, still in the harness, I notice the pictures strewn across the floor. James picks one up
and gives it to me. I stare at the photo, distressed by
what I can plainly see: a woman who is obviously
under his thrall. I am descending, I know, into a pit
vertiginously steep. Nothing good can come from
my association with this man.

Letting the photo drop to the floor, I look up and
see the panic snap, the metal clip for emergencies,
for getting out of dangerous bondage situations, and
it makes me think that I need a panic snap of my
own. I need something to release me from this situation, something to cut the chain that James is
wrapping around my soul.

CHAPTER TWENTY-ONE

For several days, misshapen bruised clouds have darkened the sky. They look like ugly wounds, look like they would bleed if you poked them too hard. Rain, this time of year, is not good. A summer rainstorm can rot the grapes, can cause patches of mold in the clusters if the fruit doesn't dry quickly enough.

But the weather holds all day, and by night I'm guessing the storm has passed us by. I go outside, ready to leave, and almost make it to my car when I hear Mrs. McGuane call out my name. I turn around.

"James just phoned," she says. She's standing in the doorframe, still wearing her reading glasses. She was looking at a magazine when I left. "He wants you to stop by his house on your way home."

I nod and wave. She says good night once again and closes the door. I've managed to avoid James all week. He summons, but I do not come. I need the distance, the objectivity. Close to him, I succumb.

The night air is cool, the moon just a faint glow hidden behind a wall of dark clouds. In the distance, I see something move, a tall figure out in the vine-

yards, far away. I wonder if it's Gina. Curious, I walk
out, down the main road, then cross into the vineyard. The figure, a black shadow, moves farther
away, and I have to walk faster just to keep her in
sight. She seems to float down the rows of vines,
like a black phantom, wandering the vineyards by
night. I'm not trying to conceal myself, but she
doesn't see me. She crosses the road, over to another
vineyard, striding rapidly, as if there's a purpose for
this late-night prowl.

I follow. I could call out, but I don't. I want to see
where she's headed this time of night, alone. In a
few minutes the rain begins, just big drops of water
at first, scattered and intermittent, but then, suddenly, it comes pouring down in slanting sheets,
raining so hard and so heavy that I can barely see
beyond the immediate row of vines. I'm not prepared for rain—I had put on slacks and a light
sweater this morning, thinking the clouds would
drift away—and the water quickly soaks through
my clothing, drenching me. The ground becomes
saturated, my tennis shoes squishy with mud and
water. I shiver. The wind picks up, plastering the
rain against my body.

I look ahead. She's gone. I've lost her. I turn
around, peering through the heavy rain, the view
blurry, everything indistinct. I don't see her. I look
all around. She's disappeared. I slog through the
mud, my fingers raw now from the cold, water dripping from my hair into my eyes. I head back to the
road. The vineyard seems vast, unending. Rain cuts
shallow gullies into the earth, and small rivulets of
water stream between the rows of vines. Hearing a
loud wail, I jerk around, startled, but no one is there.
It's only the sound of the wind, a keening cry
through the grapevines.

Turning back, I trip over a piece of wood and fall

flat on my face. I pick myself up, try to wipe the mud from my clothes, finally give up. Head down, I plod along. I seem in slow motion, the stinging wind and cold rain chilling my body. Everything is flat and gray and bleak, like a picture on an old black-and-white television set. The rain, zigzagging to the ground, has washed out all the colors.

Finally, I reach the road, begin the long, wet walk back to my car. After several minutes, I hear a car engine. I turn around and see Gina's truck. The headlights shine on my body, spotlighting me. She slows down, pulls over.

I look in the passenger window. Gina is wearing a black raincoat and black hood. She was my phantom. She was out here only to retrieve her truck. I almost laugh at my foolishness—I don't know what I expected.

She presses a button on the armrest, and the window slides down. "What are you doing out here?" she asks.

Rain rolls down my face. I hug my arms around my body, shivering. I start to tell her I was following her, but change my mind. "I was out for a walk," I say. "I got caught in the rain."

"You were taking a walk?" she repeats.

I nod. Raindrops pelt me on the face. My clothes, mud streaked and sodden, stick to my body.

Reaching over, she opens the door for me. "Get in," she says.

I slide inside the truck. We drive up the main road. Rain smears the side windows, and in the headlights it shimmers like bits of liquid silver. I think she's going to drop me off at my car, but she pulls around the driveway to the back, cuts over to the cottage.

She gets out of the truck, removes her mud-covered boots and sets them on the porch, then unzips the raincoat, looks down at her clothes. From mid-thigh down, her pants are drenched. A damp notebook sticks out of the front pocket of her blouse. Her hair, wet from the rain where the hood didn't cover it, falls loose around her face in tight, black corkscrew curls.

I get out, then go stand on the porch, dripping, hugging myself tightly in an effort to stop shivering.

"If you want," she offers, "you can take a shower to warm up before you leave."

"I'm okay," I say, and I start to head off toward my car. She reaches out for my arm. The rain pours down.

"Don't be stupid," she says, leading me toward the door. "It'll let up by the time you're finished."

I allow her to usher me inside. This is the first time I've been in here. The cottage has a warm, cozy feel to it, lived in but not cluttered. In the corners, green plants grow in wicker baskets, and a blue quilt is scrunched up at one end of the couch where Gina probably fell asleep while reading a book or watching television. Or maybe she doesn't use her bed anymore. Maybe sleep comes to her in the early hours of the morning, after a night of restlessness, when she finally dozes off on the couch. I take another look around. It's warm and cozy, but something's amiss.

She goes over to the fireplace. "I didn't think I'd be using this anymore," she says, without turning around. "Not at this time of the year." She crumples old newspapers and stuffs them beneath the logs.

While she makes a fire, I stand near the desk against the wall. On top, I see a large manila envelope, stuffed almost to bursting, a few sheets sticking out. I glance over at Gina—she's still crumpling newspapers—then slide out the top sheet. It's a poem, typewritten. Gina reaches for a box of matches. Quickly, before she sees me, I slip the sheet back in the envelope. She lights a match and holds it under the newspapers. They crackle and shrivel as they burn, sending up shoots of flames and little wisps of charred paper. The logs catch fire, burn slowly. Outside, the rain, not as heavy now, spatters on the roof.

She shows me the bathroom, sets out towels and a light blue bathrobe, then shuts the door as she leaves. I peel off my wet clothes, set them in the sink. When I open the shower door, I notice the bar of soap is down to a sliver. I put on the bathrobe, go back out to the living room.

Gina is asleep. Her body sprawls the length of the couch, her feet hanging over the edge. I wonder what it would feel like to be so tall, what perspective it would give me to look down instead of up, if I would feel stronger, mightier, more in control of the world. Her breathing is soft and regular, and I reach down and touch her, brushing my fingers lightly across her forehead, wondering if I have a sister of my own. She stirs but doesn't wake, buries her head deeper into her arms. She doesn't seem so invincible anymore.

I take another look around the living room. Then it comes to me, what bothered me about the room: it has a subtle look of benign neglect—a coffee cup, half-empty, with a scummy film on top, sits on a low table, forgotten; an old newspaper, still folded and wrapped with a rubber band, lies in the corner, one end under the couch, overlooked; the picture on the wall, a painting of a vineyard, is tilted slightly, as if she bumped into it and neglected to straighten it out. When I first met Gina, everything about her was direct and clear-cut. She wore jeans and a T-shirt, but they fit her precisely. She wore pointy-toed silver-studded boots and checkered shirts, but they made her look like an urban cowgirl, chic and tough. Even her face, angular, her expression always arranged in a no-nonsense attitude, was orderly. She would never allow untidiness, not in her appearance, not in her home. Now, however, ever since I've interrupted her life, there's a bedraggled look about her, a look of benign neglect, just like this room.

I glance at the painting again. Something about it bothers me. It looks vaguely familiar, but I'm sure I've never seen it before. Gina stirs, pulls herself up when she sees me in the room.

"Finished already?" she asks, her voice sleepy.

"There wasn't any soap," I say. I sit in the La-Z-Boy recliner near the fireplace.

"Will you lose the grapes?" I ask.

She rubs the bridge of her nose, slowly, then her forehead. She says, "We may lose part of the field. Maybe not. It's too early to tell. We won't know the extent of the damage until later. If it warms up tomorrow, if the grapes dry . . ." She shrugs, not finishing. She gets up and places another log on the fire.

The rain is just a light, muffled patter now, no sign of the storm that had come up so suddenly. I gaze into the fire, stare at the burning logs and the tonguelike patterns of hot, licking flames.

"You're in love with James," she says abruptly.

I look up. She stares at me from across the room. I see the sad expression on her face. We both want the same thing: James. She is obsessed with her brother; so am I.

The logs shift, sending up a spew of glowing, red-hot sparks. "The soap is in the hall closet," she says. "Second shelf."

Back in the bathroom, I stand under the shower, thinking of what Gina said, the hot water streaming down on me. Am I in love? The steady flow of water splashing against the tiles is hypnotic. I stay under so long, my fingertips get wrinkly and my skin flushes pink. By the time I finally turn off the water, steam fogs the room, obscuring, thankfully, my reflection in her mirror. I dry off, rub the towel over my scalp. My reflection is hazy, indistinct, the gauzy presence I prefer.

I put on the blue terry-cloth robe again, wring out my clothes, and hang them over the shower door. As I'm combing my fingers through my wet hair, straightening it out, I hear the muffled sound of voices. I open the bathroom door, slowly walk out. I stop as soon as I see to whom the voices belong: James and Gina. They're in the living room, by the door. James's back is turned away from me, his hand at Gina's waist. Neither of them see me. He's wearing a leather jacket, gunmetal gray, that stretches across the back of his shoulders and fits snugly around his arms. He leans in closer to her, murmurs something in her ear, brushes his lips, with a gentle intimacy, on the side of her face. I feel a twang of jealousy. Gina, I see, is trying to slip away now, but he restrains her with soft words I can't hear. His hand slides up her arm, up to her cheek. He strokes it lightly, whispering. She leans her head on him, on his shoulder, just rests it there, her eyes closed. His hand goes back to her arm, moves slowly up and down, a sensual caress. I hear her sigh. He wraps both arms around his sister, holds her as close as he's ever held me, their bodies pressed tightly together.

I'm out of my element, I know, way over my head. The living room seems to have shrunk. The wood crackles and snaps, glows bright red as it shifts. The rain has stopped, and other than the soft dripping sound of water on the roof rain gutters, it's quiet outside.

Opening her eyes, looking over James's shoulder, Gina sees me now. She steps away from him. He turns around, a scowl on his face. He comes over to me, grabs my arm.

"Come on," he says. "We're leaving."

"My clothes are still wet," I say, but he doesn't listen. He yanks me, barefoot and bathrobed, out the door.

"James, let her stay here," Gina calls out, but he ignores her also.

He walks me across the lawn, his hand wrapped firmly around my arm. I glance back, see Gina watching us, then she slowly closes the door. The night air is fresh, vigorous, not a trace of rain, not even a sprinkle.

He stops, looks down at me. "Did my mother tell you I called?" he asks, his voice tight, uncompromising.

I nod.

"Why didn't you come over?"

I don't answer.

"You'll do what I say, or you can leave Byblos now. Forever." His eyes are flat, cold. He stalks off, leaving me on the lawn.

My first impulse is to let him go, but then, when I think about leaving Byblos, when I think about never seeing him again, I get a hollow feeling in the pit of my stomach. I don't want to lose him now. I can't leave Byblos. Not yet. I go around the main house, clutching the bathrobe to my body, chasing after him. He's pulling around the driveway, then onto the road. I run in front of his Cherokee, make him stop. This is the second time tonight I've been caught in bright headlights. As I approach the car, he stares at me through the windshield, a predatory look. He rolls down the window.

"All right," I say. "I'll do as you ask."

He watches me, silent.

"I'll do as you ask," I repeat.

He turns off the engine, gets out of the car. I feel the tension between us, razor sharp. The moon shines brighter than before, and I hear the intermittent sound of water drops falling off the leaves.

He stares at me, unblinking. Finally, he says, "You and I, fifteen years ago, we brought out the worst in each other."

The statement hangs in the air, raw, exposed, like an open wound. I don't know what to do with it. The rainwater falling off the leaves, each drip, is slow and torturous. The time between each drop seems an eternity, time enough for a change of heart, time enough to kill.

He reaches for me, pulls me close, presses my head to his chest. Softly, he strokes my back, makes circles with his palm, then his hand moves down my spine, slowly makes its way back up, a tender embrace. Confused, I lean against him. Minutes go by. I begin to relax in his arms, lulled by his touch. He is solid, a pillar in the dark night. I put my arms around him.

"Do you trust me?" he says, gently pushing me away, holding me at arm's length. He looks at me for a minute, not moving, and I feel as though he's looking into my soul, his eyes missing nothing.

"I don't know," I say, whispering. Everything between us is so tentative, so fragile, always so dangerous.

He pulls me close once more, putting one hand inside the robe, around to my back. His fingers are warm. They spread out across the middle of my back, a gentle fan, soft like satin. I love his touch, the feel of his skin against mine. It moves me, his touch, makes me yearn for more. I wish we'd met under different circumstances, in a different place.

He puts his mouth to my ear. "Get down on your knees," he says.

"What?" I ask, thinking I didn't hear him correctly.

"Get down on your knees."

I look at him, puzzled.

He places his hands on my shoulders, forces me to the wet ground. My knees drop in a small puddle of water. He gazes down at me, steadily, his face cast in shadows, a surface of dark dips and swells, two craters for eyes.

"Ask for forgiveness," he says.

Sighing, feeling exhausted, I bow my head, lean it against his leg and close my eyes. The night is quiet. The air smells organic, of humus, the damp earth odor of recent rain. Confused, I sigh again. Absolution is not his to bestow.

He runs his fingers through my short hair. It's still damp from the shower. He touches me gently.

"Plead for forgiveness," he says again. His voice is soft, coaxing, infinitely patient.

I should be able to say the words—they are, after all, only words—but they stick in my throat. He plays with my hair, runs his hand under my chin, then tilts my head up to him.

"Ask for it," he says.

"I haven't done anything wrong," I say. He keeps his hand under my chin, forcing me to look up at him. "I shouldn't have to ask for forgiveness."

He listens to me speak. When I am through, he says, patiently, "But you have done something wrong. You dared to defy me. I expressly asked you to come to my house. You've avoided me all week. You must do what I say. Always. Those are the rules. Now, ask for my forgiveness."

I begin to cry. Before I came to Byblos, I never cried. My emotions remained locked inside, hardened. Now, it seems as if my feelings, pent up for so long, display themselves at will. I feel a teardrop run down my cheek. He takes his finger and wipes it away. I'm tired. My knees are wet and sore from the ground. I want to be in his arms, not on my knees.

"Forgive me," I say quietly, giving in.

He holds my head. "More," he says.

My eyes water. "I'm sorry," I say, the words coming out as a sob. "I shouldn't have ignored your request. I was afraid." My voice chokes. Weary, confused, I lean my head against his arm.

He doesn't say anything. I know he wants more from me.

"But that was no excuse," I add. "I should've come anyway." I feel another tear, then another. "I'm sorry," I say. "I'm really sorry," and now I mean it. I want his forgiveness, need it, but I'm not sure why. "Forgive me," I beg, my voice trembling with an emotion I don't understand. "Please, forgive me."

Gently, he strokes my cheek. After a few moments, he says, "That wasn't so difficult, was it?"

Yes, it was, but I shake my head, not wanting to disappoint him any further. My eyelashes are wet with tears. I rest my cheek against his hand. He caresses it with his fingers. Still on my knees, still genuflecting before him, I turn my head and kiss his open palm. He receives it as would a priest, as a sign of worship.

He unzips his pants. He takes out his penis, holds it in his hand. He says, "When I piss, I want you to taste it. I want you to lap at it like a dog lapping at water." He adds, "You should consider it a privilege."

He urinates on the ground next to me. It comes out strong, splashing on the asphalt road. I hesitate, then lean forward, stick out my tongue, tentatively touch the flow of his urine. It's warm and pungent, the smell of it stronger than the taste. I put my tongue out again, and I understand why he's making me do this. It is a privilege, consuming part of him. Only he's not making me—not really. If I wanted to, I could get up and leave. But I don't want to. I lap at his urine, lap at it until he's finished and it's reduced to a trickle.

"Now suck me," he says, and I do. I take him in my mouth, taste the last drops of his urine, then feel him go hard.

"Deeper," he says. "You can take it deeper," and his hands go to my head, pulling me closer, shoving his penis all the way into my throat, keeping it there for a while, then moving my head back and forth, slow at first, with an easy rhythm, then faster and faster, a desperate ache to his tempo now, jerky and frantic in his need to come, taking what he wants from me. Soon, I taste his semen spurting into my mouth, and then his words come to me once more, *it's a privilege,* and as he's holding my head to his crotch, as he's pulling me to him still, I feel as if I'm being pulled into another world, my world of years past, an earlier time of simpler desires, a time where my only thought, and my only need, was to please this man. I am changing, I know that now.

CHAPTER TWENTY-TWO

"You have no intention of leaving, do you?" Gina asks quietly.

I don't reply. She knows the answer to that question. Slowly, we walk through one of the east-side vineyards. Workers are pulling and repositioning leaves—removing any dead ones and thinning out dense foliage. Too many leaves crowd the grape clusters; too few allow the sun to scorch the skins. Despite advances in viticultural practices, I'm learning that successful grape growing is still an imprecise science, dependent on the grower's judgment and the luck of good weather.

Gina reaches down, slips her hand in mine, holds it as we walk. The gesture catches me off guard. I'm not sure what to make of it, but I don't resist. I used to think her dazzling in a sort of hard-edged, flinty way. Now, her face is brittle looking, with dark calderas of sleeplessness smudging the skin beneath her eyes. Her hair, piled on top of her head, has a few long hanks hanging loose, and some frizzy black tendrils fly out as if they'd been zapped with electricity, giving her a crazed, unsettled appearance.

"Are you and James . . ." I hesitate. Fucking?
Sleeping together?—how do I put the question?
"You and James," I begin again. "Are you . . ." Once
more, I falter.

Her hand tightens just a little around mine. She
doesn't look at me, doesn't break her stride. She
says, "Would you leave if I told you we were?"

"No," I say.

"Then there's no reason to discuss it."

We continue down the row, silent now. There's
no sign of the untimely storm. It was fleeting, a
freaky August rain, the next day's sun drying out
the vineyards quickly. Today, the sky is blue and
cloudless. Plastic ribbons, fastened to trellises and
vine supports, oscillate in the air, colorful rippling
zigzags that scare off berry-hungry birds. Each day,
the vineyards smell sweeter, more intense, more
like grapes.

"Promise me something," she says, still walking,
still holding my hand. "Promise you'll tell me if
James gets . . ." Now, she's the one who can't finish.
Stopping, she pulls her hand away from mine. She
looks down at me, her expression unreadable.

Finally, she says, "Come to me when you need
help." Abruptly, she leaves.

I look out over the tops of the vines, across the
fields. Workers are repairing the irrigation and frost-
control systems, and I see the vineyard manager
measuring the acid and sugar contents of the grapes
with a handheld instrument. A truck, hauling in a
shipment of new oak barrels, drives up the road.
Everyone is busy, gearing up for the fall harvest.

I reach out, feel the texture of a leaf between my
fingers, smell the jammy, warm-fruit aroma in the
air. The leaves are dark green; the grapes, bursting
with color, purplish red, hang heavy on the vines.

The white grapes will be the first to ripen completely, then the reds, extending the harvest from late August to late October, or even early November.

I watch Gina walk away. Both she and James were up early today, at dawn, surveying the vineyards, checking the condition of the grapes, estimating the date of harvest. I look at them in a different light now. I see them, perhaps, more clearly than before. I see their relationship to the land and the vines. They are winemakers, yes, but they're also—something which I hadn't really understood until recently—they're also farmers, rooted to the land, with the farmers' constant worry about unseasonal rain, spring frosts, droughts, harmful pests and rodents, and a myriad of other factors effecting the crops. Before, I saw mainly the privilege into which they were born, the parties, the entertaining, the business trips that seemed a luxury. Now, I see the daily struggle, the long hours at the winery and in the vineyards, their solicitude of the land.

"Out for a walk?"

I hear James's voice before I see him. I turn around. He's on the other side of the trellis, in the next row, wearing a gray T-shirt—battleship gray comes to mind—that covers his chest like an extra layer of skin. His hair, golden blond, shines in the sunlight, and I remember my first sighting of him, in the *Wine Spectator*, a picture of him taken in the autumn fields after the leaves had turned. I was mesmerized by his photograph—his look of privileged composure, his self-assurance so palpable. He was impressive looking, tall, tanned, and sturdy. He hasn't changed.

"Yes," I say, curious that I hadn't heard his footsteps. He must've been watching Gina and me, treading quietly.

He squints in the sunshine, shades his eyes. "What were you two talking about?"

I shrug. "Nothing much," I say.

He reaches over the trellis—a move so quick, so unexpected, I don't have time to react—and grabs me. I let out a small yelp of surprise. He pulls me close, up against the vines and the plastic tubing of the irrigation system. Leaves press against my face and bare arms. I feel bunches of grapes by my stomach.

"Watch yourself around Gina," he says.

Then he leans forward, and, in another sudden movement, kisses me on the lips, surprising me again. After he releases my arms, he takes a step backward, looks at me as if he wants to say more. But he doesn't. He turns and walks down the row of vines, catches up to Gina. They are a pair of giants, the two of them, imposing, towering over the vines—no mistaking the blood ties between them. He puts his arm through hers.

That night, I follow James up the spiral staircase. The diffuse light of the moon, from the arched window, paints the loft in dark, shadowy grays. James's face, faintly limned in the moonlight, is a dimly etched profile, kind of scary the way his eyes recede in hollow sockets, haunted looking. He goes over to the studio, turns on a lamp, then lifts the hanging rattan chair—the one with the plush burgundy cushions—and slides it off the hook. The long chain dangles free. He sets the chair off to the side, takes a step over to the huge arched window, and closes the drapes. Apprehensive, I remain by the stairs, watching. He said I had another lesson to learn, another step in our journey.

He adjusts the chain hanging from the rafter,

makes it shorter, clips on a panic snap, then attaches a metal-and-leather apparatus to the hook. It's different from the leather harnesses he's used before, not as elaborate. There's a long metal bar on top, and from it, on both ends, suspended from several clips, hang two wide, black leather straps, each looped on the ends. More clips, in various locations, are attached to the straps.

"Did you use this with Anna?" I ask.

He bends over, picks something off the floor, and stuffs it in his jeans pocket, where it bulges. Turning around, he sees that I'm still by the staircase. "No," he says. "Never."

I start to ask why, but he anticipates my question. "She wasn't the type," he says. "Unlike you."

The room is quiet, still. "You don't have any pictures of her," I say.

He gives me a calculated look, then slowly smiles. "You mean, I don't have any besides the ones you found while searching my filing cabinet."

Cowed, I don't respond.

He says, "I think there's a wedding album at my mother's. In the attic."

He reaches up and slowly unbuttons his shirt, takes it off, and tosses it on the rattan chair. His thighs, large and firm as boles, are snug against the material of his jeans. He walks over, puts his hand on the side of my face, his thumb under my chin. Placing my palms on his bare chest, I feel the strength of him. He reaches down and pulls the flowered jumper I'm wearing over my head. He unbuttons my blouse, slips it off my shoulders, then takes off my bra. He says, "I can do whatever I want with you."

He pushes me against the balustrade. He kneels down. I'm wearing knee-high suede boots, and he unzips them and pulls them off, then slides my panties down my legs, removes them also. The only thing I'm wearing now is the gold chain, his chain, around my ankle. Without clothes, the room seems cool. He kisses the inside of my thigh, then I feel the sharp pinch of his teeth around my flesh. I wince, try to pull away, but he holds me firmly around the waist, bites down harder. I shudder, from the slight chill in the room, from the pain.

Getting up, he reaches in his jeans pocket and pulls out a long scarf, black and satiny. He folds it over and over. "Turn around," he says.

When I hesitate, he grabs me by the shoulders, twists me around, pushes my stomach against the wooden railing of the banister. I look down, get a dizzying sensation of falling, the brick floor so far below me. I grasp onto the railing, hold on. I think he's going to bind my wrists behind my back, but he doesn't. He reaches around my head, lays the folded scarf against my eyes. He's going to blindfold me, something he's never done before. Quickly, I reach up, place my hands on his arms. I don't want to be without sight. I can't take the darkness.

He pauses. He lowers his arms, places his wrists on my shoulders. The scarf, still in his hands, drapes around the front of me, like a necklace, like a noose. "Are you afraid?" he asks.

I nod.

"The unknown bothers you?"

I think of all the unknowns in my life: the truth of my past still hidden, the amnesia that blocks out everything, the final destination of this journey I take with James. I feel his fingers on my collarbone, feel the soft fabric of the scarf against my skin. "The unknown always bothers me," I say.

He whispers, "We made an agreement, you and I. You belong to me."

He steps back. I hear him unbuckling his belt,

then sloughing off his jeans and shoes. I turn around to look at him. He's wearing white socks, nothing else. I want to step forward and touch him, but I don't. I just look, take in the priapic maleness of him, the firm and knotty calves, the stalwart flesh, the air of confidence he projects. He reaches for me, massages my breasts, gets the nipples hard, then leans down and takes one in his mouth. Of course, I respond. There's something about him I can't resist, something purely physical. I want him to fuck me. I push closer, needing more. He sucks on my nipple as if he were a small boy at his mother's breast. Putting my hand on the back of his head, I press him to me, feel the softness of his hair. I move my hand lower, down the smooth planes of his back, to the slope of his buttocks, then around the front, between his legs. His penis juts out, hard. I wrap my palm around it, slowly stroke the length of it while he sucks on my breasts, feeding. I lift one leg up to his thigh, wanting to be fucked, wanting his cock inside me, but he puts his hand on my hip, holding me back. He takes his mouth off my breast.

"Not yet," he says.

His penis is stiff in my hand. It pushes out toward me, seeking. I reach lower, snake my fingers down to the goose-fleshed pouch of his testicles, the skin of which is now stretched taut, the balls like two firm-fleshed figs rolling around in my palm. Once, I read that men ejaculate at a force equivalent to twenty-eight miles per hour. I cup my hand over him, sensing that unleashed power in the tautness of his balls, in the projecting strain of his cock. Short pubic hairs brush against the back of my hand. I need him now, but still he holds back.

"Not yet," he repeats.

"Why not?" I ask.

He looks at me, smiles, then goes back to my

breast. He sucks it harder, and I wince because it hurts, because the suction is painful, but I don't want him to stop.

He does, though. He places his mouth on mine, kisses me. "You belong to me," he whispers once more.

"Yes," I say. "I do," and he picks up the scarf from the floor, ties it around my head, tightly, covering my eyes. A flash of panic goes through me, but then I tell myself my hands are free. If necessary, I can remove the scarf. He takes my arm and leads me across the room.

"Stay here," he says, and he releases me. The room now feels warm. Tentatively, I reach out, move my arms around in front of me. I feel nothing. I try not to think about the blackness, about the dark images, formless monsters, haunting my mind, ready to invade the conscious world if only they could. Instead, I listen. Across the room, I hear him rummaging in a drawer of his dresser—or maybe in the armoire, or in the antique trunk, I can't tell— then I hear him walk back toward me. There are scraping noises, as if he's sliding a chair or table closer to where I'm standing.

"Put your arms straight out," he says, and he slips something over my hands and up my arms, some- thing soft, smooth. He fits it over my breasts, then turns me around and fastens it behind my back. When he's finished, I feel it with my hands. It's like a brassiere, but without the cups so my breasts are exposed, sticking out. He moves me forward a cou- ple of feet.

"Lean against me," he says, and then he picks up my right leg. Immediately, I grab hold of him, feeling disoriented, as if I'm going to fall. He steadies me with his hand.

"I'm going to put your leg through one of the

loops on the sling," he explains, and I feel him slipping it over my foot and all the way up my leg, near my crotch. "Hold this," he says, and he guides my hand to one of the straps.

"Now, the other one," he says, and he lifts my left leg, puts it through the other loop. The leather scrapes my leg as he moves it up on my thigh. It feels as though I'm on a swing, sitting straight up, naked, both hands holding on to the straps, my legs held open by the wide leather loops. My heart pulses faster. I feel the rush.

"I'll be back in a minute," he says, and I hear him padding across the loft, then more sounds of him rummaging around. When he returns, there's a soft thud—he's set something down, I think—and then noises of him moving around, doing something. Finally, he comes back to me. I feel his hand on my shoulder.

"I'm going to put the straps behind your back," he says. "Lean forward. You can hold on to me."

Releasing one of the straps, I reach out in the blackness and feel James in front of me, his chest, his abdomen. I release my other hand, wrap both arms around his waist. He moves the straps behind my back and shoulders, then he takes a step back. Still holding on to his waist, I move with him. He pushes me back.

"Give me your hand," he says, and he takes one of my arms, secures something around my wrist which I know, from previous experience, is one of his fur-lined cuffs.

I feel another surge of panic—if he binds my hands, I won't be able to remove the scarf—but, quickly, before I can protest, he twists my arm behind my back and snaps the cuff to one of the clips I'd seen earlier on the strap. Then he does the same to my other hand. He walks away. With both arms behind my back, attached to the straps, I tilt forward.

"James?" I call out, feeling even more panicked, the darkness overcoming me, seemingly blacker than before, but he doesn't answer. Suddenly, I feel myself rising, my feet leaving the floor. I make a small, choked noise of surprise, then I realize it's only the hoist. He's using it to lift me. I try to calm myself, breathe slowly and deeply as he taught me so many months ago. He's used the hoist before, I tell myself. There's no reason for alarm.

I pretend I'm outside, a black night without stars, no visibility. I breathe deeply. The straps around my legs are wide and hold me comfortably. Suspended like this, in the air, chest and face down, I feel as if I'm floating on water, an endless black ocean, just drifting. I wait to find out what will happen next, but don't have to wait long. I smell him, his fresh autumn-leaf-and-grass scent, then feel his hand on my face, his lips on my neck, his warm breath. Slowly, he moves his hands along my body, over my breasts, down to my stomach, between my legs. Without sight, the touch of his hand, the tactile sensation, seems heightened, more intense. Each caress carries a sensuous tingle, luxurious. The darkness no longer conjures up frightening images, but takes me to a higher place of pure sensation. I feel the texture of his palms, his fingertips, a grainy surface here, a smoothness there; I'm sensitive to every groove and line, it seems, although I know the impossibility of that. His hands go to my breasts, touch them lightly, like the brush of a feather, a mere suggestion of contact, and I hear myself moan, wanting more of him, and he responds, squeezing them now, pulling and kneading, making me sigh at the pleasure of his touch, and then I feel his mouth on my nipple, sweetly sucking. I lean my head down, feel the silkiness of his hair on my cheek. Once more, his hand goes between my legs, slides smoothly between the moist folds of skin, the wetness of me like a lotion, creamy, the choicest part.

"Your cunt is wet," he says. "The unknown frightens you—but it also turns you on." He slipslides his finger over to my clitoris.

"You like this," he says.

I nod, not knowing if he's looking at me or not. "Yes," I say. "I do."

He puts his finger inside me, then slides in another. His thumb makes circles on my clitoris.

"Fuck me," I say.

He ignores my request. He puts his mouth on mine, kisses me, then I feel him putting something on my left breast, attaching it to the cupless bra, clamping it down. Then he does the same to my right breast.

"I used to milk you," he says.

"Milk me?" I repeat.

"I wanted your complete submission—and you gave it. You surrendered your ego to me. You didn't view it as derogatory. The surrender was your gift."

"Milk me?" I repeat again, confused, feeling stupid that I'm not following the conversation, wary of where it will go.

He says, "I've always found the sight of a mother nursing her child extremely erotic. I want you to give me that. I want your breasts to be full with milk."

He pauses, then adds, "I don't want a child, of course, just the milk. Just the sight of you being milked."

"You can't have one without the other," I say.

"Wrong. It's unusual, but it can be done. Pregnancy isn't an absolute prerequisite. Certain medications, hormones, can induce lactation, but they aren't always necessary. Sometimes, a breast pump is sufficient to establish the milk supply. With you, before, that's all it took."

I listen, apprehensive, knowing what this means for me. I feel his hand on my breasts, on the contraption he has attached to my breasts. He says, "What you're hooked up to now is an electric double pump. It'll do both breasts simultaneously. It's a bit exotic looking—each breast is cupped with a clear plastic shield, like a funnel, with a small bottle attached to collect the milk. Long tubes run to the pumping machine, where a vacuum will simulate a baby's sucking action on your nipples. It'll take a couple of weeks to get the milk started. You'll need to mimic a baby's nursing pattern—put it on every two hours, for ten to fifteen minutes."

He hesitates, then says, "You did this for me before. You faithfully hooked up the pump, even when I wasn't around to make you do it. You wanted to produce milk for me. You took the pump with you when you knew you'd be gone for more than two hours, disappear in a restroom, apply the pump for fifteen minutes. Finally—I forget how long, two weeks maybe, or three, it seemed like it took forever—you began lactating."

I hear him turn on the machine. The suction pulls on my flesh, drawing out my breasts and nipples, tugging on them, it feels like, stretching them out. It's a little uncomfortable, an odd sensation, but it doesn't hurt.

"You'll do this for me again," he says, and then I feel his mouth on mine, his tongue inside me, his fingers once more down between my legs, sliding, rubbing, while the pumping of my breasts continues, the vacuum creating a heavy, pulling pressure that begins to feel sensual.

"You'll do it," he says, and his words mingle with a moist kiss. His tongue traces my lips. He keeps his fingers inside me, moving. I kiss him back, wanting him to fuck me, understanding completely, how, in the past, I could surrender to him, how my own pleasure got all mixed up with his, his needs superseding my own.

"Let me touch you," I say, when he takes his mouth from mine. "Undo my arms. I need to feel your skin."

"I know you do," he says, "but I want you the way you are."

His fingers stay inside me. His breath is warm against my skin, on my neck, on my mouth.

"There're stages to the milk," he says. "When a pregnant woman begins breastfeeding, the first liquid to come out isn't even milk. It's called colostrum, kind of a syrupy, light oily liquid, a little thicker than milk. I think it's supposed to boost the baby's immune system, I'm not sure. After a while, a few days or longer, the transition milk appears, then finally the mature milk. Since you aren't pregnant, you won't produce the colostrum, just the milk. It tastes different than the milk we buy in stores, thinner, almost like sugar water, and it's warm, of course, body temperature."

Suddenly, I feel the speed of the pump increase. Then the suction increases also, pulling harder on my breasts. His fingers continue to move inside me.

"In the beginning, it was quite painful for you. Your nipples were sore, tender all the time. But after a while, after a few weeks, they toughened up. They looked the same, there was no physical difference, no callouses, but the sucking didn't hurt you anymore. Just the opposite, in fact. You said it was a relief when I milked you. Your breasts would get full, tight, and you'd need to get the milk out of you so it wouldn't hurt. You'd leak sometimes, and you'd have to put breast pads inside your bra so the leaking wouldn't show through your blouse. You had small breasts, but when you began lactating, they became slightly larger, almost plump."

His breath is still on me, close, hot. He kisses me, moves his lips along my neck, and then he turns up the suction even more.

"It was wonderful," he says. "I had a great time playing with your nipples. Sometimes, I'd suck on them myself, feed on your breasts. Other times, I would take you to the kitchen sink, have you bend over a little, then tell you to milk yourself, using your fingers, and I'd watch as it squirted out. It would squirt all over the sink, in several directions. Occasionally, I'd make you wait longer than usual to get the milk out. Your breasts would get hard, and sometimes they'd start to leak. You'd beg me for relief. I'd take you into the bathroom, have you get up on the counter on all fours, your breasts hanging down, full, then I'd start pulling on them, first one, then the other, milking you like a cow, the liquid streaming out beneath you into the sink. It was quite erotic. I'd keep milking you until you were empty."

The pump pulls my breasts, stretches them out it seems. He says, "A woman will produce only as much milk as her baby needs. If the baby nurses frequently, the milk will increase; if the baby stops sucking, the milk decreases. So, in order to keep you producing, you had to be milked every two hours."

"You did that every two hours?" I say.

He laughs softly. "That wouldn't be very erotic, would it? Or convenient. No, you took care of it yourself. You'd use the pump to take out the milk, or you'd do it manually, with your fingers. You wanted the flow to continue—because I wanted it—

so you milked yourself every two hours." He places his hand on my stomach, on my waist, then slides it around to my ass.

"You'll do this again, won't you?" he says. His hand moves down between my legs. His thumb circles my clitoris, his fingers slide around inside me, slippery. "You'll do it for me."

And I nod, not because I want to be milked, but because I want to please him, as I had so long ago.

He says, "Sonoma is known for their lamb. I've been to restaurants in New York and Florida and Washington, restaurants all over the country, and seen Sonoma baby lamb on their menus."

I'm not thinking of food. I'm thinking of his cock, wanting it inside me.

He says, "I bought a live lamb from one of the sheep farms and gave it to you. You knew what I wanted as soon as I put the lamb into your arms. You were sitting on the couch, downstairs. You took off your blouse, put the lamb to your breast. The lamb didn't take it right away, but eventually it did. It latched onto your nipple, began sucking out your milk. When it was through with that breast, you switched it to the other. You were quite maternal. When the lamb first began sucking, you said there was a tingling sensation in your breast. You liked it."

I feel his fingers moving, feel the sweet torment of his thumb, the seductive pull he exerts on me. "You fucked me afterward?" I say, almost whispering.

"During," he says. "I couldn't wait. It was a delicious sight, the lamb slurping at your breast. I put my cock in your mouth, let you suck on me as the lamb sucked on you. Later, as it got older, I would make you kneel on the ground and offer your breasts to the lamb. It was truly erotic, you on your knees, the lamb feeding off of you, sucking and pulling on your breasts. I never completely weaned him off you—if he got thirsty, he went to you. It seemed you always had something plugged to your nipples, the lamb, the pump . . . me."

His fingers play at my crotch. The pump pulls and sucks my breasts, making them sore, making them ache.

"You'll do whatever I want," he says, kissing me.

He keeps his fingers inside me, working, his thumb making steady, rhythmic circles on my clitoris, drawing me in, until the pain from the pump gradually disappears, transforms into something increasingly pleasurable with the pulsing movement of his fingers.

"You'll do whatever I want," he repeats.

"Yes," I say, "I'll do whatever you want," and he keeps his fingers inside me, his thumb on my clitoris, rubbing, keeps at it until I come, until I beg him to fuck me, which he finally does, from behind. With me hoisted up in the air like this, we're a perfect—albeit dangerous—fit. I say it once more. "I'll do whatever you want."

CHAPTER TWENTY-THREE

This is the first time I've been in Mrs. McGuane's attic. I don't know why I never thought to come up here before. It's an enormous space contained entirely within the sloped roof framing the house. Broad beams, old and dark and roughly hewn, run lengthwise up above, with supporting rafters meeting them at a slant. Wide hardwood planks floor the room, and dull gray light pushes through several dormer windows, each of them opaque with dust and grime.

Slowly, I cross the room, looking around. The air smells stale and fusty, as if it hasn't moved in years, and silky intricate cobwebs hang in the corners and off the rafters. The entire area is crammed with old trunks and furniture no longer in style. Cardboard cartons are stacked against the walls, two pairs of dusty skis are hooked to one rafter, and forgotten camping equipment—a green Coleman stove, three rolled-up sleeping bags, an ice chest, an olive-colored tent—is stuffed in one corner, way in the back.

I lift the corner of a dingy gray cloth, peek underneath. Paintings, not framed. I throw the cloth off to the side. Dust stirs, churns in the air. Several pictures, similar to the one on Gina's living-room wall, are stacked together, each of them a view of the Byblos vineyards. Suddenly, I realize what it was that bothered me about the painting in Gina's cottage—it was missing the young girl; it was missing me. All the portraits in the shed have vineyard backgrounds, just as these do. The brushstrokes are the same, the style identical. James painted the picture in Gina's cottage, and these also. I step closer, hold one up. It's serene, even beautiful, without the girl and all her fury. He must've painted this before I came into his life.

I replace the painting and begin searching through the trunks shoved up against the walls. I find small trinkets and cheap jewelry, toys that were once favorites, carefully folded baby clothing—James's and Gina's?—that will never again be worn, but no photo albums. When I'm finished with the trunks, I start on the cardboard cartons. The first few contain a stack of drawings that James and Gina painted in grade school, Boy Scout and Girl Scout merit badges, programs of school plays and music recitals, scuffed-up report cards.

Opening another box, I find the photo albums, a stack of them. I flip through them quickly, mostly pictures of James and Gina as children, then stop when I open the last one, a cream-colored satiny album. A picture of James and Anna stares back at me, their wedding portrait. She's quite lovely, with gorgeous dark hair and large brown eyes. I feel, in her, a kindred spirit—we share the same man, perhaps the same destiny—and I want to issue a warning: be careful.

But it's too late for that, too late for her. I sit on the floor. I turn the pages slowly, see pictures of the reception, the bridesmaids and ushers and ring bearer and flower girls, all the family and friends, dancing, eating, drinking, smiling. I scrutinize each picture, Anna happy, dressed in an expensive flowing white gown, never suspecting her life was almost at its end, never knowing her killer would go free.

The attic door opens. Gina walks in. "Mother told me you were up here," she says. "She wanted to talk to you about the dinner party tomorrow night." She looks at the album in my hand.

"Was her death an accident?" I say. Gina looks away. The light from the dormer windows has faded with the shifting sun, leaving the attic dim and dusky.

"Was it?" I ask again.

"James was the only one there. He said she slipped."

A bird alights on the dormer sill, its feathers pressed to the dusty window, then flies away. "Did she?"

Gina doesn't reply. The room is quiet.

"You know him better than anyone," I say. "You know the truth. Instinctively, you know it."

She wants to confide in me—I can see it in her troubled face—but she holds back. Finally, turning to leave, she says, "Mother needs to speak with you."

CHAPTER TWENTY-FOUR

I pull up in the front of the winery. The lot is empty, my car the sole one here. The winery, with its huge slabs of stone, looks vacant and solitary in the still of the night, the only light visible coming from the glow of a pale moon. I get out of the car, check the front door. It's locked. I walk around to the side of the building, see Gina's white truck, and go over to it, looking around, nervous. I lean against the hood, stalling. She called from the winery before I left the main house, said she had something important to tell me about James. Faint strips of fog, like smoke signals, waft across the air. They are signals to me, I think, warning me away. I try to shake off the uneasiness.

The office door is also locked. I go to the back of the winery, check a door there. The knob turns. I slip in, closing the door quietly behind me. The lights are off. I take a deep breath. Standing still in the darkness of the room, I try not to let it spook me. I wait for my eyes to adjust, not moving. I know where the light switches are located, but decide not to turn them on. For some reason—a gut instinct—I want to find Gina before she finds me. From a high window, moonlight seeps in, fills the room with a craggy landscape of tall, looming shadows and hidden spaces and black crevices. Gradually, I make out the shapes in the building, the large stainless-steel tanks, dark by moonlight, ultramodern cylindrical forms lined up in a row, hovering, like giants ready to attack.

I listen, but don't hear anything. No sound of Gina. I walk down the aisle of tanks, checking the narrow spaces between them. The tanks go up to the ceiling, and they must be at least twenty-five feet high. I go down another aisle. Still, I don't find Gina.

Walking through the building, I check each room, careful not to trip over the dark, shadowy forms all around, the hoses or buckets or ladders leaning against the walls. I reach the inside entrance to the office and open the door. It's dark. I peer around but can't see anything. It's as if I'm staring into a black cavern. I shudder, start to close the door.

"Come in," James says.

I freeze, my hand still on the doorknob.

"The darkness bothers you?" he asks, and then I hear a sharp click and the desk lamp goes on, brightening the area with a glowing nimbus of light. James is sitting there, his feet up on the desk, leaning back in the chair, his arms crossed. His bulk dominates the room, and his face, in the high-wattage light, appears harsh, his jaw severe. "I've been waiting for you," he says.

Then I notice the sling in the corner, dangling from the ceiling on hooks which had once held four potted plants. The plants are on the floor now, lined up against the wall, the green leaves billowing around each pot like a lady's old-fashioned hoop skirt.

"Gina," I begin. "I'm supposed to—"

"Close the door," he interrupts.

I hesitate, stay where I am.

"Close the door," he says again.

Once more, I hesitate. Another wave of uneasiness comes over me. He watches, cocks an eyebrow, questioning, then swings his feet off the desk and slowly gets up. Crossing the room, he walks over to me. Involuntarily, I back up. A wry smile begins to form on the edges of his mouth. He puts his hand on my shoulder, restraining me.

"Does this place frighten you?" he asks. "Or is it me?" He leans down, places his lips on my cheek, kisses me lightly. He's dressed as he was earlier today, light-colored shirt, faded blue jeans. He pulls me inside the room.

"Gina," I say again. "We were . . . going out for a drink. I'm supposed to meet her here."

His hand slides down my arm, to my fingertips, then he releases it. He reaches around me and locks the door. "I know," he says. "I sent her away."

My gut clenches. I try not to think about the locked door, or being trapped, or the darkness on the other side, the feeling that ghosts of the past reside here still. He keeps his hands by his sides, not touching me.

"Stay away from Gina," he says. "Your questions can be answered only by me."

This warning of future action—stay away from Gina—brings a slender sense of relief. There is time still. Our journey is not yet over.

He is quiet for a while, staring down at me, considering. Finally, he lifts his arms, wraps them around me, holds me so close, so tenderly, that I become confused. His shirt is soft, the fibers fuzzy against my cheek. He holds me for several minutes, then steps back abruptly. I sense a shift of mood, as perceptible as the step he just took.

"Take off your clothes," he says.

I temporize, glancing around the office, feeling immured, the room sealed and locked, but then my gaze goes back to him, pulled by the insuperable sway of his will, and I capitulate once again. Slowly, I unbutton my sweater. I remove my clothes while he watches. He takes me over to the sling. Unlike the others, this one is made of a single rectangular sheet of very thick black leather—maybe three feet long, a couple feet wide—suspended by four chains, one at each corner of the sling, so it lies flat in the air. He lifts me up, has me lie on my back.

"I'm going to put you in restraints," he says.

My heart beats fast, but I don't reply, knowing he doesn't expect one. He wraps fur-lined, leather cuffs around my wrists, then attaches them to the upper chains by my head.

"Lift your legs," he says. "Bend them," and he cuffs my ankles, hooks them on the outside of the two lower chains. He moves me down a bit, so my buttocks hang partially over the sling. This device seems as though it could've been designed for women about to give birth—back supported, legs bent and knees spread open, ass on the edge of the sling so a baby can pop out into someone's hands.

"Comfortable?" he asks.

I nod.

"Good," he says. "You may be here for a while." He unbuttons his shirt, takes it off, and lets it drop to the floor. He leaves on the white T-shirt. He brings a chair over and sets it near the sling, then crosses over to the desk. He opens a drawer, comes back with a paper bag. I watch him, feeling nervous when I see the bag. He sets it on the chair.

"We're going to do something new," he says.

Immediately, I feel a twinge of both fear and excitement, the exhilarating sense of danger—controlled danger—looming. He stands in front of me, the sling waist-high for him, the material of his jeans touching my crotch. He strokes the insides of my thighs. Bending down, he places his mouth on my crotch, licks me. His tongue makes a tour of my genitals, sliding over the dips and swells, making me relax. He looks up, his hair brushing my thighs.

"Actually," he says, "it's not completely new. You've done this before. You didn't like it at first. It scared you."

Perceptibly, my muscles tense.

"Don't worry," he says. "If you did it before, you can do it again."

"Do what?" I ask, wary.

He keeps his hands on my thighs, stroking, watching me. "I'm going to put my hand inside your ass," he says. "My entire fist."

His gaze stays on me, waiting for my response. My glance darts to the chains, my arms and legs securely attached. I am wide open, helplessly exposed. I picture him forcing his fist into my ass, punching up, splitting the flesh, tearing it, bloody entrails. I feel no excitement now—only fear.

"Your hand is too big," I say, my voice shaky. "You'll rip me apart."

He continues stroking my thighs, not replying.

"Please don't do it," I say, and although I'm trying to remain calm, I hear the tremble in my voice, feel the cold sweat breaking out.

"*I'll do whatever you want,*" he mimics. "Didn't you say that? Didn't you promise me that?"

"Yes, but . . ." A drop of sweat slides down my temple. "Your hand is too big," I say again, futilely, because I know nothing I say will deter him.

"I want your ass," he says. "Easy or difficult—it's your choice. But I'll get what I want." He leans over, opens the bag on the chair, pulls out a large jar of lubricant, a roll of paper towels, a folded piece of white cloth. He puts the cloth under my ass. He tears off sheets and sheets of paper towels, lays them on the chair, on the floor. He pulls the T-shirt over his head, kicks off his shoes, removes his jeans and underwear.

"I meant what I said the other day," I tell him. "I do want to please you. But . . . I'm too small."

He doesn't listen. He takes off the lid of the lubricant, dips in his fingers, turns to me. I tense when I feel his touch. The lube goes on cold. Even though my wrists are shackled to the chains, I twist them so I can grab hold, wrap my fingers around the metal links, grip tightly. He smears the lube between my buttocks as if it were globs of thick fingerpaint. He reaches for more, pokes it in my ass.

"Loosen up," he says. "We're just beginning." He greases his hand now, rubbing it all over, between his fingers, over the knuckles and palm, across the width of the back, then spreads it around his wrist. His hand is gloved in lubricant, slimy, an oleaginous mess. Through my legs, I see his penis. The thought of what he's going to do has given him an erection. He slides a finger in my ass, looks up at me, his blond eyebrows knitting together in a frown.

"I know you can do better than this," he says. "You're not even this tight when I fuck you." He jiggles his finger around, twists it, then lets out a long, irritated sigh. He leans over me, puts his face up close to mine, his finger still inside me.

"Relax, Carly."

"I can't."

His eyes search mine, lock on my fear. "You'll have to," he says. "I'm going in—one way or another."

I start to speak, but the words don't come. My lip, my jaw, quivers. Water pools in my eyes.

Again, he sighs, this time with a little compassion. He places his head on my chest. "Breathe with me," he whispers.

I try, but I cannot. Tears roll out the sides of my eyes, slip down.

"Breathe," he says again.

I listen to the steady rhythm of his breath. I try to relax. I try to slow down my breathing, try to match his. His hair is soft on my skin, his breath warm. We stay like this for minutes.

His head still on my chest, his voice quiet, he says, "You must surrender everything to me, every part of your body. Saying the words isn't enough. Prove your obedience to me. I demand it."

He lifts his head, looks at me, a thatch of golden hair falling over his broad forehead. "I don't believe in middle grounds, Carly—you go all the way, or you don't go at all."

I find no reprieve in those cold green eyes, eyes the color of ripened limes, and even though I still feel my tears, I begin to think, no matter my fear, that he is right: saying the words isn't enough. If I could willfully pick and choose the terms of my surrender, what kind of a surrender would that be? None, none at all.

"I'm sorry," I whisper.

He watches me, waits for more.

"I'm sorry I resisted you," I say, and, anticipating the pain that will surely come, my eyes water once again. I blink back the tears, thinking I am a coward. "I do want to please you," I say.

He kisses the hollow of my neck, then places his lips on my eyelids, tastes my tears. He draws back. "Just relax," he says.

I nod.

He stands up, his finger still inside me. He moves it around, finds no resistance this time, and inserts

another finger. I close my eyes, force myself to concentrate on what he's doing right now, not on what
will come. My breath is slow, deep. His fingers slide
in and out easily. I try to enjoy the sensation, as I
have before. I think of how he fucks me, his cock
hard in my mouth, my cunt, my ass. I feel another
finger slide in. It, too, goes in easily. He's had three
fingers in my ass before. I breathe slowly, let him
push inside me, imagine it's his cock there, nudging
in, making itself known. He twists his fingers, casually fucks me with them, and then I feel his mouth
again, his tongue rooting around in my vagina, then
sliding over my clitoris, making me want more. He
withdraws his fingers and his tongue. His sudden
absence leaves me empty.

I open my eyes halfway, see through my lashes
that he's getting more lube, spreading it on his fingers, then on me. Closing my eyes, I wait for him to
continue.

He insinuates the three fingers back inside my ass,
sees that I have no trouble accepting them, then introduces a fourth—his thumb, I think. He rotates his
hand, presses against me, opening me up. He goes
out again, lubes up, comes back in, three fingers
first, judging by the feel, then all five. He squeezes
them in, twisting and turning gently. This is it, I
think, he's going in all the way, and I get scared all
over, forgetting to breathe, tightening up.

"Relax," he says.

I open my eyes and find him watching me.

"This is going to take a while. Close your eyes and
breathe deeply." His voice coaxes, as if he's a coach
wheedling a performance.

I do as he says. He works on me slowly, patiently,
his fingers worming inside at glacial speed, advancing, retreating, advancing, millimeter by slow millimeter. I don't know how long this goes on, forever

it seems. Then the pressure increases, becomes greater and more intense, and I feel I'm about to explode, that I'm stretched beyond tensile capacity. I groan, opening my eyes.

"No more," I say. "I can't take any more."

He stops. "There're lots of folds in the tissue down here," he says, "an amazing capability for expansion."

"I can't," I say, shaking my head, feeling a tear slide out of my eye.

"You will," he says softly.

Again, I shake my head. "I'll burst," I say, nearly panicked.

He surveys my body with dispassionate, cool eyes, his gaze sweeping over the pale flesh of my midriff and thighs, and then down to the bloated asshole skin, a long look there, as if he's judging the limits of my tolerance.

"I'll burst," I say again.

"No," he says, "you won't. Doctors do it all the time. The only difference here is that you're doing it without an anesthetic. Just relax your muscles, concentrate on breathing deeply, and let me take care of the rest."

I feel the sweat on my brow.

He reaches up with his free hand, touches my breast. He has lube on this hand also, and it leaves a greasy imprint on my nipple. He caresses it gently. Then I feel the hand in my ass moving again, slowly twisting, his fingers firmly ensconced. "I'm up to my third set of knuckles," he says, his voice low, as cool and dispassionate as his eyes. "As soon as I get those through, I'll be in."

I know if I allow myself to panic, it will be much worse. I breathe deeply, begging all my muscles to relax. I imagine my asshole is a rubber band with limitless elasticity, expanding, yielding, growing larger. He works on me, opening me up more and more, the pressure continuous, straining, bearing in. I feel distended and pulled apart.

"Exhale deeply," he says, his voice coaxing.

I take a long breath, let it out as slowly as I can, then suddenly gasp as I feel him slipping inside me, almost as if my ass is swallowing his hand, a gulping motion. He holds it inside me, not moving for a few seconds, watching for my response. "I'm up to my wrist," he says.

I am unable to speak. Although the pressure remains, it decreased as soon as he slipped inside, it's not nearly as intense, and the feeling now is unlike anything I can recall ever experiencing—a sensation of complete fullness and penetration, of one person cleaved to another in a carnal bond.

He smiles. He puts his other hand between my legs, finds my clitoris with his greasy fingers, begins stroking, playing with it until I respond, until I hear myself begging him to fuck me, to which he replies by moving the hand in my ass, rhythmically, pulsing, a slow steady beat, and something new overcomes me, surges like a wave rolling from his fist to my ass up to my heart, all through my body, an intense connection to James, the energy going from him to me too immense to fathom, and I find myself gasping once more, coming on his fingers, and then, when I'm through, James, who is erect once again, leaves my clitoris and turns his hand on himself, makes a greasy slide up and down his penis, jerking off, and I'm thinking he looks grand that way, his body tense and tanned and muscular, piston powered with the big fist grasping, and I'm thinking he belongs to me—or, rather, I belong to him—and a sense of pride overtakes me as I watch him manipulating his flesh, yanking, then pointing it in my direction. He takes aim and shoots his cum at me.

Afterward, he leans against my thigh, resting, his body slick with sweat. His fingers spread and flex in my ass. "If I'm not careful, this could hurt you . . . I could even kill you." He adds, "Easily."

He starts to work his way out of me, another slow progression. He glances up, his face arranged in a look of satisfaction. He says, "Maybe next time I'll insert up to my elbow."

In the bathroom, I wash myself, cleaning off the lubricant—not an easy task—then get dressed and return to the office. James is not here. The sling is gone, the hanging plants returned to their hooks in the ceiling. The office looks like an office once again, nothing but desks, chairs, filing cabinet, computer, printer.

I go back into the winery. It's dark all around, the only light coming from a high window, pale moonlight filtering in. Walking carefully through the building, looking for James, I try not to trip over the hoses or a piece of equipment on the floor. The building seems haunted at night, as quiet as a graveyard. As I'm making my way to the light switches, I see the stairs leading up to the catwalk. I stop. I think of Anna, her long fall. Whenever I've been in the winery, whenever anyone offered to show me around, to take me up the catwalk, I refused, made a feeble excuse to leave.

Now, I walk up the stairs. At the top, I look around. The catwalk is a good observation point, revealing the entire room below, but I don't spot James. Everything is dark, murky in the faint light. Obscure, fixed shadows furnish the room. Unless James is between the tanks, or behind some other piece of equipment, he's not in here.

I start to turn around, but a morbid sense of curiosity comes over me. The catwalk was rebuilt after Anna died, a lattice of metal attached to the guard-rail so no one could slip beneath it. Taking a cautious step forward, I wonder how many steps Anna took before she fell. I take another step, see the double row of fermentation tanks below me. I continue, then abruptly halt. Looking around, I peer down into the darkness of the room. I thought I heard a noise, a muffled, scraping sound, as if someone had bumped into one of the hoses lying on the floor, dragging it along a few inches. I listen. It's quiet.

"James?" I call out, hesitant, uncertain.

There is no answer. I sweep the room with my gaze, searching, but I see nothing untoward, no motion in the dark. The shadows are still.

"James?" I call out again. No reply. Silence is my answer.

I move forward, tentative steps, with a firm hold on the guardrail. I walk out to the middle, stop, look down. The concrete floor is far below me. Inexplicably, I think this is where Anna died, the very spot. A vague sense of recognition comes over me, a nagging feeling somehow related to remembrance, a sense that memory is trying to drop back into place. I picture Anna sprawled on the ground. But then I wonder if I'm only remembering my own fall. My injuries, the doctors told me, were consistent with a long fall. Anna died here, perhaps I, also, was meant to. I gaze down, a dizzying feeling taking over, a sense I've been here before. I remember someone pushing me, or hitting me, the unexpected shock of it, the suddenness. The concrete zooms up at me, and I see myself falling, helpless.

With a disorienting start, I jerk back. I look up, see someone on the catwalk coming toward me, a dark shadowy form. It's James, I think, and I want to run away, but I can't. My legs, leaden with fear, don't move.

"James?" I ask, hesitant.

"No," I hear Gina say. "It's only me."

As she walks closer, I begin to make out her form. "You scared me," I say. "I thought you were James."

"I'm sorry. I didn't mean to frighten you. I called out when you leaned over the railing. Didn't you hear me?"

I shake my head. She saw James and me in the office, I'm sure, his fist up my ass. I used to think she was spying, but now I wonder if she was just watching over me, making sure I came to no harm.

She comes closer, stands next to me, looks down over the railing, at the concrete far below.

"This is where Anna fell, isn't it?" I ask her.

"Yes."

I wait for her to tell me what really happened, but she doesn't say anything more. She grips the railing with her hands, her knuckles white. She seems on edge, frazzled more than before.

"It wasn't an accident," I say.

Gina doesn't respond. This is hard for her, giving up her twin. Finally, she says, "Anna shouldn't have married him. She would be alive today if only . . ." She pauses, then says, "I tried to warn her away. She wouldn't listen to me. Just like you."

I wait for her to continue. She doesn't.

"Tell me what happened," I say.

Still, Gina doesn't speak, just grips the railing, seems far off in her own thoughts. She sighs, a long, weary sound.

I'm afraid she'll change her mind, that she won't confess James's part in Anna's death. I say, "She was beautiful in her wedding picture."

No response.

I move closer, put my hand on hers. "She was beautiful in the picture," I say, trying to get Gina to talk.

She turns her head, looks at me. Finally, she says, "Yes, she was—even more so than the photograph revealed."

Again, she is silent, gazing into the dark abyss below. Her face, tired, worn out, clouds over.

"Did James ever paint her?" I ask, just to keep her talking.

She frowns, confused. "Paint her?" she repeats. "No, James doesn't do portraits."

"What about—" I stop. I assumed Gina knew about the paintings in the shed. Perhaps they keep secrets, after all.

Gina says, "Portraits, landscapes, still lifes—those are much too tame for my brother. You've seen the paintings on his walls. Death and destruction, that's his forte."

"There's the landscape in your cottage," I say.

"He didn't paint that."

"No, I mean the one in your living room. The vineyard painting."

Gina shakes her head. "He didn't paint that. I did."

I look at her, momentarily confused. And then it comes to me—all the paintings hanging in James's house are signed J.McG. The vineyard paintings, and the ones of me in the crates, aren't signed.

I step back, realizing what this means. The paintings in the crates, dozens of them, each one of me—Gina painted them all, not James. The obsession—and the guilt—was hers. Thinking back, I realize James never told me, specifically, that he was the artist. The darkness of the winery closes in. Panic, like a fist, grips me, clenches in my chest. Slowly, I back up.

"What's the matter?" Gina asks. She takes a step toward me, clamps her hand around my wrist.

A picture of Anna comes to my mind, lying on the ground, body broken. Then I imagine myself on the concrete floor. Gina will push me over the edge—the way she did before. Her hand is still clamped around mine.

"You almost killed me fifteen years ago," I say. "You shattered my face. You did that to me."

I see the look in her eyes—the confusion that turns to shock as she realizes who I am—but she doesn't release my arm. "Yes," she says, a ghostly whisper, her hand tightening on mine. "I did that to you."

Before she has time to act, I ram into her with all my strength. She lets out a loud *uuumph!*, then stumbles backward. I turn to run.

"Don't," I hear her gasp. "Don't . . ." and then I feel her hand on the back of my shoulder, grabbing me, yanking me back, then her arms circle my waist and she holds me tightly from behind. I struggle to break free, push her back with a sudden burst of strength, and we both crash against the opposite guardrail, then I'm falling backward, my feet slipping out, while Gina's arms are still around me, holding me tightly, and I see that I pushed too hard, that we're both going over the guardrail, toppling over the edge, falling down, her arms finally breaking away from me. I hear a scream—mine or hers? maybe both—while I'm flinging out my arms, scrambling, grabbing out, everything a blur of motion and sound, the frantic grasps, the scream, her body going down, everything happening so fast, a split second of time, yet somehow I've managed to latch onto a side post and I'm hanging on, all the while hearing the heavy pounding of footsteps, hearing the dull thud of a fallen body, and I'm hugging the post, breathing sharply, my legs and torso dangling in the air. I am gasping, barely able to breathe, my heart racing, my thoughts coming in shattered images, splinters of meaning. Gina fell. The thud. Her body hitting concrete. Footsteps? Whose were those? Blood pounds in my ears, throbs. I try to pull myself up, but I'm down too far—and I'm too scared to release a hand to give myself a boost. I hug the post tighter. It digs into my arms, the sharp edges boring into my flesh. The pounding in my ears continues, and then I realize it's not blood pounding, but footsteps, getting louder, closer, the weight shaking the platform. Gina has come back to finish the job. I hear footsteps running the length of the catwalk, see legs, then a body leaning over the guardrail. With a shock, I see it's James. Then, slowly, my confusion lifts. Gina could not withstand a fall from the catwalk un-scathed. There would be blood, broken bones.

He seems as surprised as I. He stares at me a mo-ment, finally reaches down, grabs my arms, and yanks me up. He stands back, his hands by his sides, his face as blank as stone.

He turns and walks the length of the platform, his step heavy, his shoulders squared, stiff. He goes down the stairs. I look over the guardrail, get an instant sensation of falling, dizziness, nausea. I force myself to look. Even in the darkness, I see it, the shadowy lump of a body.

I go down the stairs, walk over to James. He's sitting on the floor, cradling Gina to his chest. He rocks her back and forth, slowly, murmuring in her ear. Her long hair is tangled in his arms, flowing over, a cascade of black curls. He pulls her closer, rocking, whispering words both she and I are unable to hear.

CHAPTER TWENTY-FIVE

I've never been to a funeral before. I listen to the minister, a bald-headed man with thick black glasses, try to concentrate on his words, good words I'm sure, consoling words, but they seem to bypass me, floating up gently into the air, dissipating before any meaning can be discerned. The sounds that come to me are background noises, the shuffling feet, a cough now and then, a few sniffles, the baby cooing from somewhere in the crowd, a very large crowd.

Shifting my weight, I lean on the other foot. The cemetery is well groomed, small rolling hillocks pebbled with headstones, colorful flowers sticking out of the green grass. The minister continues speaking. I pick up a few words now and then, words meant to comfort, but they don't bring me any peace of mind. I stare at Gina's coffin, dark wood, polished, mahogany maybe, an expensive coffin. When the police came that night, James told them her fall was an accident. I didn't fill in the blanks. I wanted to, but he insisted I wait until his mother recovered from her grief. Gina goes to the grave with her reputation intact, but she can't harm me anymore. *That* brings me peace of mind.

I look over at James, find him staring at me, a strange expression on his face. He turns away before I can read it. Even in his grief, he's a formidable presence, roughly handsome in the black suit, stalwart. Next to him, his mother sways slightly, and he reaches over and holds her arm, steadies her. She's wearing a long dark dress, and her face is pallid, almost ashen. In her hand, she clutches a yellow rose, one of Gina's favorites. She listens to the minister with her eyes closed, not opening them until he's finished.

A mound of dirt, from the freshly dug grave, sits beside the coffin. When the coffin is lowered, James steps forward and throws a shovelful of dirt into the grave. It makes a soft patter when it hits the coffin. Mrs. McGuane grimaces. She moves up to James, opens her fist, lets the yellow rose fall into the hole.

I have a yellow rose also, which she gave me earlier today at the house. I step forward, lift my arm. James puts his hand lightly on my shoulder, restraining me. Pausing, my arm outstretched over the grave, the yellow rose still in my grasp, I look up at him. He bends down, puts his mouth close to my ear.

"You're glad she's dead," he says, whispering it so quietly that it takes a second before the words register.

With a start, I drop the rose. Since Gina fell, he's barely spoken to me. "No," I say, shaking my head, but he has already drawn back, by his mother's side, a pained look of grief settled on his face.

I go upstairs to get away from everyone, walk down the hall, then stand in the doorway of the room on the end. When Gina was growing up, this room belonged to her. Mrs. McGuane uses it as a guest bedroom. It's light and airy, like a spring day, with flowered wallpaper and a pale pink bedspread and a sliding glass door that opens onto a balcony with a grand view of the surrounding vineyards and distant hills. I came here in springtime, the hills lushly green from recent rain. Now, they're brown and parched. Over to the right, I see a small plot of seventy-year-old zinfandel vines, some of the oldest in Napa Valley. The vines, thick and ropy, weathered with age, endure. They are lasting, riding out the draughts and floods and all the bad times that eventually come. They will prevail without Gina. James, I'm hoping, can do the same.

Suddenly, I sense I'm no longer alone. Turning around, I see James. He yanks me into the room, shuts the door, and locks it.

"What are you doing?" I say.

He shoves me up against the wall, glares at me. His eyes are red, bloodshot from lack of sleep. "You're glad she's dead," he says, repeating his words at the cemetery.

The look on his face, the bitterness, makes me wince. I reach up, touch his cheek, place my palm on his face. He shakes it away. "No," I say. "I didn't want her to die."

His breathing is heavy, angry. "But you wanted her to pay for what she did," he insists. "You came to Byblos for that. You came for me. Then you realized it was Gina who . . ." His hands press into my shoulders, crush me against the wall.

"I wanted her to be prosecuted, not to die."

His breath is hot in my face. His hands bear down on me, pressing.

"That hurts," I say, but he ignores this, keeps me pinned up against the bedroom wall, his fingers digging into my shoulders. "Gina wanted you all to her-self," I tell him. "Her love for you, her jealousy—that's what killed her, not me."

I feel him back off slightly. He knows this is true.

"I didn't want her to die," I say.

His jaw clenches. "I saw the struggle," he says, his voice a low whisper, tense, barely controlled. "I ran to the catwalk, started up the stairs. It was too dark to see clearly, but I knew it was you and Gina. I heard a scream, then saw someone fall."

He leans in closer, his face inches from mine. "I thought it was you who fell," he says. "You—not Gina."

Without warning, he draws back his arm, his hand clenched tightly in a fist, then drives it for-ward. I let out a startled scream, sure he's going to hit me. I bring up my hands to protect my face, but his fist slams into the wall, slams so hard the wall shakes. He must've hit a stud, because the wall doesn't give. Small indents, prints of his knuckles, remain behind.

He stares at me, his face tight, a vein throbbing at his temple, then he's reaching down, grappling with his pants, still pinning me up against the wall.

"Don't, James," I say. "Everyone downstairs—"

But he doesn't listen. He doesn't care about the people who came back to the house after the fu-neral, doesn't care if he is missed, doesn't care if they hear us now. He throws off my shoes, yanks down my pantyhose, then lifts me up. The movement feels more like a seizure than an embrace, his hands clamping on. I don't resist. He shoves his penis inside and fucks me, banging my back up against the wall, fucks me with a frantic urgency, almost feverish, an angry grimace on his face, and I know, right now, at this moment, he wishes I was the one who died. He grips me fiercely, his arms like a vice. Although scared, I make no attempt to break away. He makes noises I've never heard before, wounded sounds. He's like a beast raging, fucking turbulently, as if fucking alone, the sheer angry force of it, can stave off the inevitable future, a future without his twin.

CHAPTER TWENTY-SIX

"I'm going for a walk," I tell Mrs. McGuane. She ate breakfast over an hour ago, but she's still at the kitchen table, reading one of Gina's poems. Mrs. McGuane retrieved them from the cottage the day of the funeral. Gina typed each poem on a separate sheet of paper, kept all of them in large manila envelopes at her desk. I read them several days ago, when Mrs. McGuane was sleeping. The poems reminded me of James's paintings: dark, bleak, violent. I thought she might have written about me, but she didn't. I wasn't mentioned at all.

"Would you like to come with me?" I ask her.

She looks up from the sheet of paper, thinks for a minute. Her white hair lies flat around her head, like a helmet, and her round, wire-rimmed reading glasses give her a wide-eyed, owllike expression.

"No," she says finally, and she waves me away with a shaky movement of her hand. Her nail polish, once fastidiously attended to, is chipped and peeling. "You go on without me, dear," she says, and she returns to the poem.

Since Gina died, Mrs. McGuane sits around the house most of the day, reading, and refuses to go to the winery. She's practically turned the house over to me. I pay all the bills, take care of any maintenance or repair problems that come up, run errands, do all the shopping. Now, the housekeeper and gardener come to me if they have a question, rather than Mrs. McGuane, and I even had to hire someone to help out in the kitchen so I can attend to everything else.

"The fresh air would do you some good," I say.

Again, she waves me away, not even looking up this time. "Later," she mumbles, without much vitality, as if Gina's death has sucked it all out of her. "Perhaps later."

I watch her for a moment, her forehead wrinkled in a frown, trying to make sense of her daughter's poetry, the violence and the despair of it. I think of my own mother, wondering if she grieved my loss as much. Gina's absence is felt acutely, not only by Mrs. McGuane and James, but by everyone who works here. Her death has cast a pall at Byblos, and the dolorous atmosphere won't seem to lift. I start to walk out of the room.

"Carly?"

"Yes?" I say, turning around.

"You won't leave us, will you?" She peers at me through her glasses, her face anxious. She sets down the sheet of paper, absently smooths it out with the flat of her hand. "James will come around," she says.

James, just the opposite of his mother, busies himself with work, the loss of Gina creating in him desperate bursts of energy to fill the void of her absence. If he's not at the winery, then he's working the vineyards. I rarely see him, and when I do there is a distance between us that we can't seem to bridge. Gina, in death, keeps us apart more than she did in life.

"He'll come around," she says again, sighing. "He just needs a little more time. We all do."

She gets up, comes over to me. She's lost a few pounds, and her blue dress hangs loosely around her waist, making her appear frail and insubstantial. She doesn't seem so tall anymore, although, in fact, she towers over me still. She puts her hands on my shoulders.

"You will stay, won't you? Forever, I mean. I don't want any more changes in my life. I don't want another loss." She presses my head to her breast, cradles me as if I were the daughter.

I go out the back door, pass through the fruit and vegetable gardens. In the distance, I see vineyards all around, field after field of them. Fall harvest has finally begun, and the vineyards pulsate with activity. Field hands, paid by the box, are moving swiftly through the rows with their curved picking knives, slicing off grape clusters. A tractor, towing a flatbed filled with bins of grapes, trundles across the land to the winery, where the fruit will be weighed, crushed, pressed, and pumped into barrels or stainless-steel tanks and allowed to ferment.

Crossing the lawn, I walk toward the cottage. I haven't been there since Gina died. Even now, I'm angry I was so easily duped. I thought she was my friend. Perhaps it's spiteful, since she's dead, but I want people to know her for who she really was. I want her held accountable, even in death, for the scars she gave me long ago. James still asks me to wait.

I reach the cottage. Her white truck sits in front, a constant reminder of her absence. Nobody drives it now, although someone washed and waxed it recently. It's clean and shiny, free of its usual spatterings of mud and dirt and caked-on debris.

I test the front door, find that the knob turns. Keeping my hand on it, I hesitate. Do I really want to go inside? I glance over at Gina's truck, so spotless and brightly white that it seems out of place. There should be splotches of mud on it, and dust everywhere, so much dust that it would take on a dull, fuscous hue, the grayish-brown color of dirty dishwater, but instead it sparkles, gleams in the warm morning sun, wiped clean, just like Gina's reputation.

I push open the door and step inside. The housekeeper has been here, packing away Gina's things as I instructed. Cardboard boxes lie all around, empty ones with their flaps open, some stacked against the wall with "GOODWILL" written on the sides, others, a few, marked "GINA," and then "STORE IN ATTIC." Two large, black trash bags sit by the door. James and Mrs. McGuane have already taken the mementos and personal effects they want to save.

Tentatively, I walk through the cottage. It has the hollow, eerie feel of abandonment to it, of a place forsaken. There are no pictures on the walls, no cups or magazines or newspapers on the coffee table, no blanket scrunched up in the corner of the couch. In the kitchen, the cupboards are bare, so, too, the refrigerator.

I make my way into the bedroom, see that the housekeeper hasn't begun in here yet. The room is contemporary, painted in cool colors of apple green and light blue, the honeyed oak furniture blond and modern. Gina hadn't made her bed the last day of her life, and the pastel bedclothes lie rucked up in the middle of the mattress; a tossed Kleenex lies there also, wadded in a ball.

Curious about her private life, I open the dresser drawers, see piles of silky lingerie, balls of socks, folded sweaters and jeans and sweatpants, several swimsuits. I drift over to the nightstand. The top drawer contains sex toys—vibrators, battery operated and plug-ins, dildos, two jars of lube. I wonder how the housekeeper will sort these—Goodwill, attic, or trash?

Closing the drawer, I see her boots lined up in the closet, all of them: cowboy boots, purple suede boots, brown leather ones, black ones, boxy toes and pointed. Gina almost always wore boots. Up on the top shelf, I spot a white boot box, separate from the others. I go over and pull it down. I take off the lid. Inside, there are dozens of newspaper articles—all about me. I sit on the bed and take them out, one by one. The *Davis Enterprise*, the *Sacramento Bee*, the *San Francisco Chronicle*, more. The articles, some yellow hued, others brownish, are stiff with age, crisp, fragile. Gina must've scoured all the major California papers, searching for a mention of me. I read one headline, "Young Girl Remains in Coma." Another, "Mystery Girl Without a Past." Then, "Still No Clues." There are articles here I've never seen before, from newspapers far away. I flip through them, reading the headlines, the first few paragraphs.

Abruptly, I stop. There is a photograph, a Polaroid, slightly faded and umber hued. I pick it up. This is me. I recognize the blouse—white with small blue flowers—the same blouse in many of the portraits Gina painted. At last, I have a true picture of what I looked like more than fifteen years ago. And her visage is not the one I've come to know, the one of a girl made ugly by her rage. My features here—the fragile chin and dainty nostrils and milky white translucent skin—are clearly in focus. I finally see the young girl who used to be me. She was pretty and sweet, not yet a woman, a delicate creature with smooth, flawless skin, with a fresh innocence in her face that time hadn't yet taken away. Even accounting for the age difference between us, there is no resemblance. I had no reason to fear, when I came to Byblos last spring, that James might recognize the young girl in me. The doctors did a good job rebuilding my face, but they had little from which to work. My nose, my jawline, my cheekbones—they're all different from the girl in the photo. Her features are almost perfect; mine are patched together, asymmetrical, a face made from leftover parts, a little of this, a little of that. I find myself envious of this girl in the photograph, her fresh face, her easy beauty. Any beauty I may have comes from the pain of surgery. But *beauty* is not really a word people apply to my kind of face—unusual, they call it, a bit odd, a strange attractiveness. But beauty?—no. I am not beautiful. The girl, had she survived intact, would be beautiful. I can see that clearly. I put the photo in my breast pocket.

I go through the rest of the box. Near the bottom, I see the newspaper clippings of James's wife, Anna, the reports of her fall from the catwalk, her death. I take them out. A small slip of paper falls to the floor. I bend over and pick it up. I read the typewritten words. It's one of Gina's poems, not as polished as her others, different in style, but the meaning is obvious:

> *Neither girl would heed my frown,*
> *(couldn't let my twin stray).*
> *Ashes, ashes, they all fell down:*
> *(couldn't let them get away).*

CHAPTER TWENTY-SEVEN

"You covered for Gina," I say.

James sits on the couch, coffee mug in hand. He must have a meeting with business associates today, because he's dressed nicely in dark gabardine slacks, an ivory-colored shirt, and a printed silk tie. Steam rises from the mug. His left hand is in a white cast, from the tip of his fingers to the middle of his forearm. When he slammed his fist into the wall after Gina's funeral, he cracked his knuckles and broke three bones.

He looks over at me. I hold out the poem I found at Gina's cottage. He takes it, reads it carefully, then sighs.

"In the police report, and in the newspaper, it states you were alone with Anna on the catwalk," I say. "But you weren't, were you?"

"No," he says, handing the poem back to me. He brings the coffee mug to his lips, takes a sip while watching me above the rim. He says, "I didn't see Gina push Anna over the catwalk—they were behind me—but I always suspected she did. When the police came . . ." He sets his mug on the table beside the couch, sighs once more. "I couldn't let her go to jail," he says.

Midmorning light, flat and ashen colored, filters through the arched windows. Gray motes of dust drift in the hazy air. "You knew she'd come after me," I say.

"No." A lock of blond hair falls in his eyes. He brushes it away.

"I'm not going to wait any longer," I say. "I'm going to show this poem to the police. I'm going to tell them everything."

"She's no longer a threat to you."

Across the room, I see the canvas leaning against his desk, the painting of the girl. I can't see it clearly from this angle, but I don't need to. I know it by heart, the rage, the disbelief that life could go so horribly wrong, the face distorted beyond human recognition. I go over to James. "I want . . . I want people to know who did that to me."

He reaches up, puts his hand on my arm, pulls me closer. "It'll destroy my mother," he says. "And it'll destroy us."

He pulls me onto his lap, holds me close for the first time since Gina died. "I wouldn't give her up when she was alive," he says, "and I won't now that she's dead." His right hand goes to my leg, makes a smooth slide down to my ankle, where he clasps it, gently, over the gold chain.

I change the subject. "What's my name?" I ask. "My real name."

He shakes his head, a small movement. "I don't know," he says. "You called yourself Sophie, but you made that up. You'd run away—that was fairly obvious. You didn't talk about your parents or where you came from."

"You never asked?"

"No." He puts his hand on the back of my neck, plays with the short hairs at the nape. "I'm sorry, but I never did."

In the hazy light of the room, his face looks soft, without harsh lines, even the scar at his temple only a faint etching, and his hair silky blond.

"You'll have to let Gina go," he says. "No matter that I love you, no matter how much I may come to love you, I'll never allow you to expose Gina."

I have to make a choice: Gina or him. The truth or him. I think of the professor's house. It's cold and empty. I am a guest there, like a stranger in a hotel, just passing through, as I've passed through all the other apartments and trailers and rented rooms and houses I've lived in, none of them really a home. There's no one there to greet me, no one to ask if I've had a nice day.

And then there is the McGuanes' home, a place where *family* means something. James and his mother—and Gina still—they have ties to one another that can never be broken. They love, and they are loved. In exchange for Gina, James is offering me this.

One blond eyebrow cocked, he watches me, waits for an answer.

Sighing, I nod my head. "I'll let it go," I say. I lay my head against his chest. I feel a headache coming on. I wanted justice for what was done to me. I wanted someone to pay, to suffer as did I. I wanted, at the very least, for the truth to be known. Now, there will be no final accounting. I chose James over the truth.

He leaves for work, but I remain behind. I cradle my head in my arms. My headache seems to form a fissure running from front to back. I've spent my life looking for justice, but now I've let it slip away. No one will ever know what Gina did. I sit, for hours I sit, disappointment and bitterness washing over me like a wave. Then I think of what I have: James. The room lightens with the afternoon sun, and, gradually, even though I try to hold on to it, the bitterness lightens up too. In the brightened room, my headache lifts and disappears. I feel almost weightless, as if a burden has been removed—the onus of vengeance—and a sense of relief comes over me, relief that, finally, maybe, after all these years, I can let it go.

CHAPTER TWENTY-EIGHT

It's still dark outside when James gets out of bed. I hear him walking softly across the loft, go into the bathroom. When he comes back out, he dresses in the dark, not wanting to disturb me. He doesn't know I'm awake. He'll come over and kiss me before he leaves—he always does—and I snuggle down in bed, listening to the quiet sounds of him dressing, waiting for my kiss. Every morning during harvest, he gets up before I do. Sometimes, when he wants to fuck, he'll wake me; other times, he lets me sleep.

I hear him kneeling down by the bed, then feel his arm around me, feel his lips lightly on my cheek. I open my eyes, withdraw one arm from under the covers, reach out to the shadowy bulk of him, feel the hard plaster of the cast on his left hand.

"You're awake," he says, his voice a whisper in the dark, plush, like black velvet.

I nod. His other hand feels warm on my bare back. He holds me close, his touch so familiar it seems an extension of myself. "Do you want to fuck?" I ask. "We can fuck, if you like. Or I can suck you before you leave."

In the darkness, I see him give me a soft smile,

shake his head. "Go back to sleep," he says. "It's the middle of the night."

I'd forgotten tonight was special. He's experimenting with a barrel of port, and he needs to check the fermentation. The timing, he explained earlier, is crucial. If he doesn't stop the fermentation at the precise point, all his efforts will be wasted.

He brushes his lips against my skin, whispers, "I'll see you later," and then I hear him walk across the room, down the stairs, out the front door.

I try to sleep, but can't. James gave me a key last week, when we were hiking in the mountains. Stroking my cheek, he said there was something innocent in my pale blue eyes, vulnerable too, that inspired protection whether I wanted it or not. His words surprised me. People always see an odd coldness in my face, but he saw something else. He gave me his key then, pressed it in my palm, and I realized, for the first time, that love had come.

Getting up, I almost trip on one of my hand weights that had rolled out from under his bed, where I store them now. I still work out nearly every day, building up my strength, as if weight lifting is a defensive activity, as if it could prevent future injury. But it won't.

I push the weight under the bed, thinking maybe it's time to stop preparing for the worst. I put on my clothes, grab my car keys off the table by the front door, then drive down the winding road. The night is black, the air cool. The recent change of the season is subtle—shorter days, cooler mornings, a brisk smell in the air, muted instead of bright, sun-drenched colors—but fall has definitely arrived.

I head for the winery. The black Cherokee is parked by the side of the ivy- and lichen-covered stone building, near the outside entrance to the office. I open the door. The yeasty smell of fermenting

wine permeates the air. It's overpowering, and un-
forgettable—a heady aroma of sweet fruit and pungent yeast, and a faint prickly sensation of carbon
dioxide in the air. James is at his desk, in front of
the computer—it must not yet be time to stop the
fermentation of the port grapes—and he looks up,
his face questioning, when I come in.

"I couldn't sleep," I say, crossing the room. I see
the white boot box on top of the filing cabinet.
James said I could have it. I stand behind him, put
my hands on his shoulders, then let them slide down
to his chest. His wool shirt, blue-and-gray checked,
a tartan pattern, feels soft under my hands. He's
wearing faded blue jeans, and a white T-shirt under
the wool. I like the way he looks in jeans, the denim
snug across his thighs, as if the material can barely
contain the muscularity of him. He leans back in the
chair, puts one hand on mine.

"Do you have time for breakfast later?" I ask. "I
thought I'd make waffles." I rest my head on his
shoulder, close my eyes, still tired. "Cardamom–sour
cream waffles. With lingonberry butter and pre-
serves."

He pulls me around. I straddle his legs, hiking up
my brown skirt. My buttocks and thighs are scored
with thin lines, bruises from the whipping he gave
me last night. I am wearing *his* marks. I've turned
myself over to him, surrendering not only to the
pain but also to his will. I accept whatever he gives—
and I like it. I can no longer pretend I submit solely
to gain information about my past. I may have begun this out of necessity, but I continue out of need.
His love consumes me.

I wrap myself around him. The grainy texture of
his jeans rubs against my bare skin, against the insides of my thighs. Pressing my head to his chest, I
listen to the steady beating of his heart, the reassur-

ing sound of life. I take in the heady fermenting aroma in the air. In the other room, grape juice is bubbling and churning and frothing in the tanks, turning into wine, the yeast converting the sugar of the grapes into alcohol and carbon dioxide. It's a lusty, turbulent process of change, alive and ebullient and, I think, very sexual. I move my hands lower, down to his belt.

"Tell me what you want," he says, whispering into my neck. I hear the desire in his voice, that nascent need heating up, churning like the fermenting wine. His hands span my waist, holding me firmly.

I pull my blouse over my head, then reach around and unhook my bra, slide it off my shoulders and let it drop to the floor. His good hand comes up to my breasts. He squeezes my nipples, plays with them. A surging ache, not of pain but of longing, rises in my loins. He keeps his fingers on my nipples, pulling, tugging. Milk comes out in small spurts, dribbles on his fingers, on my midriff. He leans forward, puts his mouth on my right breast, latches onto the nipple, sucks on it, drawing out my milk. I rub against him, feel the fabric of his jeans on my bare thighs. Reaching down, I touch the bulge of his penis through his pants. He sucks the milk out, drains me dry, then clamps onto the other nipple. I undo his jeans, pull out his penis, realizing there is something reckless and feral about all of this, about the way he loves, and I feel I'm on parlous grounds, a place where anomie prevails, yet I cannot back away. My future lies with him. I wrap my hand around his penis, feel its power. I move closer, rub it against my crotch, then slide down onto it, pushing it deep inside me. His love may be reckless, but it makes me feel alive.

"Tell me what you want," he says again, insistent, and I lose myself in the sound of his voice, in the solidity of his body, in the penis burrowing inside me, becoming part of me, an anchor. I understand, now, the young girl's—*my*—devotion to James, her willingness to surrender everything. I understand because, like her, I am unable to say no. His desires have become my own. In the yeasty aroma of the air, the walls seem to swell and expand, making room for new possibilities.

"Whatever you want," I answer him, whispering, wondering if I am foolish to love this way. "I want whatever you want," I say again, and he puts his hands on my hips, rocks me on his penis until we both come.

His hair is mussed—blond strands falling over his forehead into his eyes, a shock of hair partially concealing the scar on his temple—and it makes me smile. When I first came to Byblos, he seemed so composed, a man in total control, his demeanor self-assured. Even his clothes fit perfectly, as if they were tailored. Now I see his humanness, the chinks in the formidable facade, the hair drooping in his eyes like a tousled little boy. Of course this side of him existed all along, but, so intimidated by his presence, I never noticed.

Quickly, I check my own hair in the mirror. Then I pause in wonderment. When did I stop flinching at my own reflection? A faint smile appears. The visage I see in the mirror isn't so bad after all. It's normal, almost, and I realize that the past is over now, that all the scars, and all the pain, and the family I left behind—they're finally vanishing, slowly pulled into the whirling vortex of time gone by.

Outside, the night is still black. I drive up to the main house. By moonlight, I see the elaborate dark brickwork, the arched paned-glass windows, the wooden double door, the tall trees shrouding the home. I remember my first impression of the house. It looked like a large two-story country estate, impressive, with a solid feel of permanence to it, as if it was part of the land, taking root. I was envious, that feeling of permanence completely foreign to me. But as I look at the home now, I realize I've found my place. For the first time in my life, I have ties of my own, to the land, to the McGuanes. I have responsibilities. Byblos *is* my home now. This is the place where I fit in.

The boot box is on the passenger seat. Although James gave it to me, I know I should throw the box away, or at least store it out of sight. It is part of the bargain I have struck with him: a future in exchange for the past. I pick through the newspaper clippings, glance through the ones I haven't read before. I read about Anna's fall, from a newspaper in Sonoma. Then I read it again, one sentence in the last paragraph. This wasn't mentioned in the article I copied at the library, this wasn't in the *Napa Valley Register*. A knot of uneasiness settles in my chest, seems to grow. I read it one more time. A small detail, insignificant to everyone but me. And James.

I sit in my car, waiting. After an hour, a tinge of flat gray appears in the eastern sky, and the land, still without much color, seems dull and lifeless, washed out. More time passes. The morning sun rises and brightens the vineyards, and the pickers descend upon the rows of vines. Mrs. McGuane will be up now. I go inside the house, put my question to her. She thinks for a moment, remembering, then gives me the answer I don't want to hear. The past, I know now, is never truly over.

CHAPTER TWENTY-NINE

I drive up the narrow road to James's house—for the last time—and curve around the oak-covered hillock. In the vineyard on the left, pickers move down the rows of vines, their hats and heads, protruding over the trellised leaves, bobbing along. The harvest is coming to a close, the workers picking the last of the grapes. Today will be my final day at Byblos.

I go inside the house, stand by the door for a minute, take in the sparse elegance of the room, the high-vaulted ceiling, the long wooden table, the brick-framed arched windows—a house redolent of the man who owns it, masculine and solid, with an undercurrent of cool detachment. I thought I knew James, thought I finally had him figured out. I was wrong.

I take the stairs up to the loft. The drapes over the huge window are pulled back, revealing, like a movie screen, a scene of humpbacked hills lined up behind his home. Sunlight streams inside the room, giving the rattan chair, which hangs near the window, a blanched, faded hue. The chair is suspended from a stainless-steel chain attached to the hoist, the line from the hoist tied off on the metal cleat bolted in the wall. James can take down the chair easily, without lowering it, but the hook is too high for me to reach. I untie the rope controlling the hoist-and-pulley device, then lower the rattan chair and re-move it from the hook.

I cross over to the antique trunk, open it. I inspect the slings and harnesses, trying to decide which would be the easiest to use. I've seen James set up all of these, and I'm fairly sure I can do it myself. I pull out the sit sling, a suspension bar, a panic snap, several clips, then take everything to the middle of the room. I attach a panic snap to the hook on the chain, the suspension bar to the panic snap, then the sling to the bar. I go back to the hoist rope and raise the sling. I tie off the line, pull on it to make sure it's secure. I knot it again, then a third time—over-kill, I know, but I don't want it coming loose.

I return to the sling. Walking around it, I decide where I'll need clips, then I attach several to the D rings. I go back to the trunk, rummage inside for anything else I'll need. I pull out two pairs of leather cuffs—both wrist and ankle cuffs—and take them over to the sling, set them on the floor. Then, getting a second thought, I go back to the trunk and take out two sets of metal handcuffs. James rarely uses these. They're not practical; they chafe, cut into the skin. I'll use only one, but, unable to anticipate which strap he'll grab, I'll need both of them at-tached to the sling. The sit sling has two vertical straps, like a swing, and on each strap I lock one end of a handcuff, let the other end dangle open. I fiddle with the handcuffs, make sure I can close them without any trouble. I don't know where the key is. I suppose it doesn't matter.

I call the winery. Patsy, the office manager, an-swers. She locates James, but it takes several minutes before he can come to the phone. When I hear his voice, clipped, terse, I hesitate, don't speak right away.

"I'm at your house," I finally tell him. "Can you come home for a few minutes?"

He doesn't answer. His breathing is short, impatient. This is the busiest time of the year at the winery. He told me earlier he couldn't make it for breakfast.

Before he can refuse, I say, "I really need to see you." I add, "Please come."

Over the phone, I hear background noises, people talking, a scraping of metal, the buzzing whir of machinery. I picture him looking out into the winery, distracted by my call, his fingers tapping silently against his pant leg, that unconscious gesture of his.

"Give me a half hour," he says, and he hangs up.

I take off my clothes, go into the bathroom. Gazing at myself in the mirror, I tilt my head to see the faint scar under my chin. Then I look at the one below my left breast, and the one on the inside of my thigh. They aren't so bad, not really. I'm more objective now, more so than when I first came to Byblos when all I saw every time I looked in the mirror were memories of cross-stitching sutures covering my face and body, train-track scars marring the flesh. But they were psychic scars, from a soul ache not easily repaired, and I'm able to see myself much more clearly now, thanks to James. He exposed me constantly, acclimatized me to my own body. He gave me the scars, and he took them away. I am no different, really, from any other woman. I can see that now. Thanks to James.

Getting under the shower, I let the warm water wash over me, think of what will happen next, of where I will go. The fullness of my breasts begins to ache. I knead them, pull on them until the milk flows. The milk dribbles down my belly, my thighs, between my legs, a whitish bath, my skin laved with sweet mother's milk.

Except I'm not a mother.

I lather up my hair, rinse out the shampoo, then slide a soapy washrag all over my body. I stay under the hot water, let it beat down on me until my skin is flushed pink. I see the gold chain around my ankle. I'll cut it off after today. One more time with James, I think, and then I'll leave Byblos forever. I turn off the shower, dry myself with a towel. Wrapping it around me, I walk into the loft. I stop.

James is here, sitting on the trunk.

I didn't hear him come in. He doesn't speak, just watches me from across the room, his left hand, still in the white cast, on his thigh. He brushes back his hair. It's lighter than when I first met him, bleached from the summer sun, and I can't help but think— even now, with his hand in a cast—that he resembles a Nordic warrior of heroic proportions, very blond, very big, a man not easily felled.

"What's this for?" he asks, nodding toward the sling.

Walking across the loft, I let the towel slide to the floor, exposing myself. "We haven't used it for a while," I say to him. "Not since Gina died." Naked, my body still flushed from the shower, I stand close to him, resting my hand on his shoulder.

He looks at me, not moving, deciding whether he has time for this.

I lean closer, brush my lips against his. He smells of the outdoors, crushed leaves, wild grass, a walk through a vineyard. "Since Gina died," I whisper, "you hold back when you whip me. I want more." I touch his cast, my fingertips making a leisurely trail. "You still blame me for what happened to her— punish me for that. Beat me."

Grabbing me with his good hand, he pulls me down to his lap, kisses me hard. His fingers feel like talons, digging in. The cast, against the back of my shoulder, slides roughly on my skin. His tongue gropes, prods, invades. He clenches a fistful of my hair in his hand, makes my scalp burn. Suddenly, he stops. He pulls back. The light from the window changes the hue of his green eyes, gives them a yellowish tinge, chartreuse, a look of distrust.

Tentatively, I reach for his blue-and-gray checked shirt. I work the buttons out of their holes, push the shirt off his shoulders, then pull the white T-shirt over his head. I place my palm in the slope between his pectorals, to see if I can feel a heartbeat, but I don't. Smooth skin, muscle, power—but no heart. He said he loved me. Now, I wonder what that means.

I start to get off his lap, but he restrains me with a hand on my thigh. I wait. When he relaxes his grip, I sink down, slowly, between his knees. I remove his shoes and socks while he watches. I reach up and unbuckle his belt, then, for the second time today, I undo his jeans. Still, he watches. As I pull down his pants, he lifts up to help me. I slip them off his legs. I go for his penis. It's soft and wrinkly, drooping slightly to one side, fitting easily in my mouth, down to the base, but not for long. As I suck him, it grows and lengthens, elongates like one of those oblong carnival balloons, stretching out as it's blown up. It fills the space in my mouth, sounds for the depths of my throat, then dives deeper, demanding I accommodate its newly prodigious size.

Breaking away, I stand up, back off, retreat to the sling. "Will you help me?" I ask.

He comes over, holds one of the vertical straps to steady the sling. I hesitate before putting my foot through the leg strap. Reaching down, I touch his penis, wrap my hand around the length of it. I lean forward to kiss him, put my other hand on the strap near his. I feel around for the metal handcuff, find it. His tongue pushes inside my mouth, his penis slides in my fist. I snap the handcuff around his wrist. My heart beats fast. My impulse is to jump backward, out of his way, but I don't. I stay close to him, warding off suspicion, keep one hand on his penis, the other on his wrist.

He looks at the sling, at his wrist cuffed to the strap, then down at me, his green eyes quizzical but not wary. No, he's much too arrogant, this Nordic god, to think there is cause for alarm. Quietly, he says, "What are you doing, Carly?"

I turn my head, kiss his manacled wrist. "I thought, maybe, you'd like to do something different." I run my tongue along his arm. "I want to fuck you while *you're* in the sling . . . your arms and legs cuffed . . . helpless to do anything. Except be fucked." I put my hand on his chest, my tongue on his nipple, bite it lightly, then suck it.

I look up at him. "I want to be in control this time. Just this once. I want you cuffed with your legs apart—so I can suck your cock, or put my tongue inside your asshole, do whatever I wish." I pause, then add, "I want you at my mercy."

"I prefer it the other way around," he says, but the idea must not be totally without appeal, because his penis is still hard in my hand. I drop down to my knees, lick his penis until it's slick with my spit. I suck his balls. I roll them around as if they're giant marbles in my mouth. I reach for the leather cuffs on the floor.

Looking up, I say, "I'll make sure you like it. And afterward, you'll whip me, harder than before. You'll punish me for Gina."

He doesn't speak.

Slowly, not sure he'll let me, I open the cuff, then wait, but he doesn't make a move to stop me. I attach it to his ankle, then glance up at him again.

He watches me carefully, like a man on guard, assessing. The muscles in his legs are taut, his cast arm hangs loosely by his side. Reaching for his penis once more, I touch it lightly, run my finger around the rim. I attach a cuff to his other ankle. I hold out the leg strap for him to step through.

He doesn't raise his foot. Moments pass. The idea tantalizes him—I'm sure he's thought of it before, wondered what it would be like to be on the other end—but still he's unsure. I watch his face. He's not afraid, I'm positive of that. He just doesn't like the idea of the power exchange running the opposite direction. Still, he remains motionless, undecided. If he doesn't do this willingly, I know, even with one hand cuffed, there is no way I can force him.

"You'd better make sure I enjoy this," he says. "If I don't, I'll whip you until you bleed. I'll leave scars."

I nod my assent.

He lifts his foot, slides his leg through the strap. I move it up to his thigh, then hold the other strap for him. He steps through.

"Sit," I say, and he bends his knees, lowers his weight on the sling. I put his feet behind him, hook the ankle cuffs to the back of the strap. He's suspended now, his feet off the floor. I thought I might have to raise him with the hoist, but I don't.

I lean down to kiss him, let my hands roam over his chest, then down between his legs. He's only semierect now, so I play with him until he's hard once more. My tongue makes a slow slide across his lower lip. I suck on it.

"First," I say, my mouth still on his, "I'm going to stick my tongue deep in your ass. I'm going to eat you, tongue-fuck you better than I ever have before."

He kisses me, crooks the elbow of his cast arm around my neck to draw me closer. I back off, ducking under his arm.

"Not yet," I say.

I walk in front of him, pick up the wrist cuff and attempt to put it around his cast. It's too small. I get another ankle cuff from the trunk. It fits around his cast, but not very well. It slides, doesn't remain securely in one place. I move the cuff up on his arm, just above the elbow, and attach it there. I clip it to the leather strap. He watches me the entire time, not saying anything, definitely not acting submissive. He's wondering, I imagine, how this will affect us later, wondering if I will want to be more dominant in our relationship. He'll want to whip me afterward, severely, just to prove nothing has changed.

I put my hand on his burly shoulder. This seems all wrong, him shackled. I like it the other way around, he's taught me that. Months of coaching, learning the meaning of submission, giving myself over to him—it doesn't go away easily. I don't enjoy seeing him like this, diminished.

"I'm sorry I tricked you," I say.

He looks at me, questioning.

"I need answers . . . this is the only way I can get them. You'll never tell me the truth otherwise. Not willingly."

I thought he'd be furious with me, but instead he throws back his head and laughs, a loud hearty laugh, booming, one that fills the loft. I wait for him to finish.

He shakes his head, still chuckling. "Hoist by my own petard," he mumbles.

"What?" I ask, not understanding.

"Never mind," he says. "It doesn't make any difference," and again he shakes his head, chuckling. "I didn't think you were capable of this. I underestimated you."

"Yes," I say. "You did."

Standing still for a minute, I hesitate, irresolute. I'm reluctant to begin.

"Well?" he says, taunting me, drawing out the word. "What's next? Do you plan to beat the truth out of me?"

"No," I say. "That won't be necessary. Besides, I doubt if that would work."

I walk around to the other side of him. "I'm going to call your mother, ask her to come over here. I'll tell her who I really am, and what happened to me over fifteen years ago."

"You don't know what happened."

"I know Gina didn't kill Anna. How long has it been since you read the newspaper articles on your wife's death? Fifteen years?"

He doesn't reply.

"It's only in one of the articles, a brief mention, barely a sentence near the end—Gina was in San Diego at the time of the accident."

He shrugs. "A misprint."

"Your mother confirmed it: Gina wasn't here."

He starts to say something, but I interrupt. "And the poem in Gina's boot box—you wrote it. You planted it for me, just so I'd be sure Gina was the one. She wasn't, though. You killed Anna. You almost killed me."

"Wrong," he says. Then adds, "On both accounts."

I walk over to the phone, pick it up.

He glares at me, a withering look. I wait for him to begin with the truth, but he doesn't say a word. His mouth, clamped shut, forms a hard, defiant line.

I start to dial.

"You don't want to call my mother," he finally says. His face is like granite, stony, resistant, the contempt in his eyes palpable. "You won't want her to hear this."

I put down the phone. I wait.

He says, "Who shall I tell you about first—you or Anna?" He answers his own question, smiling maliciously. "I'll save Anna for last," he says. "You came to my house a week after she died, your bags in hand, insisting I marry you now that she was dead. You'd been renting a room in town, but you moved out. I laughed at you—at the absurdity of your demand—and told you to leave. It made you furious. You followed me up to the loft, yelling, screaming, saying you'd tell the police I killed Anna. Then you demanded money. I laughed, and that infuriated you even more. I started to turn around, to walk away. You grabbed the metal poker by the fireplace, hit me with it, made this big gash in my shoulder. I came toward you, angry, and you took another swing at me, got me this time on the side of my head."

I see the scar on his shoulder, and the one at his temple—the scars he wouldn't talk about.

He says, "I lunged for your throat, started to choke you, then I saw Gina out of the corner of my eye. She was in the kitchen when you knocked on my door, but she'd come upstairs when she heard the fighting. She yelled for me to stop, then grabbed my baseball bat, came at me, swinging. She'd suspected I killed Anna, and now she thought I was going to kill you. I jumped back, and instead of hitting me, Gina accidentally smashed your head, hard. You slammed against the loft window, crashed through it, fell all the way to the ground, on the concrete patio."

His words come to me with a dull thud, anticlimactic. All these years, I searched for my attacker. Now, it seems there was no attacker at all. It was an accident. He could be lying, I think, and I consider this, but, somehow, I know he speaks the truth. I'm not sure how to explain my certitude—I've been wrong on so many occasions—except to say that the words ring true. Someplace in my memory, the words have valence. I look over at the window. This is where I fell, not the catwalk.

"If Gina hadn't intervened," I ask him, "would you have killed me?"

He shrugs. "You attacked me with the poker, I attacked back. It just happened."

"Tell me the rest," I say.

"Unhook my legs first. They're cramping."

I don't do it.

"If you want the rest, unhook my legs."

Even with his legs free, he can't go anywhere. He's still in the sling, both arms manacled. I open the clips on the back straps, release his feet. He puts them on the floor, shifts around, straightens up.

"Start talking," I say.

"Gina and I thought you were dead. I couldn't find a pulse, you weren't breathing, your face was covered in blood, smashed from the concrete, from the glass, from the baseball bat, and your legs seemed broken, bent awkwardly, and shards of glass were stuck in your body, all over. Gina panicked. She wanted to call the police immediately, but I convinced her not to. I said it would look as if she murdered you, and she'd be the one to go to prison.

"I took off all your clothes and jewelry so there'd be nothing to identify you in case you were ever found, nothing that could be traced back to us. I rolled you up in a carpet, stuffed you in the trunk of my car, then I drove to Davis. I'd gone to college there, and I knew of some empty fields out on one of the old county roads. I parked behind a long stand of trees, carried you out to the middle of the field, dug a hole, and put you in. I was covering you with dirt when I saw a car driving slowly up the road. I didn't want to get caught, so I left before I finished burying you."

He stops for a minute, then resumes. "No one realized you were missing. You'd already moved out of your room in the city, and I told everyone at Byblos that you'd quit. I checked the Sacramento newspaper for any mention of a dead body in a field near Davis. Imagine my surprise when I discovered you were alive but in a coma. Gina wanted to go to the police right then, but, once more, I talked her out of it."

He clears his voice, continues. "Then, a few weeks later, another story appeared in the Sacramento paper. You'd come out of the coma, but you had amnesia. No one could identify you. Gina and I waited. We searched the newspapers every day for any mention of you. Occasionally, there'd be an article detailing your progress, but your memory never returned and soon the newspapers lost interest. The first few years, Gina was a wreck. She snapped. She couldn't stand to be apart from me, and she couldn't stand it when I was with someone else. She needed to have me all to herself, as if the enormity of the secret we shared precluded anyone else. That's why she painted all those pictures of you—guilt . . . guilt that *she* almost killed you."

He stretches his legs, glances around, at the hoist line, at the metal cleat bolted to the wall. He's looking for a way out, but he won't find one. The line is secure. He says, "She never trusted me after that. She became vigilant about my girlfriends—especially about you. She thought I would harm you.

She'd do anything to get you to leave. Scaring you with the winepress, bribing you with fifty-thousand dollars, even starting a fire in the kitchen so my mother would dismiss you—she didn't want you here."

"Gina was trying to protect me all along," I say.

He smiles, a faintly bitter, rueful expression. "Sometimes, I think she loathed me. I suppose, the night she fell, she was going to tell you her suspicions about Anna's death. Instead, you killed her."

"I didn't mean to. It seemed as if she was coming after me . . ." I don't finish.

He works his left shoulder. "Release my arm," he says. "Just the one with the cast. It hurts."

I shake my head.

"You'll still have me shackled here. I can't move beyond the radius of the chain."

He's right, of course, but still I don't release his arm. "What about Anna?" I ask.

He shakes his head. "Release my arm first," he says.

The metal cleat, where the hoist line is tied, lies beyond his reach, and he's securely attached to the sling, his other wrist locked in the metal handcuff. He can't get away. I release his cast arm, move back before he can reach me. "Now tell me about Anna," I say.

He tilts his head to the side, looking at me. I see the sneer on his face. "I was saving the best for last," he says. "You were devastated when I married Anna. You were angry, bitter. On the day she died, you had confronted us on the catwalk. You told Anna that I was fucking you, told her everything else we did. Your little confession caused a horrible argument. Furious, still screaming at me, Anna turned to leave, started running, but then she slipped. She fell under the guardrail. I grabbed her arm, started to pull her up, then, in a flash of a second, I realized her death would be the perfect way out. We had a bad marriage, I didn't love her. If she died, her money and vineyards would be mine. I hesitated just a moment, let her dangle over the edge. That's all it took, a brief pause, and she knew what I was thinking. I could see it in her eyes, the sudden realization that I wanted her to die. I looked back at you. You gripped the guardrail, your knuckles white, a shocked expression on your face. You also knew what had crossed my mind. *You knew.* You were horrified, but you didn't say a word. Not one word. Nothing. All of this happened incredibly fast. Just a flash of a second, a slight hesitation, a moment's thought of how much easier life would be without her—and she was gone. I let her go, but you raised no objection. We both killed Anna."

I take a step back, shocked. The room seems to get smaller, but it isn't claustrophobia this time. The truth is closing in. I know it's the truth, I feel it in my gut. There is resonance in the words he spoke, a mnemonic umbilical cord tying together past and present. Murder. We are accomplices in this, he and I.

He hesitates, then says, his voice gentler now, "This doesn't have to change anything, Carly. We could go on as before. We're good together—you know we are."

I think of Anna, of how I failed to speak out. A moment of desperation, a decision wrongly made, and all of our lives were irreparably altered.

He says, "We *are* good together. I alone understand you. We have the same tastes, the same hunger."

I feel lightheaded, queasy with the knowledge of who I really am—a coward, plain and simple. An accomplice. "What about Anna?" I ask.

"It just happened; I didn't plan it."

He says the words without remorse, without any sense of guilt or responsibility. It just happened—except we could've saved her. The truth seems to whirl around in the air, spinning vertiginously fast. We killed Anna. My thoughts come to me jumbled, incoherent, a blur of guilt and disbelief. I try to rationalize an excuse—I was too frightened to speak, and even if I had voiced a protest, James wouldn't have listened to me; and what if I physically tried to stop him? No, he's much too strong—but the truth is that I never even tried. I took no action at all.

"I'm going to the police," I say, feeling dizzy, in a stupor.

"With what? There's no evidence of any crime. You won't be able to prove a thing. It's your word against mine. Who do you think they'll believe?"

I don't reply.

"It happened a long time ago," he says, his voice calm. "Nothing has to change between us."

I rub my forehead, feel the pain of a headache coming on. I wanted to settle scores, punish the guilty—but the guilt belongs to me. And like a coward, I hid the truth behind a wall of amnesia. My head aches, burns with the knowledge of what I am. I want to turn all of this over to someone else. It's too much for me. "I'm going to the police," I say, and I head for the stairs.

"I can't let you do that," he says. "You'd destroy my reputation. You'd destroy Byblos . . . Gina and I worked too hard to let that happen. You won't be going to the police."

I stop, turn around. He's standing now, still in the sling, reaching up with his cast arm, his other wrist still manacled to the leather strap. I don't understand what he's doing at first, then I realize he's attempting to release the panic snap. If he can pull it up, he'll release the sling from the chain, freeing himself. I rush toward him, grab his arm, trying to pull it down, but even his one arm is stronger than both of mine. We struggle. With his legs not restrained, he's able to move several feet in all directions. He twists around, jerking me with him. I see the determined look in his eyes—and the menace. If he gets loose, there'll be no second chances for me this time. I wrestle with his arm, grapple to pull it down, but I can't. He resists my futile attempts, fumbles with the panic snap. Then I realize he can't release it. The cast on his arm goes to his fingers, almost to the tips of them. He can't get a grip on the snap. As soon as I comprehend this, I jump back— but it's too late. He reacts immediately, lunging toward me, hooking his cast arm around my waist, pressing me to him. The plaster digs into my side.

"I didn't want it to be like this," he says, "but you're living on borrowed time. You should've died fifteen years ago."

I struggle to get away. He keeps his arm clamped tightly around my waist.

"There's enough leeway on this chain so I can jump through the window," he says. He walks over to the huge arched window, dragging me along. I see the concrete patio far below, the wrought-iron table and chairs.

"You did a good job hooking me up in the sling," he says. "The chain will pull me back. I'm secure. You, however, aren't as fortunate. I'll drop you— and this time you won't survive the fall."

I dig my fingers into his skin, scratch and bite him, kick out with my legs, but he doesn't let me go. I reach for his face, for his eyes. He manages to avoid me, turning his head. He moves away from the window, takes a few steps backward, as far as the chain will allow, then stops. He's going to run for the window.

"You won't do it," I say, but I know that he will. My voice sounds like a plea, choked with fear and dread and the remembrance of how I once appeared.

He looks down at me. He says, "I suspected our journey might end like this. I know you won't believe me, but I was rooting for you. I was hoping for an ending different than this. We *were* good together."

"You won't do it," I say again, desperate, talking fast. "You love me—I know you do." I'm crying now, saying anything to make him stop, hitting him, uselessly, with my clenched fist.

He stares straight ahead. He tenses, ready to run.

"You won't hurt me," I sob. "You didn't plan to kill Anna. You're not a cold-blooded killer. You're better than that."

He glances down at me, a brief look of compassion in his eyes. But then it is gone. "No," he says, "I'm not," and he starts to move forward, runs for the window. My gut clenches. The room is a blur as he lurches forward, and all I see is the window straight ahead, looming, getting closer, and even in my panic I think something, or someone, will intervene and stop this from happening, please God stop this, but it doesn't stop, and the window is directly in front of me now, and I know I will die. I reach up as we're crashing through, the sounds of splintering glass and my screams thundering in my ears. The last thing I remember is my hand on the panic snap, pulling it up, releasing him from the chain, the look of surprise on his face, both of us hurtling through the air.

CHAPTER THIRTY

I try not to think about the verdict, try not to think about the twelve men and women who will decide my fate, but of course I can think of nothing else. I pace back and forth, in this small room they call a holding facility but which is no larger, really, than a cell. Slowly, with a limp, I walk the room, from the gray west wall to the locked door, then back again, wondering if I'll go to prison or if I'll be set free. My lawyer said the case never should've gone to trial, that the publicity surrounding it demanded prosecution more so than the evidence, but still I am here. Maybe this is where I belong. Life, I've learned long ago, doesn't come with a failsafe system. There are no more panic snaps for me.

I look up at the clock once again, through the narrow window on the door. The clock is outside, in the hallway, high up on the wall. The red second hand, in its incessant movement, ticks away the time. A verdict would come soon, everyone thought, so they chose to keep me here, in the courthouse, rather than transport me back to the county jail. It's been more than seven hours, though, and still no verdict.

I rest my head against the door, waiting, thinking. James is dead. I am responsible for this, they say. Exacting revenge for what happened more than fifteen years ago, I killed Gina and then I killed James. That's what the jury was told. They don't know about Anna. No one does. Ever a coward, I kept that to myself.

I begin pacing again, from one wall to another, my legs aching with each step. Earlier, the guards brought me to the courthouse in bellychains, padlocked in back, my wrists restrained by cuffs on the sides. It's standard procedure during transport, yet it almost made me cry. They've had me in bellychains before. The guard put them on gently, said in a soft whisper that no one else could hear, "You know I have to do this," and then locked them in the back. I closed my eyes, squeezed back the tears, tried not to give him any trouble. The guards, the ones who know me, treat me nicely, but not everyone does. The tabloids, when they heard of my case, took everything and twisted it around. They found out about the leather harnesses, the whips, the gold chain around my ankle. They found out James was the one bound to the sling, his arm manacled to the leather strap. I became the monster, he the victim. They dubbed me Madame de Sade, created a story guaranteed to sell. I came to Napa to destroy the McGuane family, they said. I succeeded with Gina and, although James made a valiant effort to survive, I also succeeded with him.

I sit on the chair, put my elbows on my knees, lean forward and cradle my head, waiting for the verdict. I have scars again, not imaginary but real—a jagged line down my left cheek, a few body etchings here and there. When I look in a mirror, I see how different I am from other women, how I'll always be different. Even though the scars will eventually fade and disappear, I will never be like other women.

Getting up again, I resume my slow, limped pacing, wait for the verdict, for twelve people to decide my future. Before I came to Byblos, I thought I'd be willing to pay any price, any price at all, if only I could find the answers to my past. But the price is too high. I lost the first seventeen years of my life, and now I may lose even more. I was foolish to think truth comes before all else.

I glance up at the clock once more, watch the red hand move. I wait alone, without family, without friends. I wait, for that is all I can do.

When I arrived at Byblos last spring, I thought the McGuanes were the perfect family. James and Gina had it all, I assumed—love, community, a secure place in the world—but I was wrong, and my envy misplaced. Gina, forever changed by that night in the loft, was consigned to a life not of her own choosing. A hermit at Byblos, she hid out in her cottage, composing her secret poems, no husband, no kids, no close friends. And James, despite his cynicism, did not go unscathed. Over and over, he painted pictures of death and destruction, themes from which he was unable to escape. They didn't have it all—perhaps no one ever does—and I, without a family of my own, was naive to think they did. Their place in the world was never secure; mine, determined by a panel of twelve, even less so.

The jury found me not guilty. It could've gone the other way.

I pull up in front of Mrs. McGuane's home, turn off the engine, and sit in my car. James and Gina were afraid I'd destroy Byblos, but the winery is doing very well. Sales have steadily increased, which means people either ignored the stories in the tabloids or bought more wine because of them. A little notoriety, I suppose, helps. Madame de Sade's spectral sells. The people in Napa have mixed reactions to the verdict. Some still believe what they read in the papers and swear I came to Byblos to destroy the McGuanes. Others accept the verdict, but their attitude toward me has subtly changed. I see the covert glances when I'm in town, hear the whisperings when they think I'm out of earshot: not guilty, but not innocent either.

Their gossiping, however, the oblique affronts and intended slights, all this doesn't torment me nearly as much as I torment myself. I did nothing to prevent Anna's death. I didn't even try. How do I reconcile who I was before with who I am now? I don't even know how to begin.

In the distance, I see workers in the fields, pruning and tying down the vines. The canes are barren, without foliage this time of year. I wonder about the vegetable garden—it probably needs a new layer of mulch—then realize it's no longer any concern of mine. I open the glove box, find what I'm looking for, palm it in my hand, then gaze out the window at Mrs. McGuane's home, stately, permanent, a family home, but it's not mine. Never mine. I reach for the door handle, hesitate, don't open it. I'm still not sure what I'll say to Mrs. McGuane.

My memories have not returned, my identity still a mystery. Occasionally, at the oddest times, when I'm in the middle of a sentence on the phone, or when I'm soaking in a bath, I'll feel a tug, ever so slight, on my memory, a slender thread of recall, vague and tenuous, trying to pull me back. Even though my doctors warned me about the elusive nature of recall, I feel betrayed by my memory, as if a best friend is holding back, or cheating, or purposely leading me astray. I used to think memory was like a jigsaw puzzle—if I filled in the pieces, a lucid picture would emerge. But it hasn't happened that way. James handed me some of the facts, but they remain disconnected from me, just fragments floating in my mind, without linking emotions. Still, I know what I am—a coward, unwilling to deal with the reality of the past. I keep the memories hidden, in camouflage, like nightmares buried in the safety of sleep. Maybe, someday, my identity will return. For now, however, I keep the name Carly Tyler, the only name I've ever known.

Except for my car, the circular driveway is empty. The black Cherokee is gone. I open my hand, see the gold anklet in my palm, the chain broken. It's no longer around my ankle, but I belong to James still. *I belong to him.* The dross of his love will stay with me forever. I wanted every kiss, every touch of his hand, all the pleasure he gave . . . and all the pain. I wanted it all because it made me feel alive. There is a price to be paid for that kind of passion. It doesn't lead to liberation. It torments, it shackles, yet I want to be set free.

I thought, when I came to Byblos last year, I would find justice and peace of mind. Neither has come. I pulled the panic snap so I wouldn't fall alone. I took James with me, a final act of revenge, something he hadn't expected. I chose to destroy us both. But he, also, did something unpredictable— he twisted around in midair, turned his body to shield mine, taking the brunt of impact. Did he do it to break my fall? Or was it unintentional? The answer will never be known. I wish I could believe that his last conscious act was one of love, that, in a sudden burst of humanity, he sacrificed himself in order to save me. I wish I could believe that, but I don't. He had no change of heart. He wanted me to die.

Years from now, my recollection of all this will subtly alter. The truth, never absolute, will be warped by time. Finally, I'm learning that memory, unlike a puzzle board, isn't concrete and never changing. It's fluid, flowing like a river, cutting new channels and swerving over time and distance, perspective changing along the way. The slippery stuff doesn't hold still. It's the event I cannot remember— callously standing by while Anna died—that is frozen in time.

I look up, see Mrs. McGuane in the top-floor window, staring down at me, her white hair brushed off to the side, her expression tinged with a sadness that can never be erased. She doesn't blame me for her children's deaths. I may not be culpable, but I know I'm the cause. If I had never come here, her family would be intact. James and Gina would be alive. I've taken them away, and Mrs. McGuane has no one now. I would stay here if she asked, I'd like to stay, but she doesn't want me around. I watch her, standing by the window, alone, a frail hand parting the curtain. At the trial, she spoke in my behalf. She accepted my version of the truth. Most people can't understand why she would befriend the woman who caused her so much grief, but what they don't realize is that she's taken on the guilt of her children: they left me for dead. I've become her albatross— much as she is now mine.

I stay in the car, watching her. I don't get out. There is, after all, nothing to say. She doesn't want me here. She lifts her hand, a silent farewell, then slowly turns away. I start the engine, pull around the gravel driveway, my stomach knotting when I realize I'll never return. Byblos is the closest I've ever come to having a home, and Mrs. McGuane to the mother I never had. Once again, I'll have to start all over.

I drive down the main road bisecting the Mc-Guane property. The vines, like hibernating bears, lie dormant now, waiting for warmer weather to reawaken them, for new life to begin. I have a job in San Francisco, if I want it.

I pass the winery, then see the entrance up ahead, the double stone pillars. An unexpected sense of relief gradually comes over me, and I breathe easier, as if the ghosts of the past are loosening their hold. I may not have a home, nor the comfort of Mrs. McGuane, but I made it out of here alive. I get another chance at life. I drive through the pillars, turn left onto the road. Of course she wouldn't ask me to stay. Releasing me from Byblos was a gift, I begin to understand now, Mrs. McGuane's gift to me.